Christmas under a Cranberry Sky

Christmas under a Cranberry Sky

HOLLY MARTIN

ZAFFRE

First published as an eBook in 2016 by Bookouture

This paperback edition published in Great Britain in 2017 by
ZAFFRE PUBLISHING
80-81 Wimpole St, London W1G 9RE
www.zaffrebooks.co.uk

A CIP catalogue record for this book is available from the British Library.

ISBN: 978–1–785–76312–0

3 5 7 9 10 8 6 4 2

Typeset by IDSUK (Data Connection) Ltd
Printed and bound by Clays Ltd, St Ives Plc

Zaffre Publishing is an imprint of Bonnier Zaffre,
a Bonnier Publishing company
www.bonnierzaffre.co.uk
www.bonnierpublishing.co.uk

For my dear friend Wendy, for always being there.

❄ Chapter 1 ❄

If I could give zero stars to this hotel I would. There is nothing good about this place. How it has been running for so long is a complete mystery to me. Everywhere is filthy.

I'm not sure what was the worst part of my stay, waking up to see a rat sitting on the broken drawers eating my free biscuit or sharing the mouldy shower with a friendly cockroach.

The staff are the rudest people I have ever met.

I feel I have walked straight into a hotel from the 1950s with the terrible décor and the complete lack of facilities. The beds are hard, the rooms are cold and dirty, and the bathroom is disgusting.

The food was inedible. If I'd had a dish of dried rabbit food for breakfast and dinner it would have been far superior to the food that was given to me…

Piper Chesterfield stared at the review and sighed. She had been a professional mystery guest for over ten years now, visiting hotels around the world and writing honest reviews for *The Tree of Life* magazine she worked for. Although she had seen some of the most beautiful places on earth she was getting weary of travelling and her patience for bad hotels was clearly wearing thin.

She'd been to a lot of wonderful hotels recently, so her luck was bound to run out at some point. Silver Blossom Hall in Edinburgh was one of the worst hotels she had stayed at for a long time, which was a pity because she loved the city. It always helped to vent her feelings like this, to pour all of the hotel's failings onto the page. She never submitted her first draft though. That wouldn't be fair. She would come back to the review in a few days, and once she'd had a chance to calm down she knew she would take a lot of her comments out and tone down the rest of it.

She looked up at the cornflower blue sky as it turned a candyfloss pink in the setting sun, a plane taking off from the airport silhouetted against the evening sky as it headed off to some far-flung exotic location. She didn't feel jealous. She had seen it all. She didn't want to travel any more; she didn't want to spend her days living out of a suitcase. She was tired and she just wanted to stand still for a little while. She had one more hotel this year, where she was going to spend Christmas and New Year, and then she was going to rent a flat somewhere in London and take six months off from the world. She couldn't wait.

Piper closed the laptop down and picked up the brochure for her next assignment. Stardust Lake Hotel was a winter resort on Juniper Island, the most northern island of the Scottish Isles. The beautifully presented brochure had wonderful pictures of gorgeous log cabins strewn with fairy lights, glass igloos for watching the Northern Lights, and it even promised an ice palace. It looked beautiful and idyllic.

Not having a home to call her own, Piper had spent Christmas in some weird and wonderful places over the years, but nothing could beat the cosy festiveness of Christmas in Britain. If there was a checklist for a perfect Christmas, it seemed Stardust Lake Hotel had it all.

She flicked through the pages of the brochure. Nestled into the hills of Juniper Island, Piper could practically feel the heat from the log fires and the gorgeous scents of the real Christmas trees, mulled wine and pine cones. The thing that made her smile most of all was the tiny town called Christmas, a collection of log cabins and stone cottages that had reinvented themselves as a permanent Christmas market.

She had been to Juniper Island once before in a different life. As a child, visiting with her best friend's family, the place had seemed barren and cold, but it had made a wonderful adventure playground for her and Gabe as they had hiked, played and traversed the whole island. That Christmas had been one of the few times in her childhood that she had been truly happy. Those days were long gone and she wouldn't let her feelings for the place affect her review for good or bad. It looked completely different now; it seemed the whole of Juniper Island had received a makeover and she couldn't wait to see it.

Right on cue, Piper's flight number was called to the gate for boarding.

Piper slipped the laptop into her carry-on bag along with the brochure and walked through the terminal. It was Saturday, the last weekend before Christmas, and the airport was filled with stressed-out families and loved-up couples who were all travelling somewhere for the holidays. Even the lone travellers were probably going back home to their families. She didn't have anyone to go back to.

She finally reached the gate, seemingly at the furthest distance from the main airport, and handed her ticket to the bored member of staff on the desk. She was directed through a door and down some steps towards the plane. She knew Juniper Island was quite small and wouldn't be able to accommodate the bigger jets that were flying out from Edinburgh airport that day.

She reached the bottom of the stairs and looked across the tarmac, her heart filled with joy at the red plane decorated with silvery stars. Scrawled across the side of the plane in cursive silvery writing were the words *Juniper Island Airlines*. It seemed the tiny island had certainly gone up in the world.

Standing at the bottom was an elderly man in a long green coat with gold buttons. He was wearing a black top hat decorated with holly leaves and berries. He smiled at her, his blue eyes creasing in the corners as she approached. She needed to get a photo of this.

'Good evening, Miss Chesterfield, I'm Stephen, I'm going to be your flight attendant today.'

'Hello, would you mind if I took a few photos before we leave?'

'Of course, go ahead.'

Piper grabbed her camera from her bag, fired off a few shots of the plane, glowing under the setting sun, and took a few of Stephen too as he waited patiently for her to finish. She quickly shoved the camera back in her bag and he held out his hand to take it for her. She was charmed already. After the staff at Silver Blossom Hall had told her that she would have to carry her suitcase up seven flights of stairs by herself as the lift was broken, things were certainly looking up.

Stephen followed her up the stairs and she walked into what was obviously the first-class cabin of the plane, where large leather recliner-type seats were dotted around the edges and a well-stocked white marble-look bar stood in the middle. Rich warm red carpet lined the floor, and the plastic interiors of the normal jets had been replaced by painted cream walls and walnut wood panelling. It was stunning and plush and completely out of her league.

'Take a seat anywhere you want,' Stephen said as he walked into the cabin behind her.

'Oh, I'm not in first class,' Piper said.

'There is no first class, Miss Chesterfield. This is the only cabin in the plane. All of our guests travel in style to Juniper Island.'

She sat down in one of the comfy chairs and smiled to herself – she had no doubt she was going to enjoy her stay at Stardust Lake Hotel if this was the kind of treatment she was going to get.

She watched as Stephen fastened the door behind him and she looked around the empty plane.

'Am I the only passenger?'

'You are. I'm not sure if you are aware but Stardust Lake Hotel doesn't open for business until Thursday. I know that you were scheduled to come then but rang last night to see if you could come early. The manager didn't want to turn you away so they made arrangements for you to be accommodated today.'

'Oh I didn't realise. I hope they haven't gone to any trouble.'

'Nothing is too much trouble for the guests of Stardust Lake Hotel,' Stephen said.

Piper smiled; they clearly had him well trained.

Stephen removed his long green coat and hat and hung them up, revealing a rich red velvet waistcoat and a burgundy cravat. He reminded Piper of a kindly old uncle, although she certainly hadn't had one of those growing up.

'Would you like a glass of mulled wine or a mug of hot chocolate?' Stephen asked.

'Oh, a mulled wine would be lovely,' Piper said. It was just over a week until Christmas, but she might as well get into the festive spirit now.

Stephen moved over to the bar and the rich fruity smells of the warm mulled wine reached her nose as he poured her a glass and a moment later passed it to her.

The plane taxied onto the runway and Stephen asked her to put her seatbelt on. As the plane took off Piper looked down at the bright lights of Edinburgh as the city fell away to fields and hills, and then mountains and lakes. Pretty soon only the silvery glow of the ocean lay beneath her. She grabbed her camera again and took a few more photos of the dazzling view of the ocean from the window.

Piper undid her seatbelt, slipped off her shoes and curled up in her chair. She leaned her head against the window as she sipped her hot wine, a warm fuzzy glow spreading through her as they flew through the darkening skies.

Stephen left her in peace, obviously sensing she wanted some time alone. She was nervous about going back and didn't know why. She had been there only once as a child, but she still had so many memories of her time there and she couldn't stop thinking about them as she flew closer.

'It's cold on Juniper Island; it was snowing when I left. You might want to dress a little warmer for our arrival,' Stephen said, after they had been flying for over an hour. 'We'll be arriving shortly.'

Having stayed at several bitterly cold locations over the years, Piper had a suitcase of gear fit for all occasions, weathers and terrains.

She pulled a pair of warm snow boots out of her bag, slipped them on, laced them up and then packed away her heels. She grabbed her hat, scarf and gloves ready for her arrival too.

'So tell me a bit more about Juniper Island. I went there once as a child but it seems to have changed a lot since then.'

Stephen paused in his job behind the bar. 'You went there as a child?'

Piper nodded. 'I came with my best friend and his family. It was Christmas time then too.'

'I thought I recognised you. I've lived on Juniper Island all my life, we must have met when you came.'

'You recognise me? It must have been over twenty years ago.'

'You have a very distinctive look.'

Piper didn't know what to do with that comment. *Freak* was one of the names she had been called over the years. She had tried to tell herself her eyes were a light brown, but in reality they were gold, making her look a bit like a cat.

'Gabe always said you were the most beautiful girl in the world, even back when you were kids,' Stephen said.

The mention of Gabe's name was like a punch in the gut. She had tried to tell herself she hadn't thought about Gabe at all for the past twelve years, but that would be a lie. She had thought of him often. For Stephen to remember she had come with Gabe and his family was even more surprising than the idea he remembered her at all.

But it wasn't just Gabe she had missed, it was his family too: his lovely older sister Neve and his mum and dad who had been much more of a family to her than her own parents had been.

Stephen walked round the bar towards her, offering her a warm mince pie covered in a sprinkling of icing sugar and a tiny sprig of holly. 'Are you still in touch with the Whitaker family?'

She took a big bite, stalling for time. 'I haven't seen or spoken to any of them for twelve years. Not since I left the little village in the Lake District where we all grew up.'

Stephen watched her carefully, then looked at his watch. 'We'll be coming into land very soon. Can I ask you to fasten your seatbelt?'

Stephen moved away and Piper quickly fastened her seatbelt again. She looked out the window and saw only the silvery waves and snow-capped shores. Any of the wonder of Juniper Island was denied to her from her current seat.

The pilot landed with barely a bump and before Piper had undone her seatbelt, Stephen was there by her side ready to help her into her coat and picking up her bag.

Stephen opened the door and a cold wind burst into the plane bringing with it sparkly snowflakes.

She smiled and stepped outside.

❄ Chapter 2 ❄

Piper got into the back of a big Range Rover as Stephen loaded her bags into the boot. He came round to make sure she was settled and offered her a thick warm fur-type blanket to put over her legs for the journey. The car was cold, so it was a lovely cosy touch to be able to snuggle under the blanket while the car warmed up.

Stephen got into the driving seat, showing he was clearly more than just the flight attendant.

'It's not far, Miss Chesterfield, and I'm sure the fire will already be burning in your lodge when we get there. We've had a power cut on some parts of the resort so they might have moved you to a different lodge. We'll see when we get to the reception.'

Stephen drove the car away from the tiny runway and onto what clearly was supposed to be the main road. Snow had been cleared from the surface and old Victorian-style lamps sent golden puddles of light over the silvery snow either side of the road.

Fir trees shadowed the roadside, their limbs heavy with fresh fallen snow. As they rounded the corner, Piper gasped when she saw the trees suddenly all lit up with twinkling, golden lights. The red and green garlands twisted around each of the lamp posts were also lit up with tiny fairy lights, and coupled with the snow it looked magical.

'It's beautiful,' Piper whispered.

'I know. Mr… The new owner of the hotel has done a wonderful job.'

Piper frowned slightly at the stumble in the conversation. Who was the owner? Had she seen it in the brochure?

Distracted by the beauty of the place, she reached for her camera but decided against it. The blur of the trees as they sped past wouldn't make a great photo; she'd walk back down here one night to take some pictures by herself. She would have a better chance of framing the perfect shot if she wasn't in the car.

The driveway to the hotel twisted down into a valley and for a moment a flash of green lit up the sky beyond the trees before the road dipped down too far for Piper to see it. Piper peered through the trees trying to take it all in. The Christmas trees were still lighting the way, but behind them she saw something move, some kind of animal, a few of them, though she couldn't make out what they were.

The road curved down to the right and the trees fell away to reveal thirty or forty large wooden lodges. Most of them were in complete darkness, but the ones further back up on the hillside were lit up, welcoming them into the resort.

As the drive curled round again, she saw the old hotel, where she had stayed as a child. Happy memories filled her of her time spent here, playing with Gabe, his sister Neve and sometimes even Luke, Gabe's grumpy half-brother. The Golden Oak hotel had been a ramshackle old building, with crumbling stone brickwork and a roof that had been half broken and falling quickly into disrepair. Piper and Gabe had shared a room and because it had been so cold and draughty, she'd climbed into his bed and they had cuddled each other to keep warm. At the ages of seven and eight it had been completely innocent, but it was there that she'd had her first kiss. Not a proper one, not like Gabe had kissed her when they were older. He'd just given her a quick kiss on the lips and promised her he would love her forever.

It hadn't worked out quite like that, though.

The Golden Oak was almost nothing like she remembered. The name was the main thing to change: *Stardust Lake Hotel* was written in beautiful fairy lights above the door. The building had obviously been extensively repaired and restored to its former glory. The large stone brickwork seemed to gleam in the light from the lamps, the steps had been rebuilt, and the car stopped on a proper paved driveway instead of a mud patch in front of the hotel. It was an impressive building made even more so by the huge gorgeous Christmas trees bedecked in large gold ribbons, lights and red glass baubles standing sentinel on either side of the door. Lights were strewn artistically around each window. Twinkling garlands and red ribbons were wrapped around the bannister that led up the stairs to the main front doors, and candles in brass lanterns stood on either side of the steps. It looked spectacular.

'The new owner wanted to keep the legacy of the old hotel while adding all the new lodges and improvements. This building now serves as the reception area and a large conservatory has been put on the back for the dining room. All the offices are in here but all the accommodation is in the lodges around the resort,' Stephen said as Piper pressed her face against the window to look at it.

Stephen chuckled at her reaction and then got out. He went round to the boot to retrieve the bags and then opened the door to help her out.

He offered his arm to escort her up the steps and she took it, though it was very clear that the steps had been cleared of all ice and snow.

The cold wind swirled around them, tiny snowflakes dancing in the air.

Piper stopped as she noticed movement at the corner of the hotel. She glanced over and was surprised to see a small herd of Shetland ponies staring at her, the freezing wind blowing their manes like something from a shampoo commercial. They were so tiny they were comical, but their cold black eyes were almost sinister.

'Oh they're so cute. I didn't realise they would have Shetland ponies here, bit silly really, given their name. Of course they come from here.'

'They roam wild over the island, Miss Chesterfield. They might look cute, but these ones are quite savage.'

Piper giggled. 'Savage. They're tiny ponies.'

Stephen shook his head. 'Normally the ponies are very docile, but this gang are quite wild. Leo is their ringleader – he is the gold one at the front. I think he thinks the island is his and he has been known to terrorise the villagers and most of the staff here.'

'Does he bite?'

'Not yet, just don't give him the chance.'

With a sinister whinny, Leo gave her an evil glare, tossed his head and turned round and walked away. The other ponies parted to let him through then followed him into the darkness.

Piper stifled a giggle. It was hard to take the prospect of tiny savage ponies seriously.

As Stephen opened the reception door, warmth reached out and seemed to pull them in. Stephen placed her bags by the sofa and went to talk to the receptionist. Piper blinked the snow out of her eyes and looked around.

A log fire was burning away in a giant stone fireplace, warming any visitors who might come in, even though Piper was the only guest. It was reminiscent of a wooden ski lodge inside, with the wooden panelling, leather sofas and bright colourful rugs. The huge Christmas tree twinkled with white fairy lights and red and green tartan bows.

Stephen returned a moment later with a young pretty blonde and a boy with brown curly hair. Both of them looked to be about seventeen years old.

'This is Iris and Jake. Iris works on reception and Jake is our porter. The owner of the hotel wishes to welcome you to the resort himself so, if you'd like to take a seat, he won't be a few minutes. And if there is anything you want to eat or drink you can let these guys know and they will get it for you. Would you like a hot chocolate or tea or coffee while you are waiting?' Stephen asked.

'A hot chocolate would be lovely.'

Stephen nodded at Jake and he quickly disappeared through a door.

'I hope your stay at Stardust Lake Hotel will be a very happy one,' Stephen said.

Piper smiled, excited to see everything and how it had changed. 'Thank you, I hope so too.'

Stephen smiled kindly at her, touched his hat and then stepped back outside into the cold and dark.

It was getting late now and she was looking forward to climbing into a nice clean bed and going to sleep so she could see the full glory of the resort in the daylight. She hoped the owner wouldn't be too long.

Jake returned a minute later and handed her a tall glass of hot chocolate with cream on the top then went back behind the reception desk with Iris. They started talking quietly, but as there wasn't any other noise in the reception, Piper couldn't help but overhear what they were talking about.

'Everyone is so worried about Thursday with all the journalists who are coming,' Iris said.

'And we still don't know which of them is the dreaded Mr Black?' Jake asked.

Iris shook her head. 'I suppose we are lucky enough that we know he's coming; normally the hotels he visits never know he's been until the review appears. You should see some of his reviews, so scathing. Hotels have closed after his visit.'

That was interesting, another mystery guest was coming to the hotel, one who wasn't as secretive as her and had clearly let slip where he was going next and Stardust Lake Hotel had been forewarned. But this man's reviews seemed to hold a lot of weight. She couldn't imagine any of her reviews holding so much significance in the travel industry that hotels would close because of her. There had been nothing positive about her stay at Silver Blossom Hall, and *The Tree of Life* magazine she worked for had a large readership, but she still couldn't imagine so many people taking her review that much to heart that it would cause the hotel to close.

'But he writes good reviews too, I've seen them,' Jake said.

'Yes he does, but his opinion is so powerful he can literally make or break a hotel with his reviews. We have to make sure that he leaves here with a good impression, we have to make sure all the journalists leave here having had the time of their lives. We get one chance at this.'

'They will, everyone here will make sure of that. As long as the power comes back on before they all arrive.'

A flicker of green caught Piper's attention outside and she stood up. The island was well known for its great views of the Northern Lights, but with the cloudy skies she had witnessed on the drive over, she doubted she would get to see the wonder of it on her first night. With all her worldly travels over the years, she still hadn't been lucky enough to catch this phenomenon. Hopefully she would see something of it during her stay.

Another flash of green on the horizon lit up the night sky and as Jake and Iris were still talking, she grabbed her camera, shoved it in her pocket and slipped outside to take a look.

The cold night air whipped around her, the snow still falling steadily, landing on her face as her feet sunk into the powdery blanket.

Several large log cabins stood either side of a path that seemed to lead down the hill towards the green light. The cabins were in darkness, as were the lamps either side of the path. A casualty of the power cut no doubt. But although there were no lights, the white glow of the snow on the ground provided enough light for Piper to see where she was going. She looked back into the cosy reception where Jake and Iris had failed to notice she had gone. She pulled her hat tighter on her head and set off down the path to investigate the green glow that was coming through the trees.

She pulled her camera out as she rounded the corner, wanting to capture some of the lodges almost silhouetted against the snow. But as she raised the camera to her face, she stopped. Dancing in the snow, her hands raised in the air as she tried to catch the snowflakes, was a little girl of about four years old, dressed only in a wispy blue Elsa dress. Her arms were bare, she had no shoes or socks on and she didn't seem to care. Her black hair cascaded behind her as she twirled and spun around, giggling as the snowflakes landed on her skin. There was something so magical about the girl, so innocent and carefree. Piper fired off a couple of shots of her before realising the girl was completely alone.

Piper ran forwards, pulling off her coat, and the girl spotted her, stopping her dancing to watch Piper with amusement.

'You'll get cold,' the little girl warned.

'I think you're more at risk than I am,' Piper said, wrapping the coat around the little girl and zipping her up, trapping her arms inside. She shoved the camera into one of the pockets and fastened it so it wouldn't fall out. The coat came down to the girl's ankles.

The little girl laughed; she struggled for a moment or two and then fed her arms through the armholes, though she laughed again when her hands didn't reach the end. Piper pulled her red gloves off her hands.

'Here put your feet in these, your little toes will snap off if you don't wear shoes in the snow.'

The girl obviously thought the idea of wearing gloves on her feet was hilarious, but she obliged Piper and offered each foot up for Piper to pull on the gloves.

Piper stood up for a moment to look at her efforts. The little girl looked down at herself too. She burst out laughing again.

'I look like a penguin.'

She did too – with Piper's black winter jacket and her red gloves on her feet she looked exactly like a penguin. Piper couldn't help but laugh too. She pulled her hat off and put that on the little girl as well.

She offered out her hand. 'Let's get you back indoors, shall we?'

For the first time the girl seemed unsure. 'I'm not supposed to talk to strangers or go anywhere with them.'

'That's very wise. I'm Piper, what's your name?'

'Wren.'

'Pleased to meet you, Wren.' Piper turned her outstretched hand into a handshake and Wren shook it formally. 'See, now we aren't strangers any more. Why don't I take you back home?'

Wren took her hand and led her along the path, but after a few moments it was quite obvious that Wren was struggling to walk in the thick snow with gloves on her feet and they were making very slow progress.

'Shall I carry you, we might get there a bit quicker?'

Wren offered her arms in the air and Piper swung her up and settled her on her hip.

'Where's your mum?'

'Mummy's dead,' Wren said, calmly as if she was reporting on the weather.

'Oh, I'm sorry.'

'She died a very, very, very long time ago.'

'Where's your dad, then?' Piper asked, praying he wasn't also dead.

'He's busy.'

'Well who's looking after you?'

'Boris, but he fell asleep.'

'Well, can you point me in the direction of your house?'

Wren thought for a moment and then pointed off down the hill and Piper followed the path in that direction.

'You have beautiful hair,' Wren said.

'Thank you.'

'It's like Elsa's hair.'

'I suppose it is a bit.'

'Same colour. I wish I had hair like yours, blonde hair is much more interesting than black.'

Piper wondered where she had heard that; she was too young to really appreciate the meaning of the saying 'Blondes have more fun'.

'I love your hair,' Piper said, honestly. 'It's like black silk.'

A memory jolted Piper but she quickly shoved it aside.

'You have beautiful eyes too.' Wren studied her carefully. 'I've never seen eyes like that before. Why are they that colour?'

'My mum used to say that maybe my real parents were angels and that's why my eyes are like gold.'

Wren looked at her in confusion. 'What do you mean, your real parents?'

'I was adopted. I never knew my real parents. The lady who raised me was my mum but she didn't give birth to me. Does that make sense?'

Wren nodded solemnly. 'My daddy was dating a girl called Sally a few months ago and Sally told me she was going to be my new mummy, but when I asked Daddy if that was true, Daddy said not on his life, which I think means no as they stopped seeing each other after that. Can someone have more than one mummy? If one dies can they be replaced with a new one? Daddy's car died a few months ago and he just went and bought a new one, do you think you can buy a new mummy too?'

Piper smiled at all the questions.

'No one will ever replace your mummy, sweetheart, but one day your daddy might fall in love with a woman and might decide to marry her and then that lady will be your step-mum. She won't be the same as your mummy, but she will love you and hug you and do nice things with you like your mummy used to.'

'I like the idea of having a step-mum; she sounds wonderful. Maybe Daddy will buy me one for Christmas.'

Oh crap.

'Oh no honey, it's not something you can buy and it's not something Santa can bring. Your daddy has to meet a woman and fall in love with her, and she has to be perfect in every way. She has to love your daddy and love you too. It's very hard to find the perfect person.'

Piper looked around, realising that the log cabins had all gone and they were following the path through the empty woods, though the green glow ahead of them was getting stronger.

'Where are we going?' Piper asked.

'I'd like to know that myself,' a deep voice said behind them. 'Just where are you taking my daughter?'

Piper turned round to explain to Wren's dad what had happened, but when she saw him her heart stopped beating and her mouth went dry. The angry expression vanished from his face as he stared at her, his mouth falling open.

'Pip?' he whispered.

She tried to say something but there were no words at all as she stared at Gabe Whitaker in shock, the only man she had ever loved.

Memories crashed through her of the last time she had seen him, the worst day of her life.

❄ Chapter 3 ❄

Twelve Years Ago

Pip woke up with the weak winter sun shining on her face, but it wasn't that that had stirred her from her sleep, it was Gabe as he softly stroked her hair. She was lying on his bare chest and she couldn't help but smile as memories of the night before came flooding back.

Her friends from school all said that the first time they made love was messy, uncomfortable and over far too soon, but it hadn't been like that for her. Maybe it had something to do with making love to her best friend or maybe she hadn't been Gabe's first and he was just more experienced at it. It wouldn't surprise her if Gabe had been with many girls; he always had an adoring fan club around school and even more so since they had gone to college.

At seventeen Pip was one of the last of her friends to lose her virginity, but it couldn't have been better or nicer. Gabe had made sure of that.

Her dad had gone down the pub again, where he spent every night, sometimes not returning until later the next day, and Gabe had lit candles everywhere in her room before he led her upstairs and kissed her all over. He had gone so slowly, making sure she was happy at every step. She hadn't been nervous, it had seemed so perfect, so right between them. And when he had finally made love to her, he had held her so reverentially, whispered how much he loved her and she knew what they had was forever.

She'd heard her dad come home in the very early hours in the morning, banging into things as he made his way to his room, and Gabe had held her tight and promised her that soon they could get a place together and she could move out of her dad's house for good.

Pip hated her dad, but it seemed that the feeling was entirely mutual. He hadn't always been like this, he had been a good, kind man until the day her mum died. Pip was only seven years old at the time, and her dad had turned to the bottle for comfort and never surfaced again from his grief. He was permanently angry and bad-tempered and, although he had never hit her, the screaming and shouting was often far worse. The only reason they had managed to coexist for so long was because he spent most of his days and nights down the pub, leaving Pip to her own devices.

Gabe's family had almost adopted her as their own, and she spent much more time in their happy family home than in her own.

Gabe kissed her on the head and slid from the bed. 'I have to go, I said I'd help Dad on the farm today. Will you come over tonight? Mum has asked that you come over for dinner.'

Pip nodded, stretching her weary limbs. 'I'd love to.'

'You could stay if you want to, Mum won't mind and your dad probably won't even notice.'

'OK.' She eyed him as he got dressed. At the age of eighteen he was already tall and muscular from helping out on the farm most days. His strong body against hers the night before had been one of the nicest feelings ever.

He leaned over the bed and kissed her on the lips just briefly. 'I love you. I'll see you later.'

Pip smiled as he quietly left the room and then went over to the window and watched as he cycled up the hill towards the Whitakers' farm.

She got dressed and opened the door to go and have breakfast, but her dad was standing at the top of the stairs waiting for her. His eyes were cold.

'Get your shoes on, we're going into town.'

The last thing Pip wanted to do was get in a car with her dad. He drank so much that he was probably still over the limit. 'I have some work I need to do for college.'

'It wasn't a request, get your shoes on now.'

Desperate to avoid another fight, she did as she was told and got in the car with a huge sense of unease. The roads were icy; it wouldn't take a second for him to lose control.

They took off up the drive.

'Where are we going?' Pip asked, noticing that they weren't taking the usual route into town.

'The train station.'

'Why?'

'I don't want you in my house any more.'

She stared at him. He had threatened to kick her out on many occasions but he had never gone this far before.

'Why, what have I done now? I clean the house, I cook for you. Who will do all of that for you if I'm gone?'

'I saw Gabe leaving your bedroom this morning. I'm not going to wait around until you get pregnant. There is no way I'm having a screaming baby in my house. If you want to be a whore you can do that in London.'

'Are you insane, where would I go in London?'

The car bumped over the wooden bridge that led over the frozen lake towards the train station.

'That's not my problem.'

'Fine, if you want me out, I'll go and stay with the Whitakers.'

'They don't want you,' he spat. 'I went to see them yesterday and asked them to take you and they said no.'

'You're lying. Lizzie loves me.'

'I spoke to Lizzie Whitaker. Would you believe I offered her five thousand pounds to take you off my hands and she refused? Five thousand pounds and that still wasn't enough to get her to take you

in. Your own parents didn't want you – that's why they dumped you in the orchard – the Whitakers don't want you and neither do I. No one wants you.'

Pip stared at him in shock. The Whitakers were like family to her, why wouldn't they want her to stay with them? Had she really been burdening them with her presence all these years and they were just too polite to tell her to go away? She felt sick. Luke, Gabe's older brother, always rolled his eyes when she turned up for dinner. Did Neve and their parents feel like that too?

Suddenly her dad groaned and slumped over the steering wheel. The car swerved off the road and crashed straight through the wooden railings of the bridge. Pip screamed as the car slammed through the ice on the lake.

Her dad didn't move as water splashed over the windscreen and all she could see was the murky green of the bottom of the lake. Water covered all the windows and Pip could feel the car was sinking. She undid her seatbelt and tried to rouse her dad who was unmoving and unresponsive. Water sloshed in around the footwell as the car came to rest at the bottom of the lake with a soft thud.

'Dad, wake up,' she shouted, shaking him again. He didn't even make a noise.

She tried to undo his seatbelt as the water was now up to her knees, but it was jammed. She shook him again, desperately trying his seatbelt which was now underwater too. No matter how hard she yanked at it, it wasn't coming undone. The water was so cold, she could feel her breath was ragged, coming in short sharp bursts. She had to get out.

She tried the door but it wouldn't open. She swivelled in her seat and kicked out at it with her legs, but it still wouldn't budge.

'Dad!' Pip screamed, but he didn't move.

The water was already covering her legs and slowly creeping up her stomach. She tried her dad's seatbelt one more time but it still didn't give way.

She felt round his neck, desperately trying to find a pulse, but whether there was one or not she couldn't find it.

The cold was like ice, her legs and feet going numb. She shook her dad one more time, but when he remained unresponsive she knew she had to leave. She undid the window and the water poured in. She took a deep breath and, as the car filled to the top with water, she swam out of the window and made for the surface. If she could get help she might still be able to save her dad. The lake was thankfully quite shallow. Enough to cover the car but not much deeper than that. Within a few seconds, the surface was in sight, but as she reached up her hand thudded against thick ice. She was trapped.

Panic ripped through her as her lungs screamed in protest at the lack of oxygen. She kicked out against the ice but it didn't budge. The car had broken through the ice when it crashed through the bridge, she just had to find the hole it had made. She moved around desperately trying the ice every few seconds but it stayed resolute above her. Black spots popped in her vision and her arms and legs refused to work, and just when she thought it was hopeless, her head broke the surface of the water and she sucked in huge mouthfuls of air.

The danger wasn't over yet; she had to get out of the water and get warm quick.

With great difficulty she managed to get to the side and climb out, heaving and panting as she rested for a few seconds on the grassy verge.

She had to get help. The Whitakers' farm was at the top of the hill. It was the closest place with a phone.

Her feet, legs, arms were painfully numb with the cold and she could barely walk as she staggered up the hill on shaky legs, half crawling, half walking. Her breath was laboured and painful as she struggled to go on.

How long would it take her dad to drown? Two minutes, maybe three. How long had it been since she had opened the window and flooded the car? Three minutes, four minutes, maybe five. Maybe if she hadn't opened the window the car wouldn't have filled with water. Had she killed him by trying to escape? If her dad hadn't already been dead. Something had happened to make him swerve off the road, a heart attack maybe. Sobs burst from her throat, making it harder to breathe.

The last ten years since her mum had died had been hell, but he was still the only dad she had ever known and there was a tiny part of her that had hoped that the kind, wonderful dad who had raised her until she was seven would return at some point. Now it seemed he was gone for good.

She started counting down the seconds as she struggled up the hill. Over five minutes went by before she reached the farm. Added to the three or four minutes that had already passed since she'd left her dad in the car, it was becoming more and more hopeless. She felt sick. She should have dived back down to get him out. Why had she left him there to die?

The Whitakers would help her. Doubt slammed into her mind. What if they wouldn't help? The last words her dad had spoken played again and again in her mind. They didn't want her.

She staggered into the farm, trying desperately to summon enough energy to shout for help, but she couldn't.

She saw movement in the barn where she and Gabe always hung out and she pushed the door open and stopped dead. There was Gabe with his arms wrapped around Jenny Maguire, one of her friends from college. He kissed her on the forehead, just as he had done to Pip a thousand times.

Pain seized her heart and she turned blindly and half staggered, half ran from the farm, sobbing so hard she could hardly breathe. Her dad was dead and she was utterly alone.

❄ Chapter 4 ❄

'Pip? Is that really you?' Gabe said, watching his daughter lean her head on Pip's shoulder as if Wren had known her all her life.

Pip tried but failed to rearrange her facial features to cover the shock at seeing him again.

The small sliver of hope he'd felt, that she had come to Juniper Island to see him, quickly died. She'd clearly had no idea he owned Stardust Lake Hotel or that he would be here. A thousand questions swirled in his head but he couldn't find the words to voice any of them.

Snowflakes danced between them thick and fast and neither of them spoke.

Finally Pip recovered herself.

'My name's Piper Chesterfield. I haven't been Pip for twelve years. I would say it's nice to see you again, Gabe, but that would be a lie.' She stepped towards him, clearly angry with him over something, though he had no idea what. She gently passed Wren into his arms. 'Your daughter was outside in only her dress, no shoes, nothing warm and no one to watch over her. What a wonderful father you must be.'

She stalked past him up the hill, heading back towards the main part of the hotel.

'Where are you going?'

'The owner of this place wants to see me, I'm sure he is waiting.'

'Pip, I'm the owner.'

She stopped dead in her tracks, her shoulders slumping a little in defeat. She turned to face him.

'Well, what did you want to say to me?'

There were a million things he wanted to say and none of them were anything to do with the hotel. This was the wrong time to say any of that, though. She was tired, it was late and she'd just had a huge shock seeing him again after all this time. Plus they were standing outside in the cold and he was carrying his daughter who was staring between them with wide curious eyes. If they were going to talk they would have to be alone to do it.

The power cut had thrown everything into disarray. If it hadn't happened he might have paid more attention to the guest's name, he would have been there to see her arrive and maybe had more chance to prepare himself for the onslaught of suppressed feelings that were suddenly crashing over him.

Gabe looked over at his lodge shining brightly in the darkness. Annoyingly all the staff quarters hadn't been affected at all by the power; it was only the guest lodges that had been cut off. Remembering he had to talk to his first proper guest about the power cut, he called on all his professional reserves.

'There has been a power cut in all the lodges and none of the guest rooms have any electricity. It's a temporary measure I'm sure and I'm very sorry for any inconvenience but for tonight we have made alternative arrangements for you.'

'Fine, just show me to my room.'

He glanced over to his lodge again and back at his beautiful best friend standing before him. Professionalism be damned.

'I have a spare room in my lodge. It's very comfortable, you can have free access to the lounge and any of the facilities. The bedroom is very spacious with great views over the lake. I can arrange for dinner and breakfast to be served there if you wish or you can eat in the dining room. Of course we will offer you compensation for the inconvenience.'

Pip stared at him in shock. 'I'm not sleeping in your house.'

What had happened between them for her to hate him so much? He hadn't seen her since the day her dad had died; did she somehow blame him for that?

'There is nowhere else for you to sleep. And it's only for one night.'

She stared at him for longer than necessary for her to come to a decision before she finally nodded.

He sighed with relief.

'I'll just call down to reception and get them to bring the bags up.' He walked up the path, holding Wren in one arm. He pulled out the walkie-talkie from his pocket as Pip walked at his side.

He pressed the button for Jake's walkie-talkie and a second or two later Jake answered.

'Hello Mr Whitaker?'

'Hi Jake. Can you tell Boris I've found Wren and can you also bring Miss Chesterfield's bags to my lodge please?'

There was silence from the other end before Jake finally answered. 'Sorry, Mr Whitaker, did you say your lodge?'

He cursed to himself. 'Yes, that's right. As we discussed earlier, my lodge is the only one with the spare room. Perhaps you weren't there when we made the decision.'

There was silence again and Gabe prayed that Jake didn't question it any further. Pip was listening to every word.

Finally the walkie-talkie crackled to life again. 'That's fine, sir. I'll bring them straight over.'

Gabe climbed the few steps to his front door, stamped his feet a few times to get rid of the snow and then pushed the door open. He placed Wren down and undid Pip's coat and removed the gloves from her feet.

'Go get into your pyjamas, Princess, and I'll be in to read you a story shortly.'

'Piper could read me a story.'

'No, she's a guest in our house and she's had a long day. Besides, you know I want to find out what happens to the dragon in the story we're reading as much as you do.'

Wren grinned and ran off towards her bedroom.

He stood up and turned back to face Pip. She was so incredibly beautiful, even more so than the last time he'd seen her. He swallowed down the lump of emotion that had stalled in his throat.

'I'll show you to your room.'

He led the way upstairs to the back of the house where the spare room had been made up for his mum and dad's arrival in a few days' time.

The bedroom was nice and had lovely views; it even had an en-suite. It would be no hardship for Pip to sleep there. It was going to be harder for him to have her under the same roof after all this time. She looked around her new room and sat down on the bed.

'Are you hungry? I could arrange for something to be brought over?'

She cleared her throat and it was quite clear when she spoke that she was forcing herself to be nice. 'A sandwich would be great. If it's not too much trouble?'

They were being so polite to each other when in reality he wanted to kiss her and shake her at the same time.

'I'll see what I can arrange.'

He stared at her for a few moments and went back downstairs, just as Jake arrived with the bags. To his credit he didn't even ask why Pip was staying with him and not in the village as originally planned.

'Thanks Jake, can you take the bags up to the back bedroom and would you mind waiting with Wren for a few minutes? I won't be long.'

'Of course, Mr Whitaker,' Jake said, without question.

'Jake!' Wren called from over the top balcony. 'Will you come and be my prince?'

'Hey Munchkin,' Jake laughed. 'I'll be there in two minutes.'

Gabe left them alone and raced over to the main reception. As he feared, his sister Neve was waiting for him, her hands on her hips.

'What the hell are you playing at?' Neve demanded. 'What was that big speech you gave the other day where you said no member of staff is to have any kind of relationship with the guests other than a professional one? Five seconds with our first guest and you've already invited her to stay in your lodge. Jake said she was pretty but damn it Gabe, I expected more of you than this.'

'Neve, listen—'

'No, I won't. What happened to putting the guest in the house in the village as we discussed? The boys have been working for the last few hours to get the place ready for her arrival, the house is clean, the bed is made, they have even lit a fire. But obviously your sexual needs far outweigh the good of the hotel. And have you thought about Wren at all in any of this? Are you just going to put your daughter to bed and then shag our first guest in the room next door? Christ Gabe, you are not one of the added extras for our guests. We are not that kind of resort.'

'Neve, it's Pip.'

She stared at him in shock and the anger faded from her face immediately. 'Pip Silvers?'

'Yes, she's going under the name of Piper Chesterfield now, but it's her.'

'She's married?'

'No, I don't think so. I don't know. I think Chesterfield was her mum's maiden name.'

'But… What is she doing here?'

'I don't know, she had no idea we were here. But she is mad at me for some reason when I'm the one who should be angry at her.'

'So...what? You're just going to pick up where you left off ten years ago?'

'Twelve years. It's been twelve years since I last saw her and, no, I don't think that's an option. I just need to talk to her, I need to know what happened and where she's been and I can't do that if she's down in the village and I'm up here.'

Her face softened. 'You need closure.'

He sighed and pushed his hands through his hair. Neve knew what he had gone through. She had watched him grieve for her and now all those memories had come flooding back. 'I think I do. I never had that. She was my best friend. We were in love. I was going to propose to her and she threw all of it away. We never broke up, she never said goodbye. She just vanished. She broke my heart and I spent so long hoping she would come back and now she's here, I need to know why she ran away. It won't affect the hotel or Wren, I promise. I just...I need to talk to her.'

'Then go talk to her. With any luck the power will be back up tomorrow and you'll have no excuse to keep her in your lodge any longer.'

Gabe nodded. 'I need to get her some food. I've left Jake babysitting, so I better go and rescue him before Wren has him dressed up in a prince's costume. Can you get the kitchen to make a sandwich and a portion of chips and send it over?'

Neve nodded.

Gabe raced back over to his lodge, only to find that Jake was on his hands and knees giving pony rides to Wren in the lounge. Wren was shrieking loudly as Jake deliberately banged into the furniture. Gabe plucked Wren off Jake's back and threw her over his shoulder. She squealed in delight as she hung upside down.

'Thanks Jake, I'm relieving you of your horsey duties.'

Jake stood up, brushing the dust off his uniform. 'No problem.'

He let himself out and Gabe ran up the stairs to Wren's room and dropped her on the bed. He pulled his coat off and kicked off his snow boots and socks.

'Right, Princess, get into bed.'

Wren lay down and Gabe lay down next to her, covering them both with the duvet. He grabbed the book they were reading from the drawers next to her bed and turned to the right chapter as Wren snuggled into his shoulder. He kissed her on the head and started reading.

He needed to talk to Pip, but Wren needed to be asleep first. It would give him time to plan out what he wanted to say because right now he had nothing.

❄ Chapter 5 ❄

As Gabe walked out of Wren's room, Jake arrived again with a plate under a silver dome. Gabe took it off him and Jake left, without question. Gabe had originally thought that Jake was too young to be a professional porter in his resort, now he could see how wrong he was; the boy might even earn himself a pay rise before the week was out.

He left the plate in the lounge and went upstairs to tell Pip the food was here. The bedroom door was closed and when he knocked softly there was no reply.

He knocked again. 'Pip. Erm, Miss Chesterfield.' He rested his head against the door in frustration. The line between professional and personal was already blurred. He had deliberately invited her to stay in his lodge so he could finally get some answers; there was nothing professional about that.

There was still no answer. Was she upset over seeing him and now refusing to answer the door? Was she asleep?

He knocked again and when there was still no answer he opened the door just as Pip walked out of the en-suite bathroom stark naked, drying her hair.

'Damn it Gabe, did you not knock?' She quickly wrapped the towel around her, but unfortunately the towel was so small it barely covered any of her modesty.

'I did, there was no answer.'

'So you just walked in? What kind of hotel are you running here, where guests are forced to stay with members of staff and privacy is reduced to a minimum? If I was writing a review for this place, it wouldn't be very good.' She struggled to keep the towel closed and every professional bone in his body was screaming at him to leave the room. He should have left the second she walked out the bathroom yet he was still there, his feet glued to the floor. Twelve years had done nothing to quell the feelings he had for her.

'There's a robe in the wardrobe,' he said, his voice strangled.

She let out a sigh of impatience as she moved to the wardrobe. 'Turn around.'

He did as he was told and inadvertently stared straight into a mirror as she ditched the towel. He quickly looked down at the floor. He knew every inch of her body. The night they had first made love he had spent hours kissing, stroking and caressing every single part of her. Wonderful memories of that night came flooding back.

'Did you want something?' Pip said from behind him.

He chanced a brief glance at the mirror and, seeing she was suitably covered, he turned around.

'Just to say the food has arrived. It's in the lounge.'

He should have offered to bring it to her room but he needed answers and he intended to get them.

'I'll be down in a minute.'

He stared at her for a moment – her eyes were ablaze – and then he stepped out and closed the door behind him.

❄

Piper stared at the closed door, feeling the tension in her shoulders. Gabe Whitaker was here. Infuriatingly he had got even better looking than when she had last seen him. He had filled out in every way, his arms and legs were huge and strong, those piercing sea-blue eyes under that black messy hair were bluer than she had remembered. He was beautiful and she hated him a little bit because of it.

She had thought about him so often. She had known him her entire life, they were best friends growing up and that friendship had grown into something beautiful and wonderful, something that was supposed to last forever. She had fallen head over heels in love with him and that love had been impossible to switch off no matter how angry she was at him for betraying her.

In the months after her dad's death, when she had been staying with her aunt in London, she had often thought about calling him to get some explanation for what she had seen that day. But every time she thought about him and Jenny Maguire she found herself thinking about the events that had happened that day – her dad, the accident, being trapped under the ice – and it was easier not to think about any of that. She'd had horrible nightmares and panic attacks and her aunt had arranged counselling, but in the end it was easier to file all those memories in a box marked 'Do not open', and Gabe and Jenny Maguire were part of that.

She should have demanded an explanation there and then in the barn, but she'd felt so let down, not just by him but by the Whitaker family's refusal to take her in when her dad no longer wanted her around. She had always considered them to be like a second family, but she had clearly been a burden to them and not one they wanted. She couldn't help thinking Gabe might have been part of the reason that they had said no. Maybe having her there permanently would have cramped his style with the other girls he was secretly dating.

After seeing him with Jenny Maguire, she had managed to make it to the drive leading up to the farm where there was a payphone, which was closer than going up to the farmhouse anyway. She had called the emergency services and hysterically explained that her dad was dead.

The next few hours had been a blur as she somehow managed to make it back to her own house, get changed and answer questions from the police when they arrived. Divers had come to retrieve the body, though she wasn't there when they pulled him out, and when there was nothing left to be said or done, they' asked if she had anyone nearby she could stay with. She'd shaken her head, told them she had no one but that an aunt in London was expecting her. She packed her bags, they took her to the train station and she left the tiny village in the Lake District behind forever.

She had locked away all those memories from that fateful day, but now they were back and she didn't know how to deal with them. Though keeping herself shut away in her bedroom was certainly not going to help.

She got dressed and went downstairs.

Gabe was sitting on the sofa waiting for her, the log fire burning merrily in the fireplace making the whole room seem cosy, even though Piper felt cold.

She sat down in the furthest corner away from him and pulled the plate onto her lap. She took the lid off, curled her legs under her and started eating, feeling Gabe's eyes on her the whole time.

To his credit, he let her finish eating before he spoke.

'What happened, Pip? It's been twelve years. You just disappeared. No phone calls, no letters, nothing. I had no idea where you were. The last time I saw you was the morning after we had made love for the first time. How could you walk away from that?'

She stared at him in shock. He had no right to be angry. 'Funny, the last time I saw you, you were wrapped in the arms of Jenny Maguire.'

He stared at her in confusion. 'Jenny Maguire? Who the hell is Jenny Maguire?'

'Oh, I'm glad you threw away what we had for someone so special.'

He frowned and then his face suddenly cleared with recognition. 'Jenny Maguire is Anne-Marie's daughter, my mum's best friend. Nothing ever happened between me and her. I don't know what you saw but it certainly wasn't…' He stalled, his face suddenly turning to guilt and horror. 'That day. You saw us in the barn?'

Piper nodded. 'The worst thing was, when my dad crashed the car into the lake, when the water was seeping into the car from every crack, when I was desperately trying to rouse him and free him from the seatbelt, when I got out and was trapped under the ice, all I kept thinking about was you. How I couldn't give up because I couldn't be without you. Then when I got out of the lake, I just wanted to see you, to feel your arms around me and hear you tell me it was OK. As I struggled up the hill to your farm to get help, I knew if I could just find you, everything would be OK. And I did find you and you were in the arms of someone else.'

Gabe stared at her in horror. 'You… You were in the car?'

'Yes. The worst day of my life and seeing you with another woman was probably the final straw.'

'I didn't know. God, that week was a mess. We didn't hear about your dad's accident until a few days after he died. We heard that you'd gone to stay with your aunt in London, but I just assumed you would be back after a few days. I had no way of contacting you to see if you were OK. I tried to phone you, I emailed, but you just vanished.'

'Why would I come back? I had nothing for me there.'

Gabe winced. 'My parents adored you, you could have stayed with us.'

'Your parents tolerated me. They certainly didn't want me living with them on a permanent basis.'

Gabe looked more hurt about that than anything else. 'They loved you, they always loved you.'

'Did you know that my dad asked them if I could move in with them? He offered them five thousand pounds if they took me in. They turned him down.'

'I don't believe that for one second.'

'All my life, I'd dealt with rejection, the knowledge that my birth parents never wanted me and even my adopted dad only agreed to take me in because my mum wanted me. Something he reminded me of almost daily after my mum died. But I always consoled myself with the fact that you and your family loved me even if no one else did. But it turned out you guys didn't want me either. That was the hardest rejection for me to take.'

'That's bullshit. My mum and dad loved you. Mum was always asking me to ask you round to dinner, they took you on holiday with us. Can I remind you that your dad was vile to you after your mum died, always putting you down and making you doubt yourself? Whatever crap he told you about my parents not wanting you is an absolute lie. They'll be here in a few days, you can ask them yourself.'

Piper shook her head, all the hurt and confusion she had felt after that fateful day came crashing back now.

'The day your dad died, it seems the Grim Reaper was out in force. Jenny's dad had died earlier that morning. His car had slid on some ice and collided with a wall. He was killed instantly. My mum and Jenny's mum, Anne-Marie, were best friends and Anne-Marie was apparently a complete wreck. She'd sent Jenny to get my mum to come over. I'd seen Jenny when she walked past the barn and I could see she was upset. She told me what had happened and she was crying. I was giving her a hug to say I was sorry, I promise it was nothing more than that. I loved you, you were the only one I ever loved. There was never any other woman for me.'

Piper stared at him, feeling the tears prick her eyes. It couldn't be true. Had she really thrown away the love of her life over that?

She had been so young and traumatised over the accident. For months after she had tried to cope with the guilt of what had happened under the ice, reliving the moment she had flooded the car so many times in her head and in her dreams, desperately trying to figure out if she could have done something differently. It didn't matter that the autopsy revealed her dad had died of a severe heart attack and had probably been dead before he even hit the water. It didn't matter that her dad had been horrible to her for the last ten years of her life, or that he was driving her to the train station to get rid of her with nothing more than the clothes on her back, she had still been racked with guilt.

While she had tried to come to terms with that, it had been easier to be angry at Gabe for not being there when she needed him and at his family too. It had seemed better to pick herself up and move on with her life, never staying still long enough to build relationships with anyone, never putting her trust in anyone again for fear of being let down. And now to find out that the one person she had trusted and loved in her life hadn't let her down at all?

'I thought…'

'You honestly thought that I would betray you like that, after spending the night before telling you how much I loved you, how much you meant to me? How could you possibly believe that I would be with another woman a few hours after I left your bed?'

Piper stared at him.

'You never trusted me. I should have guessed that you would have run at the first bump in the road. You kept asking me why I was with you when I could have anyone, you never believed me when I said I only wanted you. You were waiting for me to let you down just like everyone else had and when you saw me with Jenny it was all the proof you needed to know you had been right all along.'

Piper had nothing she could say. She felt so tired all of a sudden.

'I'm…tired, I'm going to bed.'

He watched her leave but made no attempt to stop her.

❄

Gabe watched Pip's bedroom door close, feeling so angry.

He switched the lights off and went upstairs to his own bedroom. He got undressed and caught his reflection in the mirror, his eyes falling on the tattoo he'd had done across his chest. Four savage-looking scars clawed across his chest as if it had been ripped open by an animal. At the age of eighteen it had seemed a good idea at the time, a symbolic reminder of the pain he'd been in when the only girl he had ever loved walked away and didn't look back, ripping out his heart and taking it with her on the way out. He was obviously one for theatrics when he was younger; not content to just cry and move on, he'd got a tattoo to signify his pain. He smiled, rolling his eyes at his younger self.

He had moved on, though. After bumping into Pip's aunt several months after her disappearance when she came to sort out Pip's house and hearing that Pip was never coming back, and later, after he'd got out of hospital, he had vowed it wasn't going to destroy him. He'd gone to university, thrown himself into his studies in business management and astutely ignored any woman who tried to get to know him better. The agony had stayed with him and eventually he had tried to get over her by sleeping with any woman who would have him. The pain eventually went away and looking back now it was unlikely they would have even lasted, that their love was anything beyond puppy love, but yet he still thought of her often.

And although the tattoo was a reminder of a period in his life that he never wanted to go back to, he was in a much happier place now than when he had permanently tattooed his pain across his chest. Since Wren's mum had walked out on her when she was tiny, Wren had been his entire world and he didn't need anyone else. Pip being back wouldn't change that. He had closure now and he realised that Pip was too messed up to ever be able to sustain a proper relationship. She was not someone he wanted to get involved with again and certainly not someone he wanted around Wren.

Tomorrow, if the power was not back up, he would move her to the lodge in the village they had prepared for her arrival. He would treat her just like any other guest who stayed in his hotel and he would secretly count the days until she left and he wouldn't have to see her again.

❄ Chapter 6 ❄

Gabe lay in bed staring at the bright moon as it lit up the hills and woods around the hotel, cursing that seeing Pip again had prevented him from finding any sleep.

A stupid misunderstanding had been the reason he had lost his best friend. Now that most of the anger had receded, it broke his heart that he hadn't been able to be there for her after the accident, that she had seen him comforting a girl who meant nothing to him instead. If Pip had arrived five minutes before or five minutes after, none of this would ever have happened. But he was angry that after seventeen years of friendship and a love as deep and intense as theirs, she would throw it away after seeing him hug someone else. Her insecurities over being abandoned at birth obviously ran deep and she had been waiting for him and his family to reject her all along.

But now he had the answers he needed, although he still didn't feel any better for it.

Suddenly a cry for help rang out in the darkness. Gabe leapt out of bed and out onto the landing and was running for Wren's room as fast as he could when another cry for help came and this time he knew it was from Pip's room, not Wren's. He peered round his daughter's bedroom door just in case, but when he saw her lying sprawled out like a starfish in her bed, snoring softly, he quickly ran to Pip's room. As another moan came from the other side of the door, he burst in and saw her fast asleep too, struggling against unknown forces as, somewhere in her dream world, things were not good.

He hurried to the side of the bed and gently shook her awake. She woke with a jolt, let out a little yelp at seeing him leaning over her and shuffled quickly off the bed away from him, backing into the wall.

He quickly flicked the bedside lamp on, illuminating the room in a soft warm glow. Pip was standing against the wall, clutching the duvet to her chest, her eyes wide and terrified. But when she saw it was him and where she was, she let out a sigh of relief and sank to the floor.

Gabe was still angry at her and he didn't want to be in a position to comfort her. He would simply check she was OK and then leave. He stared at her as she pushed a trembling hand through her hair. It hurt him to see her like this.

He still cared about her.

That thought was like a punch to the gut because he certainly didn't want to feel like that. He hated himself for being so weak and hated her a little bit for stirring all those feelings up in him that had long since been dead and buried. He would just go back to bed. But as he continued to watch her, the need to protect her outweighed the need to protect himself. She needed someone right now and he was all she had.

He moved over to her side and, after a moment's hesitation, he sat down next to her.

She sighed, leaning her head back against the wall. 'God, Gabe, I haven't had those nightmares for twelve years. I had them for months after the accident, but then they just stopped. I guess seeing you again today has jolted all those memories back to the surface.'

'Do you want to talk to me about the accident, would it help?'

'I don't know. Maybe.'

He sat in silence for a while. If she wanted to tell him, she would. After a while she spoke. Telling him everything about that fateful day and he felt even guiltier about not being there for her when she needed him the most.

'I'm so sorry that you went through that. I can't even imagine what that was like for you. What about the dreams? What are they about?'

'They vary. Sometimes I'm trapped in the car and my dad leaves me to save himself. Sometimes I'm just trapped under the ice. Sometimes I'm standing on the side of the lake and I can hear my dad banging on the car door trying to get out.'

'Your dad died of a heart attack, he didn't drown. There was nothing you could have done to change that.'

'I know.' Pip closed her eyes and leaned her head against his shoulder. For a second it was just as it had been twelve years ago, when they'd sit in the barn or at her house, with her head on his shoulder as they talked about anything and everything. Sometimes they'd talk about their future and the big house they would have, the children they wanted and what they hoped to do with their lives. It was heartbreaking that in the blink of an eye all of that had changed.

It didn't seem right now, having her cuddle up to him. So much time had passed, so much resentment on both their parts.

He moved his arm to wrap the duvet around her, forcing her to lift her head, but when he moved back into his position he ensured he was far enough away from her that she wouldn't be able to lean against him.

He thought he had been subtle, but she had clearly noticed. Hurt crossed her face for a second but then it was gone.

'I'm sorry I ruined everything,' Pip said.

He looked out into the snow-covered darkness. 'It wasn't your fault, not really. You'd had a shock, you weren't thinking straight. Your dad had died and you'd been trapped under the ice. If you had found me and Jenny hugging on any other day, I expect you would have been a lot more rational about it. Instead, with the trauma of the accident, it seemed worse than it was and with your grief you didn't have a chance to be logical about it.'

She sighed.

'And who's to say that we would have lasted anyway,' Gabe said, practically. 'If we'd gone to university, travelled, would the puppy love of two teenagers really have been enough to keep us together all this time?'

'Maybe you're right. At the time I thought what we had was forever.'

'I did too,' he said, softly.

'I also thought that Myspace was really cool and Brad and Jennifer would last a lifetime.'

He smiled. 'A lot has changed in twelve years.'

They were silent for a while but it wasn't awkward, silence had never been awkward with her.

'We could still be friends, though. When I leave here we could keep in touch,' Pip said.

Could they be friends again?

She looked at him hopefully and then her face fell when she saw his doubt. 'You're probably too busy to have a pen pal.'

'I'd like it if we stayed in touch.'

He cursed himself. Why would he want to stay in touch with her? But there was something about sitting here with her. Now she was back, he didn't want to lose her again. He knew they could never be in a relationship again, but they could be friends. He wanted to be friends with her.

'You would?'

'I really would. I've missed you. We were best friends long before we were in a relationship and although we can never go back, maybe we can move forward as friends.'

Her face lit up into a big smile. 'OK, so we're friends. Tell me what you've done for the last twelve years. You're a dad now, were you married to Wren's mum?'

He shook his head. 'Ellen was never someone I would have wanted to spend the rest of my life with. She was someone I was seeing, she was fun, a bit of a party girl, but it never would have lasted. We'd been seeing each other for about three months when she told me she was pregnant. She was supposed to be on the pill, so it came as something of a shock. I wanted to get married: if I was going to be a dad, I wanted to do it properly. She wasn't interested in that at all. She was too busy enjoying herself. When Wren was born her party lifestyle barely changed at all. She hung around for six months before she left me to raise Wren alone. It was something of a relief. We argued constantly and she was never going to win any mother of the year awards. She drifted in and out of our lives for the next year, visiting occasionally, sending the odd present. She died in a jet-ski accident when Wren was eighteen months old. Ellen was drunk and…well, it was an awful accident. I really felt for her family.'

'I'm so sorry.'

'It's OK. I felt sad for Wren that she would grow up without a mum but…I know it's horrible to say, but I think Wren is better off without her. I love her so much, she is the best thing that ever happened to me and we're doing great with just the two of us. She doesn't need a mum.'

'That didn't stop Sally from trying to take the role.'

Gabe laughed. 'You did have a nice little chat with Wren, didn't you?'

'She told me that Sally had told her she was going to be her new mummy.'

'Not on my life.'

Pip laughed. 'Wren said that too.'

'I liked her but she lied to me. Frequently. And it's important I have people around me that I can trust. I've made some good decisions over the years and I now own a few hotels. There are... certain financial benefits that come from dating me. I guess there are quite a few women that would see me as good husband material because of it. Sally was one of those women that saw pound signs when she looked at me. She was just a bit of fun.'

'So have you ever dated someone seriously? Anyone you loved?'

'There's only ever been one woman I fell in love with.' Immediately he regretted saying that. He didn't want to give her any hope that they could rekindle their relationship.

'So you're not seeing anyone at the moment?'

'No.'

For a brief moment he thought he saw hope flare in her eyes and that annoyed him a bit. After what had happened, after what she had done, she couldn't possibly think they could just pick up where they left off.

'I like it that way. I've been with lots of women over the years, but dating someone when I have a daughter just isn't practical. I'm not going to hand her over to a babysitter every night just so I can go out with some random woman. It's bad enough that I have to do that when I work, I don't want to do it in the evenings too. I'm certainly not looking for anything serious. Someone who thinks they can swoop in and play step-mum to my daughter, I don't think so.' He ignored the hurt in her eyes and decided to change the subject slightly. 'What about you, any serious boyfriends or husbands?'

He wasn't sure why he wanted to know the answer to that question when he had no plans of pursuing anything romantic with her, but there was something inside him that needed to know.

'Not really.'

He looked at her. She was so beautiful, he imagined there must have been several men over the years, even if none of them were serious. That thought alone filled him with a pang of jealousy. 'You must have had men swarming around you.'

'Hardly, but then I've perfected the "If you don't leave me alone, then you might lose body parts" look.'

'Ouch.'

'Plus I sometimes wear a wedding ring, it deters most men.'

'You push them away?'

She paused before she spoke. 'Let's just say, I have trust issues.'

Guilt gnawed at his gut. Partly because of her terrible upbringing and partly because of him, she hadn't allowed herself to trust anyone since she had left her home twelve years before. There was something really sad about her never letting anyone in and spending her whole life alone.

'Besides, I've never really stood still long enough to have any kind of serious relationship.'

'What have you been doing for the last twelve years?'

'I lived with my aunt for a while, but she didn't really want me around either. I stayed with her long enough to sell Dad's house – my aunt gave me all the money and told me to go and see the world.'

He forced down the anger that someone else had let her down. 'You always dreamed of travelling.'

'I did. And I never really stopped. I was lucky enough to get an amazing job which involved a lot of travelling and I've been doing that for ten years.'

'Oh? What's the job?'

'I'm…a photographer. I take pictures of hotels and holiday destinations for travel brochures.'

'You're living your dream. You always wanted to be a photographer. I'm so pleased for you.'

She smiled sadly, but he couldn't interpret it. He had noticed the pause too when she had said what she did for a job. Was it not what she had imagined it would be? Pip had always wanted to be a photographer, travelling the world and taking beautiful photos of the different countries, not just the views but the people. Maybe her job didn't allow her to be as creative as she wanted.

'So you own hotels? How did you get into that?' Pip asked.

He sensed she was changing the subject away from her job, but he decided not to push it.

'When my grandad died he left us all a ton of money. No one really knows where this money came from, though there were rumours it had something to do with North Sea oil. I'd been doing business and tourism at university so I knew I wanted to move into the hotel industry. I invested the money in a small London hotel, bought it cheap, did it up, changed how it was run, and sold it on for almost four times what I paid for it. I repeated the process several times over the years, got good people to come and work for me, made the hotels the best they could be. Some I sold, some I kept. I currently own four hotels, one in London, one in California, one in New York and now here.'

'I bet your family are so proud of you,' she said and he noted the wistful tone in her voice.

'I hope so. Mum and Dad used their money to travel the world, so I only see them every few months.'

'And Neve, how is she? Is she still into horses? She had such a way with them, I always expected to see her on the Olympic equestrian team over the years. Wasn't she working at the stables where the British Olympic team trained?'

'Yes.' He hesitated, not wanting to impart the full story because it wasn't his to tell. 'That ended badly for her. She works for me now, she's here as my hotel manager and she's completely brilliant. I'd be lost without her.'

'She's here?' Her whole face lit up. Pip had always adored Neve. She was two years older than Pip and so they were never really properly friends, but Neve would do Pip's hair and make-up. Pip looked up to Neve like the big sister she never had and he knew for Neve the feeling was mutual, that she loved having a little sister figure to talk to and look after.

'I bet she'll be really pleased to see you again,' Gabe said, encouragingly.

Her face fell a little. 'Oh, I don't know about that. She was always very protective over you. I imagine the welcome might not exactly be a warm one after I left you the way I did.'

'You don't need to worry about her.' He hesitated. 'Luke on the other hand…'

The smile completely fell from her face this time. 'Is he here too?'

Luke, his half-brother, was six years older than him and they'd never had the easiest of relationships growing up. He seemed to hate everyone, and that extended to Pip too. Gabe was much closer to him now, but he was still such a closed-off person.

'Yes, he mainly helps with all the animals but also with a few of the manual labour jobs, construction and repairs. He's gone through a really rough time recently and I think he came up here hoping to get some solitude.'

'God, he hated me growing up.'

'He hated everyone. I wouldn't take it too personally. He was like you in many ways, he had an awful start to his life.' Despite Luke being the older brother, Gabe still felt really protective over him and worried about him. He certainly wasn't winning any friends around the resort at the moment. The only friend Luke had made in the three months since he had been here was Audrey, one of the girls who ran a shop in the village. That was going to end in disaster as well. She was completely head over heels in love with him and he had no idea. He was going to end up hurting her and pushing her away too. He sighed. 'Don't worry about him, you probably won't even see him while you're here. You know he keeps himself to himself.'

'Well, I'll certainly keep an eye out for him.'

Gabe sighed. That would be another thing he'd have to worry about while Pip was here. That and the fact that he was enjoying talking to her again way too much.

'So you must have seen some fantastic sights on your travels, where have you been?' Gabe asked.

Pip's face broke into a huge smile. 'It's been amazing. I've travelled around the world and the seen the most beautiful things...'

He smiled as she talked and for a while everything seemed right with the world. He had his best friend back. He would ignore the fact that she would be leaving again in just over two weeks and he'd probably never see her again.

❄ Chapter 7 ❄

Piper woke up to the bright winter sunshine streaming in through the window. She opened her eyes a crack and realised she was lying on the floor with her head in Gabe's lap. How did that happen? They had talked all night, catching up on what they had been doing for the last twelve years and it had been almost like old times, as if that gap had never happened. At some point she must have fallen asleep, but she wasn't sure how she had ended up like this.

Suddenly she realised something else: Gabe was stroking her hair. The feelings she'd once had for him but suppressed came crashing back now at this sweet, intimate gesture. She couldn't fall for him again. She had spent almost her whole life believing she couldn't trust anyone, that she wasn't loveable or worthy enough. To find out Gabe had truly loved her and she had thrown that away was utterly heartbreaking. He would never love her like that again, so falling for him would only lead to rejection, and she couldn't face that.

She felt him stir and stretch slightly under her and she quickly closed her eyes, hoping to prolong the moment with him just for a few seconds.

'Hey beautiful.' Gabe's voice was all croaky and sleepy but also filled with love and adoration. 'What are you doing in here?'

Odd question. It was her room after all.

'You weren't in your room, Daddy, and then I saw Piper's door open,' Wren said and Piper realised it had been Wren stroking her hair, not Gabe. Gabe had clearly just woken up. 'I'm combing her hair and making it look like Elsa.'

'That's very nice of you. Oh, you've brought all your snowflake hairgrips in here too. I'm sure Pip will love that when she wakes up,' Gabe whispered.

Piper smiled and kept her eyes closed for a moment, intrigued to listen to their conversation.

'Will you plait her hair for me? I was going to do it but plaiting is hard. Then I can put all the snowflakes in the plait.'

'Erm, we might wake her up if I plait it and she had a long day yesterday, I'm sure she's really tired.'

'If you do it gently she won't wake up and it'll be a nice surprise for her to be Elsa when she wakes up.'

Gabe clearly hesitated for a moment as he weighed up doing what his daughter wanted and doing something that could be considered to be quite intimate with Piper.

'OK, then, but we must be really quiet,' Gabe whispered and Piper stifled a smile. He had a beautiful way with his daughter. She had overheard him reading a story to her the night before and it made her heart ache at how much he clearly loved her.

She felt him lift her hair carefully and gather it gently into a ponytail and then his fingers were moving deftly through her hair. His touch at the back of her neck sent goosebumps down her spine.

'She's so pretty, isn't she, Daddy?'

'Yes she is.'

'And she has golden eyes that the angels gave her.'

Gabe's fingers paused in their work. 'Is that what Pip told you?'

'Yes, she said that her mummy told her that her real parents might be angels.'

After a moment Gabe's fingers carried on moving through her hair. 'Yes, her mummy said that often when Pip was little.

Pip noticed that her eyes were a different colour to everyone else and she worried about being different. Pip's mummy told her that she was a gift from the angels and that's why her eyes were gold.'

'Is it true, Daddy?'

Piper regretted saying that now – it was an offhand comment – but she certainly didn't want to confuse Wren.

'When I was about your age, I heard people talk about Pip being adopted and I asked my mummy and daddy what it meant.'

'Nanny and Pops?'

'Yes, and they told me that Pip's real parents were unable to look after her so they gave her to Louise and Simon because they knew that they would love her and care for her better than they could.'

That wasn't true of course. She'd been left in a wooden apple box in an orchard when she was only a day old. Her birth mum hadn't even cared enough about her to arrange for a proper adoption or to leave her somewhere she would be found more easily.

'Louise and Simon desperately wanted children of their own but couldn't have them, so they applied to adopt a child and they were given Pip to raise as their own daughter. Long before Pip was old enough to ask about her eyes, Louise always said that she was a gift from Heaven, her perfect little Pip.'

Piper felt the lump in her throat as she listened to Gabe explain about her past. Her mum, Louise, had loved her even if her dad hadn't. She forgot that sometimes. Louise had died when Piper was only seven years old and it was hard to remember the good times they'd had when the next ten years had been blighted by so much darkness.

'Nanny and Pops also said that Pip needed us to love and look after her too because when she got older she might be sad that her real mummy couldn't keep her, but if we showed her how much we loved her then she might not be sad any more.'

Tears formed behind Piper's eyelids at this beautiful gesture from Gabe's parents.

Gabe's fingers stopped plaiting and Piper felt the end being secured with a hair tie. She felt Wren's tiny fingers press things into the plait.

'And did you love her, Daddy?'

'I loved her very much.'

'Like you love me.'

'In a different way to how I love you.'

'And did Louise and Simon look after her and love her too even though she wasn't really their daughter?'

There was a pause from Gabe. 'Louise loved her a lot. But both Louise and Simon died a very long time ago.'

Wren's fingers continued to press and twist things into Piper's hair. 'But who looks after her and loves her now if they are both dead?'

'She's grown up now, she doesn't need anyone to look after her any more.'

'But, Daddy, you still have Nanny and Pops to look after you.'

'They don't really look after me. They love me but I can take care of myself now.'

'And Neve looks after you.'

'Yes, I guess she does.'

'And I look after you.'

'Yes you do, Princess, you do a very good job of looking after Daddy.'

'And Piper has no one to look after her?'

Gabe hesitated again. 'No, I don't think she does.'

'We could look after her.'

'It doesn't work like that, honey. She's not a pet, we can't keep her.'

'She needs someone to love her. Nanny and Pops said that if we love her she won't be sad.'

'They meant when Pip was a child, not now.'

'She doesn't need loving now?'

Piper would have laughed at this awkward conversation had it not been so heartbreaking.

'She does, but she is only staying here for just over two weeks, then she will be leaving. It's hard to love someone who you don't see.'

'But you don't see Nanny and Pops very often, but you still love them?'

Gabe sighed. 'Yes I do... Do you want some breakfast?'

'Yes, I'm starving. Can I have pancakes?'

'You can have whatever you want.'

'Why do you call her Pip when her name is Piper?'

'It's a nickname, Princess. Just like my name is Gabriel and everyone calls me Gabe. Pip is short for Piper. I've always called her Pip, it would be difficult for me to think of her as Piper now.'

'What should I call her?'

'Why don't you ask her that when she wakes up?'

Piper felt a slight weight lean over her and then Wren whispered in her ear, 'It's time to wake up.'

'Wren, I didn't mean wake her up now,' Gabe said, sternly.

'But if she doesn't wake up now, she'll miss out on the pancakes.'

Piper stretched and sat up, feeling slightly guilty that she had pretended to be asleep and overheard their conversation but secretly glad she had.

Gabe looked at her with concern, obviously wondering how much she had heard.

‘I certainly wouldn’t want to miss out on any pancakes,’ Piper said.

‘I made your hair like Elsa’s,’ Wren said. ‘Daddy helped too.’

‘Oh.’ Piper pulled the plait over her shoulder to inspect it and tried to act surprised when she saw all the tiny snowflakes entwined with her plait. ‘It’s beautiful.’

‘Go and get dressed, Princess, and we can all go over to the dining room for breakfast together.’

‘OK.’

Wren ran out the room excitedly but a second later she came back. ‘Piper, shall I call you Piper or Pip?’

‘You can call me Pip. All my friends call me that.’

Wren nodded happily at this answer and ran off.

Piper returned her attention to Gabe who was watching her carefully.

‘I’m not sure how much of that you heard…’ he said.

‘A little.’

He rubbed the back of his neck. ‘I think Wren would like to see us together, I was just explaining that—’

‘That’s not going to happen,’ she finished for him, swallowing the sudden hurt she felt over that.

‘We can’t go back to how we were, Pip. It’s been twelve years. It would be silly to think we still loved each other after all that time. We’ve both moved on with our lives, had different partners, lived hundreds of miles apart. We’re different people now.’

‘Of course we are. As you said, it was just silly teenage puppy love anyway. It would never have lasted.’

He looked hurt at that and she couldn’t help feeling a little disappointed that they were both pushing each other away. But what did she honestly expect to happen; it had been twelve years, he had a child, there was no way that he would want a relationship with her now. What he’d said the night before about being with lots of different women stuck in her head. She had never been able to move on from him but he had moved on with a whole multitude of women by the sounds of things. He hadn't hung onto her memory. So maybe he hadn't loved her at all.

She sighed.

'I'm sorry that I ended up sleeping on you,' she said, trying to diffuse the sudden awkwardness between them.

'It's OK,' he shrugged. 'We're friends. We used to hug and do stuff like that all the time. You slept in my bed many times and long before we got together.'

'It's a bit different now.'

'Yeah it is,' he said, sadly.

He stood up and then offered her his hand to help her up too.

'Why don't you get dressed too and meet us downstairs when you're ready.'

Without another word he walked out and left her alone.

❄

As Piper finished getting dressed, her phone rang. She smiled when she saw it was Wendy, her editor at *The Tree of Life* magazine. She'd never met her, but over the ten years Piper had worked for the magazine, Wendy had become the closest thing Piper had to a friend. She quickly answered the phone.

'Hey, beautiful girl. I've just read your review for Silver Blossom Hall, that place sounds appalling,' Wendy said, the busy noise of the office in the background.

After leaving Gabe in the lounge the night before, Piper had been unable to sleep and had spent a while composing a particularly scathing review before sending it into Wendy.

'It was, I think it was probably one of the worst hotels I've been in and that's saying something. Thank you for getting me in here at such short notice.'

'Couldn't have you staying in squalor now, could I? What's Stardust Lake Hotel like?'

Piper hesitated.

'It's beautiful. The attentiveness of the staff, the food, the hotel itself, it's a wonderful place to spend Christmas…' she trailed off.

'Honey, I know you, what's that tone of voice for?'

'I know the owner, Gabe Whitaker.'

'Oh, that's awkward. Do you know him well?'

'He's the only man I've ever loved,' Piper said, quietly.

There was silence from Wendy as she digested this. They never really talked about personal stuff; they chatted about the hotels, the places, the sights, some of the funny things that had happened to Piper. They talked about stuff that was happening in the office, about Wendy's new boss Marcus and what an ass he was. Piper had told her how disheartened she felt about travelling the world and it had been Wendy who had suggested the six-month sabbatical. She'd also been the one who had convinced Marcus that it was a good idea too. But Wendy didn't know anything about Piper's past and sadly Piper knew next to nothing about Wendy's personal life either.

For the first time ever, Piper realised how sad it was to have no one she could talk about these things with. In a stupid rash moment, twelve years before, she had thrown away the sisterly bond she shared with Neve, the relationship with the man she loved and her relationship with his parents, the only people who had ever shown her any love. She'd cut off any other friends from college and when she had started travelling she closed herself off from ever having any kind of friendship or relationship with anyone. And now she had reached out to Wendy, the closest thing she had to a friend, and Wendy was probably trying to work out how to get off the phone as quickly as she could before

Piper had a complete meltdown. Piper had crossed a boundary and their friendship wasn't strong enough for personal problems.

'Piper, can I put you on hold for a second?'

'Um, sure.'

The line clicked and the awful hold music of 'Greensleeves' was piped through the speaker. Wendy had probably gone off to deal with something far more important or was desperately trying to come up with a polite way to get rid of her.

The line clicked again and Wendy came back on. 'Sorry about that, I've just put you through to the meeting room so I can talk to you privately. Are you OK?'

Piper was staggered by this. Did Wendy actually really care?

She cleared her throat. 'Yes, I think so. I haven't seen him for twelve years, it's so weird seeing him again.'

Piper tried to stay nonchalant, but Wendy was clearly having none of that.

'I always got the sense that you were running from something. No one wants to travel for that length of time without wanting to come home at some point unless they have no home to return to. Was he the reason you ran?'

Piper sighed. 'There was a whole host of reasons, but he was a huge part of it.'

'Did he cheat on you?'

'No, I thought he had, but he didn't, which just makes the whole thing so much harder. I made a terrible mistake running away from him and now he's here and all these feelings are coming back.'

'Do you want to pursue something with him, see if you still have anything there?'

'I don't know. We're different people now, we've grown and changed so much, but there's a part of me that wonders if we can fall in love all over again.'

'Honey, go for it. What do you have to lose? If you try and it doesn't work out you can come back to London and start your sabbatical just like you planned. We can meet for lunch and you can tell me all about him, the good, the bad, the ugly. We can get drunk over a bottle or two of wine and slag him off for not realising how wonderful you are.'

Piper laughed. 'I'd really like that.'

'In all seriousness, you don't want to live your life with regret. Trust me honey, I'm old enough and wise enough to know that's no way to live, looking back on what you should have done. You made a mistake but here's your chance to fix it. You don't want to be looking back in years to come and wondering why you didn't take that chance at happiness. Just see how it goes over the next few days. You might hate him after spending a few days with him, but keep an open mind. Don't close yourself off to possibilities.'

Piper smiled at how well Wendy did know her after all.

'Thank you. And I'm going to hold you to that lunch date.'

'I look forward to it,' Wendy said, honestly.

They said their goodbyes and Piper hung up.

She quickly finished getting ready, threw her camera and other things into her bag and walked downstairs to wait for Gabe and Wren.

Giggles, thuds and the deep murmurs of Gabe's voice could be heard from upstairs, though she couldn't make out what he was saying.

She wasn't used to waiting around for other people. She had spent over ten years eating when she wanted to eat, seeing the sights she wanted to see and not being accountable to anyone. Though to be honest that was one of the things she was growing weary of. Travelling was wonderful and exciting, but not having anyone to share that joy with, no one to make memories with or to look back and reminisce with, was lonelier than she ever imagined.

She didn't know whether to get on with some work while she waited. Normally, after the first night in a new hotel, she would be writing notes in her journal about her arrival and her first impressions. She would then use those notes to help write her review at a later stage.

What could she write, though? Could she really write an unbiased, professional review when the man who owned the hotel was her ex-best friend and ex-boyfriend?

For over ten years she had always written honest reviews and she had never let any personal feelings or attachments affect that. Not that she'd had any of those before.

When she had used the money from her dad's house to travel, she had started a blog of places she'd visited and seen. It had gathered quite a bit of interest, but the posts that interested people the most were her honest reviews of hotels. Some funny, some great, some terrible, but those were the posts that received the most comments.

When *Tree of Life* asked her if she wanted to do the reviewing as a job, she'd leapt at the chance. They'd pay for all her hotels, food and flights in return for her honest review. The pay wasn't very much, but, other than clothes and the odd expenses here and there, she didn't need much when everything else was paid for.

It was only meant to be a few months, maybe a year or two, before she was going to go to college or university to get a photography qualification. But she had never stopped, always taking one more job and the next and the next. Stopping would mean settling down, getting a house or flat, making friends and attachments, and she had worked very hard at not doing that.

She felt bad that she had lied to Gabe about her job, but she could hardly tell him the truth that she was here to review his hotel.

With still no sign of Gabe or Wren, she pulled her journal from her handbag and sat down to make some notes.

- Flight from Edinburgh to Juniper Island was wonderful, treated like a first-class customer.
- Stephen was charming, every hotel needs a Stephen.
- The drive to the hotel was magical, giving a wonderful first impression of Stardust Lake Hotel.

Piper stared at the empty bullet point and sighed as she thought about everything that had happened after her arrival, the memories and feelings that had suddenly reappeared.

She put her pen next to the bullet point and wrote something else.

- I think I'm falling in love with my best friend again.

She stared at the words in shock just as Gabe and Wren came thundering down the stairs. She quickly snapped the journal shut and shoved it into her bag.

'Sorry, we were playing a quick game of Dragons while we were waiting for you,' Gabe explained, holding a giggling Wren under one arm like a log. He deposited her on the floor and Piper smiled at the *Frozen*-themed all-in-one snowsuit she was wearing, complete with *Frozen*-themed wellies.

'How do you play Dragons?'

'Oh, the princess is trapped in the tower, guarded by the evil dragon and the handsome prince has to come in and fight the dragon and save the princess,' Gabe explained as if it was perfectly normal for a man of his size and importance to be playing a game with princesses and dragons.

Piper smiled. 'Sounds like fun.'

'We can play it when we come back if you want,' Wren said, excitedly. 'Pip, you can be the princess and I'll be the evil dragon.'

'That sounds great. Who normally plays the evil dragon?'

'Winston.'

'Who's Winston?'

Gabe gave a whistle and a second later Piper could hear the clatter of tiny feet. A few moments later a tiny sausage dog came galloping into the room, wearing a set of green scaly wings.

Piper burst out laughing and looked at Gabe who was smiling too.

'I kind of pictured you with a manlier-looking dog, not a dachshund.'

'Winston is Wren's dog, not mine,' Gabe said.

'Why didn't I meet Winston last night?'

'Because I left both Wren and Winston with Boris for half an hour while I was going to greet our first guest. But both of them fell asleep and Wren made her escape. She's good at doing that. Boris brought him back this morning.'

Winston bounced around Piper and she bent down to scratch his head. 'He doesn't exactly look like a fearsome dragon, though. I don't imagine he puts up too much of a fight.'

'Oh, I don't know about that. Winston, growl.'

Winston let out a tiny bark.

'Winston, Dragon.'

Winston leapt up onto his back paws, standing vertically with his front paws in the air.

'Winston, play dead.'

Winston rolled over onto the floor with all four paws in the air and Piper laughed again.

Wren giggled endlessly. 'Can we take Winston to breakfast too?'

'No, he'll get lost in the snow, but we can bring him back a sausage.' Gabe hoisted Wren onto his back and moved to the front door.

Piper grabbed her bag and followed him, pulling her hat on her head.

'Daddy, it's only seven days until Christmas.'

'I know.'

'I counted the days on my advent calendar this morning.'

'What did you get in your advert calendar today?'

'Chocolate.'

Gabe laughed. 'I know that, but did you see what chocolate shape it was before you snaffled it? Was it a chocolate reindeer or a snowman?'

Wren laughed. 'It's chocolate. It tastes the same no matter what shape it's in.'

Gabe nodded to concede this.

As the door closed behind him, he plonked a wriggling Wren on the ground and she ran on ahead, dancing and jumping in the snow.

Piper glanced at Gabe as he watched his daughter. It was clear he absolutely loved her. He realised she was looking at him and turned to face her.

She smiled and looked away.

'Still writing in your journal, then?' Gabe said, walking by her side.

'Oh, no, it's just a few notes I'm making for work.'

'Shame. I read your journal once.'

Piper stared at him in horror. 'You didn't?'

'Sure I did. I was sixteen and it was open on the bed. The curiosity was too much.'

'What did you read?'

Gabe smiled. 'About how much you loved me.'

Piper blushed, feeling her cheeks go blood red. Things really hadn't moved on at all.

'Neve!' Wren called out and Piper watched as the little girl ran into the arms of a tall thin woman with long black curls cascading down her back.

The little girl inside Piper wanted to do the same. She had missed Neve and she hadn't realised quite how much till now.

Piper swallowed nervously as Neve turned round to look at her. She hadn't changed much, same cute freckles, same effortless beauty. Piper had such fond memories of Neve. Piper had always looked up to her, adored her in that kind of way little girls idolise an older sister, but Neve being two years older than her had meant they never really hung around together a lot. Neve had always been kind, lending her clothes in the way that an older sister would. Piper remembered her own love of Westlife came about because Neve's walls were plastered with posters of them. They'd sit and listen to the albums sometimes and pore over magazines that included interviews with the band.

But Neve adored Gabe, and Piper worried what she would make of Piper coming back into Gabe's life after all this time, even if it was just for a few weeks.

Neve waited for them on the path ahead with Wren balanced on her hip.

As they drew closer, her eyes flicked between her and Gabe and for a second she looked anxious before a warm smile spread across her face.

'Pip, it's so lovely to see you again, it's been too long.'

Piper wondered if that was a barbed comment, but the smile on Neve's face was genuine.

Neve reached out and kissed her on the cheek.

'You look well,' Neve said, studying her carefully. 'God, you grew up to be so beautiful; you were just a scrawny little kid the last time I saw you. And what are you doing with yourself these days, what brings you here?'

Piper hesitated with the lie she had told Gabe the night before but knew it was too late to change her story. 'I'm a freelance photographer. I take pictures for travel brochures.'

It was a well-rehearsed lie and one she used at any hotel that started asking questions.

'Oh, which one?'

'Several different ones.'

'We have deals with all of the big-name holiday companies. Though they all sent photographers months ago. We had to stage an early Christmas so the photos would be ready for the winter brochures in time. The place wasn't anywhere near finished, but we were very clever about what we allowed them to photograph. I'm surprised the companies are sending you again now. I'm not sure if snow and Christmas trees are a good look for the spring and summer brochures. Which company sent you?'

'Ocean View,' Piper quickly plucked the name of a big holiday company out of the air.

'I'll have to give them a call, make sure they know our prices for the next year. They are always ahead of the crowd, though. They are probably organising the winter brochure for next year already. Actually it's good that you came; you can take pictures of the ice palace and the glass igloos, none of those were here when the last lot of photographers came. I can take you round, show you the best bits. I'll give you a list of all the things we'd like featured…'

'Pip promised she would play Dragons with me,' Wren said, quietly. 'I don't want her to work, everyone works and no one ever has time to play.'

Neve stalled with what she had been going to say, her face flooding with guilt.

'I know we've been really busy, sweetheart, it won't be like that forever,' Neve said.

'Neve, why don't you give Pip a chance to find her feet first?' Gabe said. 'She's here for a few weeks, I imagine she could take all the photos she needs in a matter of days. I'm sure she would like some holiday time too; it is Christmas after all. Plus she has been doing this job for over ten years. I'm sure she knows what looks good and what photos the brochure needs.'

'I just want the world to see Stardust Lake Hotel in the best possible light. You've worked so hard to make the resort what it is, Gabe, we all have, and I want everyone to see how wonderful this place is.'

'I know, I do too,' Gabe said, softly. 'But Pip isn't going to do anything to paint us in a bad light.'

Neve nodded. 'I know she wouldn't. I'm just worried about Thursday and all those journalists coming, especially Mr Black.'

The dreaded reviewer again. Piper wondered who he was and who he wrote for.

'We are going to show all our guests the time of their lives so they only walk away with good things to say about Stardust Lake Hotel. But Pip is our guest too, and we need to show her a good time as well. I'm going to take her round the resort and the island over the next few days and maybe Pip can take a few photos then once she has got a feel for the place.'

Piper smiled encouragingly to put Neve at ease, wondering if she could just not do the review at all and start her sabbatical early.

As soon as she had that thought she knew that was what she had to do. She wouldn't have to worry about blurring the lines between professionalism and friendship or worry about what she would write. She would email *The Tree of Life* the first chance she got and explain, which meant she was now officially on holiday and she was going to enjoy every second of it.

❄ Chapter 8 ❄

Gabe watched Pip as Wren pointed out the sights from the dining room, their faces pressed up against the glass.

He loved this room, how it was lit up only by the natural light that streamed in from the glass roof and walls. At night, each table was lit up by candles. During the day the light from the windows was all the room needed, lending a superb outlook over almost the entire island, the valleys and the huge lake below that gave the hotel its name. Out in the distance you could even see the sea too. There wasn't a single building in sight of the dining room; the island was completely unspoilt and beautiful from where they were sitting. He could look out on that view forever, if only he had the time. But now his eyes were fixed only on Pip and he smiled at how she was completely taken with the view too. She must have seen some incredible sights on her travels over the years, but the fact that this little island clearly held so much beauty for her as well touched him. He wondered if for her too the island would always remind her of the holiday they had spent here and all those wonderful memories.

Neve moved her head to intercept his gaze and he dragged his eyes from Pip to his sister.

'I take it you two have talked.'

Both Pip and Wren were far enough away for him and Neve to be able to talk without them hearing, but he still lowered his voice when he spoke.

'We spent the whole night talking.'

‘And you now have closure? You can stop wondering and move on with your life?’

He focused on his mug of tea because the last thing he had was closure.

‘I have moved on with my life, I’ve not exactly been waiting around for her to come back. I’ve lost count of the number of girlfriends I’ve had over the years.’

‘All women that you deliberately chose for some fun, never anyone that you wanted a serious relationship with. You’ve been holding back and I don’t know whether it’s because you’re scared of getting hurt again or because none of them were Pip.’

He glanced over at Pip again. Was that really the reason that he’d never fallen in love since Pip had left? Because he was subconsciously comparing every woman he met to his best friend and none of them could meet his high standards? Had he put Pip on a pedestal over the years, made the memory of her better than the real thing? Though he’d seen nothing since she’d come back into his life to think he’d oversold her.

‘She broke your heart,’ Neve said, softly. ‘I can tell by the way you are looking at her that you’re falling in love all over again. I don’t want you to get hurt.’

‘It was a silly misunderstanding that drove her away, it wasn’t her fault, not really.’

He quickly explained what had happened that day, how terrified and upset Pip had been after the accident.

‘That must have been terrible for her, and I hate that she went through that, but it doesn’t excuse what she did. She cut you out of her life with no word, no explanation. She should have had the courage to end things with you properly.’

‘She was seventeen. Did you not make mistakes when you were seventeen? Christ, we’ve both made mistakes all our lives. I don’t think someone should be judged on one rash moment twelve years ago.’

Neve had the grace to look embarrassed. Neither of them had squeaky-clean pasts.

'So, what? You're just going to start dating again?' Neve asked.

'No. I don't know.'

'So just sex, then?'

'No.' He didn't know the answers.

'What do you think will happen if you guys get involved again? Spend cosy nights together by the fire? She is leaving in just over two weeks. You'll fall in love and she'll leave just like she did last time. She has spent the last ten years or more travelling the world, seeing the most wonderful things on planet earth. Do you honestly think this tiny one-town island would be enough to make her want to stay? There's nothing for her here. The bright lights of the big cities, the beautiful beaches of Thailand or Australia, the rainforests, the great canyons and mountains, we don't have any of that. And the worst thing is that it won't just be your heart that will get broken all over again; this time it will be your daughter's heart too. Pip hasn't even been here a day and Wren adores her.'

Gabe looked at Neve and wondered if she was scared of getting hurt too, of letting Pip in again and watching her walk away at the end. They had all been hurt by Pip's departure when she was seventeen. It had hit him the hardest but he knew they all had felt her loss, almost as if she too had died in the lake that day.

'Wren has never got attached to the women I've dated before.'

'You've not had any of the women you've dated live with you before. Wren never got a chance. Don't get me wrong, I like Pip, I really do, but this is not going to end in the way that you hope it will. She has been running her whole life and a few weeks with you is not going to change that.'

'I know.'

'Why don't I take her round the island over the next few days? If you're not with her all the time it might be easier for you when she leaves.'

Pip glanced over at him and flashed him a brilliant smile.

'You're right, I know you are. But if I let her go without giving us a second go, I'll always be wondering if I missed my chance, whether she really is the one that I'm meant to spend the rest of my life with. We could spend the next few days together and realise there's nothing left between us, maybe there's no spark at all, and we'll just end up being friends. If that's the case then I'd finally be able to let her go. But I have to know whether there is something there worth fighting for.'

'I don't think spark will be a problem; it practically crackled between you over breakfast.'

Gabe smirked. Neve was right. The little glances and smiles between him and Pip as they had eaten breakfast, it seemed all new and exciting all over again, like riding a rollercoaster and making their way to the very top. He knew he was going to get hurt again but there was also nothing he could do to stop himself as he tumbled over the other side.

❄

Piper stood outside the main reception area while she waited for Gabe. She quickly finished writing the email to Wendy, explaining that she didn't think it would be a good idea to do this review, that there was too much of a conflict of interest for her and she hoped that after ten years of exemplary service, Marcus would allow her to start her sabbatical early.

She shoved her phone back in her bag and looked around. Fresh snow had fallen overnight and the lodges looked so pretty in the grounds of the hotel. Fairy lights were strewn from all the roofs though she was yet to see them lit. Apparently, the power still hadn't been restored to the guest accommodation.

In the daylight everything seemed bright and clean, the winter sun sparkling off the snow and ice. The sky was a beautiful cornflower blue with not a single cloud to dull the effects of the sun. She pulled her camera out of her bag and fired off a few shots of the trees, the lodges and her and Gabe's footprints in the snow.

Gabe had promised to show her around and she couldn't wait to see it all, although secretly she knew she was more excited about spending time with him.

It didn't make sense to feel this way about him after all this time, it didn't make sense that when she saw him with Wren it made her want to weep that she could have had a child with him and she had missed out on that. She had never wanted to be married or have children, she was perfectly happy on her own, or so she had told herself over the last twelve years. Looking at him now, she couldn't help imagining what could have been and hopelessly imagining what still could be, which was ridiculous – as he'd said himself, they could never go back.

There was something more between them now that had never been there before. She had fallen completely in love with Gabe when she was younger and of course she was attracted to him, but the chemistry that was zinging between them over breakfast was almost tangible and not something she had ever felt before. Maybe it was years of suppressed feelings that had built up or maybe it was just something more basic than that and nothing more than lust and desire, just two people who were attracted to each other wanting to do dark and wonderful things to each other. She smiled at the glorious thoughts that were suddenly running through her head. Being just friends was going to be torture.

A noise in the trees made her glance over that way and she noticed Leo and his gang of reprobates were back, glaring at her through the leaves of the fir trees. It was silly for the islanders to be scared of such tiny ponies and she couldn't possibly imagine any trouble these animals could cause, but as she endured their endless gaze she felt a shiver down her spine. Was it her imagination or were they all staring at her as if they were planning her untimely demise?

Leo stepped forward towards her and bizarrely started scraping his foot against the floor as if he was a bull about to charge at her.

The door opened behind her and she looked round to see if it was Gabe. She was startled to see the most gorgeous, blond male model walking towards her, looking like he had just stepped out of a catalogue advertising winter ski holidays. He had the most incredible blue eyes and those chiselled cheekbones that could cut glass. She quickly turned back to the ponies, not wanting to be caught off-guard and mowed to the ground, but the blond model had clearly scared them away as they disappeared back into the trees.

She looked back at the model again and as he saw her he smiled.

'I think you just saved me from the evil ponies,' Piper said.

'Ah, their attitude is worse than their bite.' He strode towards her and bent to kiss her on the cheek.

'You must be Pip, you are more beautiful than Gabe described,' he said exuberantly. He had a foreign accent, Swedish maybe or Icelandic. He surveyed her at arm's length, smiling knowingly.

'I'm Boris, I'm a groundsman here and snowmobile instructor. I have many jobs actually,' he smiled again.

Piper couldn't help but smile too. When Gabe and Wren had talked about Boris the night before, she'd imagined an old man, not this sprightly vision of loveliness.

'It seems I also owe you a debt of gratitude; you looked after Wren last night when I was supposed to be watching her. It had been a long day, shovelling snow and getting ready for your arrival and I was so tired. I closed my eyes for five minutes and when I woke up she was gone. I was horrified.' Boris put his hand to his chest.

'It was no problem, I saw her dancing in the snow and I just wrapped my coat around her and took her back to her home.'

'Wren loves the snow. Chester doesn't really like it so much. That's my son. She was playing with him, but then, from what I can gather, they were playing hide and seek and Chester climbed under the bed and fell asleep. Wren couldn't find him and I was asleep, so she went outside to play in the snow alone. Mikael was furious with me. Oh, here he comes now. Shush, don't mention about last night, he has only just forgiven me.'

Another blond sexy hunk of a man came out and down the steps towards them, clutching a sweet little blond boy on his hip. The boy had the most massive blue eyes and was sucking his thumb.

'Mikael, this is Gabe's Pip. Pip, this is my husband Mikael and our son Chester.'

Chester stared at her with unblinking eyes and Piper tried hard not to smile at the fact Boris had said she belonged to Gabe.

Mikael, clearly not as affectionate as his husband, offered her his hand and a small smile. 'Hello, pleased to meet you. I hope my husband has apologised for last night. We are not negligent parents or babysitters.'

'I didn't think you were, these things happen and I'm sure Wren was perfectly safe. If I hadn't found her, I'm sure some of the other staff would have. The island seems like a very safe place to raise your children.'

'It is a haven,' Mikael said, softly.

The door opened again and Gabe appeared at the top of the steps, carrying Wren over his shoulder. As soon as Chester saw her, his whole face lit up.

Gabe trotted down the stairs towards them. He plonked Wren on the ground and Chester wriggled to be out of Mikael's arms. Mikael put him down and Chester immediately hugged Wren, giving her a kiss on the cheek. Wren hugged him back as tightly as she could when they were both wearing padded snowsuits and then, holding hands, they ran off together to play in the snow nearby.

Something jolted inside Piper. She and Gabe had been exactly the same when they were little, going everywhere together, holding hands and cuddling each other. That affectionate relationship had never worn off; in fact they had just grown closer and closer over the years.

Gabe watched them go with a smile and then turned his attention back to Piper. 'Are you ready for the tour?'

She nodded.

'I thought we'd take the snowmobiles. There's quite a lot to see and it's certainly faster and more fun.'

'That sounds great.'

'I have two ready for you, boss,' Boris said. 'And if you want to leave Wren with us, we'd be happy to look after her. I know Chester would be pleased too.'

Boris looked at Gabe hopefully, clearly wondering if Gabe had forgiven him.

'We would take very good care of her, Mr Whitaker,' Mikael promised.

'Of course she can stay with Chester if that's what she wants. And I don't want you to feel bad about what happened last night. She keeps wandering off all the time; I've had a stern word with her about it this morning. It's so different here from where we used to live. We had a small garden with six-foot high fences, she was always outside playing but she was safe, she couldn't wander off. Here there are no fences and I think she sees the whole island as her back garden. But I trust you both. I know you'll take care of her.'

'Thank you, Mr Whitaker,' Mikael said.

'Gabe, I keep telling everyone to call me Gabe but it's not sinking in.'

'You are Mr Boss Man, that's why,' Boris said.

Gabe sighed. 'Let me see what Wren wants to do.'

He called her over and she came running back to him. He knelt down and she threw herself into his arms.

'Wren, I'm going to take Pip round the island. You can come with us if you want or you can stay here and play with Chester, Boris and Mikael.'

Wren didn't hesitate for a second. 'I want to stay with Chester.'

'That's fine, honey. I'll see you later. Remember what I said to you this morning. No wandering off.'

'No, Daddy, I promise.'

Gabe stood back up and smiling his thanks to Boris and Mikael, he waved goodbye to Wren and motioned for Piper to follow him.

They were silent for a few moments, until Piper knew they were out of hearing distance of Boris and Mikael.

'You're a good man.'

Gabe looked at her with surprise as they walked. 'Why?'

'Because Boris was clearly upset about the whole thing and you just put them both at ease. Other parents wouldn't be quite so understanding.'

He shrugged. 'Wren is my entire world, but there's no need to be an arsehole over her safety. Accidents happen and the exact same thing happened to me three weeks ago. I woke up early in the morning and found her gone, rushed outside and she was playing on the slope outside our house. She knows not to go too far. I told her off more about going off with a stranger than for leaving Boris's house.'

Piper winced. 'That was my fault. I told her that I wasn't a stranger because we knew each other's names. I just wanted to get her in the warm.'

Gabe considered her carefully. 'It's fine at the moment because she knows everyone here so there are no strangers for her to be worried about, but in a few days the place will be filled with guests and I can't bear the thought of her wandering off with one of them.'

'I'm sorry.'

'It's OK. You were only doing what you thought was best.'

They walked on in silence, the only sound their boots crunching on the snow as they headed round the outside of the main reception and down a track.

'What made you come here, build this resort? From what you told me last night you're used to developing hotels in much more glamorous resorts than this,' Piper said.

'The Golden Oak was my grandad's. Do you remember him?'

'Oh, I remember the old man that ran the place, I didn't remember he was your grandad.'

'That's because we never called him that; he was always Andrew, never Grandad. He said "Grandad" made him feel old.'

Piper smiled. 'I remember him. He was wonderful, funny, always had some scary story to tell us around the fire. And so much energy, walking all over the island with us.'

'We spent many holidays up here with him, some of the fondest memories of my childhood took place here. It was hugely popular in the summer. Lots of people used to camp up here on the hills and fields. When he died the place just fell into ruin. I didn't have enough money or experience then to try to start over with this hotel. But it was always my plan to improve it and relaunch it as something better. I never realised how much of a vital part my grandad played in the tourism of the island. He'd rent out bikes, organise horse rides, he even took people out in his boat. There were decent shower facilities for the campers and many of them would pay to have breakfast in the hotel too. Without him here there was very little for people to come back for. The summer months have always been popular with the whales that migrate up here, plus the puffins and other rare birds, but the tourists can see a lot of that from the other Shetland Islands and the other islands had much better facilities.'

They rounded a corner and Piper saw what appeared to be some stables up ahead.

'The island was dying and I knew we had to do something to return it to its former glory. I just didn't want my grandad's legacy and hard work to die with him. I knew if we were going to bring the tourists back here, it wasn't enough to provide good facilities for the bird watchers and whale watchers in the summer months; I had to develop something that would be attractive to tourists all year round and the whole island had to be a part of that. We had a meeting with the islanders and we agreed that we would turn the island into a winter and Christmas resort.'

'A town called Christmas. I think that's a wonderful idea.'

Gabe nodded. 'Everyone wanted to be a part of it. We fitted out the houses in the village so they look like wooden lodges, even though they are mostly stone or brick underneath. The villagers all run a Christmas-themed shop from their own front room, but we worked hard to make sure that each shop is completely different from any other in the village so there is no competition, everyone sells something unique. We have a house that makes crêpes of all sorts of different flavours, one that sells candles, one that sells hats, scarves and gloves. A lot of the products they sell they make here on the island. We also advertised for a few artists and craftspeople to come and live in the empty houses, giving them a place to live and sell their wares but also expanding the market and not leaving any houses empty, either.'

'So you have a year-long Christmas market?'

'Yes. People love Christmas and one of the things I noticed about the gift shops in the hotels I own, the one thing that sells consistently well all year round are the Christmas decorations. Obviously the market won't just be Christmassy; it'll be more winter-themed than anything. Hot chocolates, fudge, jewellery, those things will sell well all year.'

'People will love it. What about the hotel itself? The lodges look great and the main reception area and dining room are so pretty. What else have you changed?'

'One of the big draws of the island are the Northern Lights. Or the Merry Dancers as the villagers call them. We see them so frequently up here and they are an attraction that so many people want to see. Have you ever seen them?'

Piper shook her head. 'Never. Whenever I've been somewhere that's north enough to see them and at the right time of year, I've always been really unlucky with the weather.'

'You'll see them while you're here. I guarantee it.'

Piper laughed. 'You can't guarantee it.'

Gabe nodded. 'Juniper Island is magical, can't you feel that?'

'Feel what?'

He stopped and turned towards her and she stopped too. He was a few metres away as he looked around for something to prove his point. His gaze fell on her.

'Close your eyes.'

She frowned at him for a second but closed them anyway.

'Don't open them until I tell you,' Gabe whispered.

'What am I supposed to do?'

'Just...feel.'

She didn't know what she was supposed to feel as she listened to the silence of the woods around them.

Suddenly she knew Gabe was standing there right in front of her. He hadn't made a sound, she couldn't feel his warmth, but she knew he was there. Excitement thrummed through her at his proximity, goosebumps dancing down her spine. She smiled. But a few moments later she knew he had stepped away.

'Open your eyes,' he said.

She opened them and he was exactly where she had seen him last, though he was grinning at her.

'Did you feel it?'

'I felt something, I'm not sure it was the island.'

'Sure it was. There are many explanations for the Northern Lights, lots of myths and legends. My grandad said they were spirits in the sky who would light their torches to guide lost travellers home.'

Piper swallowed as he stared at her. Had she really been lost all this time? 'I like that explanation.'

'Home isn't always a house and it isn't always where you grew up; sometimes it's just a feeling.'

He stared at her and she couldn't take her eyes off him and despite the fact he was a few metres away this time, that same feeling crashed through her, that same spark she had felt moments before. Eventually he looked away, letting out an embarrassed chuckle.

Piper looked around too, for want of something to do other than stare at him. 'I can see a lot of people will want to discover the magic of the island themselves. It's a beautiful place.'

'It is.' Gabe continued to walk down the path and she joined him at his side. 'People will make the journey purely just to see the Northern Lights, but I wanted to give them somewhere warm and comfortable to watch it, considering that the most likely time to see it is in the winter months. We've made glass igloos and put large glass roof windows into most of the bedrooms in the lodges. With regards to other entertainment, there is a sledging and donut run at the back of the resort. We're also going to have an outdoor ice-skating rink. We have snowmobile trails for the winter and we'll have bike trails and horse riding in the summer, just like my grandad used to have. But the cherry on top of our cake is the ice palace. It's not cold enough to have a real ice palace like they do in Sweden or Quebec, so ours is made from glass and fibreglass. But inside, the ice carvings, walls, seats and slides are all made out of ice. Wren can't wait to see it, she's convinced it's actually Elsa's ice palace.'

'She's not seen it yet?'

'I wanted it to be special for her, so I said I'd take her Christmas Eve. That's where she was taking you last night – she'd clearly decided to take matters into her own hands and to go see it herself.'

Piper laughed. 'I like her style. Do you think though, that all this will only attract guests in the lead-up to Christmas?'

'No, hopefully not. We are trying to hold an event every month of the year. We are having a big ice-and-snow carving competition in January and a big ice festival too, with different entertainment. We're encouraging weddings all year round, especially in the ice palace, but we also have a licence for the dining room. We have a few weddings booked for next year already. Our first one is booked for Valentine's Day. We have lots of shows booked throughout the year, using the ice palace as an auditorium when we won't have ice carvings; we even have a Cirque du Soleil coming in May. We also have the Great Island Race in the spring, which will see a boat race between here, the most northern island, and the other Shetland Isles, and hopefully the wildlife will bring people back in the summer.

'We also offer free and cheap boat tours to the other islands. I didn't want to be that arsehole who steals all the tourism from the other islands. I'm hoping that if people come here that perhaps wouldn't have considered a holiday in the Shetland Islands before, free boat rides will tempt them to visit the other islands too. We'll also offer whale-watching boat tours and scenic boat tours around the islands. We're going to offer helicopter rides over the islands as well, although guests will have to pay for those as an added extra.'

'And what about the grand opening? I've heard some of the staff talk about it, they're clearly very excited. What do you have planned?' Piper asked.

'We're having a Christmas carnival on the evening that all the guests arrive. There'll be a procession from the hotel, down to the ice palace and round to the lake where there will be a firework display. The procession will take in all the sights and facilities of the resort but will also showcase the spectacular views of the island. All the villagers and staff will be involved and wearing Christmas costumes, some of them will even be performing. We have fire-breathers, dancers and other entertainers flying up here for the night. It will be quite the show and I know everyone here is looking forward to it.'

'Sounds like a lot of fun, I'm sure the guests will love it. You've worked so hard, people are going to flock here.'

'I hope so. We've poured so much into developing it, so much time and money. It has to work now, I can't let the islanders or my grandad down.'

It was so important to him and she was touched by his passion to save the island. This would never be a good moneymaker: it was so remote and hard to get to that it could never make as much as his New York, California or London hotels. But he knew that and he was still pouring everything he had into it.

She had slipped her hand into his before she even realised what she was doing and he faltered in his step as he felt her touch.

'It'll work, I guarantee it.'

He looked down at her. 'How do you know?'

'Because the island is magical.'

He laughed.

'And because you want it to work so badly, you won't possibly let it fail.'

He stared at her and then down at her hand. She went to pull away, but he held her hand tighter.

'Wanting something badly doesn't always mean you get it. Sometimes you can do everything humanly possible to keep something and you still lose it.'

She knew he was no longer talking about the hotel.

'And sometimes it's no one's fault, fate just has a knack of getting in the way,' he added, sadly.

'And maybe sometimes fate has a way of making up for it,' Piper said.

He nodded thoughtfully as he walked. 'A second chance?'

She hesitated before she spoke. 'If you're willing to take the risk.'

He gazed down at her and then loosened his fingers from her hold. 'I'm not sure if I can.'

She took a step away from him. Her being there was difficult for both of them, she understood that. She would just accept the friendship from him and not push him for any more than that. It was her fault that they had ended up in this situation and she couldn't expect him to throw himself into her arms again just because she had come back after twelve years.

'It's not a great time, Pip. We have the grand opening in a few days, the place will be filled with journalists. There's still stuff we need to get ready. I can't afford to take my eye off the ball. Plus there's Wren to think about and…' he trailed off.

'It's OK. I get it.'

'You do?'

'No second chances.'

He pulled a face. 'I'm not saying… I just… You leave just after New Year's Day and…'

'It's fine,' Piper reassured him. 'It was silly to even suggest it. Seeing you again reminds me of all those memories and feelings. I know you feel it too. But we really are better off as friends.'

He stared off into the distance and sighed.

'And you certainly don't need to babysit me or feel you need to be with me if you have other things you need to do. I don't want to be in the way. But I'd be happy to help you with any last-minute preparations if you want me to.'

'You're on holiday.'

'I'd like to help. That's what friends do, isn't it?'

He was silent for a moment. 'There are probably a number of things you can help me with over the next few days. I stupidly gave most of the staff a couple of days off ahead of the Christmas rush and there are still a few things that need to be done.'

'That's settled then. You can give me the guided tour today, so I know where everything is, and tomorrow you can put me to work.'

He smiled. 'OK.'

❄ Chapter 9 ❄

Gabe smiled at his best friend as she walked next to him. He liked the idea of working alongside her again. She used to help him on the farm all the time when they were younger; she was a hard worker and they made a good team. Although it did mean spending more time with her and that, he suspected, would only lead to further complications.

What Neve said had stuck with him. Whereas before he had been willing to give his relationship with Pip another go, Neve's words had now settled into his brain. She was right, Pip was leaving in just over two weeks and she was unlikely to give up travelling the world to stay on Juniper Island with him. He had loved Pip so much when they were younger and it still hadn't been enough to keep her. Maybe she was too damaged by being abandoned by her birth parents and then when her adopted dad turned against her it was too much. Coupled with twelve years of solitary independence, not relying on anyone else, she had been on her own for a long time. Maybe she could never put her trust in a relationship again. And quite honestly he didn't know whether he trusted her, either.

They approached the stables where they would eventually keep the ten horses that were being delivered in the spring. There were only two horses there now, poking their heads over the stable doors as they walked past, their hot breath forming billows of steam in the cold air.

'This is Shadow and Knight,' Gabe introduced the black and silvery grey horses. Pip smiled as she stroked their velvety noses.

'Neve's pride and joy. The plan is we will offer horse rides or pony trekking in the spring and summer once we can no longer use the snowmobiles. We'll offer bikes for hire too, so people can explore the island. We have ten horses coming at the end of March and Neve has said she will be happy to take people out on treks or pony tours. I think her plan is to offer pony-trekking holidays for the horse-mad like her. I'm not sure if Neve will let anyone ride Shadow or Knight though, they're her babies. Luke has ridden Knight a few times. I don't think anyone apart from Neve has ever ridden Shadow.'

'They're lovely.'

'Do you ride?'

'I have ridden. I wouldn't say I was a great rider.'

'Yeah, me too. I've never had a great affinity with horses. Neve though, horses are in her blood.'

'I remember the horse she had when we were little, Diamond, he was a little ginger pony.'

'He was a strawberry roan, he was adorable.'

'Neve used to let me ride him when we were kids,' Pip said.

'Oh, she must have liked you a lot, she never let us ride him.'

Pip smiled at that. 'Well you boys were probably too big. Luke was a giant even back then. Though I remember Luke had this special way with animals. Like he could talk to them. I caught him once, hand-feeding a fox.'

'He still has that kind of affinity with animals now. His dream was always to work at London Zoo. He worked hard at university and went straight from there into his dream job. Worked there for almost eight years I think.'

'And now he works here? What made him leave?'

He hesitated. He was sure Luke would not appreciate Gabe talking about his personal life behind his back. 'Let's just say that things went wrong and the zoo felt tainted for him.'

They left the horses and walked into the barn opposite where they kept the snowmobiles. There were twenty in total, though he would order more if there was the demand for it.

Two sleek black snowmobiles were sitting out the front waiting for them, though Gabe wished he'd asked Boris to leave out only one so he could have Pip on his. He shook his head. What was he thinking? Pip had practically offered herself to him and he'd turned her down and now he was envisioning what it would feel like to have her body wrapped round his again.

'Do you know how to ride one of these things?' Gabe asked, laying out a thermal suit, gloves and a helmet for her.

'I've done it quite a few times over the years. I had some great instructors.'

He didn't want to know what was so great about the instructors she'd had. The thought of her with other men was not a pleasant one, though he knew it was hypocritical to be angry about it considering the number of women he'd been with over the years.

'We'll go round the perimeter of the island first; it won't take too long but I'd prefer to be back here when it gets dark. Then I'll show you the resort once we get back – it looks better in the dark when it's all lit up.'

She nodded and he watched her get kitted up. He moved to make sure her helmet was on securely and she stared up at him with those beautiful golden eyes. Having her here was going to be trouble.

'Why don't you go in front,' Gabe said, as they walked back outside. He watched as Pip put her camera in the compartment under her seat. 'There's only one trail, so you can't get lost.'

'Do you want me to go in front so you can stare at my bum?' Pip laughed.

That made him smile. She had grown in confidence since she was seventeen. She had always been quiet and shy, especially when it came to things like kissing and sex.

She sighed, probably at his lack of reaction. 'Sorry. I was just joking. This is so weird for me. The last time I saw you, you were making love to me and now we're just friends. It's… '

'Awkward? Yeah, for me too.'

She stared at him for a long moment. 'Would you prefer it if I wasn't here? We could arrange for the plane to take me back to Edinburgh tomorrow. Tonight probably if you're super keen to get rid of me.'

'That's the last thing I want.'

'Then lighten up and stop staring at me like I'm breaking your heart all over again. This is difficult for me too.'

She got on the snowmobile and roared off down the path. He stared after her. He almost didn't recognise this new Pip, but it didn't stop him from wanting to rekindle their romance all over again.

He hopped on his snowmobile and followed her. Any worries about her not being able to control the snowmobile were unfounded as she careened around corners at high speed, whooping with delight and manoeuvring the machine with skill and bravery.

Finally, on a long stretch, she slowed down a little and he caught up with her. She didn't say anything as they coasted along the path and he didn't, either.

They passed a herd of Shetland ponies on a field, eating the fresh food that had been put out for them earlier that morning.

'What's the deal with these ponies? Stephen said they were savage,' Pip said, her voice raised slightly so she could be heard over the noise of the engine.

Gabe laughed. 'That's probably a little bit of an exaggeration. Most of the ponies stay out of the way, and don't wander into the village at all.'

'What about Leo and his gang?'

'They're a bunch of thieves.'

'What?'

'They come into the village and around the resort and they steal things.'

'Like food?'

'Like anything. Clothes, jewellery, money.'

'Are you serious?'

He nodded. 'They're not so bad in the winter because the doors and windows are closed. In the summer most of the houses, especially those that overlook the sea, have their doors open. Leo's gang started walking into people's homes and stealing things. Anything they could get their mouths on before they were chased back out. We're a bit worried about the Christmas market, whether they'll strike once the shops are open to the public. We might have to fence off the town and put cattle grids over the road.'

'What are they doing with all the things they steal, opening a black market of stolen goods or selling them over the internet?'

'I think they might be raising money for sex and drugs.'

Pip laughed. 'Proper little bed of sin you have going on up here. Does no one try to stop them?'

'Well, that's what has Stephen all upset about them. Leo came into his house a few months ago, stole the TV remote. Stephen tried to stop him and Leo made a run for it, trampled Stephen's feet. Apparently Leo broke a bone in Stephen's toe in the attempt to get away and he still made it out with the TV remote.'

Pip giggled, shaking her head in disbelief.

Gabe smiled at her. He had missed this and he'd forgotten how much. Just being with her, chatting to her, it felt so good.

'Oh, pull over there, there's a great viewpoint,' Gabe suggested.

Pip did as she was told, cut the engine and climbed off the snowmobile as Gabe did the same.

She grabbed her camera and she stood on the edge of the cliff tops staring out at the sea as the icy cold coastal wind whipped around them. It was one of Gabe's favourite views in the world.

There was silence for a long time but Gabe didn't feel the need to fill it. She was just enjoying the view and he loved seeing that look of happiness and contentment on her face. His eyes stayed on her not the sea as she started taking photos and he could suddenly see himself staring at this view with his best friend for the rest of his life. He had always told himself that he wasn't looking for marriage or a long-term relationship: he'd have fun with women but he never looked for anything serious. He realised now that was because he only ever wanted that with Pip. Now she was back he didn't want to let her go. He wanted that second chance with her, he wanted to see how things would go between them with no holding back, but was there enough time to build something strong enough to make her want to stay in a few weeks' time? Would he be enough to make her want to stay?

Realising that he was staring at her, Pip looked over at him, her eyes meeting his curiously. That same chemistry sparked between them and he ached to reach out and touch her, stroke her face, kiss her hard and feel her body against his. Neither of them moved or said anything, but her eyes fell to his lips and he knew she was thinking about kissing him too.

Eventually Gabe dragged his eyes from her and looked out over the sea. 'We're at the southernmost point of the island, and you can see some of the other Shetland Islands. In front of us is Unst and to the side of it, in the distance, you can see the very edges of Fetlar and Yell.'

'It's beautiful,' Pip said, returning her gaze to the view.

'You think so? You must have seen so much beauty on your travels.'

'But this is so…raw. I don't know, there's something so peaceful and tranquil about this place and so barren and remote too. It feels safe here.'

'Would you stay?' Gabe blurted out then immediately regretted it. 'I mean, could you honestly see yourself living here?'

She shifted her gaze from the view back to him.

'Hypothetically,' he added.

'I don't know. The world is a big and wonderful place, there's lots I haven't yet seen. Where would you be in this hypothetical situation? Would you go back to your hotel in New York once this place is up and running or the one in California, or move on to a new venture?'

'I'd be here. I want somewhere safe to raise Wren. As much as I love the bustle of New York and the warmth and beauty of California, I want somewhere for Wren where I don't have to fear for her safety. The world is a crazy place and every time I open up the papers and read about people killing each other I just want to find a private island somewhere for me and her to live out the rest of our days. This is as close as I can get to that private island.'

'You can't think like that, though. You can't live in fear of what might happen. People die in car accidents all the time, people trip and die from a bang to the head, and there are so many horrible illnesses and diseases out there that people die of all the time. Life is short and precious, the world is a beautiful place full of wonderful and rich experiences, and you need to share that with her.'

'I will. I want to. You inspire me so much, travelling the world on your own, doing your own thing, and in many ways I want that for Wren, I want her to see it all. But right now she is so tiny and I want to protect her for as long as possible. I want to give her stability too, and there has been a lot of travelling with my job. I don't want to be dragging her around the world and away from her friends. I want her to have what we had, not necessarily fall in love with her best friend but to have a best friend she can turn to, always.'

'I understand that.'

He waited for her to answer his previous question but the conversation seemed to have moved on and he didn't want to push her. It was stupid even to ask.

'We should move on. It gets dark so early up here and I'd like to get back before it gets too late.'

He climbed back on his snowmobile and she followed him.

❄

Pip laughed as she beat Gabe in another race. She wasn't sure if he was letting her win or whether she was just more confident on the snowmobiles than he was, but it felt good to have this with him rather than the intense looks and feelings that had been crashing between them when they had stood on the cliff top.

He had been going to kiss her, she was sure of it, and she wouldn't have done anything to stop him.

There was no way they could spend the next few weeks together and not let anything happen between them, the chemistry was too strong. But if something did happen, could she stay? Would he want her to? The question circulated around her head and then took hold. If she did, it wouldn't be a teenage romance any more where they would just hold hands and kiss. They couldn't exactly go out on dates; living on the island meant there was really nowhere to go for that. It would be unlikely there would be anywhere for her to live either, as she couldn't stay in the guest accommodation and the village probably only held twenty or thirty houses, all of them probably occupied. She would have to live with him and that meant being in a proper relationship. She wouldn't just be living with him either: there was his four-year-old daughter too and that all seemed very sudden and scary.

She smiled as she thought about it some more. Yes, it felt scary but wonderful too.

Gabe pulled alongside her again and he was laughing too. 'You're too good for me, you don't seem to have any fear.'

'Life is too short to be scared.'

Pip smiled as she applied that to her last thought.

'Seize the day?' Gabe said.

Pip nodded.

'Oh, pull over here, there's another great viewpoint.'

Pip pulled over where she was directed and they both cut the engines and climbed off the snowmobiles.

Pip moved to the edge of the cliff tops and could see nothing but the endless sea as it stretched for miles in every direction. The water was a deep navy here, instead of the lighter blue on the southern side. The waves crashed angrily on the rocks below, the water rough and tempestuous.

'We are standing on the northernmost point of the British Isles.'

'Oh. Not many people can say that.'

'No. I think it's pretty special and look…'

He pulled his phone from his pocket and swiped a few keys. He moved the phone around slightly as if trying to align it with something. Finding what he wanted, he moved behind her still holding the phone out in front of her so his arms were around her. She found her breath catching in her throat at his warmth and proximity. His wonderful scent washed over her, filling her with so many memories of the times he had held her in his arms before. His scent was like fresh-cut grass, of trees and rain, mixed with the citrus scent of his body wash, oranges and limes. It was divine and she wanted to stay there all day.

He was still fiddling with his phone and she forced herself to glance down at it as he clearly was trying to show her something. She realised there was a compass on the screen.

'There, see the arrow pointing to the north? Follow that arrow out into the sea.'

She nodded, not trusting herself to speak.

'There is nothing between us and the North Pole, no land, nothing but sea. Over to the north-west we'd come to the Faroe Islands, Iceland and Greenland and over in the north-east there is Sweden and Svalbard, but there is nothing to the north of us. If we could fly from here in a straight line we'd soon be standing on top of the world. I think that's pretty special.'

She swallowed the lump of emotion that had stalled in her throat. She felt the shift of awareness in him as he realised that he had his arms wrapped around her. He didn't move his arms, though. The moment stretched on and she knew that neither of them was looking at his phone or out to the horizon any more.

Pip closed her eyes for a second. Seize the day.

She turned round in his arms and stared up at him. His eyes darkened as he gazed at her.

She needed to say something. She had to tell him they needed to explore these feelings between them before it drove them both mad, but before she had time to open her mouth to speak, he bent his head down towards her and his mouth came down hard on top of hers.

❄ Chapter 10 ❄

Oh god, his kiss. Pip had almost forgotten what it was like to kiss him, but as he moved his soft lips over hers every memory of every kiss came flooding back. They'd had chemistry before, how had she forgotten that? She'd remembered the affection, the friendship, the love between them but forgotten this. This intensity, this need had been present in every kiss they'd had.

She felt him fumble around, trying to put his phone back into his pocket before his hands were around her waist, pulling her against him so there was no gap between them. She wound her hands round his neck, running her hands through his hair. But Gabe's hands moved lower, as he lifted her. Instinctively she wrapped her legs around him as he moved backwards away from the edge of the cliff.

He sat down on the side of the snowmobile so she was straddling him and she rearranged her legs so they were hanging over the other side of the snowmobile. His hands moved to her hair, stroking it back from her face and the urgency continued as if the kiss wasn't enough. His tongue slid into her mouth and the taste of him was wonderful, sweet and tangy all at once. A moan escaped his throat and it sent a kick of desire straight to her stomach.

'Gabe,' she whispered as his mouth went to her throat, his hands traversing over her body, desperate to touch her, but they were both clearly wearing too many clothes to be able to do what they wanted to do.

His mouth moved back to hers but it was slower now, less urgent as he kissed her softly, carefully. She could feel how much she meant to him as he kissed her so reverentially.

Eventually he pulled back slightly, leaning his forehead against hers and she could see his eyes were closed.

He opened his eyes and stared at her in confusion. 'Well, that wasn't supposed to happen.'

'I'm really glad it did,' Pip said, finding it hard to catch her breath.

He smiled slightly. 'So much for just being friends.'

'Friendship is overrated.'

His smile grew as he looked at her fondly. 'What are we going to do about this? You leave in a couple of weeks.'

'Can we just see where it goes? Let's not worry about the future yet. We need to see if there is anything serious between us. If it's just lust…' She kissed him deeply but briefly and he moved his hands to her hips, pulling her tighter against him. 'Or if there's something more. You said you couldn't fall in love with me again…'

'Maybe I was wrong.'

She stared at him, thoughtfully, clearly as confused as he was. 'So let's see what happens, and we'll worry about the future when it gets here.'

He nodded and pulled her into a big hug. She leaned into his chest, feeling the solid muscle underneath the thermal suit. He rested his head on top of hers as he stared out over the sea.

'I missed you so much, Pip.'

'I missed you too.'

They sat like that for so long, clinging onto each other like their lives depended on it. The icy north wind gusted round them but she didn't care as she felt warm in his arms. She knew she was falling in love with him all over again, but she had no idea if he felt the same way for her. Lust and love were very different things. She had broken his heart when she ran away and it would take a lot for him to trust her again.

Eventually Gabe pulled back slightly. 'We need to get back, it'll be getting dark soon and I don't want you freezing to death.'

She nodded and with a bit of effort she managed to untangle herself from him and stood up.

He smiled at her, waiting for her to get on her snowmobile while he climbed on his. 'There's lots to show you, but I think we can see the rest after lunch. Besides, Wren will be wondering where we are.'

They started the snowmobiles and made their way down the track following the coastline and Pip couldn't help but smile at the wonderful turn of events.

The trees fell away and Pip saw snow-covered fields and hills spreading out in front of her. Nestled into one of the valleys near the coast was the town, a few tiny lights sparkling from the distance, although it was too far away to see anything more. In the fading light as the sun began its descent in the sky, the island was painted with a rosy glow, the snow twinkling in the shadow of the sun.

'We'll go to the town tomorrow,' Gabe called. 'They're opening up the Christmas market for you.'

'Just for me?'

'Consider it a trial run for when our guests arrive in a few days.'

'I can't wait to see it.'

The track curved round and soon the lodges of the resort could be seen peppering the hillside.

'Over there are our glass igloos,' Gabe pointed out, and she glanced over at the large domes glistening in the evening sun. 'They have curtains around the bottom so our guests still have privacy. We have twelve of those, six large ones for four people, six smaller ones for two people.'

She smiled over at them. Nothing could be more romantic than lying next to your husband or wife as they fell asleep under the stars or the Northern Lights.

'If the power comes back on, we could stay the night in one later this week, before we open to the public,' Gabe said.

She turned to look at him and he blushed, running his hand round the back of his neck with embarrassment.

'I didn't mean…we could just… I mean, you could stay there on your own or we could, erm…'

'I'd love to stay in one.'

He smiled but she made no promises of what could happen if he stayed with her. It was a big leap to think about making love to him when they had only just kissed for the first time in twelve years. Although she would be lying if she said she hadn't already thought of that and how much she wanted it. Part of her knew they had to go slowly, they were almost starting from scratch and they had both changed so much over the last few years. She didn't want to do anything to hurt him again. But if they were going to find out if they had anything worth fighting for, making love was going to be part of that too. Her heart leapt at the thought of it. God, she wanted to make love to him. It had been so perfect between them the first time: surely it would be just as wonderful when they did it again.

They slowed their snowmobiles down as they approached the barn and Gabe cut his engine just outside, so Pip did the same.

'Just leave them here, Boris will put them away later,' Gabe explained.

They moved into the barn to get out of their thermal suits and Pip could hear the phone in her bag beeping plaintively to let her know that an email had arrived.

Gabe moved closer to her, his hands on her shoulders as he smiled at her. He looked like he wanted to say something to her or kiss her or both. He bent his head down to kiss her just as there was movement at the door.

'Hello!' Boris called, strolling in holding onto Wren with one hand. Gabe leapt back from Pip as if he'd been burned.

Pip stepped back and smiled at Wren who didn't seem to think anything was amiss with her dad about to kiss another woman. Boris, on the other hand, was horrified.

'Oh, sorry, boss, erm...we saw you come back and Wren wanted to come and see you. I didn't realise...'

'It's OK,' Gabe said, clearly embarrassed.

Of course he wouldn't want Wren to see him kissing Pip. Pip had no idea how to define their current relationship, so how would Gabe explain that to Wren? It didn't stop Pip feeling a little hurt about how quickly he had stepped away from her.

'Daddy, me and Chester built the biggest snowman. Boris said we might have to take it down before the guests arrive, but we can keep it, can't we, Daddy?'

'Yes of course, Princess, I'm sure the guests will love to see him.' Gabe swung her up into the air and kissed her on the nose. Wren giggled and snuggled into his shoulder. She eyed Pip. 'I told Chester I wanted to call the snowman Pip, but he wanted to call it Buzz, so Boris said we can call it Buzzpip.'

Pip laughed. 'Wow, I love that name. Can I see it?'

Wren wriggled to get down and as soon as Gabe plonked her on the floor, she grabbed Pip's hand and tugged her out the door. Pip picked up her bag on the way out and she heard Boris apologising to Gabe again as they left the barn.

Wren pulled her along the track back towards the main reception and as they rounded the corner Pip laughed at the biggest snowman she had ever seen. This thing had to be over eight foot tall, with a bottom, middle and head and huge branches for arms. Boris and Mikael had obviously been keeping the children busy. Wren pulled her round to the front of it and Pip laughed even more when she saw the wonky eyes and smile made from lumps of coal and a bent carrot for the nose. He looked like he'd had way too many mulled wines.

'Pip, this is Buzzpip. Buzzpip, this is Pip.'

'Pleased to meet you, Buzzpip,' Pip said, gently shaking one of the branches.

Gabe rounded the corner with Boris and stopped when he saw it. 'Oh, it is big, isn't it? And right in front of the reception too.'

Pip snorted as Gabe's face fought the battle between the fake smile for Wren's benefit and the look of horror as he imagined the guests' reaction to Juniper Island's own answer to the abominable snowman.

'I can take it down, boss, it's no bother,' Boris said, quietly.

'No, Daddy said we can keep him,' Wren said, a little pout forming on her lips.

'Of course we can, honey, but you know snowmen don't last forever. If the weather turns mild, Buzzpip might melt.'

'I know, Daddy,' Wren sighed, sadly.

'Let's go have some lunch,' Gabe said. 'I heard there's jelly for pudding.'

Wren cheered and ran off towards the dining room.

Gabe took another look at the scary drunk snowman and sighed. 'Let's just hope we have really hot weather between now and Thursday.'

❄

After lunch Pip excused herself from the table to check on the email that had arrived. She didn't get many emails and the ones she did get were always work-related. She went upstairs to where all the old bedrooms used to be, now offices if she remembered what Gabe had said correctly. There was no one around and she sat down on one of the sofas and opened up the email.

She groaned when she read it.

Hey honey,

I explained the situation to Arsehole Marcus and asked if you could start your sabbatical early. He had some choice words to say about that, none of which I wish to repeat, but the polite version was that The Tree of Life *have paid for your stay there, the flights and even agreed to pay for the longer stay of two weeks so you could be there over Christmas and New Year, and the whole booking wasn't particularly cheap. Honestly, I can kind of see his point. If it was just starting your sabbatical two weeks early, I'm sure I could talk him round, but he isn't going to pay for you to stay in some uber-posh resort at the most expensive time of the year and not get anything back.*

I explained about the conflict of interest and he said, not so politely, that you've been doing this job for over ten years and that you should be professional enough to write an unbiased and honest review.

I suggested that you might want to pay back the money we had spent on your reservation so you would effectively be paying for your own stay there. Arsehole Marcus didn't like that idea either. He said if that was the case, he would have to seriously reconsider your six-month sabbatical and whether he would be able to keep your job open for when you came back. Apparently he wants to run a six-page spread on winter holidays and resorts and he wants to feature Stardust Lake Hotel and your review, which will be great coverage for your friend.

My advice. If the place is as beautiful as you said, you shouldn't have any problem writing a good review. It'd be awkward if you had to write a bad review, but as that's not the case, just write something good now and get it out of the way, then you don't have to worry about any kind of conflict of interest.

Sorry not to have better news. Hope you've snogged your gorgeous ex-boyfriend by now. I found his picture, and he is hot.

Love you loads,

Wendy x

Pip sighed. She didn't have the money to pay the magazine back. The pay she got from them was next to nothing, though she had never really needed much money before as all her accommodation, food and travel was covered. Over the years she had saved up all of her wages and she had just enough to pay for her rent and bills for her six-month sabbatical. She didn't really want to have to touch that to give the money back to *The Tree of Life.*

Although Gabe had said the night before they would give her some compensation for the inconvenience of staying with him, she'd not heard any more about that and she certainly didn't feel right about asking him.

She remembered Gabe's conviction and determination that Stardust Lake Hotel would be a success. There was no way she could let him down. If *The Tree of Life* was going to feature it in a proper article that would be amazing coverage for him. Pip just had to ensure that it was the best review she had ever written. She would make sure Stardust Lake Hotel shone. She had already told the magazine that she couldn't write the review because her friend owned it and it would be a conflict of interests. If they insisted she wrote the review anyway she wouldn't feel guilty for even a second that it might be slightly biased.

She stared out of the window at the beauty of the resort; it was like something from inside a snow globe. It wouldn't actually be a far stretch to say it was perfect in the review. The resort was gorgeous, the food was excellent and the staff were friendly. She laughed to herself as she remembered just how friendly one of the staff had been when she had been out on the snowmobile. And if there was anything bad that might crop up over the next few days she would just have to conveniently forget about that.

She slipped her phone inside her bag and stood up. but as she moved back to the top of the stairs she heard crying from behind one of the doors.

She moved towards the doors and saw one of them was left ajar. The crying was definitely coming from there. She peered round the crack and saw Neve sitting at her desk crying into her hands.

Her immediate reaction was to rush in and comfort her. This was someone Pip had grown up with, who had looked after her like a big sister. Neve had been there for her on countless occasions. She had picked Pip up after she had fallen, held her after her mum had died and comforted her when her dad had yelled at her and she'd ran to the Whitakers for solace. If Pip could offer some comfort now, then she wanted to be able to help her.

Pip put her hand to the door to push it open and then hesitated. She didn't know the Neve on the other side of the door. She hadn't seen her for twelve years. Neve probably wouldn't thank Pip for sticking her nose in. Pip had seen the way Neve had looked at her over breakfast, and although Neve had been polite and friendly, Pip could see she wasn't thrilled that Pip had shown up out the blue like this.

Maybe she should go and tell Gabe – he would want to know if his sister was upset. As she watched Neve continue to cry, her heart broke for her and whatever pain she was going through. Neve could tell her to get lost but Pip couldn't leave her like this.

She gave a soft knock on the door and pushed it open slightly.

Neve jumped and quickly wiped her eyes.

'Sorry to disturb you. I just came up here to, erm, make a call in private and I heard you crying. Are you OK?'

Neve nodded then shook her head. 'Not really.'

Pip inched into the room. 'Do you want to talk about it? I mean, just tell me to get lost if you don't, but maybe I can help.'

Neve didn't say anything as she wiped the tears away, but she didn't tell her to get out either, so Pip stayed.

'No one can help, thank you for offering, but there's nothing anyone can do,' Neve said.

'Is it the hotel, are you worried about the opening or this Mr Black coming?'

Neve let out a small smile. 'I wish it was that. No, I…I broke up with my boyfriend before coming out here. I've regretted it every day since I left him.'

Pip stood awkwardly in the middle of the office. Matters of the heart were not something she was experienced in or particularly good at. She had run away from the only man she had ever loved and there had been no one for her since.

'How long has it been?'

'Since I broke his heart? Eight weeks, two days and, oh, probably fifteen hours.' She let out another sob.

Pip moved round the desk and knelt on the floor, taking her hand.

'Breaking up is hard, but sometimes it's the best thing for both of you. Do you think it was the right thing to do?'

'I don't know. I think it was the best thing for him. He's younger than I am and has this huge bright career ahead of him. He's fulfilling his dream and I didn't want to get in the way of that. I thought I'd be holding him back, especially if he has to keep travelling over here to see me all the time. I didn't think he was ready for commitment with me. I wanted marriage and kids and he just wasn't ready for any of that. But maybe I didn't give him a chance. Maybe it was too soon and he would have got there eventually.

We had only been going out for ten months. I don't think I will ever stop loving him. God, I hurt him so badly, I could see that, and his sister has just emailed me begging me to reconsider, saying that she has never seen him so miserable before. I thought I was doing the right thing for him. Now I don't know what to do.'

'If you are doubting your decision, maybe it isn't too late to change your mind.'

'He's in Hollywood, I'm here.'

'Hollywood?'

'He's an actor.'

'Oh.' The comment about his career suddenly made more sense.

'He was filming in London and I was travelling up here so often to get things ready for the grand opening, but it didn't matter, we made it work. He knew I'd be moving up here permanently and he was leaving to go to Hollywood, but he was still convinced we could still be together. He said he'd fly over every chance he got or fly me over there, but in reality it was never going to last and I just thought I'd be holding him back. Then I found out…'

Neve stopped talking and Pip didn't know whether to push her or not.

'Maybe, it's for the best,' Neve said.

'You're both miserable, that doesn't sound like it's for the best to me.'

'This email from Sofia…God, I know what it's like to see my brother's heart break. When you left I would have done anything to bring you back. It ruined Gabe. I can't bear the thought of doing that to Oakley.'

Pip felt the stab through her heart at what she had put Gabe through. *She had ruined him?* It had hurt him as much as it had hurt her. That thought was almost crippling.

Neve didn't seem to realise she had said anything untoward. 'He's going to hate me,' she said quietly.

Pip squeezed her hand tighter, trying not to focus on the thought of how much she had hurt Gabe.

'I think if he loves you, then he'll forgive you. Look at me and Gabe: he probably hated me for twelve years for what I did to him. I don't know if we'll ever be able to go back to how we were but he has forgiven me.'

Neve stared at her through her tears. 'I don't think Gabe ever stopped loving you. That was the problem. That's what ruined him. He has carried that heartbreak with him for the last twelve years and he never ever got over it.'

Pip stood up, stung.

'You need to think carefully before you get involved with him again. I see the way you are looking at each other and if you let things happen and then walk away in a couple of weeks it will break his heart all over again. I don't know whether he would recover from it a second time.'

'I have no intention of hurting him.'

'See that you don't. He might have forgiven you, but I certainly won't if you break his heart again.'

Pip felt like she had just been slapped. She had no words and she quickly turned and walked out. She stood out in the corridor for a moment trying to catch her breath before she turned around and marched straight back in.

Neve looked up as she returned.

'It is absolutely none of your business what Gabe and I get up to. And he is a grown man, not a child; he is responsible for making his own choices. If we want to shag each other's brains out right here on your desk we will and there is nothing you can say to change that.'

'What's going on?' came the deep voice of Gabe from behind her.

Pip spun around and saw him standing in the doorway. He didn't look happy. Wren was standing next to him, her hand in his, her eyes wide with shock and confusion.

❄ Chapter 11 ❄

Neve stood up. 'Nothing, Gabe, it's just a misunderstanding.'

He moved into the small office, filling the space.

'You've been crying.' He looked at Pip accusingly. She couldn't find any words to defend herself. Had she been wrong to say what she'd said to Neve? Her relationship with Gabe was hard enough to navigate for them, let alone factoring in an over-protective big sister. And she wouldn't be made to feel guilty for a decision she had made when she was seventeen years old.

Pip sighed, suddenly desperate to make her escape. 'Why don't I take Wren down to play in the snow and you two can have a nice chat about what a terrible person I am.'

Nobody said anything so Pip crouched down to talk to Wren. 'Fancy coming with me? We can see if we can make a friend for Buzzpip.'

Wren looked up at Gabe, clearly unsure if she should go with the person who had just been shouting at her aunt. 'Can I, Daddy?'

Gabe nodded and Wren took Pip's hand and they walked out. The office door closed firmly behind them and Pip wanted to stop and listen to see what was said, but Wren was already tugging her down the stairs.

Pip made sure Wren had her hat and gloves on before they stepped outside into the cold. But as soon as they had made it down the steps, a snowmobile suddenly roared to a stop in front of them.

Pip stepped back, scooping Wren up into her arms to protect her, but as she took in the huge man sitting on its back her heart leapt then fell with recognition. It was Luke. He was huge now. He was sitting down, but she guessed when he stood up he would be nearing seven foot. Everything about him was big too, his thighs, his arms, his hands. He was like a giant bear. His hair was shaggy; even his stubble was four or five days old and had a straggly quality to it.

He was seven years older than Pip and had never had any time for her before. In fact he had always made it clear just how little he had thought of her growing up. She remembered him as a child, angry with her, angry with the world, but as they both had got older there had been more of a tolerance from him. They had never been friends and they'd never had the closeness she shared with Neve. But there had been a few times that the girls in the village had mocked her for the colour of her eyes and Luke had told them to leave her alone. She had never felt comfortable around him, but she was surprised by the scathing look he was giving her now.

A face peered round Luke's massive shoulders, a pretty redheaded girl about Pip's age with sparkling green eyes and a large smile which made the scowl on Luke's face even darker by comparison.

'Pip.' Luke nodded his acknowledgement.

'Hi Luke.'

There was a tense, awkward silence for a moment and the redhead rolled her eyes. In an obvious attempt to clear the air, she stuck her hand out towards Pip with a smile.

'I'm Audrey, I own one of the shops in the village.'

'I'm Pip, Gabe's friend.'

'I guess we'll be seeing you tomorrow when we open the Christmas market for you?'

'Yes, I'm looking forward to seeing it.'

Luke was still watching her and then he turned his attention to Wren. 'Fancy coming to see the puppies with us?'

Wren practically burst with excitement and climbed on the back of the snowmobile in between Audrey and Luke without any further hesitation. Audrey helped her on and said something to Wren that made her laugh. Pip bit her lip nervously; she looked so small on the snowmobile and none of them were wearing helmets.

'Gabe asked me to come and get her,' Luke said, casting a derisive look her way and stopping any anxious thoughts dead. 'Clearly he doesn't trust you to look after her.'

Without another word Luke roared off on the snowmobile, and they all disappeared through the trees a second later.

Gabe didn't trust her.

Of course he didn't. Why would he? She had broken his heart. She didn't know Wren or have any experience with childcare. Wren was his entire world, of course he would only want people he loved and trusted to look after her.

She felt tears sting her eyes as she pulled her coat around her and set off down the track alone.

❄

Gabe watched Pip walk off down the track. Ignoring the stab of guilt he felt at asking Luke to come and get Wren, he turned back to face Neve.

'What happened?'

Neve sighed. 'Nothing. She was being lovely and kind and I snapped at her for no reason. I worry about you that's all. I think getting involved with her is a mistake, but I forget sometimes that you're not my little baby brother any more and you don't need me to look after you.'

Gabe sat down, rubbing his head, which had started to ache. 'Stay out of this, please. I appreciate your concern but if it's a mistake to try again with Pip then it's my mistake to make. I know she's leaving in a couple of weeks, but if we have something worth fighting for then we'll make it work. Look at you and Oakley, you're thousands of miles apart and…' He trailed off as Neve's face dissolved into tears again.

'We broke up a few weeks ago,' she sobbed.

'Oh Neve, I'm so sorry.'

'Well, more accurately, I broke up with him.'

'Why?'

'I don't know. I didn't want to hold him back. Acting has always been his dream and I felt that seeing me would get in the way of that. I was scared I didn't mean as much to him as he means to me. I wanted to get out before I fell completely in love with him, although it's already too late for that. I think my fear of the past repeating itself meant I couldn't see a future with him.'

'You can't let your past cloud your future. Don't let what happened with Zander rule how you live the rest of your life. You deserve to be happy, don't spoil that for yourself.'

She stared at him and sniffed back the tears. It broke his heart to see his sister like this: she was normally so together, so calm and professional. Every conversation they'd had over the last few weeks had been about the hotel. She took her job as hotel manager so seriously, but he hadn't realised that she'd been hiding her heartbreak by throwing herself into her work.

'I want you to be happy too Gabe, and if you honestly think Pip will bring you that then I won't stand in your way. If you really love her then don't throw it away like I did.'

He nodded.

'Now get out of my office, I have work to do,' Neve said, wiping the last of the tears away and straightening her shoulders.

She took a deep breath and switched on her computer. He knew she would say no more about her and Oakley, at least not now.

He stood up. 'Are you OK?'

'I'm fine. Go and talk to her.'

He hesitated and she made shooing gestures with her hand. He smiled and walked round the desk, placing a kiss on her head.

'I love you and if Oakley was crazy enough to let you walk away from him then the man's an idiot.'

She smiled sadly, but as she opened her mouth to speak the phone rang on her desk.

'I better take this, I'll talk to you later.'

She picked up the call before he could argue and when he realised the call was evidently something to do with the hotel, he left her to it.

❄

Pip walked through the trees, following the path down into the valley. The only light seemed to be from the green glow up ahead of her, which she guessed was the ice palace. The icy cold stung her cheeks and made her eyes water. The wind whipped through the trees with a soft moan, causing snow and ice to swirl up into her face. She shoved her hands into her pockets and with her head down against the wind, she walked on.

It had been a weird twenty-four hours since she had landed on the island. Seeing Gabe had changed everything. He had to trust her again and so far she had given him nothing to trust. She hadn't promised she would stay at the end of her holiday, she hadn't told him that she thought she was falling in love with him all over again.

The prospect of being with him again, of having a future with him, was wonderful and terrifying all at once. If she was honest with herself she couldn't tell him any of those things because she knew she had to find it in her to trust him too.

He had never done anything to make her doubt him, but she had spent her whole life believing that no one wanted her or loved her. When she and Gabe had fallen into a relationship she had always been waiting for it to end, for him to reject her just like everyone else. When she had found him in the arms of Jenny Maguire, in the back of her mind it hadn't been a great surprise. If this was going to work she had to let go of those fears once and for all and she didn't know whether she had it in her.

The trees fell away and as she moved further down the valley the wind dropped; somehow she was protected from it in the gap between the hills. She carried on walking, the green glow getting brighter, and suddenly over the brow of the hill she saw it.

The ice palace was huge, a great castle made of glass. It had tall elegant turrets and towers and seemed to stretch up into the sky, encompassing several floors. The glass roof was domed, probably where the auditorium was. Fibre-optic lights lit up the insides with a green and blue glow, casting an aurora into the sky, which made it look magical. It didn't matter that it wasn't made of ice; it was an incredible work of art.

She pulled her camera out of her bag and took a few photos, capturing the moon as it peeped out behind the palace in the darkening sky.

As she walked closer she could see that the glass parts she had presumed were opaque were actually engraved with hundreds of snowflakes, making the palace look like it was frozen. Wren was going to get such a big kick out of this when she saw it.

She pushed the door open – thankfully it wasn't locked – but if she thought she was going to get in away from the cold she was mistaken for as soon as she stepped inside a cold wind swept round her, even icier than the arctic air she had just walked through.

The room was almost in darkness apart from the spotlights on the floor. Large iced snowflakes and snowmen littered the path ahead of her, lit underneath by spotlights, giving the whole room a lilac glow. It was completely silent, almost making Pip want to tiptoe. She walked through a large ice archway and into an enchanted forest made entirely from ice. It was like nothing she had seen before. Trees and bushes grew from every surface, their tiny ice leaves almost fluttering in the breeze. Fairy lights were strung from the branches, casting golden puddles of light over the snow below. Hanging from almost invisible wires were iced dragonflies and fairies flying through the air. It was incredible.

Pip pulled off her gloves and reached out to touch one of the trees, feeling the tell-tale burn of ice though surprisingly it wasn't wet at all. She took a few photos, hoping that she could capture the beauty of the place, though she doubted the camera would be able to do it justice.

She moved through the trees and slowly the trees became Christmas trees, all decorated with baubles and stars that were trapped within the ice. Several ice reindeer were grazing or peering out through the forest of Christmas trees and she even saw a couple of Shetland ponies, which made her smile.

'It's beautiful, isn't it,' came Gabe's voice, though she had no idea where he was. His voice seemed to echo round the room.

'It's amazing.'

She carried on through the forest, passing candy canes that were lit up from below with red spotlights to give them their distinctive striped colouring. She saw movement through the trees, but when she quickly looked in that direction there was only her reflection staring back at her from a wall of icicles.

'We flew an ice carver up from White Cliff Bay, which is somewhere on the borders of Devon and Cornwall. Penny Meadows won some ice-carving competition last year, so we put her in charge of creating this. She didn't do it alone though; she hand-picked a team of carvers to do the job with her.'

Pip came to a large iced bridge that even had tall Victorian-style lanterns with golden lights casting their glow over the icy river below. The path led up the stairs and over the bridge, although there was a white rubber mat on the parts she was supposed to walk on.

'She did a brilliant job. How long will these things last?' Pip called through the trees.

'As long as we want them to. We have the snow and ice-carving competition in January, so I imagine we'll keep them here then. We have a large walk-in freezer out the back so we can put some of the things into storage and bring them back out as necessary. Most of the larger pieces are on wheeled crates so we can manoeuvre them quite easily.'

'You know you're spoiling the magic for me.'

Gabe laughed and she instantly knew he was somewhere up ahead of her.

She followed the route off the bridge and through the trees and smiled at the ice husky dogs that were running along the side of the trail. Large iced presents and oversized baubles also punctuated the path either side, as well as a few elves with large pointy hats and shoes too.

She rounded the corner and saw a large igloo up ahead. The opening was big too, and she barely had to duck to get in. Inside was a large spectacular golden throne made of ice, a big sack of iced presents and a couple of reindeer were grazing. The room was lit by lights strewn about the domed interior, but she had eyes only for the man sitting on the throne watching her with fondness as she stopped. In the light his ice-blue eyes seemed to sparkle and dance as he stood up and stepped down the few stairs towards her.

'This is Santa's Grotto. When the guests arrive, we'll have a Santa in here for a few hours a day for the children to visit,' Gabe explained, resting his hands on her shoulders.

'What will you be asking Santa for?' Pip asked.

He smiled at her, then kissed her forehead softly.

'There's only one thing I want,' Gabe said, as he stared into her eyes.

Pip looked down, suddenly scared by the intensity of his gaze. She didn't want to hurt him again, but what if she was incapable of trusting him?

'I'm sorry about Neve…' he said.

'Don't be. She's looking out for you. I wish I had someone to look out for me.'

He put a finger under her chin and brought her face back up to look at him.

'You do. You have me.'

She smiled, sadly, and looked over his shoulder at the throne. 'Do you remember when your mum took us to see Santa when we were kids? It was the year that my mum had died and your mum obviously knew that my dad was never going to take me. We sat on Santa's lap, obviously in the days before political correctness made that impossible, and told him the things we wished for most in the world.'

'I remember. The guy was the best Santa I ever saw, his beard was real and his suit was perfect. All you wanted was a rocking horse. A grey one with silvery hair and a red saddle.'

Pip stared at him in shock. 'How do you remember that?'

'Because that's what I asked Santa for. I knew your dad would never get it for you, so I asked Santa for it so I could give it to you.'

She had no words at all to convey about that beautiful gesture. She swallowed the emotion that was clogging in her throat and wrapped her arms round his neck.

'Do you know what I asked for that year?'

'You didn't ask for the rocking horse? Jeez, I thought if we both asked for it we stood more of a chance.'

'No, I wanted something more. I asked that you would be my best friend forever.'

Gabe's eyes softened as he slid his hands down to her waist and then wrapped them round her back, hugging her tight.

'I think we will be. Whatever happens between us in the next couple of weeks, I always want to be your friend. Let's make a pact now. Whether this thing that's bubbling between us develops into something more or not, whether we shag each other's brains out on Neve's desk every day for the next few weeks and you still walk away at the end of your holiday back to your glamorous life of travelling the world, let's promise each other now, we will always be friends.'

'I promise,' Pip said, smiling at his use of her words.

'Good. Now can I kiss you again before certain bits of me freeze and snap off completely?'

Pip laughed and nodded and under the golden light of a grotto made from ice, Gabe kissed her softly and sweetly just like a best friend should.

❄

Gabe was woken again by screams later that night, but this time Pip was screaming for him. He ran as fast as he could to Pip's room and just like before she was thrashing around in the bed.

Learning from his mistake the previous night, this time he hit the light before gently shaking her awake.

She shot up, her eyes flying open. He could immediately see she had been crying. He quickly knelt on the bed, pulling her into his arms, and she clung to him, sobbing with relief.

'It's OK, Pip, I'm here. It's OK.'

'God, Gabe, this dream was different. This time it was you that was trapped in the car with me and I couldn't get you out. I swam up to the surface and when I went back down to look for you I couldn't find the car. I could hear you screaming for help and I couldn't find you. I've never been so scared before.'

'It's OK. It was just a dream.'

He sat on the bed and she cuddled into his chest, holding him tight. As he stroked her to calm her down, after a while the sobs subsided and her breathing returned to normal.

'I'm so sorry to wake you again. I bet you'll be glad when the power comes back on and you can get rid of me.'

'I never want to get rid of you. I love having you here. Nothing you could do could push me away.'

'What about Wren, did I wake her too?'

'No, nothing can wake her once she goes to sleep. Once, when we were living in California, a car blew up right outside our house, the emergency services came, all their sirens blaring, and she slept through the whole thing. She'll wake up sometimes to go to the toilet, but she never gets woken by noise. You could scream all night and it wouldn't disturb her.' He paused and noticed she was more settled. 'Are you OK now?'

She didn't answer straight away, then she looked up at him. 'Would you stay with me for a little while?'

'Of course.'

He shuffled around so he was lying down and she lay next to him, with her head still on his chest. He wrapped his arms round her and stroked her hair just like he used to.

It wasn't long before she was fast asleep again, but he had no intention of leaving her for the rest of the night.

❄

Pip woke up in the very early hours of the morning, when the sky was just turning grey. At some point the lamp had been turned off and she had rolled the other way, but Gabe hadn't left her. He was curled round her back with one arm tight around her stomach; it made her heart soar. If this was what could happen if she stayed, if she could spend every night like this, she would be happy for the rest of her life.

Suddenly she was aware of movement in the room and her eyes shot open. Wren was standing next to her, sniffling a little.

'Hey sweetheart,' Pip whispered, instinctively pulling back the duvet for her. Wren immediately crawled into the bed and wrapped her arms round Pip's neck, crying a little but not properly.

Gabe carried on sleeping behind Pip, obviously exhausted at being woken two nights in a row.

'Are you OK?' Pip whispered, holding her tight. Wren's tiny body was warm next to hers and Pip felt something unfurl inside her.

'I had a bad dream and Daddy wasn't in his room.'

'Well, it's OK now. I've got you and I won't let anything hurt you, I promise.'

Wren made little huffs against her neck, but Pip knew she wasn't really crying any more.

'Did you have a bad dream too, is that why Daddy is cuddling you?'

Pip hadn't even thought about what Wren would make of finding her dad in bed with a woman, or whether Gabe's lifestyle of dating lots of women meant that Wren had seen this sort of thing many times before. For Wren's sake, she hoped Gabe had been a little more discreet than that.

'Yeah I did,' Pip said, honestly.

Wren nodded, wisely. 'Hugging Daddy always makes me feel better when I've had a bad dream.'

'He gives the best hugs, doesn't he?' Pip said.

'Yes, but you smell nicer than Daddy.'

Pip laughed. 'I do?'

'You smell of flowers and cherries.'

'Oh. What does Daddy smell like?'

'Like a stinky boy.'

Pip had to hold a hand over her mouth so she didn't laugh out loud at that. Wren let out a little giggle, clearly seeing that Pip was laughing at her comment.

'I like the way your daddy smells.'

Wren became all serious again. 'Do you love him?'

Oh God, what a question.

'Do you love Chester?'

Wren nodded. 'He's my best friend.'

'Well, Daddy is my best friend too.'

'When I grow up, I'm going to marry Chester.'

'Are you? Does he know?'

'I told him. He didn't like it, but I said he had to do as he was told and he had to marry me. Will you marry Daddy when you grow up?'

So much for distraction tactics. 'Well, if he tells me I have to marry him, then I suppose I'll have to do what I'm told too.'

'Then you'll be my step-mummy.'

This conversation couldn't get any worse. Pip had to remember to think twice and three times before making some offhand comment, as everything would be stored in her tiny mind for future use.

'I don't think your daddy will ever get married. He loves you too much and there's no room for him to love someone else too.'

'Well that's silly,' Wren said, with all the wisdom of someone five times her age. 'He can't marry me, can he?'

'No.'

'And I'll be married to Chester, so who will look after Daddy then?'

'I don't know.'

Wren frowned slightly. 'Maybe Chester can live with me and Daddy once we get married. Then we can both look after Daddy.'

'That sounds like a good idea. Why don't you try to go back to sleep for a little while? It's not time to get up yet.'

Wren snuggled into the side of Pip's neck, making her smile.

Wren was silent for a while and Pip thought she had gone off to sleep very quickly.

'And Pip, tomorrow we can tell Daddy the plan,' Wren said, sleepily.

'What plan, sweetheart?'

'That you're going to marry Daddy and I'm going to marry Chester and we will all live here together.'

Pip cringed. Gabe was going to kill her. If there was one thing guaranteed to dull his affections for her it was Pip inadvertently staking a claim over his life and somehow leading Wren to believe she would be her step-mum.

Wren shifted closer to Pip and she stroked the little girl's hair. It was silly to think about marriage and being part of Gabe's family so soon after coming back into his life, but right now there was nowhere else she'd rather be.

❄ Chapter 12 ❄

Gabe woke up to a dull grey light outside and snowflakes swirling past the window. He smiled when he saw Pip lying on her back with her arms tight around Wren who was curled up on her chest. Wren was sucking her thumb and looked utterly content. His arm was wrapped round them both and he had never felt so complete as he did right then. This was how it was meant to be. Winston had even moved into the room during the night and was curled up round Gabe's feet. It felt like they were the perfect little family.

He moved a stray hair off Pip's face and kissed her softly on the forehead. She stirred slightly but didn't wake. Instead she rolled towards him, still holding Wren so she ended up between the two of them. Wren didn't stir at all.

'Pip,' Gabe whispered.

Pip's eyes opened slowly, her golden gaze fixing on him as she smiled.

He motioned for her to be quiet as Wren slept on unknowingly between them and he leaned forward and kissed her.

She moaned softly and stroked his face.

'Yay. I knew you two loved each other,' Wren said and Gabe snatched his mouth from Pip's.

His daughter was sitting up, her eyes wide with excitement.

'And now you're going to get married and Pip will be my step-mummy and I can be bridesmaid.'

Wren leapt to her feet, bouncing on the bed between them. Winston yapped with excitement and Gabe grabbed her and pulled her onto his lap, tickling her mercilessly, anything to stop her talking about marriage. She squealed and giggled and when he finally relented he hoped that the subject would be dropped.

'Will you get married in Elsa's ice palace, Daddy?' Wren said, as she gasped for breath, sprawled across his lap.

'We are not getting married, you silly thing. Pip and I are just friends.'

He glanced over at Pip and she smiled briefly before getting out of bed and heading for the bathroom. She closed the door behind her and Gabe sighed. Nothing was ever simple.

'Right, Princess, let's get dressed then we can go over to breakfast.'

He stood up, swinging a giggling Wren over his shoulder, and left Pip's room.

❄

Pip had been a bit quiet over breakfast and Gabe didn't know if it was because he had denied that they were getting married or whether it was something else. Wren had chattered enough for all three of them. What Wren had said was certainly playing on his mind.

He finished his mug of tea and stood up.

'Would you mind keeping an eye on Wren for a second? I just need to have a word with Neve.'

Pip nodded, though he was sure he heard her mutter something about getting Luke to watch Wren as he walked away.

He found Neve in reception, talking to Iris. He waited until they'd finished talking then took her to one side.

'Can you watch Wren for me today?'

'I can this afternoon. Why, what's going on?' Neve was immediately suspicious. She knew him too well.

'I think you were right. I'm worried about her getting too attached to Pip. Wren has already talked about Pip and me getting married. I ended up sleeping with Pip last night and...'

'What?'

'Sleeping, just sleeping. Pip had a nightmare about the accident and I went to see if she was OK and ended up staying with her. Wren got up in the middle of the night and found us together.'

'Gabe, you need to be careful about exposing Wren to that kind of thing. She doesn't need to see you lying in bed with a string of different women.'

'She has never seen me in bed with a woman before and we weren't doing anything, just sleeping next to each other.'

'Well, if Pip is the first woman Wren has properly seen you with, it's no wonder she is getting so excited about it. It's a novelty for her.'

'I know. I woke up this morning and the two of them were cuddled up in bed together like...like mother and daughter – except Wren's mother never cuddled her like that. And then Wren saw us kissing and has now got it into her head that we're going to get married and Pip will be her step-mum and she's all excited about it and it's just got into a big mess.'

Neve's face softened. 'Wren gets excited about everything, Gabe, the snow, the ice palace, her new *Frozen* wellies, Buzzpip, the puppies. She is also a very resilient child. Nothing ever keeps her down, she just bounces from one day to the next, taking it all in her stride. If Pip leaves, Wren will probably have forgotten her by the time we are celebrating the New Year's Eve ball. I know I was worried about her getting attached, but if Pip stays then she needs to know that life with you comes with a child and what that's actually like.'

'Pip has treated Wren with nothing but patience and kindness. Pip knows that I come with Wren and it hasn't put her off yet, where other women would run a mile. I just think that the less time that Pip and Wren spend together the better, at least for the next few days.'

Neve nodded. 'That's fine. I have some stuff I need to sort out this morning, but I can take her this afternoon. We can make mince pies together or do some kind of baking.'

'Thank you.'

A noise behind them made him turn and Pip was standing there with Wren.

'Sorry, we were just going to go outside, I didn't realise you were here, I thought you would be upstairs.'

'No bother, we've finished talking anyway,' Gabe said, praying that Pip hadn't heard anything. 'Shall we go and see the reindeer?'

Wren cheered and ran towards the door, and Gabe caught her and swung her up onto his hip.

He waited for Pip to catch them up. 'You have real reindeer?'

'Yeah. We thought it would be a good draw for Santa's Grotto. Santa and his reindeer. They are in a paddock round the back of the staff quarters at the moment, but when we have our guests here we'll move them to the enclosure outside the ice palace. Luke and Boris are busy building a shelter down there for them.'

They stepped outside and the snow was still falling gently around them. He took a little path round the side of the reception that led through the trees and behind the staff quarters.

'Wren, you're going to stay with Neve this afternoon, is that OK?'

'But I want to play with you and Pip.'

'You can if you want to, Princess, but Neve needed some help making some mince pies and cakes and she asked if you would like to do it. It's only six days until Christmas and there's lots of cakes and biscuits to make. Neve will be very busy if she has to do it all on her own.'

Wren clearly thought about this for a moment. 'I'll help Neve. I like making cakes.'

'That's very kind, Neve will be very grateful.'

They approached the paddock and he watched the frown disappear from Pip's face as she saw all the reindeer. They were all wearing shiny red harnesses with their names embroidered in gold. The harnesses had bells on and the bells rang softly as the deer nestled in the straw or moved around eating the food that had been laid out for them. He had considered taking the harnesses off until the guests arrived but there was no way he would remember which reindeer was which without the harnesses and he didn't want to confuse the animals by calling them the wrong name. They had been trained to pull sleighs and, although he hadn't tried it yet, he assumed the animals would cooperate more if they were at least called the correct name.

'Meet Dasher, Dancer, Prancer, Vixen, Comet, Cupid, Donner and Blitzen,' Gabe said, pointing each one out.

Pip laughed. 'Are you serious?'

'Yes, of course, they're Santa's reindeer.'

'They're beautiful.'

'They're very tame, feel free to stroke them.'

Cupid came plodding over to see if they had any treats and Pip reached across the fence to scratch between her ears. Wren reached out and stroked her nose. Wren had already met them several times, though she found it all a bit confusing that they were there and Santa wasn't.

'I wonder if you would mind taking on their feeding while you are here. I have a couple of girls from the village that come up and muck out their shelter twice a week, so that's taken care of. Normally Luke would be feeding them, he's in charge of all the animals, but I need him to help Boris with some of the hard labour jobs over the next few days. Most of the staff have gone off for a few days' holiday before the guests arrive.

They've all worked so hard to get everything ready and as we are pretty much fully booked until April, now was the only time that I could let them go. In hindsight, I should have kept a few of them back to help with maintenance, so I need Luke to help me.'

'Everything looks perfect. What is there left to do?'

'They are trying to get some of the houses in the village ready for our guests in case we need them. We own six small houses down there that we were going to open to guests in the busier periods, but we didn't intend to open them this year. With the power down, I want to make sure that we have the option of putting some of the guests in the village if we need to. The weather is only going to get worse over the next few months and even if the power does come back on, it might go off again. Once Christmas is out of the way, I need to look at getting a more reliable power supply. But anyway, if you could free Luke up by taking on the feeding that would be really useful. Twice a day. There's a great big container in the shelter. Just take four buckets of it and fill the trough here and half a bucket for Rudolph.'

'Rudolph?'

Gabe looked across to the next paddock, but the reindeer in question was nowhere to be seen. Probably still sulking in his shelter that he had been separated from his harem.

'The stag. These are all girls, Rudolph is the boy. The breeder and trainer I bought them off said that the reindeer mating season is normally until the end of November, beginning of December, but sometimes it can vary because of the mild or cold weather, so he suggested to be on the safe side that I keep them separated until the new year. Rudolph isn't happy. Next year I'll probably breed them. I'm sure the visitors will be delighted to see baby reindeer wandering around the place, but this year it's just another thing I would prefer to do without.'

'Poor Rudolph. The lack of action is probably making his nose turn red.'

Gabe laughed. 'Let me just show you where everything is and then I'll introduce you to the puppies.'

He opened the gate, and as most of the reindeer were still busy with their breakfast, they didn't even look up when Gabe and Pip walked into their enclosure. Wren ran on ahead into the shelter and Gabe shut the gate behind them.

'Food is there, the buckets are next to it. If you could wash the buckets out at the end of the day and then leave them upside down to drain out...' He glanced over at Pip, taking it all in. 'Are you sure you don't mind doing this? I feel bad, you're supposed to be a guest.'

'I'm your friend, of course I don't mind helping. What about the houses in the village? Is there anything I can help with down there? I'm probably not any good at building and repairs but I can help with the painting.'

'That's very kind. I think most of the painting has been done, it's just the external repairs and renovations now.'

'What about decorating the houses for Christmas, I can do that?'

'That would be really helpful. I'll have a word with some of the boys to make sure you'll have everything you need delivered down there. Thank you for this. The guests all arrive on Thursday; it's just three days away, and I just want to make sure everything is perfect.' He watched Wren happily splashing in the puddles in the entrance to the shelter and smiled. 'This is so different to any hotel I've bought before. The hotels were all running when I bought them and though I spent a lot of time making the hotels bigger and better, I worked with what I had and improved on it. Here it feels like I'm starting from scratch. The other hotels have been glamorous and luxurious with spa facilities and everything the guests need, at least they were when

I had finished with them. Here it's a different feel entirely and I just hope I've captured the essence of a winter resort correctly. There's no skiing or snowboarding here, so that's one of the main things that stands us apart from other winter resorts and not in a good way.'

'People are going to love it.'

He smiled at the confidence she had in him.

'Let me introduce you to Rudolph.'

He took her hand and led her out the shelter and across the paddock to the adjoining gate. It was only when he went to open the gate that he realised what he'd done. He stared down at their entwined fingers. It had felt so natural to take her hand, just like he'd always done.

He glanced at Pip to see what her reaction was, but she was smiling at him. She reached up to stroke his face briefly; it was all they could do when Wren was hovering nearby. It was all the encouragement he needed.

Still keeping his hand in hers, he pushed open the gate and as soon as Wren was safely on the other side he closed it behind them.

He led Pip into the shelter; Rudolph was standing in the corner, nibbling on a ball of hay. He was a big proud beast and he glanced up briefly at their arrival and then away again as if they weren't worth bothering paying any attention to.

'This is Rudolph. You can buy his affections with carrots and parsnips from the kitchen. Though to say he has a mind of his own would be an understatement.'

'Hi Rudolph,' Wren sang, though Rudolph didn't even look up as she approached and ran a tiny hand over his belly and up his neck.

'Your guests are going to fall in love with the reindeer,' Pip said.

'I hope so.'

'Can I ask why you are opening so late? People would have been up here from the beginning of November to celebrate Christmas and see Santa.'

'We were supposed to open mid-October but we had a fire and it just put everything behind.'

'Oh god, was anyone hurt?'

'No, thankfully. It was gutting, though. It happened in the middle of the night and ripped through a row of six of the smaller guest lodges before anyone noticed and could put it out. We didn't want guests to come up here and see the ruins, so we had to cancel or postpone many of the guests. We lost thousands of pounds but hopefully, with the grand opening on Thursday and all the journalists that will come and report on it, it will be great exposure for us and our rooms will be filled this time next year.'

'Can we go and see the puppies now, Daddy?' Wren said, when Rudolph was still failing to acknowledge her presence.

'Of course we can, sweetheart.' He held out his other hand for Wren and when she took it he smiled to himself at the perfect little family unit they appeared to be, all holding hands. If only it could be this way forever.

❄

Pip followed Gabe and Wren along the track as Gabe chased his daughter and Wren shrieked with laughter every time she was caught. It was clear to see Gabe adored his daughter and enjoyed the time he spent with her. It would be difficult for him to add another person to the mix when it had been just the two of them for so long. But to actually not want Pip to spend any time with Wren was hurtful. She'd heard him say that to Neve and it had stung. He didn't even trust her to look after Wren for longer than a few minutes, which was why he'd asked Luke to look after Wren the day before.

It was confusing as hell. One minute he was kissing her and looking at her with puppy-dog eyes and the next he was deliberately trying to keep her and his daughter apart. What possible chance did they have for a future together if he wouldn't let her in? And if he didn't want a future, what did he want from their two weeks together: friendship, friends with benefits or something more? Pip sighed. It was still early days, she knew that. And just as Gabe had started from scratch with Stardust Lake Hotel, in many ways she was starting from scratch with him. But could she stay if all he could offer her was a snatched kiss now and again?

They were heading away from the resort now and the lodges were left far behind them. Pip saw a little stone cottage tucked into the trees, smoke swirling from the chimney. The house had stunning views over the frozen lake which spread out from almost right in front of the cottage door.

Without even asking, she knew that was where Luke lived. Whereas Gabe lived almost right next door to the main reception area, wanting or needing to be there for any problems that might occur, Luke had always been quiet and withdrawn and this location was perfect for him.

The man himself was sitting on his doorstep, eight husky puppies sitting at his feet, not moving as they stared up at him. He slowly fed each dog a treat, one at a time, and the other puppies didn't move or try to get the food first; they just sat patiently waiting for their turn. He obviously had them well trained.

He looked up at their arrival and dismissed the puppies with a wave of his hand and, just like a switch had been flicked, the dogs returned to their normal puppy state, jumping over each other, gambolling, pouncing on each other's tails as if they had just caught their prey. They were fluffy and adorable.

Wren ran on ahead, bursting into Luke's tiny garden without any fear she would be turned away and, sure enough, Luke grabbed her and threw her into the air, catching her seemingly just before she hit the ground to great shrieks of approval from Wren.

Gabe opened the gate, letting Pip go ahead of him.

'Hey Luke, how's it going?' Gabe greeted him cheerfully though it was clear Luke wasn't happy to see them, well, probably more accurately, her.

'Morning,' Luke nodded at his brother, eyeing Pip suspiciously. She gave him her best smile but it did nothing to change his features.

'I thought Pip might want to see the puppies.'

Luke's shoulders fell a little as he clearly sighed with defeat. 'Wren, why don't you introduce Pip to the puppies, you know them all so well.'

With that, Luke disappeared inside his house. Gabe gave her an awkward smile then walked into the house after him.

'This is Blue,' Wren said, pointing to one of the puppies that did seem to have more of a smoky blue colouring than the others. 'This is Coal,' she said, pointing to one that was almost entirely black, though he still had those distinctive blue eyes. 'This is Jemima, Honey, Diva, Rex, Ray, and this is my favourite, Blaze.'

Pip kneeled down and the puppies leapt all over her, yapping and wagging their tails excitedly. Though above the yapping, Pip could hear raised voices coming from inside the house.

'I thought she could feed the puppies for you, maybe walk them, free up a bit more of your time,' Gabe said, defensively.

'I don't want her in my house or anywhere near my dogs.'

'Luke, that's unfair and really nasty and I'd never expect that from you.'

'Why is Blaze your favourite?' Pip asked, trying to keep the emotion from clogging her throat. Why was she so unlikeable that she had been rejected her whole life? Luke had never had any time for her when she was growing up, but now it sounded like he hated her. She fought the tears that sprung to her eyes.

The arguing continued inside but Pip blocked it out.

'Because I like his diamond in the middle of his head and because he keeps escaping like I do. Luke says that he must be copying me.' Wren giggled then looked at Pip more closely. 'Are you crying?'

'No, no honey, I'm fine. Sometimes the cold makes my eyes water and it's really cold down here.'

Wren studied her and then threw her arms round her neck and hugged her, just as Gabe and Luke came walking out the house.

'Daddy, Pip is sad because she hasn't got anyone to love her.'

Pip's eyes bulged. Holy shit, the kid was insightful.

'No, I'm fine,' Pip laughed awkwardly. 'It's just windy and cold down here and it's making my eyes water.'

Luke looked at her and she immediately saw guilt and regret wash across his face. Gabe clearly wasn't happy.

'Come on, I've got some other things to show you before we go to the Christmas market this afternoon.'

'Oh Daddy, we just got here,' Wren said.

'Luke has a lot of work to do in the village and I don't want us to be in his way.' Gabe scooped Wren up so there could be no further argument and walked out the gate.

Pip stood up and faced Luke properly. He towered over her, but she refused to be intimidated by him.

'I'm not sure what I did to make you hate me so much, but I'm sorry.'

She turned away but he snagged her arm and pulled her back. 'I don't hate you. I'm sorry if you overheard what we were talking about in there.'

Sorry that she'd overheard, not sorry that he'd said it.

She removed her arm and walked away.

'Pip, I'm just an arsehole. You're better off staying away from me.'

She caught up with Gabe and Wren. Wren was on Gabe's shoulders, holding onto his head.

Gabe looked at her and smiled, sadly.

'Daddy, what's an arsehole?'

❄

It was a while later when Gabe escorted Pip down to the village. He'd shown Pip around a bit more of the resort, they'd had lunch and then Wren had skipped off quite happily to help Neve with the cakes.

He looked down at his hand holding Pip's, their fingers entwined, and smiled. He had no idea who had instigated that but he had a vague recollection of their hands slotting together automatically like two magnets as they made their way down the track.

She looked up at him and smiled and he felt his heart melt a little more. He wondered where he and Pip would be in their relationship now if he didn't have to worry about protecting Wren and he had no brother or sister to put a dampener on things. Neve and Luke being rude to her was not helping Pip come to the decision to stay. He wanted to whisk her away from everything, just for a little while, and truly discover whether they had something between them, whether going back was even an option. He tried to clear his mind of what would happen if they were completely alone. Making love to his best friend had been uppermost in his mind since he had set eyes on her again. But there would be no coming back once he had. If he was scared he was falling in love with her now, making love to her would seal the deal completely.

He cleared his throat as he tried to block out that glorious and wonderful thought.

'So this card will bill directly to your room account,' Gabe explained, handing her a plastic credit card. 'It seemed impractical to expect the villagers to pay for a credit-card machine and lots of our guests will only have credit cards, not cash, so we came up with the idea of these room cards. That way we only had to buy scanners for all the shops. It links straight back with the hotel and gets applied to your room, and when you pay it gets refunded back to the relevant shop.'

'That's a really clever idea.'

Gabe shrugged. 'It's how they work on cruises. Every excursion, souvenir or drink is charged to the card and then they just get a bill at the end; it's more efficient for our customers. I've given you two hundred pounds' credit to go some way towards the inconvenience of not having the lodge you paid for. You'll probably be with me for another night at least, which hopefully will not be too much of a hardship.'

He really hoped the power wouldn't come back on; he was enjoying having her live with him.

'I think I can suffer it.'

He laughed. 'And you know, if your room isn't comfortable enough we can perhaps find you alternative accommodation.'

'What's the alternative?'

'My room.'

She laughed loudly at this and he loved the sound of it.

'But where would you sleep if I was sleeping in your room?' she teased.

'Oh well, I'm sure we can come up with some kind of sleeping arrangement that's beneficial for everyone.'

'I'm sure you can.'

They were flirting and he loved it.

The icy wind raced through the trees and as she shivered in the cold, he found himself instinctively putting his arm round her shoulders trying to warm her up. He knew they had fallen into a close relationship way too quickly, but he was enjoying every moment. He had his best friend back and he knew he hadn't been this happy in years.

❄ Chapter 13 ❄

Pip looked at the village as they approached it from the only road. Whoever had built it all those years ago had chosen a great location, something she hadn't appreciated when she'd come here as a child.

The hills that populated the middle of the island served as a great backdrop for the village and made the place very picturesque, but they also protected the houses from the arctic wind that must blow in from the north on an almost daily basis.

The sea was on the other side, far enough away that the residents didn't get the cliff-top winds but close enough that every house in the village could experience sea views.

They passed a cluster of six houses that was a little way out of the village. There were several men busily working on the outside of them, hammering and sawing and drilling. Pip guessed these were the houses they were getting ready for the guests. Luke was among them, his huge size making him stand out from the rest.

'Would you be helping them if you weren't looking after me?' Pip asked.

'Yes, and I'll be helping them tomorrow I'm afraid. We have to get them finished before the guests arrive in three days.'

'You don't need to worry about entertaining me. Besides, I'll be down here too, helping with the Christmasifying on the inside.'

'Thank you for that.'

She smiled as she leaned against him. He had put his arm around her to protect her from the cold, but although the wind had dropped since they'd walked into the shelter of the hills, he hadn't relinquished his hold. It felt right though, being in his arms, as if no time had passed between them.

They drew closer to the village. All the houses were two storeys. She remembered they were once old stone houses, but they had been given a new lease of life and covered in planks of wood to make them look like the ski lodges up in the resort. Strings of fairy lights hung from the roofs and from above the shop windows. Lights hung from the lamp-posts too and zigzagged across the street.

Every shop had large windows with leaded square panels. Each glass square was about a foot wide interspersed with the thick black edging that reminded Pip of the Victorian era. The windows glowed gold, spilling their light onto the snowy street. Sweet scents of chocolate and sugar filled the air and smoke billowed from all the chimneys. It was picture perfect and she quickly grabbed her camera and took a few photos, though she knew the camera wouldn't capture the true essence and smells of the place.

'It's wonderful Gabe, you've done an incredible job. People are going to love it.'

'Thank you.'

She looked around. 'So all the villagers just gave up the downstairs of their homes?'

'We've built extensions onto the backs of people's houses, so the room that now houses the shop has been moved to the extension. It was a big ask, and their whole lives and homes were completely disrupted this year, but surprisingly everyone was willing to take part. None of these people wanted to leave the island, but without income coming into it they would have had to at least try to seek work on the other Shetland Islands and there's not exactly a lot of spare jobs going up here. They'll make money from the goods they sell, but they'll be paid too. Whatever money we make in the resort, a percentage of that will go to pay the villagers for the use of their homes. The Christmas village is going to be a big draw for the tourists and guests and it didn't seem right that we would almost solely benefit from tourists coming here to see it so hopefully their sacrifice will be worth it in the end. Which shops would you like to visit?'

'All of them.'

He grinned down at her. 'I was hoping you'd say that. I know they'd be disappointed if you didn't at least pop in and have a look around. Don't feel you have to buy something from every store, though. But if you end up buying a lot or big things we can arrange for them to be collected by the Range Rover and taken back to the hotel later so you don't have to carry them.'

'Is that a service you'll provide for the guests too?'

'Yes, we don't want anyone to be put off buying big and heavy things because they have to carry them all the way back to the hotel.'

'You've thought of everything.'

'I hope so. Shall we walk up this side and then we can walk back down the street on the other side?'

'Sounds like a plan.'

'Come and meet Mikki O'Sullivan. I think the tourists will love her shop but I think you'll love it especially. Mikki is a bit… kooky, but there's no denying she has a real talent for her art.'

'Kooky?'

Gabe put on a spooky voice. 'She can see into the future.'

Pip laughed. 'What makes you think she can't?'

'Well, if I could see into the future, I think I would look at the winning lottery numbers. I'm not sure she would be living in a tiny house on a remote Scottish island if she had won the lottery.'

'Why not? You're doing quite well financially and you've chosen to live here. Sometimes you don't need the luxurious trappings to be happy in life. It's about the places and the people you're with. Anyway, from what I can gather from the people who claim to have that gift, they don't choose what they see, they don't have any control over it, the visions just appear in their head.'

'Are you telling me you believe in that sort of thing?' Gabe asked.

'I'm saying that fate sometimes works in mysterious ways. Maybe there are things beyond our knowledge and understanding, maybe some events are predestined and, if that's the case, maybe some people can see that destiny in front of us. There are many stories out there about couples who have got together in weird and wonderful ways. There was one man who had a photograph of him playing on the beach as a child and in the background was his wife playing on the same beach, though they didn't meet until years later. I don't know how it all works. But I do feel that some couples are meant to be together, like two halves of a whole. Life sometimes gets in the way, but fate will always bring them together in the end.'

He stared down at her and smiled. 'It is odd that of all the hotels in the world, you get sent here where I am. Maybe fate did play a part after all. Even if we are only supposed to be friends in the grand scheme of things, I'm glad you're back in my life.'

Pip frowned slightly. Was friendship the only thing he really wanted? But then what was with all the kisses?

As they walked to the first house, Pip noticed the name above the door, painted in gold curly writing on a wooden plank, 'Stardust Snow Globes'. On closer inspection all the lodges had beautiful names like 'Emerald Emporium' or 'Pancakes & Port'. It was very cute.

She pushed open the door and was met with a wall of warmth and the smells of freshly baked cookies, which she noticed were on a plate by the door along with a handwritten note asking her to help herself.

'Mikki makes amazing cookies,' Gabe said, grabbing one and taking a huge bite. He nodded his encouragement for her to take one, which she did, and then stepped further into the shop.

A log fire was burning merrily at the back of the shop and, like the ice palace, the room was almost in darkness apart from the spotlights that lit the displays from underneath. Wonderful snow globes of every shape and size filled the room. They were displayed beautifully, not just row upon row on shelves but standing on black boxes, cascading down the walls and jutting out of the floor like cave formations or the Giant's Causeway. The snow globes were incredibly detailed with tiny houses and buildings inside and many of the larger globes had real lights in the windows and streets. Each snow globe was completely unique, showing tiny snow-topped villages, towns or great cities. As Pip moved around to admire the pieces she realised they were representations of real towns and cities of the world and that she had visited almost every one of these places. The snow globes were grouped into countries, making it easier for Pip to find the places she loved the most.

'These are incredible,' Pip said, noticing Gabe was watching her carefully.

'I knew you'd like it.'

'It's like a reminder of all the wonderful places I've visited. I could spend all day in here. How does anyone choose which globe to buy?'

Gabe laughed. 'Most people don't have the extensive travel experience you have. Most people will choose their favourite place or their home town or maybe one of here as a souvenir. Mikki makes them all herself.'

'Really?'

'Let me introduce you.'

He took her hand and moved towards the back of the shop. If Pip had been expecting an elderly lady with a headscarf and a crystal ball she would have been very disappointed. Mikki O'Sullivan was stunning; she looked like a younger Cindy Crawford. She was crouched over the makings of a globe, painting the intricate detail of what was obviously Stardust Lake Hotel, the surrounding lodges, the glass igloos and the ice palace.

'Mikki, this is my friend Pip, Pip this is Mikki, one of the most talented artists I know.'

Mikki stopped what she was doing and sat up smiling. 'Pip, I'm so pleased to meet you.'

Pip smiled at the gorgeous Irish lilt in her voice.

'Stephen told us all about you when you arrived, how you had come here on holiday when you were little and that you were friends with Gabe.' She glanced down at their joined hands and smiled even more. 'Very good friends it would seem.'

'Just friends,' Gabe said, smiling, though it was obvious he was a little embarrassed by her comment.

Pip couldn't help feeling a little hurt by the denial even though, in reality, they were nothing more than friends at the moment. She wondered if they would ever be anything more.

'Gabe has worked so hard to get this place ready, but we've all been worried that he has neglected his personal life in favour of it. He needs a lovely woman to look after him.'

Pip tried to suppress a smile at the not-so-subtle matchmaking.

Gabe laughed awkwardly. 'I don't need anyone to look after me, Wren and I are doing fine on our own.'

Mikki returned her attention to the snow globe she was painting. 'I've created a wedding scene for this one.'

'Great idea, we have several weddings booked for next year. I'm sure they will be very popular.'

'I think Pip might like this one.' Mikki held it aloft and Pip smiled at the tiny bride and groom emerging from the ice palace. Though as she looked more closely her smile fell off when she realised the groom had black hair, the bride was blonde with golden eyes and in between them was a tiny black-haired girl dressed in a *Frozen* Elsa dress. 'To remind you of Juniper Island,' Mikki said, mischievously.

Gabe had clearly seen the likeness too as he frowned.

Not wanting any more awkwardness, Pip leaned forward to whisper in Mikki's ear. 'I won't need a reminder of Juniper Island or of Gabe and Wren if I'm living here with them.'

Mikki laughed. 'That is true, my dear. Maybe I'll keep it as a wedding gift, for the, erm…appropriate guests.'

'I'll take the one of St Vitus Cathedral,' Pip said quickly. 'I love Prague.'

'You don't want one of Juniper Island?' Gabe said, clearly a bit disappointed by that.

'She won't need it,' Mikki hooted, returning to her work.

Gabe looked between them in confusion. 'Look, grab the globe you want and I'll scan it and then Mikki can send it up to the lodge for you.'

Pip did as she was told and then Gabe escorted her out onto the street.

'What was that about?' he asked.

'I think Mikki would quite like to see us married off.'

'That's a bit optimistic.'

Pip sighed, feeling more confused than ever.

With his hand still in hers, Gabe escorted her to the next shop, simply called 'Chocolate'. The mouth-watering sweet smells were deliciously inviting as the warmth of the shop swirled around them as soon as they stepped inside.

Chocolate fountains of several different shades of brown and white stood in the middle of the room as hot liquid chocolate cascaded over several tiers. The smell was divine and Pip resisted the urge to stick her face into one of the chocolate flows and drink it straight from the fountain.

Before she'd had a chance to look further round the room, Pip spotted Stephen dressed in a very Christmassy waistcoat with a matching bow tie. He was sitting at the back of the shop by the fire, presumably with his wife who was actually sitting in a rocking chair, knitting. Pip suppressed the smile that was bubbling inside. With her little gold-rimmed half-moon glasses and her grey hair in a bun, she looked like she had googled what 'Mrs Christmas looked like' and decided to dress and act accordingly.

Stephen looked over at them as they walked in and stood up to greet them.

'Miss Chesterfield, how lovely to see you again.'

'Please, call me Pip.'

'Pip.' He smiled and his smile grew even bigger when he saw that she was holding hands with Gabe.

A thought struck her. 'Why didn't you tell me that Gabe lived here when we talked about him on the plane?'

'You talked about me?' Gabe said, clearly intrigued by this.

'I mentioned that I had been here before on holiday with my best friend. Stephen remembered me and that I'd come with you. He didn't mention that you were here, though.'

Stephen looked sheepish for a moment. 'There was something about the way you looked when I mentioned his name. It made me think you wouldn't welcome seeing him again. I wondered if you would have been so excited about coming here if you'd known he was going to be here too. I feared you might just tell me to turn the plane around.'

'I probably would have done.' Pip laughed when she saw Gabe's face. 'What? You broke my heart. I didn't know at that stage that my heartbreak was completely self-inflicted.'

'Then I'm really glad I didn't tell you if it's brought you two together again. Please, come meet my wife.'

Stephen ushered Pip across the room.

'This is my wife Deborah, Debs this is Gabe's friend, Pip.'

Deborah stood up and peered over her glasses at them. 'Did you say girlfriend? I told you, didn't I, Stephen? We saw the Merry Dancers last night, the Northern Lights for you English folk; it was very brief, only a few minutes, but some of it was red, which is a sign of new love. I said to Stephen that it was red because of you two, though he said it wasn't.'

'We're just friends,' Gabe insisted.

It felt so weird to hear Gabe define them as that when they seemed to be so much more than that already. They'd kissed and hugged, they'd held hands, they'd slept in bed together. How could he only see her as a friend?

Deborah exchanged confused glances with Stephen and then pulled on a smile. 'Well, it's lovely to meet you, Pip.'

'Pleased to meet you too,' Pip said, brightly, trying to mask her confusion as well. 'I had the pleasure of meeting your husband on my trip over here. I don't think I've ever stayed in a hotel where I've had a finer welcome than the one I received on the plane from Stephen.'

'That's so nice to hear,' Deborah said, smiling proudly. 'He thought he was too old, said it would be better to have some-one younger representing Stardust Lake Hotel, but I told him if Gabe chose him to do it, then he must have his reasons.'

'He's perfect for the job,' Gabe agreed. 'I can't think of anyone who would do a better job than he will. Our guests will love him.'

Pip could tell that Stephen was getting embarrassed by the attention, so she quickly changed the subject. 'Why don't you show me around your shop?'

'Well, it's just a chocolate shop, dear,' Stephen shrugged.

Deborah batted her hands at him affectionately as she abandoned her knitting to give the tour.

'We have eight chocolate fountains: the black is our bittersweet chocolate with a ninety-nine percent cocoa, the dark brown…' she pointed '…has a seventy percent cocoa mix; it still counts as dark chocolate but it's not as potent as the bittersweet fountain. Then we have milk chocolate and white chocolate. We also have a mocha fountain here, half coffee, half milk chocolate. This one is chocolate caramel, this one is mint chocolate and this is chocolate and rum. We can make you a hot chocolate with a shot of any of these liquid chocolates mixed with hot milk. Which would you like?'

Pip smiled at the choice and at the assumption that she of course would want one. 'I've never had a hot white chocolate before. Or is it a white hot chocolate? Either way, I'll have one of those.'

Deborah grabbed a paper cup and held it under the flow of white chocolate for a second then moved to a nearby machine that looked like it belonged in one of the poshest coffee houses. Steam billowed from the machine as Deborah filled the cup up with hot milk.

'Would you like cream and marshmallows?'

Pip nodded and a few moments later Deborah returned with a cup topped with a towering mound of cream and marshmallows.

Pip took a sip. It was warm, sweet and incredibly delicious. 'This is wonderful. I can't believe I've never had anything like this before.'

Deborah beamed.

'We also have chocolate fruit kebabs on sale.' Deborah pointed to a collection of ready-made fruit kebabs that had a mixture of grapes, apples, oranges and other fruits. 'These are three pounds for a kebab and you can dip it under any of the fountains. Or you can make your own. You can add marshmallows too. Or there are those Haribo sweets the kids love. You can get a cup of those and just pour chocolate over the top. It's entirely up to you.'

Pip hesitated while she made her choice. She wasn't really hungry but didn't feel she could turn the kebabs down. They sounded delicious and Deborah was obviously keen to please.

'Pip's not long had lunch. She might not have room for a kebab too.' Gabe tried to rescue her from being forced to have a kebab. 'We have lots of other shops to visit this afternoon, maybe we'll come back later and get one if we're hungry.'

Deborah looked so disappointed that Pip knew she couldn't walk away without having one. Even if she couldn't finish it.

She picked up a kebab that was mainly orange segments and apple pieces and stuck it under the chocolate and rum fountain. The chocolate oozed over the pieces of fruit and Deborah passed her a tall empty cup to put the kebab in and some napkins.

Pip gave Deborah the hotel card and she scanned it.

'Thank you so much for showing me around,' Pip said. 'And it was lovely meeting you.'

Deborah smiled. 'I hope we'll be seeing more of you in the future.'

'I hope so too,' Pip said, as she left the shop with a cup of chocolate goodness in each hand.

Gabe closed the door behind them.

'You don't have to buy something from every shop, you know.'

'Of course I do. Besides, I have two hundred pounds of hotel credit; I can't take it with me when I go. But you might need to call the Range Rover to take me back to the lodge. At this rate, I'll be five stone heavier by the time I've visited every shop.'

'That can be arranged.'

She looked down at her chocolate-covered kebab wondering how she was supposed to eat it when her other hand was taken up by the cup of hot chocolate.

'I think you need tables and chairs in there so people can sit and enjoy the hot chocolate and kebabs. It's awkward to buy and eat both while you're walking around.'

Gabe quickly held her cup of hot chocolate as she was clearly struggling with the two cups.

'Also, I'm not sure if you want people to walk around the rest of the village and put their sticky hands on other people's goods. Tables and chairs might prevent that.'

'I'll speak to them to see if they are open to it and then I'll put an order for tables and chairs in today.'

She stared at him. 'You don't need to listen to my opinion. It's just a thought.'

'It's a good thought.'

She slid one of the pieces of chocolate-covered orange off the stick and popped it in her mouth. 'Oh god, this tastes so good.' The chocolate had that kick of rum which she could taste only after she had swallowed the chunk of orange. But the burst of orange juice, chocolate and rum worked wonderfully together. She slid another piece off the stick and offered it up for Gabe to try.

He smiled, then opened his mouth and took it from her fingers, sucking her fingertips momentarily to get all the chocolate. Desire slammed into her stomach. It was so quick, almost so innocent as if he hadn't meant to make her a quivering mass of need-filled jelly. But the dark look in his eyes showed he had deliberately done it.

'Tastes good,' he said, softly, and with the way he was looking at her she didn't think he meant the chocolate.

She looked away and took the hot chocolate off him again so she could take another sip.

'You need bins out here too. You don't want your lovely village ruined by litter.'

He nodded as he walked by her side. 'That thought never even occurred to me. I'll get it sorted before our guests arrive.' He slid his hand into hers again. 'I'm glad you're here.'

She smiled, not sure if he'd said that because she could road test the place before the guests came or because he genuinely liked having her there, but she'd take it either way.

❄

Gabe watched Pip as she peered through the window of the last shop on the first side of the road. She was finishing off a mince-pie-flavoured crêpe topped with brandy cream as she stared at the wooden carvings.

She had taken the time to chat to every shopkeeper and member of the village she had met so far. She wasn't just being polite either: she genuinely enjoyed talking to them about their lives, the crafts they were selling and their experience of the island. In one shop she had spent over an hour looking at all the photos of Caroline's new grandson and at no point had she seemed bored or tried to get away. They had all been so desperate to make a good impression on their first visitor and she had sensed that and indulged them all in listening to them talk and show off their crafts and produce. True to her word, she had bought something from each shop. Everyone had been completely enchanted with her, falling in love with her as she laughed at their jokes, complimented them on their food or admired their wares. She was wonderful to watch as she engaged with them all and Gabe knew he was falling a little bit in love with her too.

It had been awkward, though. Everyone had mentioned their relationship and he just didn't know how to define it yet so how could he confirm it to others? To confirm they were a couple when they had only been sort of together for a day might scare her off. It was better all round if everyone just assumed they were friends.

Pip finished the crêpe and licked her fingers and then grabbed his hand to lead him into the shop.

As Joy, the wood carver, looked up at their arrival and then immediately down at their joined hands, he relinquished his hold on her to try to avoid any more awkward questions. He'd hoped Pip wouldn't notice but, by the tiny frown that creased her brow, he guessed she had.

'Pip, this is Joy Mackenzie, our wood carver and one of the artists that we contacted to come and live here. Joy, this is my friend, Pip.'

Joy stood up and, impossibly, her large baby bump looked even bigger than the last time he had seen her a few days before.

'Pleased to meet you,' Pip said, shaking Joy's hand. 'Did you carve all these pieces yourself?'

'Yes, it's something I've been doing for years. I started my career chainsaw carving on much bigger pieces of wood, but I really like the fine detail required for these tiny pieces. Gabe offered me the opportunity to come and carve Christmas decorations for a year and I thought it'd be great to give it a go for a while. I'm trying to get a ton done now because this little one will be here soon and I might be a bit busy after that.'

Gabe smiled, knowing how hard a newborn baby would be. The shop was already filled with hundreds of beautiful hand-carved pieces and, while it would be nice for the tourists to come and see Joy actually making the decorations, he'd be quite happy for her to take some much-needed time off when the baby arrived. She had been working like a Trojan since her arrival on the island. Her husband Finn could man the shop or there were some teenagers in the village who would be more than happy to get some extra work.

'Do you know what you're going to have?' Pip asked.

Joy rubbed her belly, affectionately. 'A boy. We'll have one of each then. Rebecca is five now and she can't wait to have a little brother to play with. I did explain it might be a while before she can actually play with him, but I'm sure she'll figure out a way. Oh, here she is.'

Gabe looked up to see her husband, Finn, walking into the shop with Rebecca on his hip.

'Mummy, are you coming to have dinner with us?' Rebecca said, completely unfazed by the visitors in her home. Gabe grinned. Wren adored Rebecca and would come down to the village to play with her every chance she got. They were going to school together after Christmas and he'd already agreed with Joy and Finn that they'd take it in turns to take the girls over on the boat to the school in Yell.

'I'll be there in a minute, sweetheart,' Joy said. 'This is Gabe's friend, Pip. This is my husband Finn and our daughter Rebecca.'

Finn smiled by way of greeting. He was always very quiet, but it was obvious he couldn't be prouder of Joy's skills and ability.

Rebecca held out her hand to shake Pip's and Gabe suppressed the laugh.

'Hello Rebecca, your mummy sure has a ton of talent. Are you going to learn to carve when you're older?' Pip asked.

'No, I'm going to be a princess.'

'Well, that sounds like a lot of fun. Now, maybe you can help me choose which of these beautiful tree decorations I should buy.'

'All of them,' Rebecca said, seriously.

Finn laughed. 'We'll make a saleswoman out of you yet. Why don't you show Pip your favourite ones?'

He placed her down on the floor and she walked with purpose to a shelf in the corner of the room. 'I like this one with all the ponies on it,' Rebecca said, offering it to Pip, who knelt down to examine the large wooden bauble.

'It's lovely. This one reminds me of Leo,' Pip said, pointing to one of the ponies.

'It is Leo,' Rebecca said.

'Have you met him?' Pip asked, turning the bauble over to inspect the wonderful craftsmanship.

'Yes, a few times,' Rebecca said, then leaned over to whisper in Pip's ear. 'He's not as scary as everyone says he is.'

Pip laughed. 'I'll bear that in mind.'

She had such a lovely way with Rebecca; he'd seen it with Wren too. She didn't talk to them like they were babies, but there was something about Pip that both girls found so engaging.

She stood up and picked up another tree ornament from nearby, one that had a couple entwined with each other as if their limbs and bodies were joined. It was stunning and looked like it should be in a modern art museum not in a Christmas decoration gift shop. He loved Joy's carvings – they varied from the commercially popular carvings of Santa, reindeer, angels and the ponies to something incredible and breathtaking like this.

'I'll take these two,' Pip said decisively, handing over her hotel card.

'Great, thank you,' Joy said, scanning the card. 'And which cabin should I send them to?'

Pip opened her mouth to speak but Gabe beat her to it. 'Just mark it for the attention of Pip. We'll make sure it gets to her.'

'I'll let you get on with your dinner,' Pip said. 'But it was wonderful to meet you all. I'll be working in the houses at the end of the village over the next few days, but I'd love to come back and look at some of your other carvings.'

'Please do, you'd be welcome any time.'

Gabe opened the door for Pip but as they walked out he heard Finn say quietly, 'Are they together?'

'I think so,' Joy whispered back.

Pip had clearly heard it too, as she blushed when they walked outside.

He sighed. The town's people were convinced they understood the complexities of their relationship when Gabe didn't have a clue.

❄ Chapter 14 ❄

Pip walked back towards the hotel with Gabe by her side. She had spent a lovely few hours getting to know all the villagers and looking around all the shops. She had stuffed herself silly at the lodge selling sweets and fudge, and at a different shop selling churros and doughnuts. She had filled up on several glorious cups of mulled wine and had a wonderful time buying wooden crafts, handmade tree ornaments, jewellery and patterned glass lanterns. She had no idea how she would take all these things with her if she did leave, but she would deal with that when the time came. She had never bought souvenirs from any place she had visited before, but there was something so compelling about the people selling them. She loved chatting to them and they had all been so friendly and approachable.

'I think it's safe to say that the Christmas market is going to be a big hit. If you had taken the time to interview and hand-pick the villagers, you wouldn't have been able to get a bunch of nicer people. The products they sold were unique and beautiful and they all took the time to chat to me. Your guests are going to love them as much as the things they are selling.'

'They're brilliant, aren't they? I want Stardust Lake Hotel to work for them, not just for me. And they certainly seemed to like you.'

Pip smiled. She liked them too. Several of the shopkeepers had hugged her when she left. They were all warm, kind and genuine people. But almost every single one of them had either subtly hinted or blatantly talked about her and Gabe being a couple and how wonderful it was.

Gabe had repeatedly said that they were just friends as if he was a stuck record and after the first few shops he had dropped her hand and not held it again, though that still hadn't stopped the questions or comments.

They walked back into the main reception area and Pip stamped her feet to get rid of the snow.

'Any messages?' Gabe said to Iris.

'No, but the power has come back on. We have power in all the lodges now.'

Gabe went very still.

Iris turned to Pip. 'You can move back into your lodge tonight if you want. Jake can help you take your things over. Do you want the key now or would you prefer to move tomorrow?'

Pip had no idea what the right answer was. Would it be better to move into the lodge so she would be out of Gabe's hair? He kept insisting they were just friends, after all.

He looked at her waiting for her answer when she was hoping he would help her with that decision. If he wanted her to stay with him she would. When the silence stretched on she made the decision herself.

'I'll take the key now; at least I can have a look at the place. Then I can decide later whether to move tonight or tomorrow.'

Iris nodded. 'Of course, whatever is easiest for you. Just give us a call if you want Jake to help you.'

Iris handed over the key.

'I'll show you where it is,' Gabe said, quietly.

They walked out of the reception and down the path towards the lodges. Strings of lights hung from the roofs, confirming the lodges did have power; they looked so pretty.

Gabe didn't say anything as they walked down the path and she somehow got the idea she had made the wrong decision, at least as far as he was concerned.

They stopped outside a large lodge that was opposite Gabe's, though Gabe's was set back much further from the path than hers.

Gabe opened the door and let her in. It was cold inside, not having had the benefit of heating for several days, and Gabe immediately set about building a fire in the log burner as Pip looked around.

In many ways the lodge was similar to Gabe's though on a slightly smaller scale. There was a lounge area that led through to a tiny kitchen and stairs leading up to a balcony that overlooked the lounge and, by the looks of things, it led up to two bedrooms and a bathroom. There was a large, beautifully decorated tree in one corner and garlands of lights and greenery hanging from the balcony. It was warm and cosy and the thought of staying there alone was actually a good one. Having some space from Gabe would give her time to figure out what she wanted and, maybe, if she was clever enough, she could figure out what he wanted too.

'Well, this is lovely. I think I'll pack my things up and stay here tonight.'

Gabe stared at her, anger, disappointment and hurt warring in his eyes. 'Fine,' he snapped. 'I'll get Jake to bring your case over as soon as you're ready.'

He turned to walk away.

'Hey, what's wrong with you?' Pip asked. Though it didn't take a genius to work out, but he had been sending her some very mixed messages.

'Well, you running away from me the first chance you get isn't exactly a positive sign.'

'I thought you'd be happy.'

'Why would I be happy?'

'I've woken you two nights running with my stupid nightmares and if I'm over here then I'm away from Wren. I know you don't want me anywhere near her, which by the way is not exactly a positive sign either.'

He stood there staring at her. 'That's not… You've misunderstood. I loved seeing you two in bed together this morning; it's wonderful to see you play and talk and how good you are with her, but I don't want her getting attached to you if you're going to leave after Christmas. You've given me no indication of whether you plan to stay. It's going to be hard enough for me to let you walk away from me a second time, I don't want Wren to go through that too.'

He was protecting Wren from getting too attached. She hadn't even thought of that.

'You've given me no indication of what you want from me either,' Pip said. 'If you want me to stay then you need to give me something to stay for. You've already told Wren we wouldn't get married.'

'Of course we wouldn't. If you stayed, marriage would be a long way away.'

'And you've repeatedly told everyone in the village that we're just friends.'

'Why are you misunderstanding everything I'm doing? We used to be so in tune with each other.'

'That was twelve years ago, Gabe, we've both changed so much.'

'I didn't want you to feel pressurised by them. I didn't want them going on about us getting married and being together in case it scared you off or made you feel like you had to make some sort of commitment that you don't want to make. It is hard enough for us to think about starting again after all this time. As you've said, we have changed. I have a little girl to think about now. You have your dream job travelling all over the world and I'd never want to get in the way of that. If we do properly get back together it has to be the right thing for both of us and I don't want to guilt you into anything or push you into staying if you don't…' He swallowed. 'If you don't have any feelings for me.'

She stepped closer and he looked at her warily. 'I think we've established that we both have feelings for each other. We've shared some pretty heated kisses over the last day or so.'

'Is it just lust and sex, though?' he asked.

'I don't know. Is it? Hell, we're not even doing that at the moment.'

'Is that what you want? Do you want me to just lie you down in front of that fire and make love to you right here and right now?' Gabe said, clearly annoyed.

Pip opened her mouth to protest but no words came out. She stared at him then stared at the rug in front of the fire. There was a huge part of her that wanted that more than anything right now. Gabe stepped closer, his scent and warmth capturing all her senses. She looked up at him and the anger he'd shown had suddenly gone. 'Is that what you want?' he repeated, softly.

She couldn't move, she couldn't breathe. But finally she found her voice. 'No. It's been many years since I've been with someone. I decided a long time ago that I wouldn't just sleep with someone for the sake of sex and I don't want that with you. I don't want to have a quick shag with you just to quench this spark between us. If we're going to be together in that way then it has to be for the right reasons.'

His eyes softened and he moved his hands to her shoulders. 'I don't want to do anything to hurt you. I think we're both scared of taking that next step. But all I can think of is you leaving here the day after New Year's Day and I feel like I'm holding myself back from getting hurt again. I don't want to fall in love with you again and watch you walk away.'

She knew she had to give him something. If they were really going to give their relationship a chance, then she had to give him something to trust in.

'I could stay. If that's what you want. I have a six-month sabbatical from work. I've worked for them solidly for over ten years and you're my last job before I take six months off. I was going to rent a flat in London and see what staying still feels like for a change. If you wanted I could stay here for a month or two or however long we need to find out if what we have is lust or love.'

His face split into a broad grin. 'You'd stay?'

'If you want me to.'

'I do.'

Gabe kissed her. The taste of him, the feel of him was just magnificent. Every time they kissed the need for him ripped through her like he was a drug she couldn't get enough of. The heat and urgency in his kiss was such a turn-on, the way he was tasting her and holding her against him. He moved his hands to her hair, running his fingers round the back of her neck. His hands wandered back to her hips and he lifted her against him as he lowered them both to the floor in front of the fire.

She let out a little moan of protest, but now he was pinning her to the floor her heart wasn't really into denying him any longer. He felt glorious pressed against her.

'I'm just going to kiss you for a while, nothing more I promise,' he said.

She nodded and he kissed her again.

It was hot there, the flames flickering just a few feet from where they lay and he wrestled himself out of his jacket without taking his lips from hers and then helped her out of hers. There was something about him undressing her which was such a turn-on even though she knew he wouldn't take it any further.

As the kiss continued his questing hands took the time to caress and stroke her, his touch velvety soft, and she found herself moaning against his mouth.

Finally he pulled away slightly, though he didn't get off her. He just stared down at her.

'You'd really stay here?'

She nodded. 'I don't have to live with you. I get that you don't want me to get too involved with Wren, but hopefully there's somewhere else I can stay…'

'I want you to live with me. We'll go slowly. You can sleep in your room and I'll sleep in mine, but I want to spend my evenings getting to know you again. And I'll let everyone in the village know if you want.'

Pip laughed.

'I want you to get to know Wren too,' he said, softly. 'I didn't handle that the right way and I'm sorry. I've always kept Wren away from the women I date. She's met them but never really spent any time with them because I knew it wasn't going to last. She adores you and if this is going to work between us then you both need to get to know each other.'

'I want to spend time with her too. I think she's lovely.'

He smiled and then stood up, holding out a hand to help her up.

'So shall we take the key to this lodge back?'

She nodded. 'I'd like that. But everyone will talk.'

'Let them. This is between us.'

'I like that there's an "us" again.'

He grinned. 'I do too.'

❄

'She's asleep,' Gabe said, as he walked back into the lounge after putting Wren to bed. After leaving Pip with Wren for fifteen minutes while he responded to an email and made a phone call, he had returned to a full production of *Frozen* being re-enacted in Wren's bedroom. All her teddy bears had been lined up in rows to watch, Wren had got changed out of her pyjamas and back into her Elsa dress and the *Frozen* soundtrack was being belted out as Wren sang the words over the microphone. Pip was running around the room alternating between playing every other character apart from Elsa, which was obviously Wren's job, while Wren directed proceedings over the microphone in between singing. Wren had been giggling helplessly at Pip's attempts at playing Sven the reindeer and Olaf the snowman. It had been incredibly endearing to watch while simultaneously beyond frustrating that, after giving a sleepy Wren a bath and tucking her up in bed, he had left Pip to read her a story and returned to this cacophony of a disaster zone. It had taken him over half an hour to get her calm enough to climb into bed and nearly an hour after that to get her to go to sleep.

Although Pip had never had any experience of looking after children, she had a natural way with his daughter that Wren was drawn to. Pip was like the fun-time aunt who knew how to have a good time with her: she knew how to make Wren laugh and how to talk to her but had no idea how to actually be a parent – when to be strict and not give in to her demands. But then she'd only been around Wren for three days, he couldn't expect her to suddenly be mum of the year. But mothering skills would come with time. He knew she was good for Wren. But Pip was good for him too.

Pip winced. 'I'm really sorry. I didn't mean to wind her up. She said she always sings *Frozen* songs before she goes to sleep. I didn't think she would lie to me. She looks too wholesome and cute for that.'

'Oh, she always lies. Especially if it helps to get her an extra portion of pudding or *Frozen* songs just before bedtime. You just got played.'

Pip giggled and Gabe felt the frustration seep out of him. There was no harm done. He plonked himself down next to Pip and slung his arm round her shoulders, running his fingers through her hair. She felt so warm and soft next to him and if she hadn't had her laptop balanced on her lap he would have pushed her down on the sofa and kissed her until all that warmth and goodness seeped into him.

There were only three more days until the guests arrived and he could feel panic and worry burning inside of him. He knew that, apart from a little bit of work on the houses in the village, the place was ready, and with Pip staying with him, that freed up another one of the lodges in the grounds of Stardust Lake Hotel. The power was back on. There was a fresh delivery of food arriving the day before the guests came. Every lodge was beautifully decorated. Even the snow seemed to be clean and sparkling. But these guests would be the making or breaking of the place, especially the dreaded Mr Black who had written more bad reviews recently than he had good ones.

When they'd found out he was coming, Gabe had spent a few hours looking at every review he had written in the last year, taking note of the things that Mr Black liked, the things he didn't and making sure that there would be nothing lacking in those areas. But lately the reviews had been getting more and more scathing, as if Mr Black's patience was wearing thin. They would just have to make sure there was nothing that he could find fault with. If only they knew which of their guests was Mr Black, that would help massively.

There were three things that Mr Black consistently liked to eat. From the reviews, Gabe knew that Mr Black had a wide and varied taste, enjoying a plethora of exotic and wonderful dishes, but whenever mushroom soup, pasta carbonara or crème brûlée was on the menu, Mr Black always had them so he could compare the recipes the world over.

Gabe had made sure that the first night the guests arrived those three things would be on the menu, among other things, and they were going to be the best that Mr Black had ever tasted. Gabe had one of the finest chefs he had ever worked with living here now and Uri had been refining his recipes on those dishes in particular over the last few weeks. Gabe had tasted more mushroom soup and crème brûlée in the past weeks than he'd ever had in a lifetime, but he was sure that Uri now had it down to a fine art.

Not only was the offer of these foods going to be a good way to welcome Mr Black to the resort, but it was one sure-fire way to identify who Mr Black was once and for all or at the very least narrow it down. There couldn't be many people who would order that exact starter, main course and dessert out of all the other options on the menu, but Mr Black wouldn't be able to resist in order to compare Stardust Lake Hotel with the other hotels in that particular field.

He sighed as he ran his fingers round Pip's neck. He had to make a success of this. He didn't know whether it was his grandad's legacy he wanted to protect or whether it was the fact that he'd pretty much had to start from the beginning with this project and he had poured everything he had into it, but this felt more important than any other project he'd worked on before.

He just had to sit back now and let his staff do the jobs they had been hired to do. Although quite a few of the islanders had been employed to work in the hotel, in one capacity or another, he had also brought several members of staff with him and he knew he had one of the best teams he'd ever had here. Everything was ready. Though that still didn't stop the nerves from twisting his gut. He needed a distraction and Pip had arrived at the perfect time to provide that.

'What are you doing?' he asked, as Pip clicked on tiny icons on the laptop and moved them into different folders.

'I'm just sorting out my photos.'

'The photos you take for work?'

She hesitated for a second before she answered. 'No, these are my personal ones. There's a set format with the photos I take for work: bedrooms, pools, reception areas, the outside of the hotels, a few individual aspects, like a garden or the ice palace, for example. There isn't much room for creativity. So after the boring ones are taken, I always end up taking loads of my own.'

'Can I see them?'

'My photos? Oh, they aren't anything special. I've been to so many beautiful places over the years, seen such incredible things and I don't want to forget about them. These are just a way to capture my memories of the places I've been.'

'You were always good at taking photos when we were younger. I'd love to see them.'

Pip hesitated for a moment or two before she clicked open a folder. 'OK. I have folders for each country and then sub-folders for areas or states within that country. I also have beach folders, city folders, sunset folders. This one is just a mix of everything, all my best bits of the places I've been to.'

She shifted the laptop onto his lap and then curled up into his side, leaning her head on his shoulder. It was such a natural gesture and one that felt so completely right.

He clicked open the folder and then clicked on the slideshow icon at the top so the photos would scroll through automatically. The first photo was of a deserted beach, the sand flat and undisturbed and the waves reflecting the plum and gold tones of the sun-streaked sky above it. It had been taken at just the right angle so the sun was dead centre and the rays seemed to explode through the clouds like a spider's web. It was beautiful. He pressed pause at the top of the screen and stared at it.

'This is stunning.'

'Oh, I got lucky with the clouds that day,' Pip said, dismissing the compliment.

'I doubt luck had anything to do with it; it's about having an eye for what makes a good photo and being able to capture it in the best light and the best angle. Did you have lessons?'

Pip shook her head. 'I always wanted to, but there never seemed to be any time.'

'I don't think you need any. This is beautiful.'

He clicked on the next photo and he saw row upon row of silver birch trees presiding over a carpet of bluebells. The tiniest glint of sun was peeping through the trees. It was simple and pure, and breathtakingly good.

'You're very good at this. Have you ever sold any?'

She shook her head. 'No, they're nothing special. They're just for me.'

'These are special. You have a real talent. People would pay good money for things like this.'

She smiled. 'Thank you, that's very sweet of you to say, but there are hundreds of photos out there just like this one.'

'Hundreds of photos that somehow miss the mark. But this has a rare quality.'

She shook her head and clicked through to the next one.

This one was different because there were people in it. Three elderly nuns sitting on a bench, with the Vatican in the background. They were all enjoying an ice cream and they were laughing at some unknown joke. Pip had captured them perfectly at the exact moment when one of the nuns had thrown her head back with laughter and as another nearly lost her ice cream into her lap. He couldn't help but smile at the picture.

'I really like this one,' Gabe said.

'Sometimes the real beauty in the world is through the people, their day-to-day lives, what makes them tick. There was something so innocent and carefree about these ladies enjoying an ice cream. The best thing was they were laughing because some fit, gorgeous guy had just ridden past on his bike, no top, tight little shorts and probably a quarter of their age. They all watched him go with obvious appreciation. Then they all noticed each other watching him and they all just burst out laughing. They were speaking to each other in Italian and I had no idea what they were saying, but I didn't need to. It was quite obvious they were talking about him and his cute little bum. This one kept making bum-pinching gestures and the others were howling at her. It made me laugh just watching them and I wanted to capture this perfect moment forever. I'm not sure I did it justice.'

'You really did, you captured the very soul of them.'

The next photo was a close-up of a field mouse eating a dew-topped strawberry. Somehow the angle of the camera and the mouse mid-mouthful made it look like the mouse had the biggest smile on its face.

'I was staying in a small hotel which had its own strawberry farm. I woke up really early one morning and decided to get some shots of the sun coming up over the strawberries. I went down to the middle of the field, set up my camera and then I noticed this little guy. That was the only photo I managed to take before he ran off. I'm not very good at close-ups, it's not something I normally do, but this one just sort of worked.'

As Gabe clicked through photo after photo he found himself staggered with how incredibly talented she was.

'You really need to think about selling these. I would buy these off you in a heartbeat and put them in my hotels. I'd hang them in each room. The guests would love them.'

She clicked on the next photo, ignoring him. She had no idea how much talent she had.

He found himself smiling at the huge towering redwood forest that grew hundreds of feet into the air, the roots so big you'd need ten or more people to encircle them. The ground was touched with the morning mist and staring right at the camera was a great stag.

'That's one of my favourites,' Pip said.

'Why? I mean apart from the fact that you have captured the deer and the giant scale of the redwoods so magnificently. Why is this one your favourite when they are all beautiful?'

'I don't know. These trees have been around for hundreds or thousands of years and long after we've left this earth they'll still be there. Life gets on top of us sometimes and we have to remember that the paths we make, the choices, our problems are quite minor in the grand scheme of things. Life will continue as it always has, as it always will, until it stops and then we won't be around to worry about it any more anyway. Life is precious and short and I think we have to do what makes us happy and stop worrying about what might happen.'

He stared at her and smiled. He loved her insight, the way she saw the world. And she was right. He had to stop worrying. He had done everything he could for the hotel. It would be a success or it wouldn't and worrying wasn't going to change that.

He clicked through to another one of a little thatched beach cabana next to a bright blue sea.

'You've been to some amazing places over the years. Will you miss seeing these sights when you're on your sabbatical?'

'I will. There's still so much of the world that I haven't seen and I want to see it all. But sometimes you need to step away from something to completely appreciate it. I feel I've been on holiday for the last ten years and I guess I need a break from that. I love my job, well at least the travelling part of it. I never want to stop discovering the little hidden gems of the world.'

He frowned slightly. There was nothing for her here that could compete with the beauty of the rest of the world.

She must have seen his frown because she kissed him on the cheek. 'Sometimes it's the people you meet along the way that make life special; having someone to share these wonderful things with is much better than discovering them on your own.'

He kissed her forehead and she looked up at him. 'Let's go to bed.'

She arched an eyebrow. 'Together?'

'Just to sleep, I promise.'

'What about Wren?'

'She's already seen us in bed together, I don't think it'll be a great shock to her.'

A tiny smile spread over her face. 'OK.'

She took the laptop off his lap, closed the lid, and left it on the table. She stood up.

'I'm just going to brush my teeth.'

He nodded. 'I'll just get a glass of water and I'll be up.'

He watched her go upstairs and disappear into her room. As soon as she was out of sight, he flipped open the lid on the laptop, firing the machine back into life. Luckily the folder was still on the screen. Quickly he made a zip file of all the photos in that folder and emailed it to himself, then he closed the laptop lid and ran upstairs.

He got changed and climbed into bed, just as she appeared in his doorway dressed in her pyjamas and looking decidedly nervous. He peeled back the duvet and after a moment's hesitation she climbed in by his side. He reached over her and switched the light off, plunging them into momentary darkness. He didn't move off her though, pinning her to the bed with his weight.

She let out a little giggle. 'Very smooth.'

'I try.'

She ran her hands round his neck and as the moonlight outside slowly lit up the room, picking out the gold in her eyes perfectly, he kissed her.

❄

Pip woke the next day wrapped tightly in Gabe's arms. They had kissed for hours the night before until eventually neither could keep their eyes open any more. She hadn't had any more nightmares, but she didn't know whether that was because Gabe had held her all night or she was just too tired to dream properly.

She opened her eyes to see Wren standing next to the bed watching them curiously.

'Hey sweetheart,' Pip said as she tried to shift off Gabe's chest but his arms were unrelenting.

Wren pulled back the duvet and climbed in next to them, reaching out to stroke Pip's hair. 'Did you have another bad dream?'

Thankfully Gabe stirred underneath her at that point because Pip didn't want to lie to her.

'Hey Princess,' Gabe said, shifting one arm around Wren and pulling her against him without relinquishing his hold on Pip.

'Wren wanted to know if the reason I was in your bed was that I had a bad dream.'

Gabe looked at Pip and back at Wren. 'No, honey. Sometimes when adults really like each other they might sleep in the same bed so they can cuddle each other. Like Nanny and Pops, they sleep in the same bed.'

Pip decided that Gabe could handle this on his own.

'And Boris and Mikael?' Wren asked. 'They sleep in the same bed.'

'Yes.'

'I asked Boris why he slept in the same bed as Mikael and he said it's because they love each other very much.'

'That's right, they do,' Gabe said.

'And because they're married and Boris said that's what married people do, they sleep in the same bed.'

'Yes, that's right.'

'And Nanny and Pops are married.'

'Yes.'

'But you and Pip aren't married.'

'No, we're not.'

Pip suppressed a laugh.

'Do you and Pip love each other very much?'

'Sometimes adults might sleep in the same bed as each other before they get married to see if they like it,' Gabe explained, patiently.

'Oh. And if you like it, then you'll get married?'

'Yes, that's normally how it works.'

'So did you like it?'

'Yes, very much.'

'So you're going to get married?' Wren asked.

'It's too early to tell yet. Usually, adults might sleep in the same bed for quite a few months before they decide to get married.'

'Why does it take so long to decide?'

'Well, you know how *Frozen* is your favourite film now, you love it, don't you?'

'Yes, Daddy, it's the best film in the world.'

'Well, in a few months' time, it might not be your favourite any more.'

'It will always be my favourite film, Daddy, always. I love it with my whole heart.'

'Right, well…'

'I love it as much as Boris loves Mikael and Nanny loves Pops and Winston loves sausages.'

Winston gave a little bark from somewhere near the floor; obviously he had joined in the party too. Little ripples of laughter were shaking Pip's body as she tried to hold them back.

'Do you love Pip as much as I love *Frozen*?' Wren asked.

Pip glanced up at Gabe and he smirked at her.

'I don't think anyone could love anybody or anything as much as you love *Frozen*,' Gabe said. 'But I do like Pip very much.'

'I like Pip very much too, so can she sleep in my bed tonight with me?'

'No. There's not really enough room for her in your bed.'

'You lie in my bed when you read me a story, there's plenty of room for you.'

'But you like to have Winston in your room to keep you company. I have Pip in my room to keep me company.'

Wren clearly thought about this for a moment. 'You can have Winston tonight and I can have Pip.'

Pip snorted into her hand and then turned it into a cough.

'You have your sleepover tonight with Chester and Rebecca. It's Chester's birthday.'

Wren's eyes grew wide with excitement. 'That's tonight.'

'Yes, you're going round there after lunch and then staying all night. So why don't you go and get yourself dressed.'

Wren scrabbled out of bed and ran out of the room and Pip finally let out the laughter she had been holding in.

'You think that's funny, do you?' Gabe said, though he was clearly laughing too. 'You could have helped me out.'

'You were doing fine on your own. Besides, I probably would have said something wrong. I certainly wouldn't have told her we are trying each other out to see if we like each other enough to get married. It wouldn't have occurred to me at all to answer her questions like that.'

'Oh, and what would you have said?'

'That you were helping to keep my nightmares away or that we were cuddling because we were cold.'

'You didn't have any nightmares last night, did you?' he asked, concern clouding his eyes.

'No, you must be my cure.'

'I like that I'm your cure.'

She smiled. 'I do too.'

'So with Wren round at Chester's tonight, we could have a sleepover of our own. How do you fancy sleeping in one of the glass igloos tonight? We might not see any Northern Lights, I'll have to check the weather, but it'll still be wonderful to sleep under the stars.'

'I would love that.'

He bent his head down and kissed her softly, before pulling away.

'We better get up too, there's lots of work to be done today before we can go to the igloo.'

He got up and stretched, showing a tiny bit of his toned stomach in all its glory.

He smiled when he saw her checking him out. 'Fancy taking a shower with me?'

Pip felt her eyebrows shoot up, not sure if Gabe was teasing or not.

'I think Wren would definitely have something to say about that.'

Gabe nodded. 'You're probably right.'

'Daddy, Boris and Chester are outside, can I go and play with them before breakfast?' Wren called, running into the room, struggling to put on her snowsuit. Gabe knelt down to zip her up.

'Do you want help putting your wellies on?'

'No, I can do it.'

Wren ran out of the room and a second later Pip heard the thunder of feet as she ran down the stairs followed by a yapping Winston.

Gabe walked out of the bedroom and Pip watched as he moved to the front window to check on Wren as she ran outside. He laughed, then came running back to the bedroom.

'Quick, get dressed, they're having a snowball fight out there.'

Pip got out of bed and Gabe threw her one of his hoodies, which she pulled over her pyjamas, then she raced downstairs and pulled her snow boots on. Gabe was hot on her heels having also got dressed. Pip could see Boris and Chester throwing snowballs at Wren outside, though she could see that Boris was deliberately trying not to hit her but just aiming them very close. Chester, it seemed, didn't have any such scruples.

Gabe managed to get his boots on before Pip and ran outside, gathering snow in his hands. Pip watched as he lobbed the snowball at Boris, much to Boris's surprise.

Pip ran out and grabbed a snowball and threw it at Gabe. It exploded against the back of his head with a satisfying splat.

He turned round to look at her in shock. 'You're supposed to be on my side.'

'Nope. I'm on Boris's side. He saved me from the evil Shetland ponies the other day.'

Before Gabe could argue she threw another snowball at him and this one hit him square in the chest. He picked one up and threw one at her as she darted out of the way and joined Boris on his team. Wren quickly joined them, so Gabe was on his own. Chester and Wren were laughing helplessly as they joined Pip in throwing snowballs at Gabe. Boris clearly wasn't sure about throwing snowballs at his boss until Gabe threw one that landed straight in Boris's face. After that Boris joined in the fight with much more gusto.

Although Chester and Wren's snowballs didn't often make contact with Gabe, every single one of Boris and Pip's snowballs hit him in the chest, legs, hair, face, until he was utterly dripping, whereas Pip had escaped relatively unscathed. Gabe started making a row of snowballs ready to attack as Boris continued to pelt him.

As Pip ran to the side to get more snow, Gabe started throwing a volley of snowballs at her back, some exploding in her hair, some on her legs. She turned around so she could see them coming and have a chance of avoiding them, but as another snowball came straight for her face she swerved and ducked, lost her balance and fell backwards into a six-foot drift of snow. The snow collapsed on top of her so she was completely buried, apart from her legs, which were sticking out the drift.

She laughed as she tried to get herself out but she was stuck fast. The snow had managed to get everywhere, down her pyjama top, in her pyjama bottoms.

A moment or two later she heard heavy footsteps approach and Gabe's laughter as he grabbed her ankles and unceremoniously dragged her out of the pile of snow.

'You alright?' he said, grinning as he stood over her.

'Bit wet.'

He offered her a hand to help her up and she took it. She brushed some of the snow off herself but she was soaking now.

Gabe turned round to Boris. 'We're just going to get changed before breakfast, you guys carry on out here. We'll be out soon.'

Still holding her hand, he pulled her back inside the house while Wren and Chester carried on chasing each other around in the snow.

Gabe pulled her upstairs to the bathroom and then yanked off his jumper and T-shirt so he was topless. Her eyes cast down his perfect body, hungrily. He was toned all over, strong arms, large capable hands. He had that sexy V-shape that disappeared under his jeans, but what caught her attention were the tattoos on his chest and over his left shoulder. Four distinct deep red claw marks slashed through his skin as if he had been attacked by a big animal. It looked so real for a moment that she had to look twice before she convinced herself that it wasn't. Instinctively she put out her hand to touch them, running her fingers over the tattooed scars across his chest.

He caught her chin and tilted her face up to look at him. 'They're very old.'

'Did they have some meaning to you?'

He shook his head. 'Just seemed like a good idea when I was young. Make me look hard and sexy for the ladies.'

She smiled, though she knew he was lying.

She ran her fingers down them and stopped when she reached the middle of his chest. There was a single teardrop exactly where his heart was.

She frowned.

'That's very old too.'

'Is it a tear?'

He didn't answer, so she looked up at him in confusion. He moved his hands round her waist and studied her face, taking her all in. He bent down to kiss her briefly. 'It's not a tear, it's a pip.'

She felt the gasp escape her mouth before he kissed her again, pulling her tight against him as if he never wanted to let her go.

He pulled back slightly. 'You're soaking wet, we need to get you out of these clothes.'

Pip giggled as she swiped him. 'You're such a pervert.'

He chuckled. 'I reckon we have about five minutes before Wren comes looking for us. Have a shower with me.'

She arched an eyebrow at him. So much for going slow.

He laughed. 'Believe me, honey, when we make love for the first time in twelve years, I'm going to do a lot better than a quick five-minute shag in the shower. Look, we can even keep our underwear on so no bits accidentally end up in wrong places.'

She burst out laughing. 'You have such a way with words, no wonder the women are all queuing up to be with you.'

He stepped back into the bathroom and undressed until he was wearing only his tight black boxers. Then he stepped into the shower, switched it on and turned round to face her as the water sprayed over his body. He smirked, challenging her to join him.

She stepped into the bathroom and closed the door behind her. She slid her pyjama bottoms down, but thankfully her pyjama top was long enough to cover everything. Then she stepped into the shower with him, soaking herself to the skin in seconds.

'I'm not wearing any underwear, so this will have to suffice.'

His eyes darkened as he pulled her against him. 'There's nothing under this shirt?'

She shook her head.

'So if this shirt accidentally came off, you'd be stark naked.'

She smiled. She loved the way he was with her, tender, kind and protective; she loved the banter they had, the funny comments he would make and the chemistry that continually sizzled between them. She knew she was falling in love with him again and she wasn't scared any more.

'I don't think my shirt is going to accidentally fall off. That doesn't normally happen. I don't walk down the street and suddenly find my shirt has come off.'

'No, admittedly that would be a bit of a problem. But maybe the water might make these buttons slippery and one might pop out of its hole, accidentally of course.'

She watched as he ran his fingers up the front opening and with very little effort the top button came undone in his hands.

'Wow, that's never happened before.'

He moved his fingers to the next button, and slid that one from its hole too.

'Maybe the shirt is faulty, if these buttons keep coming undone like this,' he said.

'It's possible. Check the next one, see if that button is faulty too.'

He smirked and kissed her as she felt each button pop out of its hole. He ran his hands back up to her neck and slowly slid the shirt off her shoulders until she felt it splat against the floor. His kisses were sweet and soft, but he didn't take his hands from her face.

Gabe stepped back slightly to look at her and she could see nothing but desire and hunger in his eyes. His mouth came down on hers again, hard, his kisses suddenly urgent and needful as his hands caressed her body.

He felt so good, his touch driving her wild.

He pulled back slightly, his breathing erratic as he looked at her. 'I need to be with you, Pip. Let me make love to you. Not now, we haven't got time now, but soon.'

Nerves slammed through her. How many women had he been with since they'd last been together? What if she wasn't any good?

'Gabe, it's been a while for me. It might be a bit rubbish for you.'

'I want you so much, it's not possible for it to be rubbish for me.'

'Well you know, you might have to show me where everything goes.'

He laughed as he looked down affectionately at her. 'It can't have been that long. You're so beautiful, Pip, I'm sure you've had your pick of the men over the years.'

'None of them were you.'

He stared at her for the longest moment. 'When was the last time you slept with anyone?'

She swallowed. 'It was you, twelve years ago.'

His eyes softened. 'Christ, Pip. You've never been with anyone else? When you said you'd never had a boyfriend I thought you meant you'd never been with anyone serious. I didn't realise you meant you'd never slept with anyone.'

'I couldn't. I didn't trust anyone enough to make love to them. I was too scared to get involved with anyone in case I was rejected again.'

'Do you trust me? I know it's been twelve years, but do you trust me enough to know that I would never hurt you?'

She nodded. She did.

'Let me make love to you tonight.'

She pushed aside her nerves. 'OK.'

He kissed her softly before they heard a door slamming downstairs. 'Daddy, are we going for breakfast, my tummy is rumbling.'

Gabe stepped back, smiling. 'And I promise, tonight, there will be no interruptions.'

He grabbed a towel, quickly patted himself down and then wrapped it round his waist, clearly to hide the significant bulge in his pants.

He walked out, leaving Pip in the shower, filled with a need that was not going to be quelled for several hours. She ran a shaky hand through her hair. How was she going to concentrate on doing any work today when she knew what the evening had in store?

❄ Chapter 15 ❄

'Are you sure you don't mind looking after Wren for a little while?' Gabe asked as they stepped outside after breakfast.

'Of course not. I love spending time with her,' Pip said, as she watched Wren try to repair bits of Buzzpip that had fallen off. She was looking forward to spending some time with Wren and getting to know her a little better. If things were going to work out with her and Gabe then Wren would have to get used to having Pip around and she wanted to make sure Wren was OK with that.

'And it's only for an hour. Joy and Finn should be back from the doctor's in Unst by then and they're going to have her until after lunch, then Boris is coming to collect her and Rebecca this afternoon for Chester's birthday party and sleepover,' Gabe reassured.

'I don't mind, honestly,' Pip said.

'I feel bad, you're here on holiday and I have you feeding the reindeer, decorating the houses and now babysitting my daughter.'

'And I volunteered to do all those things. I wouldn't be offering to do them if I didn't want to. I want to help you, I want this place to be a success for you and for the people in the town and if I can help with that I will.'

'I know you must think I'm a terrible dad. Shifting her from person to person. I had a nanny for her, so at least she had some stability and would be with the same person every day. It worked fine. I'd get up in the morning, have breakfast with Wren and I'd always make sure I was back to have dinner with her, bath her and put her to bed in the evenings. Wren adored her and then last week the nanny just quit. I was going to get another one, but Wren starts school in January and, after the official opening of Stardust Lake Hotel, it will hopefully get easier and less busy.'

'I don't think you're a terrible dad at all. You're raising her on your own and trying to co-ordinate the opening of a brand new hotel – of course it's going to be stressful.'

He stepped closer and kissed her on the forehead. 'I'm not looking for a new mum for her, or a new nanny, that's not why I want to be with you.'

She reached up and placed her hand on his cheek. 'I know. That thought hadn't even crossed my mind. Stop worrying. We'll go and feed the reindeer and then make our way down to the village. Go and help with the repairs, I'll see you down there shortly.'

Gabe bent his head to kiss her, just as Wren careened into them both, wrapping her tiny arms round both their legs and hugging them both.

'If you get married, can I have a baby brother? Rebecca is having a brother and I think I'd like one of those too.'

Gabe smirked and bent down and scooped Wren up. 'Will you look after Pip for me this morning? Show her how to feed the reindeer?'

Wren nodded.

'And after you've seen the reindeer, Pip will take you to play with Rebecca for a bit.'

'OK, Daddy.'

Gabe peppered her face with hundreds of kisses, resulting in Wren giggling loudly before he plonked her down on the ground.

'Now kiss Pip like that.'

Gabe smirked and gave Pip a brief kiss on the cheek, whispering in her ear, 'I intend to kiss you all over tonight.'

Pip blushed and with a little wave he walked off down the track towards the village.

Wren took Pip's hand.

'Don't worry, I'll look after you,' Wren said, seriously.

'Thank you, I was worried about being on my own but now I don't need to be. Shall we go and see the reindeer?'

'Yes, and after, Daddy said we can go and see the ice palace,' Wren said, following Pip down the track towards where the reindeer were kept.

Pip laughed. 'He did not. Daddy did not say that because he wants to take you to see it himself on Christmas Eve.'

'But that's ages away.'

'It isn't that long; it's only five days until Christmas, so four days until Christmas Eve. I'm sure you can wait four days.'

'I'll try.'

Pip smiled as they pushed open the gate to walk into the reindeer enclosure. The reindeer clearly knew they were about to get fed as they all ambled over towards them. Wren handed over baby carrots that Uri, the chef, had given her. She wasn't fazed at all when some of them started nudging her to get a second one. In fact she even started to tell them off, though that didn't stop them. When the bag was empty, apart from the one Wren shoved in her pocket for Rudolph, the reindeer left her alone and went back to nibbling on the hay.

Wren joined Pip and they went into the barn.

'They need four buckets of food,' Wren said knowledgeably, although Pip already remembered the instructions from the day before.

'That's right, will you help me to fill the buckets up?'

Wren nodded and they worked together to fill up two buckets of food.

'Are you going to be my step-mummy?' Wren asked, suddenly plucking the question from the air.

'I don't know, honey. Remember what I said on the first night I met you, that the person your daddy marries has to be perfect in every way. It may take a while for your daddy to know whether I'm perfect for him or not.'

'I think you're perfect,' Wren said, trying and failing to lift one of the buckets. Pip tipped a tiny bit out into another bucket so Wren could carry that one.

'Thank you. So if I was your step-mum, you wouldn't mind?'

It was a bit optimistic to think that far ahead, but she knew she was falling in love with him all over again and, with the way he looked at her, she wondered if he was starting to feel the same.

'Daddy needs someone to look after him,' Wren said, lifting the mostly empty bucket. 'And so do you.'

Pip smiled at the wisdom of someone ten times Wren's age as she walked out of the barn. They poured the food into the troughs and went back to get some more. Once they had finished giving food to the girls, Pip poured half a bucket for Rudolph.

The man himself was watching them and the other reindeer astutely, obviously wondering when it was going to be his turn for food.

Pip opened the adjoining gate and Wren was following her through, when suddenly Rudolph charged towards them. Pip dropped the bucket and scooped Wren up out of the way, stumbling backwards and landing in a pile of hay with Wren on her chest. Rudolph thundered past, not even giving the food a second glance.

'Are you OK?' Pip quickly turned her attention to Wren.

Wren nodded. 'I think Rudolph wants the other reindeer's food.'

Pip glanced over at Rudolph and swore softly.

Rudolph had mounted Blitzen and was pounding away at her as if he was in a race. Blitzen didn't even look up from the food. Clearly not impressed by her lack of reaction, Rudolph dismounted her and mounted Dasher instead. Dasher let out a bellow, obviously not expecting to be snuck up on from behind, but Rudolph didn't let go, his little furry bum going up and down like a pneumatic drill.

Pip quickly stood up.

'What are they doing?' Wren asked.

'Rudolph is just really pleased to be with the girls again,' Pip explained, lamely. 'Let's get him back in his own pen, shall we?'

Pip raced over, but Rudolph wasn't wearing a harness like the girls were so there was nothing to grab to try to stop him. She clapped her hands, she shouted at him, but he was undeterred, his eyes taking on a glaze as he focussed on the job in hand. Dasher had resumed eating again, obviously as equally unimpressed with his sexual prowess as Blitzen had been. And no wonder: a second or two later his body rippled to show he was clearly finished and he grunted and then dismounted.

'Brilliant,' said a voice from behind her, dryly. She turned round to see Luke walking towards the fence. 'We've managed to keep Rudolph away from the girls for the last three weeks. You look after them for five minutes and he's probably got at least one of them pregnant if not two.'

'Pregnant?' Wren said, her eyes wide. 'They're going to have reindeer babies. Daddy will be so excited.'

'I hardly think so,' Luke muttered.

'I didn't think he would charge at me,' Pip said defensively, as she rubbed her hip where she had landed hard on the ground.

Luke came through the gate, towering over her like an angry bear. 'Are you hurt?'

'No, I'm fine.' Though that wasn't to say her pride wasn't hurt.

To her great surprise, Luke unbuckled his belt and dragged it off his jeans. In the next moment he looped it round Rudolph's neck and with some gentle words of encouragement walked him back into his pen.

'Can you get some more food for him?' Luke said. 'The boy is going to be hungry after all that.'

Pip scowled at Luke for taking over and because it looked as though she couldn't even feed the reindeer without needing help. Though she had to admit that she'd never have managed to get Rudolph back in his enclosure by herself.

She quickly grabbed the bucket and went back into the barn and filled it up about halfway, then returned and poured it into Rudolph's trough. Luke was busy stroking Rudolph and whispering soft endearments to him and the stag stood there, listening to him patiently. She walked back out of the gate, returning all the buckets to the barn. When she came out Rudolph was already munching away on his food and Luke was closing the adjoining gate firmly behind him.

He scowled at her and she scowled straight back. 'I thought you were down in the village helping Gabe with the houses. Or did you come down here to check on me?'

'I would have been but Blaze escaped again and I had to find him. Looks like today is the day for escapees. Good job I was here really.'

'Yes, I'm beyond grateful,' Pip said sarcastically, and his eyes narrowed as his scowl deepened.

He strode out of the enclosure, grabbing Wren's hands and swinging her onto his back in one swift movement. Wren laughed.

Pip reluctantly followed him, making sure she closed the gate firmly behind her.

'If you're going to the village, I can give you a lift,' Luke said, climbing back on his snowmobile and transferring Wren in front of him by dragging her over his shoulder so she was upside down. Giggling helplessly, Wren righted herself and sat astride the snowmobile too.

'I'd rather walk, thanks.'

'Don't be stubborn. If you really want to help Gabe, then saving yourself the half-hour walk and using that time down in the village would be the best thing right now.'

Pip conceded this. She reluctantly climbed on behind Luke. He passed a giggling Wren over his shoulder and Pip sat Wren in front of her, wrapping her hands round her tiny stomach. However, Luke grabbed her hands and wrapped them round his stomach, which made more sense as Wren was now trapped between them.

'Hold on, I'll go slow.'

Luke fired the engine and took off and she was grateful that he kept to his word. Though they reached the village in five minutes she knew he could have gone a lot faster.

He pulled over by the six houses. 'I'll take Wren to Joy and Finn's. You can go and see Gabe and find out what needs to be done.'

She didn't want to argue with him, but she didn't like the way he was taking over and bossing her around. Knowing when to pick her battles, she slid off and as she walked away he roared off in the direction of the village.

As she approached the houses she could see there were six men working on one house, painting or hammering or repairing the roof. Gabe was among them.

'Great, you're here.'

He hopped down from a ladder as she got nearer and kissed her on the cheek. 'I can't wait for tonight,' he whispered, causing Pip to blush.

She was trying really hard not to think about the night ahead because every time she did it made her shake with nerves. It was silly, she knew Gabe, and she'd already made love to him before, albeit twelve years before. But in reality, the thing that was probably making her most nervous was that after making love to him she knew there would be no going back. She was falling in love with him all over again and making love to him would cement that bond between them. What if he turned around in a few weeks or months and rejected her? She would be devastated all over again.

Not knowing the turmoil that was tormenting her, he took her by the hand and led her to the nearest house. 'If you start in this house then work your way through them all. Some of them may need a bit of dusting and hoovering before you decorate, the tall cupboard next to the bathroom should have all the cleaning gear you need. There's a tree inside each house and there are two big boxes of decorations in this one, but you'll need to make sure there are enough decorations for all six trees so go sparingly. There's also a box of garlands which you could use around the room, over the fireplace or on the windows, and there're some candles and other things too. It's basically just window dressing. Is that OK?'

She saw the look of concern in his eyes.

'Yes, it's fine, stop worrying.'

Just then Luke roared up on the snowmobile.

'Did you tell him the good news?' Luke asked, getting off the snowmobile and walking towards them.

'No, I… Not yet.' Pip glared at him, trying to suppress the urge to smack him in his stupid smug face.

'What news?' Gabe said.

'You're soon going to be hearing the pitter-patter of tiny feet.'

'Who's pregnant?'

'Probably Dasher, possibly Blitzen too.'

Gabe turned back to her in confusion. 'How did that happen?'

'Rudolph got in the girls' pen while Pip was feeding him.'

Pip stared at Luke as he sold her down the river. What an ass.

'Wait. You let him through the gate? Did you not try to stop him?'

'To be fair to her, she was too busy getting Wren out of the way of being trampled. Rudolph was on a mission, I doubt anyone could have stopped him,' Luke said.

Well, that was a quick about-turn. Had Luke just defended her?

'He knocked Pip over too, she banged her hip. You might have to kiss that better later.'

With that Luke sauntered over to join the other men.

'Are you OK, were you hurt?' Gabe asked.

'No, I'm fine. I'm sorry. It just happened so quickly and the only thing I cared about was Wren.'

'It's OK. Don't apologise. The last thing I'd want is you or Wren getting hurt. Besides, baby reindeer will be a good draw for the tourists. I was going to breed them at some point anyway, we'll just get there a little earlier than expected, that's all.'

'Gabe,' Luke shouted. 'Give us a hand with this, will you?'

'I better go, I'll see you later,' Gabe said as he jogged over to join his brother.

Pip let herself into the house and looked around. It was like a much smaller version of the lodges up at the resort. A small lounge area with a bedroom and bathroom off the lounge, plus a tiny kitchenette at the back. It had the same wood walls and cosy sofas, with brightly coloured cushions and throws. The large empty Christmas tree stood in one corner ready for her to work her magic.

The place did need a clean. It wasn't filthy, but there was a thin layer of dust over every surface. She found the cupboard and set about dusting and wiping down all the surfaces and then gave the floor a good hoovering.

Just as she had put the vacuum cleaner away, her phone rang. She dug it out of her pocket and smiled when she saw it was Wendy. She answered it and then put it on loudspeaker so she could continue with her work.

'Hey honey, how's it going?'

'I'm working on the review,' Pip lied. There had been no time for that and at the moment she didn't feel the slightest bit guilty about it. She would do it and she would hand it in before Christmas, but at the moment she was just enjoying spending time with Gabe again. For the first time in ten years, work was taking second place.

'I don't care about the review. I want to know how it's going with your gorgeous ex-boyfriend or was it ex-husband?'

Pip smiled as she turned her attention to the boxes of decorations and started to divide them equally into six piles in order to see what the allocation was for each house.

'It's going good,' Pip said, vaguely. 'And no we weren't married. He was my best friend and then he was my boyfriend.'

'I need more than just "It's going good." I've just sat through the most boring meeting in the history of all boring meetings and I have another one to go to shortly where Arsehole Marcus will no doubt drone on about how wonderful he is. Give me something to make me warm and fuzzy. Are you two giving it another go?'

'Yes we are. I've agreed to stay here for a few weeks or months to see if we have anything worth fighting for. It was hard to get involved with each other when we both knew that I was leaving in two weeks.'

'Aw honey, I'm so happy. Everyone needs a bit of love in their lives. Even if this isn't forever, it'll still do you good to have someone who cares about you for a little while. Have you kissed yet?'

Pip blushed. Was this what it was like to have real friends, to talk about stuff like this? There was a part of her that wanted to shout about it from the rooftops, but there was a part that wanted to keep it private, just something special between her and Gabe.

'Yes, a few times.'

'And? Was there pizazz?'

Pip laughed. 'There definitely was that.'

'And, um…have you done anything else?'

'We're taking it slow, Wendy,' Pip lied, knowing that if she told her that they planned on sleeping together that night, Wendy would be ringing up at nine o'clock the next morning to get all the gory details about their night of passion.

'Of course, yes, good idea. Don't want to rush things. But you already know him. You can skip most of the preliminaries. No, you're right, be careful. Have you told him you're there to review the hotel?'

'Oh god, no. He doesn't need to know that. Everything is so fragile between us, I don't want to rock the boat if I don't need to. He is already so stressed about the journalists coming in two days and apparently there's a big hotel reviewer among them who is making him worried. I'll tell him once things are a bit stronger between us and things have calmed down at the hotel. I'm sure he'll laugh about it. But as the review is going to be the best review I've ever written, it won't affect him, so I don't think he really needs to know.'

'Honey, if you are going to be in a relationship, honesty is really important.'

'I know. I will tell him, but maybe in a few days when he isn't so worried about the hotel.'

'Well, I'm sure you know best. Go and have fun with him and then let me know all about it.'

'I will. Well, most of it.'

Wendy laughed and they said their goodbyes.

Pip draped garlands over the fireplace and hung them in the windows, placed candles around the bottom of the fireplace and over shelves around the room, then she turned her attention to the tree decorations. Among the gold baubles and red ribbons there were hand-carved wooden ornaments that Joy had obviously created. There were also mini glass snow-globe type baubles which Mikki had clearly made. There were other decorations that had obviously come from some of the other village shops too. It was a lovely touch; not only was it great buying products from the village to support the shops, but it helped make the Christmas trees local and more personal. It might also encourage some of the guests to go and buy some of the decorations as souvenirs.

She draped the lights over the branches, working her way up towards the top and then slowly she started adding decorations, being careful to intersperse the different decorations across the tree. It took a lot longer than she'd thought it would. She'd never decorated a tree before – spending every Christmas since her dad had died in a hotel in different locations across the world meant that the hotels were already decorated. After her mum had died, her dad had never wanted to decorate the house for Christmas; he hadn't even wanted to celebrate it. Pip had no memory of whether she had decorated a tree before her seventh birthday, but she guessed not; her mum liked things a certain way.

There was something almost sad about reaching the age of twenty-nine and having never decorated a Christmas tree. She wondered if Gabe decorated the tree in his home with Wren or whether the professional Christmas decorators they'd hired to bedeck the lodges up in the resort had done his house too. What would it be like to be part of a family, decorating the tree together, maybe making mince pies, spending Christmas Day together unwrapping presents? She had envied Gabe and his family growing up because they had all that togetherness that she simply didn't have.

Pip stepped back to admire her work. It looked good, the tree sparkling and twinkling with the lights and decorations.

The door opened and she turned to see Luke filling the room. God, the man was so big he'd give Hagrid a run for his money.

'Lunch has just been delivered, thought you might want a sandwich, there's ham or turkey.' He offered a sandwich in each of his hands.

'Turkey please.'

He tossed it over to her.

'Gabe's gone back to the hotel to deal with something, he said he'd be back soon.' He looked around. 'The place looks good, not as good as the lodges the professional decorators did, but you know, it looks OK.'

Pip let out a laugh of indignation. 'You're such an ass.'

His eyebrows shot up at this before she saw the first smile she had probably ever seen from him. 'Mind if I join you?'

She did mind. She would much rather eat alone than have to deal with his company, but if things were going to work with Gabe and she stayed here on the island, then she and Luke would have to learn to put aside their differences and at least be civil to each other.

She nodded and he sat down on the sofa. She sat down on the chair facing him.

A silence descended on them, and where silences with Gabe were never awkward, this was tense and weird. She watched him as he ate his sandwich, but it seemed he had no intention of talking to her.

She decided to see if she could get to the bottom of this angst between them. She had no idea what she had done wrong.

'Why do you hate me? What did I do?'

Luke paused in eating his sandwich. 'I don't hate you.'

'OK, you don't particularly like me very much. Even growing up you made that very clear.'

'That was different. You weren't the only one with issues growing up, Pip. You think you have the market on crappy parents; you don't.'

This surprised her. Lizzie and David had always been such loving, doting parents to Gabe, Neve and Luke. Although she had to remember that Lizzie wasn't Luke's mum. She'd never really considered Luke to be Gabe's half-brother before and neither had the rest of the Whitakers, though technically he was.

He sighed. 'I didn't hate you, I was jealous of you. You fitted into my family so easily. They all adored you and I didn't feel I fit at all.'

'That's not true. Lizzie loved you.'

'I know that now. I have a better relationship with her now than the non-existent one I have with my real mum. But when I was a child it was easier to hate her for breaking up my parents' marriage.

Pip didn't know how David and Lizzie had met; she had been too young to really ask. They had been together before Pip was born, so she hadn't really comprehended that there was a whole other life that had happened before then.

'Did your dad have an affair?'

Luke bit into his sandwich and chewed slowly. He swallowed and took a swig from his water bottle.

'Yes. Mum and Dad were always arguing, screaming at each other. Well, it was mainly my mum who was screaming at him. When I was five he came home and announced he was leaving. That he'd been having an affair with Lizzie and that he loved her and wanted to be with her. The only thing I got from that conversation was that he no longer wanted to be with us. From what I can gather after talking to Dad years later, Mum wouldn't let him visit or see me after he left. Mum got together with a new man very quickly and…' He swallowed. 'Well, long story short, this new guy used to beat the crap out of me every chance he got and Mum…well, she used to let him.'

All the anger she felt towards Luke vanished in an instant. Her dad had been an arsehole to her, treated her like scum, but he had never once raised his fists to her. 'I'm so sorry you went through that.'

He shrugged, though she knew he was trying to be blasé about it. 'The school knew that I wasn't living with Dad any more and that Mum had this new guy. When I was getting changed for PE one day, the teacher spotted the bruises and called my dad in. I went to live with him after that and I barely saw my mum again. Lizzie lavished me with attention and love, but I just blamed her for everything that happened. She was already pregnant with Neve by that point and the baby, when she arrived, became their new focus. Gabe quickly followed and they were this perfect little family unit with me as the third wheel. They never made me feel like I was the outsider. I know now that those feelings were more about me than about how I was treated, but it was easier to hate all of them and you were part of that. As far as I could tell, Lizzie loved you more than she loved me, probably because you were cute and adorable and I was a brat.'

'I had no idea you felt that way towards me.'

'I didn't always. By the time I hit my teens I had grown up enough to realise that I was pretty damned lucky to belong to such a great family and that my mum was probably the root of my parents splitting up, not Lizzie. By that time my hatred towards you, Gabe and Neve just turned to frustration at having all these little kids around. I was fourteen; you were seven. We were years apart. You were the annoying little sister that was always hanging around. Although to be fair, you only remember the times I was an arse to you, you don't remember how many kids I threatened to beat up who were giving you a hard time or Thomas Campbell who called you a freak and I punched him in the face.'

Pip smiled. 'I remember him coming to school with a massive black eye the day after he called me that. I didn't realise you were the one who had stuck up for me.'

'Of course I did. As far as I was concerned you were my kid sister. The only one allowed to give you a hard time was me.'

'So what changed? OK, you didn't hate me when we were teens, but what's with all this angst now?'

He finished his sandwich and wiped his hands on his jeans, which were already dirty. She'd probably have to hoover the sofa again once he had left.

'As much as I found Neve and Gabe annoying growing up, I love them and want to protect them too. I was the big brother, that was my job. Gabe loved you so much, it was ridiculous how much he loved you. When you left, you physically broke him. He was a mess. But that day your aunt came up to sort out your dad's house, Gabe saw her car in the drive and came down to ask where you were. She told him that you were never coming back. He came back to the farm absolutely heartbroken. He collapsed and we had to rush him to hospital.'

Pip felt her breath catch in her throat, her heart missing a beat. Gabe had never told her this.

'He kept on having these panic attacks, heart palpitations, blacking out. The doctors didn't know what was causing it. It went away after a few days and they released him saying it was likely to be stress. And although it didn't happen again, he was broken for years after.'

She had destroyed him. It broke her heart to hear that. She swallowed down the emotion, determined she wasn't going to cry in front of Luke.

He looked like he wanted to say something else but was wrestling with it.

'My wife had an affair,' he said, eventually.

That threw her. Where was he going with this?

'The only woman I ever loved, the only one I have ever trusted and she betrayed me. I was working at the zoo when I met her. I loved my job, never wanted to leave. She was working there during the high season and we met, fell in love and married eight months later. My job at the zoo wasn't enough for her. I wasn't good enough for her. We had enough money to get by but she wanted me to leave and get a job that was bigger and better paid. We argued about it constantly. In the end we had a big row and she left.' Luke took a swig of water. 'She came back three months later, pregnant and in tears, claiming the baby was mine, said that she was a fool and she loved me and wanted to get back together again. I knew that kid wasn't mine. We hadn't had sex at all in the last few months we were together. I also knew that she had been sleeping with one of the big corporate sponsors of the zoo. And I knew he'd kicked her to the kerb when his wife found out, so she'd come crawling back to me, and you know what I did?'

'Told her to sling her hook?'

'I took her back. Because stupidly, I still loved her and I thought maybe she still loved me too. She wouldn't let me sleep with her though, said she didn't want to hurt the baby. A month later, I come home and find her screwing the baby's dad in our bed. She came back to me with nothing, no home, a child that wasn't mine and I took her back and then she betrayed me with the bloke who dumped her as soon as she found out she was pregnant. As he was screwing her, I heard him say how he wanted to keep seeing her but they had to be careful that his wife didn't find out again. He wasn't man enough to end things with his wife and be with her; he wanted the best of both worlds, his adoring wife and his illicit affair, and I could hear her agreeing to it. She had told me that I wasn't good enough for her, but the bloke she screwed behind my back was complete scum, so what kind of arsehole does that make me if this lowlife she was sleeping with was better than me?

'I kicked them both out but it destroyed me. They say that anger is one of the stages of grief. Well, I've been stuck on anger ever since she left six months ago and I don't seem to be able to move on from that. I'm sorry if you caught the brunt of it. But you turn up after all this time and I could see it all happening again with Gabe. You left, broke his heart and then he was taking you back as if nothing had happened, just like I did.'

'I'm sorry you went through that and I'm sorry that I hurt him so badly, you have no idea how guilty I feel.' She hated that her voice had caught in her throat and that Luke had clearly heard it. 'But it wasn't exactly a walk in the park for me either. As far as I was concerned he had cheated on me. I was heartbroken too. And yes, looking back, I should have asked him about it. I should have talked to him but I was seventeen and my dad had just died.'

Luke nodded. 'I can't hate you for it or even blame you. When you first got here I didn't want anything to do with you. But Gabe told me what happened and I know you must have gone through hell. I just don't think he should get involved with you again. As much as it wasn't your fault and I'm a firm believer in second chances, I honestly don't think you are capable of having a proper relationship. Talking from experience of being abandoned and rejected as a child myself, I know that fear of abandonment never goes away. I don't think you'll ever be able to trust someone enough to be in a relationship with them.'

'That's not fair to judge me on one mistake I made when I was seventeen years old. A lot has changed in twelve years. I would hope I've grown up a little since then. I really like Gabe and I'm going to do everything I can to make this work again.'

'I'm not saying it because I'm an ass. But just because you really want it to work doesn't mean that you can trust him enough to put aside all those deep-seated fears of rejection. My guess is the first bump in the road and you'll run and you'll break his heart even harder than last time.'

'I don't want to hurt him, that's the last thing I want. I really hope you're wrong.'

'For Gabe's sake, I hope so too.'

❄ Chapter 16 ❄

It was dark by the time Pip had finished with the third house. The sounds of the men working and talking had long since disappeared. She hadn't seen Gabe again and evidently he hadn't come back.

Making sure that everything was packed away, Pip stepped outside and locked the house behind her.

It was pitch black outside and although that should have made Pip nervous, she felt safe here, sort of removed from the rest of the world.

The wind whistled over the cliff tops and she could hear the sound of the waves crashing below her, but other than that there was no other noise at all.

She waited for her eyes to become accustomed to the dark as she slowly made her way back towards the road. She would have to have a word with Gabe about getting some light down here; maybe he could put out some solar lanterns to light the way back to the hotel. But as her eyes became used to the dark, with the moon glistening off the snow and lighting up the features of the island, she realised how beautiful the place was in the darkness. She also realised that she wasn't alone. Sitting on a bench, staring out at the sea, were Luke and Audrey, talking softly. Not wanting to interrupt she walked past them quietly, but as soon as Luke saw her, he stood up.

'Pip, wait up,' he said.

He turned back to Audrey and said something that Pip couldn't hear. Audrey nodded and with a smile and a wave at Pip, Audrey disappeared off towards the village.

'Thought I'd give you a lift back, don't want you stumbling over in the dark,' Luke said, as he walked towards her.

'You didn't have to wait, I would have been fine on my own.'

Luke shrugged as he walked over to the snowmobile and Pip followed. 'Just because I don't want you getting involved with my brother again, doesn't mean that I hate you or that I wish you any harm. Some of the paths are quite steep and slippery between here and the hotel. I would prefer to know that you got back to the hotel safely.'

'Well, thank you.' Pip didn't know how to feel about this sudden protective side to him. Maybe after their talk earlier he had decided she wasn't such a horrible person after all.

He didn't say anything else, he just got on the snowmobile and Pip climbed on behind him.

He started the engine and as the snowmobile moved, Pip instinctively wrapped her arms around his chest.

'So you and Audrey—'

'Are friends,' Luke said, clearly having fended off that question before and not having any interest in discussing it further.

Silence fell on them again and Pip didn't dare push him any further.

'I understand you have a date tonight with Gabe,' Luke said.

Clearly it was OK for him to talk to her about her love life, but it wasn't OK for Pip to talk to him about his. Pip blushed at the thought of the night ahead and was glad that Luke couldn't see her. She wondered what Gabe had told him.

'I'm not sure if I would call it a date. Gabe wanted to show me the glass igloos so…' She trailed off, not wanting to go into much more detail about what the rest of the night would hold.

'Well, Gabe said he was going to dig out his tuxedo, so I gather it was something a bit more than just giving you a guided tour of the place.'

'He did not say that, you're pulling my leg,' Pip said.

'No, I promise. He's arranged a romantic dinner and everything. Probably shouldn't have said anything but I didn't think you'd want to turn up in your jeans if Gabe had made all that effort. Though knowing how Gabe feels about you, I doubt he would care.'

Pip smiled. 'Is that why he didn't come back to the village, because he was planning the date?'

'No, there's been staffing issues. One of the staff has quit. The reservations manager. Neve has been handling the reservations over the last few days, but it's not something she can do long-term as well as managing the hotel. One of the receptionists has called in sick too, broke her leg apparently, so she won't be back until after Christmas. I think Neve and Gabe have been trying to sort out replacements all afternoon.'

'Oh no, that's the last thing they need. Maybe I can do something to help.'

Luke was silent for a moment as they turned into the drive leading towards the hotel. He pulled up outside Gabe's lodge and cut the engine. 'I appreciate your help. I know you're not doing it for me, but I still appreciate what you're doing nonetheless. All the staff will be back tomorrow, so there's probably not a lot you can do. Lizzie and Dad will be here tomorrow as well, and I imagine they will pitch in any way they can. But thank you.'

Wow, the grumpy brother had disappeared and had been replaced by a complete stranger.

She climbed off the snowmobile.

'I'll feed the reindeer tonight. Gabe asked me to tell you to meet him in Igloo Eight at seven o'clock, that's the igloo the furthest away from the reception, but you'll see it as it'll be the only one with the lights on.'

Before she could say anything else, he roared off and disappeared through the trees. She looked over at the igloos that were up on the hillside quite a way back from the main hotel. Even at this distance she could see one was glowing gold against the darkness. It seemed she had a date to get ready for and she had no idea what she was going to wear.

She pushed open the door and was surprised to see Neve waiting for her. Pip hadn't really seen her since she had stormed out of her office two days before. If Neve was going to warn her off ahead of her date with Gabe that night, she didn't want to hear it.

Neve stood up. 'I hear you have a date with Gabe tonight.'

Pip nodded, not sure how to act around her when Neve had been so off with her the last time they had spoken. She also felt she should apologise to Neve for snapping at her.

Neve stared down at her hands for a moment. 'I thought perhaps you might not have a dress so I brought some of mine; you can borrow them if you want. I know I'm taller than you but I have some mid-calf or knee-length dresses that would probably fit you.'

Pip had no words at all. She certainly hadn't been expecting that.

'Gabe has been a nervous wreck all day, so I know tonight is important to him. I figured it would be important to you too. I thought, if you want, I could do your hair, like I used to do when you were younger,' Neve said.

Pip stared at her.

'I know you're not a child any more but…' Neve trailed off and sighed. 'Pip, I'm sorry for being such a cow the other day. You were being so nice and you absolutely didn't deserve me having a go at you. This thing with Oakley has me not sleeping, not eating, I'm over-emotional, stressed-out and I took it out on you. I'm really sorry. I've made plenty of mistakes in my life and I'd hate to be judged on them years later. It's not fair on you that I still hold over you what happened twelve years ago. Gabe has been happier over the last few days than I've ever seen him and I know that's because of you. I want this to work for him, for both of you… I brought wine, thought we could have a few glasses while you get ready.'

Pip smiled. 'Apology accepted. And I'm sorry too.'

They stared at each other for a moment, neither of them knowing what to say next.

'Let's crack open that wine,' Pip said.

❄

'…So I'm lying there in bed, and the couple in the next room are going at it so hard, their headboard is banging against my wall and my bed is shaking with their exertions. Obviously our rooms shared the same floorboards or something. They're moaning and screaming and when they'd finished he literally whooped with joy. And then he says, "Did the earth move for you, darling?" I mean, who says that, really? I nearly shouted through the wall, "Well it certainly moved for me,"' Pip said, taking a big sip of wine.

Neve laughed and Pip was relieved that over the past hour all the tension between them had slipped away. She wasn't a big drinker, so after two glasses of wine she was feeling all warm and fuzzy inside. Although maybe she'd had more than two. The wine bottle was nearly empty and Neve didn't seem to be touching her glass at all.

'It sounds like you've stayed in some really weird places over the years,' Neve said.

'Oh I have, I could write a book.'

'Oakley has to travel a lot with his job and he used to tell me about some of the horrible hotels he stayed in. I'm surprised some of these places haven't been closed down.'

Neve looked suddenly sad at the mention of Oakley's name and went to take a big swig of wine but changed her mind at the last second.

'You miss him?' Pip said, softly.

Neve didn't say anything, but after a while she nodded. 'So much. Every day I dial his number ready to tell him I love him and I want him back and every day I hang up before it rings. It's agony. I thought I would be over him by now, but I feel worse now than I did when I broke up with him. The pain doesn't seem to be going away at all.'

'You loved him,' Pip said, her heart breaking for her, knowing how hard it was to walk away from the man you loved.

'I still love him. I don't think that will ever change.'

'Why don't you call him and tell him you made a mistake? If he loves you as much as you love him, I'm sure he'll be on the next plane over here to sort things out.'

'I've left it too late now. He hates me for what I've done and I don't think he would ever take me back even if I begged him.'

Pip reached over to take her hand, not knowing what she could possibly say to make it right. Neve smiled, sadly, then glanced at her watch.

'Oh god, look at the time, you need to get ready for your date.'

Pip looked over at the clock and realised it was a lot later than she'd thought. She and Neve had chatted for nearly two hours about the hotel and her worries about Mr Black, about Gabe and the funny stories about him raising Wren as a baby. Neve had told her about her love for California and how she had worked out there for a while. She'd never really had this kind of relationship with Neve before, Pip had never had this relationship with anyone before, but she got the sense that Neve needed this relationship from Pip as much as Pip needed it from her. Neve worked so hard for Gabe and the hotel that she clearly didn't have time to form proper relationships, and right now, with everything that had happened with Oakley, it was clear Neve needed a friend.

'Here, I'll do your hair quickly, I'll plait it for you. Are you wearing the green dress?'

Pip nodded as Neve moved behind her, her fingers deftly moving through her hair.

'Good, you look beautiful in it,' Neve said. 'I don't have any shoes that will fit you though, your feet are so tiny.'

'I don't think I can wear any kind of heels in this weather anyway. Think it might have to be the snow boots.'

Neve giggled. 'Well, promise me you'll take them off when you get there. It might ruin the look otherwise.' She added a few grips and clips to her hair and then patted her on the shoulder. 'There, you're all done.'

Neve grabbed her phone and took a photo of the back and showed Pip what it looked like. In a matter of minutes, Neve had achieved a twist of several plaits overlapping one another; it looked elegant and pretty.

'Thank you, it looks wonderful. Did you teach Gabe how to plait Wren's hair?'

Neve laughed. 'Yes, I did. It's not something I thought I'd ever have to do, teach my brother how to plait a girl's hair, but it's part of the job when you're a dad. Though I suspect if things go well between the two of you, that might become your job in the future.'

'Then you'll have to teach me too.'

Neve smiled. 'I'd be happy to. Now I better go. Throw your dress on and have a lovely date tonight.'

Pip hugged her and for a second Neve stood frozen, before she hugged her back. 'Thank you.'

'I think you coming back will probably be the best thing that has ever happened to my brother. I don't want to stand in the way of that.'

Pip smiled.

'Now go and enjoy your night,'

Neve waved at her as she left, but as soon as she had gone the nerves for what the night would hold returned.

❄

Pip trudged through the darkness towards the igloos, the only sound the noise of her boots as they crunched over the snow.

Gabe's lodge had been too quiet while she had finished getting ready. With Wren staying the night with Boris and Chester, and Gabe getting things ready for their big date in the igloo, it had been completely silent. In the short time she'd spent there, she had grown used to the noise and laughter that filled the house and it felt weird not to hear it.

She followed the path, the gold light of the igloo welcoming her in. The sky was completely clear, the moon and the stars sparkling as they presided over the event.

She walked past the other igloos, which were in darkness for now, and she was surprised at how tall they were. There were curtains around the bottom half that must have gone about ten feet up the side of the igloos, which would afford the occupants total privacy, but the rest of the structure was entirely made from glass to give the guests wonderful views of the night sky and hopefully the Northern Lights. It looked like the guests could even pull back the curtains to give them the stunning views over the entire island too.

She reached the gold-lit igloo and stopped outside the door, taking a few moments to catch her breath. Her heart was thundering with nerves about what the evening would hold, but she wasn't scared enough to turn and run away.

Pip took a deep breath, knocked on the door and then let herself in as she looked around. Candles flickered from every surface casting gold shadows over the glass ceiling. In the middle of the room was a giant bed covered in what looked like a silvery wolfskin blanket. There was a table set with candles and mysterious plates under silver domes. But Pip barely noticed any of that as Gabe was standing in the middle of the room dressed in a tuxedo.

Her breath caught in her throat. He looked beautiful.

'Gabe, this looks wonderful,' Pip said.

'I wanted it to be special.'

'It certainly is that.'

Gabe stepped towards her and kissed her on the cheek as he helped her out of her coat, then he looked down to admire her.

'You look incredible tonight. But then you always were the most beautiful woman in the world to me.'

Pip lifted her green velvet dress off her feet to show him the big furry snow boots she was wearing underneath and he laughed. 'Do you still fancy me wearing these?'

'Of course. But why don't I help you take them off.' He took her hand and led her over to the bed and she sat down on the edge. She was perfectly capable of taking her own boots off but she was intrigued to see what he would do. He captured one foot and slowly undid the laces, his eyes on hers the whole time. As he ran one hand down her leg he slid the boot off leaving her barefoot. He ran his finger up her bare sole and her breath hitched in her throat. He repeated it with the other foot and for some reason him undressing her this way, even though it was just her boots, was sexy as hell and a wonderful prelude for what was to come. He massaged her bare foot gently, running his fingers over her toes and down to her ankle and just when she was wondering or even hoping that they might skip the dinner and head straight for the dessert, he took her hand and led her over to the table. He pulled out a chair and held it for her as she sat down.

'I didn't know what to make for you, so I hope you like it.'

He pulled the silver domes off the plates and she laughed when she saw the pizza with ham and pineapple, her favourite topping when she was a teenager. And then it hit her. They'd had ham and pineapple pizza the night they had first made love and with the candles dancing in the darkness she realised he was trying to recreate the magic of that evening. That made her even more nervous. They were such different people now; could they really just pick up where they had left off and expect everything to be the same?

Gabe sat down opposite her.

'How are the lodges in the village looking?' he asked, dishing up the pizza.

'I decorated three today and I cleaned them too, so they are ready. I'll do the other three tomorrow. From what I gather from Luke, the boys only have one house left to finish off and they'll be finished tomorrow too.'

'That's great. The guests arrive the day after tomorrow, so I think everything will be ready for them.'

Pip bit into her pizza. 'Oh, this is delicious.'

'Care of Uri, my chef. Sadly we don't get Pizza Hut or Domino's up here. If you want pizza, you have to make your own.'

Pip took another bite. 'Luke says you're having staffing issues. Is there anything I can do to help?'

Gabe smiled and took her hand. 'I really appreciate you offering but no, we have it all in hand. I've made Iris the reservations manager; she knows our systems like the back of her hand. She'll still do a few shifts on reception too. I've got my head receptionist from my hotel in London to come up here and cover until Chloe can come back to work at the end of January and one of the girls from the town is going to help out on reception with a few hours here and there too. I've also got Adam, one of the deputy managers from London, to come up and give Neve a hand for a few months. They were a great team when they worked in London. This is Neve's first job as hotel manager, her and Adam were both deputy managers in London. I think she is finding it all a bit overwhelming, although she would never admit it. Plus this situation with Oakley isn't helping. Between you and me, I'm hoping Adam will also provide the distraction that Neve needs.'

She stared at him for a moment, in confusion.

'You're trying to distract your sister from a broken heart with sex? I think that's the last thing she needs.'

'I didn't mean sex. I just meant someone she can have fun with. She gets on really well with Adam, they always had a laugh together.'

'Oh. Sorry.'

He smiled. 'It's OK. I don't think being with another man will help her. She's completely in love with Oakley. That kind of love never goes away.'

'You don't think they should have broken up?'

'No, definitely not. It breaks my heart to see her so upset over it. I don't know what I can do to help her. I wonder if I should contact Oakley and ask him to come here. I know I shouldn't interfere, but I don't want her to live the rest of her life wondering and regretting like I did.'

It was like a punch to the gut and she could see that Gabe regretted saying it as soon as he'd said it.

Gabe picked up a bottle of wine from the cooler and poured some into both glasses.

'Luke told me about you going into hospital,' Pip said, quietly.

His face darkened. 'He shouldn't have done that.'

'He cares about you. He thinks we're making a mistake by getting back together.'

'It's none of his business,' he sighed. 'It was years ago. I was in hospital for three nights. It was hardly anything to worry about. I was run-down. It was probably some viral infection. The doctors thought at one stage it might even be an ear infection causing me to feel dizzy and not regulating my temperature properly. It wasn't you. Please don't think it was you. I know you feel terrible over what happened, but I don't blame you at all. You were a kid and you went through the worst time in your life. If being together is wrong when we still have such strong feelings for each other then it's our mistake to make. Can we just concentrate on us and not worry about what others think of it?'

Pip nodded, though she still couldn't help worrying. Gabe was right though; it was hard enough for them without factoring into the situation other people's opinions of it. She picked up her wine glass and held it up to him. 'So, let's drink to us.'

He smiled and picked up his glass too. 'To us.'

She took a sip of the wine and the bubbles danced on her tongue.

'Would you like some dessert?' Gabe asked. 'I have coconut ice cream.'

Pip smiled. 'I love coconut ice cream.'

'I remembered that you did. I hoped you hadn't gone off it in the last twelve years.'

Gabe dug a tub of coconut ice cream out of the cooler and dished it up into two bowls.

'Wait a minute, are you telling me you have shop-bought stuff for our special date tonight? I would expect Uri to make it fresh for us.'

Gabe laughed. 'He does make his own ice cream, but it takes a little longer than a few hours for him to pull that together. Besides,

I don't think even Uri could make coconut ice cream this good. And if you tell him that I'll have to kill you.'

'My lips are sealed.'

She scooped up a large spoonful and popped it in her mouth. It tasted divine. As she glanced over the table at Gabe she realised he was watching her.

'Thank you for tonight, this is all so wonderful.'

'It's my pleasure.'

She ate a few more spoonfuls and Gabe tucked into his own. 'So your parents are coming tomorrow. Are you looking forward to seeing them?'

'Very much so, it's been over two months since I last saw them. Wren absolutely adores them and the feeling is very mutual. I know they'll be delighted to see you again.'

Pip focused her attention on her ice cream for a moment. 'So much of my feelings after the accident, regarding you and your parents, revolved around what my dad had told me just before he crashed the car. I was heartbroken to hear that your mum and dad didn't want me. Although my dad had been verbally abusive to me for over ten years, and in hindsight I shouldn't have listened to him, he was so vehement about them turning down the five thousand pounds to take me in that I couldn't help but believe that it was true.'

'I can't believe that for a second. But they'll be here tomorrow and you can ask them about it.'

Pip nodded. 'I will. I need to know. Where are they staying?'

'I'm not sure. They were supposed to sleep in your room, but I think I may move them to your lodge.'

'But if I'm in your room every night, they could have my room.'

Gabe pulled a face. 'As much as I'm looking forward to seeing them and spending time with them again, once all the guests arrive I'm going to be very busy. Call me selfish, but I'd like the few spare hours a day I'll have to myself to spend with you without them being there too. I have enough interference from Neve and Luke without them sticking their oar in as well.'

'Do you think they will be against us being together too?'

'Knowing my mum, as soon as she finds out that we're together again she'll be helping you to pick out a wedding dress and buying a great big hat.'

Pip laughed. 'OK, them staying in my lodge does sound like a better idea.'

They finished off the ice cream and Gabe stood up and offered his hand. 'Would you like to dance?'

Pip took his hand. 'I'd love to.'

He pulled her to her feet and then moved to the stereo to select a track.

As Ed Sheeran's 'Photograph' drifted out through the speakers, he moved back to her and took her in his arms. As Ed started singing, Gabe joined in too, staring at her as he slowly moved around the room with her wrapped tightly in his arms. The lyrics of the song were telling their story, about their past and how hard it was to love sometimes but you do it anyway because you have no choice. It was a beautiful song and Gabe couldn't have picked anything more appropriate. As the words came to an end, Gabe stopped moving as he looked down at her.

She reached up and kissed him and he ran his hands round her back as he kissed her, sweetly. God, she could spend the whole night kissing this man and never ever grow tired of it. Although as his hands moved to the zip at the top of her dress and started to slide it down, she knew he had other ideas.

❄ Chapter 17 ❄

In a movement that was swift and confident, Gabe slid the dress off her shoulders so it pooled on the floor, leaving her only in her lacy briefs.

He stepped back a bit to admire her for a moment before he was kissing her again, his hands caressing all over her body as if he wanted to stroke her everywhere at once.

She reached up to slide his jacket off his shoulders and then started trying to undo the buttons on his shirt, but she was shaking so much that her fingers refused to do the job required of them.

Gabe realised this too. 'You're shaking.'

'I'm just a bit chilly.' It wasn't a total lie. The room wasn't cold but it was far from warm and toasty either. Her nipples had already hardened and it was only partly out of arousal.

'Well we can't have that.'

He scooped her up and carried her to the bed. He laid her down, covering her with the fur blanket, then he quickly divested himself of all his clothes apart from his tight black boxer shorts. Pip's eyes fell on the tattoo again and a stab of guilt punched her in the stomach, and lay there among all the nerves she had over that evening. He climbed under the covers with her, taking her in his arms.

'Body heat is the best way to keep warm,' he said, and she giggled against his lips, trying not to let any thought other than being with him invade her brain.

But although they were warm and cosy under the covers, the shaking hadn't stopped, in fact it had probably got worse.

As Gabe ran his hands down her body, he stopped and pulled his mouth from hers. 'Pip, you're trembling like a leaf, what's wrong?'

'Nothing, just a bit nervous… And excited and scared all at once.'

He pulled back completely, his face clouding with concern. 'What are you scared of?'

'It's OK. I'm just being silly. Don't stop.'

'It's not silly, what are you scared of?'

'Oh god, everything. That I won't be good enough for you, you've been with all these women and I've had sex once, twelve years ago, and I probably wasn't that good then. I'm scared you'll sleep with me and there'll be no spark at all for you and then you'll decide that you don't want to pursue this after all. I'm scared that making love to you will make me fall in love with you again and I'm worried that you won't feel the same. And I'm scared of hurting you, of you falling in love with me and me being incapable of loving you back. I'm scared that I'm too messed up to ever have a proper relationship and that somehow I'll find some way to cock this up and hurt you all over again.'

He smiled as he ran his hand down her side. 'I'm scared about all those things too. Except about there being no spark. I'm not worried about that at all. We have that, we've both felt it when we've kissed.'

He hooked his finger in the waistband of her knickers and slid them slowly down her legs. His hand travelled back up the inside of her thigh and when he reached the top, she knew he could feel how much she wanted him. His eyes darkened as he stroked over her most sensitive part and her breath caught, but then he slid his hand away, back down her leg, reaching the back of her knee and hooking it over his hip as he lay on his side. Immediately, she could feel how ready he was for this too.

'We have spark, Pip, that's very clear, and yes it might be lust and passion and need and not love yet, but there's no way sex can be rubbish when we feel like this for each other. And as for the rest, this is a second chance for us; let's not spoil it with recriminations and regrets and thoughts of what we should have done or what could have been. If this doesn't work out between us it'll be because we're two different people now, and probably shows that we wouldn't have lasted anyway. But it won't be because we didn't give it our all or because we were too hung up on the past to enjoy what we have now. If you walk away from this or it ends for whatever reason, it won't break me. I'm a grown man and I'm big enough and ugly enough to look after myself.'

She smiled.

'And I don't think you're messed up at all. You had a rough childhood and you weren't loved as much as you should have been. It doesn't mean that you're incapable of love now. In fact, I would assume the opposite. You know what it's like to be in a non-loving relationship, you know what was missing and I imagine, subconsciously maybe, you will strive to fill those holes.'

He ran a gentle finger down her cheek.

'I want you to trust me and feel safe. I don't want to push you into doing something you're not comfortable doing. We can just spend the night together tonight and we can kiss and cuddle just like we did last night, and when you're ready in a few weeks or a few months from now, we can make love then. I don't want to rush this and risk scaring you away.'

Pip was just about to argue. There was no way she was not going to make love to him tonight, not after looking forward to it so much. But she was interrupted as the room was suddenly bathed in a bright cranberry glow.

She looked up at the sky through the glass roof and gasped as the pinky red lights danced and flickered across the sky.

'Oh my god, is that really the Northern Lights, or is it just a trick of some LED lights in the glass roof?'

Gabe smiled. 'It's the real thing. I was wondering if this would happen tonight, long-range forecasts predicted that it would, but you can never tell what the weather is going to do.'

Pip rolled onto her back to watch it properly and as she marvelled at the shimmering lights as they slowly rolled across the sky, turning through shades of green, turquoise and even with hints of purples and blues, Gabe held her hand.

'I've never seen anything like it, I've seen photos and videos but this is just…magnificent,' Pip whispered. 'I'm so glad I got to share it with you.'

Gabe squeezed her hand. 'I'm glad too.'

After watching it for the longest time and with no sign of it stopping, Pip rolled back onto her side to look at Gabe and he rolled onto his side too, entwining his fingers with hers.

'Remember what you said about some people believing that the Northern Lights are spirits in the sky, guiding the lost travellers home?'

Gabe nodded.

'You are my home Gabe, I firmly believe I was supposed to come back to you, it just took a lot longer than we would have liked. I want to be with you tonight, I want to make love to you: there is nothing I want more right now. Yes I'm nervous, but those nerves would be the same if I waited six months to make love to you. I just want it to be perfect, but I'm with you, so it can't get any more perfect.'

He swallowed and shifted closer, his hand on her hip bringing her closer to him.

'Are you sure?'

'Absolutely.' She smiled as she glanced up at the Northern Lights again, briefly, as they danced and swirled in the darkness. 'Do you know that the Chinese believe that couples who make love under the Northern Lights will be lucky in love, that they'll stay together forever?'

He grinned. 'I've not heard that one before. But if it's true, it seems a shame to waste this opportunity. Who knows when the Northern Lights will appear again?'

With his hand round the back of her neck, he kissed her, half rolling on top of her as his other hand slid between her legs. She moaned against his lips as soon as he touched her, the nerves and fear suddenly vanishing. It felt so right being with him, like somehow his lips and his body were made for hers. She wrapped her arms around him, needing to feel his body pressing into hers. He was so familiar in so many ways; though his body was broader, and stronger, it was still the Gabe she knew and loved. She knew his kiss, the way he smelled, it was exactly like coming home. His hands were more skilled now, he knew exactly where to touch her and how to elicit a reaction from her and she loved the confidence he had with her body, and in no time at all she was tumbling over the edge, panting and moaning unapologetically.

He pulled back slightly to look at her, his face filled with adoration as he simply stared at her as though he was studying her, taking her all in.

He leaned over to the drawers and grabbed a condom. 'I came prepared.'

She laughed. 'I'm so glad.'

Gabe knelt up between her legs and she watched as he rolled the condom on. Amazingly, he seemed bigger there too.

He leaned over her, bracing himself on his forearms, and she wrapped her legs around him as he slid slowly inside her. He felt indescribably good. She reached up to stroke his face, feeling the stubble under her fingers. He slowly lowered himself on her and she knew there was no greater feeling in the world than being pinned to the bed by his weight. He kissed her softly, barely moving at all, and she guessed he was waiting to give her body a chance to accept him, which it did very quickly, her whole body melting into his.

He started to move, slow, careful, reverential strokes as if he was afraid she might break. He didn't take his eyes off her for one second. He was being so careful and she loved him for that. She was falling for this man and judging by the way he was looking at her, he was falling for her too.

Gabe captured her hands in one of his and stretched them out above her head, causing her to arch against him, which made him go deeper inside and cause him to press against the most sensitive part of her.

'Gabe,' Pip whispered, feeling need building in her again, which surprised her when it hadn't been that long since the first time he had made her come. She pulled him in tighter with her legs and he smirked as he started moving harder and faster against her. She glanced above his head at the red shimmering lights that lit up the room, hopefully somehow blessing them with all the luck in the world. Seconds later her orgasm ripped through her with such ferocity that she shouted out his name as she trembled against him.

He paused as he released her hands and she wrapped them round his neck, gathering him as close as she could. But as the feelings in her subsided and she felt her body go soft and pliant, it seemed that Gabe was far from finished.

❄

Gabe woke and stared up at the sky above them as the first hints of a candyfloss sunrise started to appear. Pip was lying fast asleep sprawled out on his chest. Though he wasn't surprised she was sleeping, they had made love for hours the night before. They'd stop and kiss and talk for a while, but he found he just couldn't lie in bed with her naked and not make love to her until she screamed out his name again. He was never going to get enough of her. Sex had never been like that before. How could he ever think that he could fill the void she had left with those other women when nothing would ever feel as good or as right as being with Pip?

They would have to get up soon. He had promised Wren he would have breakfast with her and there was still a lot to be done to prepare for the guests' arrival the next day. His parents were arriving too, but locked in the warmth of Pip's embrace he could forget, just for a moment, that there were all these stresses to worry about.

He breathed her in and sighed.

He shifted out of her arms and she moaned slightly as he got out of bed and then re-covered her with a blanket. He used the bathroom and then came back out to the bedroom. She was lying face down with her bare shoulders showing and as he climbed back into bed with her, she opened one eye to look at him.

He stroked her hair. 'Did you have any more nightmares last night?'

She shook her head. 'You really must be my cure. Though there wasn't much time for sleeping. It's not time to get up yet, surely?'

'We've probably got half an hour before we need to get ready.'

'A half hour more sleep sounds lovely,' she mumbled, sleepily, closing her eyes again.

'Who said anything about sleeping?' Gabe said as he moved on top of her, sweeping her hair off her shoulders and kissing the very top of her spine.

'Gabe, I can't move, I don't have it in me to do it again,' Pip said, though when she opened one eye to look at him over her shoulder, he could see she was far from sleepy any more.

'Lucky for you, I have enough stamina for both of us. You just have to lie there, angel, and I'll take care of everything.'

He grabbed the last condom and then trailed kisses down her spine, nudging her legs open as he knelt between them. He slid his fingers between her legs and let out a breath of need when he felt how ready she was for him. He lifted her hips slightly and slid inside her in one swift movement. She felt so good, so hot, and she fitted him perfectly. She let out a moan that was urgent and animalistic and it turned him on so much.

He leaned over her, his arms either side of her head, caging her in his embrace as he kissed her spine again. He thrust into her again and she writhed under him, very quickly falling into a rhythm as they moved against each other in perfect sync. He was surprised though when he could feel her body quickening, getting closer to her orgasm. She was so responsive and it took so little time to send her over the edge. He had never been with a woman who had multiple orgasms during sex, but Pip seemed to be the expert, and every time she looked shocked, like she couldn't believe it was happening again, that her body was capable of it. For Gabe, he saw it as a challenge; he liked to see how many times he could make her come before he gave in to his own release.

As her body tightened around his and she moaned and clawed at the pillow, he reached up and took her hands in his, holding her to the bed as she screamed and shook beneath him. No sooner had her body stopped trembling, he pulled out and rolled her onto her back before sliding back into her again. She looped her arms round his neck and looked at him in shock as he continued to move against her. He kissed her softly and smiled against her lips as he felt her building again. He pulled back to stare into those beautiful golden, vulnerable eyes and knew he was falling in love with her all over again.

❄

Pip stared up at the empty tree. Hanging just above where the star would be was a gigantic spider. This thing was practically a tarantula, with thick black hairy legs. She swore she could actually see its eight eyes staring at her. She hated spiders.

After breakfast with Wren and feeding the reindeer – with thankfully no sexual antics from Rudolph this time – she had spent the morning decorating the houses in the village. Everything had gone smoothly until she had to face this monster. She couldn't kill spiders, they grossed her out too much, and she certainly couldn't pick them up. But she couldn't decorate the tree with it hanging over her either.

She climbed the three stairs up the stepladder and reached up towards the monster, swiping just above it with a piece of paper to try to catch the web. The spider flinched and she leapt back a bit, but still he hung there as if he was floating in the air. She swiped again and the spider suddenly fell from its web, slithered down the piece of paper towards her and straight down the sleeve of her top.

Pip screamed and yanked her top off, throwing it across the room and straight into Luke's face as he came through the door holding what looked like lunch. She yelped at him seeing her in just a bra, tried to cover herself, and as the stepladder wobbled precariously she toppled backwards into the tree, hitting the branches and feeling the stab of the tiny needles against her bare skin as she fell to the floor.

'Christ, Pip, are you OK?' Luke said, rushing over to help her.

He grabbed her hand and retrieved her from the tree, but one of the branches caught on her bra strap and as she was pulled up, her bra was yanked up too. She grabbed her bra just in time to stop it from coming off and Luke, realising what had happened, immediately dropped her, slamming a hand over his eyes.

She yelped as she hit the floor again.

'Sorry.'

He quickly handed her back her T-shirt which he was still holding in the other hand and when she struggled to put it back on from her upended position inside the tree, the bloody tarantula climbed out of the head hole towards her.

Pip squealed and threw the T-shirt out of the tree.

Luke chanced a glance through his fingers. 'What happened?'

'Don't look.'

Luke clamped his hand over his eyes again and as Pip untangled herself from the branches she could distinctly hear him chuckling.

'It's not funny,' Pip said, trying to stand up.

Luke must have known she was struggling, because he offered out his free hand and when she took it, he pulled her out. 'It really is. I only came in here to see if you wanted a sandwich, I didn't expect to get a strip show.'

Pip felt the laugh bubble from her throat too.

She marched over to her T-shirt and, seeing the tarantula scuttle underneath a chest of drawers, she picked her top up and pulled it on.

'OK, you can look now,' Pip said and smiled when Luke was still laughing. He didn't laugh or smile very often and it made her feel good that she had helped to ease some of his pain, albeit temporarily. He tossed her a sandwich and went to sit down on the sofa. She sat down opposite him.

'You're the second person I've rescued from a tree today. Well, I say person, it was Blaze. Stupid puppy escaped again and got himself wedged in a tree, I have no idea how, but his howls and yelps made him pretty easy to find.'

'He's a handful then?' Pip said, unwrapping her sandwich.

'Blaze is certainly a character. I love him, but he's completely useless for what I got him for. We bought them to pull sleds for the tourists; dog sledding is hugely popular and I'm going to train them in the summer to do it, but Blaze has no discipline at all. I might as well send him back to the breeder but Wren would kill me if I did, she absolutely adores him.'

'Aw, poor Blaze, he just needs a little love.'

'Believe me, he has that in bucket loads. At the moment, me spoiling him with love is not working and he's corrupting the other puppies too. I can teach him to sit, stay and come when called, but beyond the basics he's useless. You can have him if you want.'

Pip stopped chewing. A puppy would require commitment and stability. She couldn't take responsibility for a puppy and then leave it in a few months' time. She had always just been responsible for herself, but suddenly the thought of looking after someone or something else appealed. If she stayed she'd have Wren to look after too and although that was an even bigger responsibility than a puppy that didn't scare her off, either. She wanted the family that she'd never had and the bigger the better – puppies, cats, maybe even children of her own one day – and she wanted that with Gabe.

She glanced over at Luke who was watching her with a slight smile, clearly knowing what she was thinking. That was a big statement from him. Offering her a puppy when he knew she couldn't take Blaze with her was almost equivalent to asking her to stay, which was a bit of a U-turn from the day before.

Luke shrugged. 'Think about it.'

'I will.'

❄

Pip stretched as she looked at the finished tree in the final house that she'd decorated. It had taken her all day to do the last three houses but now it was done. Although Gabe had helped with the outside of the houses in the morning, he'd disappeared back to the hotel before lunch and she hadn't seen him since.

She had seen the red plane arrive on the island several times throughout the day, bringing with it all the staff and probably Gabe's parents too. She knew she would have to face them at some point, but she wasn't looking forward to the conversation that she knew she would have to have with them. They had been under no obligation to take her in when she was seventeen years old, they had every right to turn down the five thousand pounds that her dad had offered them, but she still couldn't help feeling hurt over the rejection. She needed to know whether it was true and, if it was, the reason why. In hindsight, and with the maturity of age, Pip could understand that the lack of space and money could have been an issue, but she still couldn't help feeling let down as they were always more of a family to her than her own family had been. In truth, part of the reason she had run away was not just Gabe's rejection but the rejection from his parents too.

She quickly tidied up any of the debris left over from decorating and left the box by the door to be collected by the maintenance team later. She stepped outside into the cold. It was just starting to get dark and it was clear that the men working on the houses had finished and packed away some time before. But as with the previous night, Luke was waiting for her on the snowmobile.

'Thanks for waiting,' Pip said as she approached.

Luke shrugged. 'Are all the houses finished now?'

'Yes, that's the last one. Hopefully we won't need them, but if the power goes out again then we have a back-up plan.'

'It's good of you to help.'

Pip climbed on the snowmobile behind him, wrapping her arms around his chest. 'I want to help Gabe, he's worked so hard for this, you all have. I want it to be a success. If things work out between me and Gabe, then I'll be staying here. I'm not sure what skills I have to offer, but I want to contribute.'

'Do you think it will work out between you? It's no secret that you spent the night together last night.'

'We've spent every night together since I've arrived here, last night was no different.' Apart from the hours of incredible, mind-blowing sex, but she wasn't going to tell Luke that.

Luke was silent for a moment. 'The boy is falling in love with you, anybody can see that. Just be careful with him.'

'I will. I don't want to hurt him, that's the last thing I want.'

Luke nodded as he pulled into the drive. There was a flurry of activity around the hotel and lodges. Pip had got used to the place being quiet and empty, but Gabe had said there were nearly fifty staff returning that day and it seemed they all suddenly had jobs to do.

'Dad and Lizzie are here, I know they're keen to see you,' Luke said, interrupting her thoughts.

Pip didn't know what to say. It was the weirdest feeling of being so desperate to see them again after all this time and dreading seeing them too.

Luke seemed to sense this. 'They loved you, Pip, don't ever think otherwise.'

They stopped outside Gabe's lodge and Pip climbed off.

'We're having a big family dinner later, I suspect I'll see you then,' Luke said.

'I'm not family. I doubt they will want me there.'

'You are family, you always have been.'

Luke roared off into the darkness before Pip could answer. She turned and walked up the stairs into Gabe's lodge. If she was going to dinner with the Whitakers later she needed to speak to Gabe's parents before then.

She pushed open the door and before she had even stepped one foot inside, Wren launched herself at her from across the room, throwing her arms around Pip and squealing with delight that she was home. Pip kneeled down and hugged Wren to her.

Wren stroked Pip's hair, soothingly, almost as if she knew that Pip was worried. Pip had never really thought about having children before – having children meant trusting someone enough to be in a serious relationship and she had vowed many years ago that that was never going to happen. But with Wren's tiny warm body wrapped in her arms, right then Pip could think of nothing better than being a part of this little girl's life, being there for her and watching her grow up.

'It's four days until Christmas, Pip. I'm so excited. Daddy says I might burst with excitement.'

'We don't want that, there would be bits of you everywhere.'

Wren giggled.

Gabe wandered in from the kitchen, smiling broadly. He had a tea towel thrown over his shoulder and as Wren let her go and went back to playing with Winston, and Gabe came over to greet her, she smiled at the idyllic image of domestic bliss that Gabe and Wren presented.

Without any hesitation, Gabe took her face in his hands and kissed her. Pip jumped a little that he would display such affection in front of Wren, but because Gabe didn't seem bothered by it Pip closed her eyes and enjoyed the kiss. Wren let out a little giggle at seeing them together, but after a second she carried on playing with Winston as if her daddy kissing Pip was completely the norm.

'Well, that's a lovely welcome,' Pip said, smiling up at him when he eventually pulled back. 'I certainly didn't expect that.'

'I missed you, we both did. Wren has been asking when you were coming home.'

'Well, I'm home now and I'm yours all evening, Wren.' She looked back at Gabe. 'I know you're going to dinner tonight with your family. I can look after Wren if you want me to.'

Gabe looked confused. 'But you're coming to dinner too, we all are. Mum and Dad are dying to see you again.'

'It doesn't seem right, Gabe. I'm not part of your family. I don't want to be in the way.'

'Of course you're part of the family. It wouldn't be right if you weren't there.'

He looked down at her, trying to understand what she was worried about. His face cleared a little. 'I'm just making some hot chocolate for Wren in the kitchen. Why don't you come through and talk to me about your day and Wren can play in here with Winston.'

Pip nodded and Gabe took her hand and led her through to the kitchen. 'What's wrong? Do you not want to have dinner with them tonight?'

'I need to talk to them before I sit down to dinner with them like one big happy family. It'll be awkward otherwise.'

'Then let's go talk to them. They're staying in your old lodge. We can go now. We still have a few hours until dinner.'

'I think I need to do this by myself.'

Gabe nodded. 'OK, if you're sure.'

'I'll go now.'

Gabe kissed her on the cheek. 'They adore you Pip, you have nothing to worry about.'

Pip smiled and walked back out through the lounge.

'Are you leaving already?' Wren asked, sadly, as she looked up from playing with Winston.

'I'm just going over to see your grandparents, I won't be long.'

'Can I come?'

Gabe came in with a mug of steaming hot chocolate. 'I just made you this. Do you not want it now?'

'Did you make it with cream and marshmallows, Daddy?'

'Of course I did. You can see Nanny and Pops again later at dinner. You need to have a bath first.'

'OK, can Winston have a bath too?'

'Maybe not tonight, but we can bath him another day.'

While Wren was distracted by the hot chocolate and the prospect of bathing Winston, Pip slipped out and crunched across the snow to the lodge where Gabe's parents were staying.

She stood outside the door for a few moments before plucking up the courage to knock on the door. She could hear Lizzie and David laughing and talking inside and her heart jolted with a recognition and an ache for them that she didn't even know she had.

A second later the door was flung open and she stared into the familiar eyes of Gabe's mum. They stared at each other in silence for a few seconds before Lizzie threw her arms around Pip and held her tight.

'Oh my darling, we have missed you so much. Come in out of the cold and let me have a look at you.'

Before Pip could protest, Lizzie had dragged her into the lounge and closed the door behind her. David was standing by the fire and his face split into a huge smile when he saw her.

'Pip, it's so good to see you,' David said, walking towards her and grabbing her into a big hug.

Pip felt a lump of emotion lodge in her throat at the warm welcome from both of them. Where Neve and Luke had both been guarded, protective and somewhat hostile towards her at first, Lizzie and David welcomed her with open arms.

David released her and held Pip at arm's length. 'How have you been?'

'You grew up to be so beautiful,' Lizzie said. 'It's no wonder Gabe is falling in love with you all over again. God, I can't believe you're here after all this time. Broke my heart when you left, I felt like I had lost one of my own children. Gabe told us what happened, that you were in the car with your dad when it crashed. Why didn't you come to us?'

Pip found her voice. 'If Gabe told you what happened, then you'll know that I did come to you and saw him in the barn with Jenny Maguire.'

'Yes, he did say that's what you thought but…'

'Did he also tell you what my dad said to me on the day of the accident?'

Lizzy looked confused and David shook his head.

'Dad was driving me to the train station when the accident happened; he didn't want me to live with him any more. He had threatened to kick me out many times before but he'd never actually done it. This time he was serious. I said that if he didn't want me, I'd live with you guys instead. Just before he crashed the car, he told me that he had offered you five thousand pounds for me to move in with you and you told him that you didn't want it.' Pip swallowed. 'Or me.'

Lizzie paled and looked aghast and Pip could see immediately that what her dad had told her had been the truth.

'Oh my darling, come and sit down,' Lizzie said and Pip followed them to the sofa. Lizzie sat down next to her, taking Pip's hand.

'Your dad did come and see us and he did offer us five thousand pounds to take you in the day before he died. And it's true that we turned him down, but it's not for the reasons that you think. We had no idea that your dad had been threatening to kick you out before then. I turned him down because I thought you would be heartbroken to find out that your dad didn't want you any more. That kind of rejection was the very last thing you needed. We knew you carried the fear of being rejected with you after being abandoned as a baby and we feared this would only make things worse for you. We ended up having a massive row with him. I told him that he needed to face up to his responsibilities as a parent and that we understood his grief for your mum but the time had come for him to be the dad your mum would have wanted him to be. He didn't want to hear it and he stormed out,' Lizzie said.

Lizzie looked over to David and he picked up the story. 'We felt so guilty afterwards. We knew that living with your dad had always been hard for you and here was a way out. We loved you and it would never have been any hardship for you to come and live with us. We talked about it for hours after he left, and when Gabe went out to meet you that night we asked him to get you to come round for dinner the following night so we could discuss what you wanted to do. We were going to tell you that you would be very welcome to live with us and that we would love to have you, but we wanted it to be your choice rather than it being forced upon you. If I'd known that he was going to kick you out anyway I would have moved all your things into our house that very same day.'

Pip stared at the flames dancing in the fire. They had wanted her after all.

'Please tell me that you didn't move away because of that?' Lizzie asked, her voice catching in her throat.

It would have been so easy to lie, to say that it didn't have anything to do with her decision. But she wanted them to know that she didn't run away from what she had with Gabe lightly. She wanted their approval for her and Gabe to be together again, she didn't want them thinking that she was flighty and undependable.

'It was part of the reason. I just didn't think I had anything left for me there any more. I would never have hurt Gabe like that. I just wasn't thinking straight after the accident and you have no idea how much I regret the way I handled it.'

Lizzie squeezed her hand.

'It was no one's fault, you can't blame yourself,' David said. 'We certainly don't.'

Silence fell on the room, the only sound the crackling of the logs in the fire, and she wondered if they were also thinking about how it could have been.

'So you and Gabe are back together again?' Lizzie asked, but there was no judgement from her, and certainly no anger as there had been from Neve and Luke.

'We're trying again. When we met it was clear there were all these suppressed feelings there that never went away, for both of us. It's hard, we're different people now, and we're both cautious of getting hurt again but…things are going really well so far.'

Lizzie smiled hugely and Pip remembered what Gabe had said about Lizzie having them married off before Christmas.

'There's Wren to think of as well now. It's a big responsibility to raise a child who isn't yours,' David warned.

'David!' Lizzie said. 'We're not talking about Pip raising Wren as her daughter. Gabe and Pip have only been back together again for a few days. Let them have some fun first before we start walking them down the aisle.'

Pip smiled. 'I adore Wren. And maybe I haven't really thought about the consequences or responsibilities of raising a child yet or what it will mean if I do stay, but it hasn't felt like a burden or an inconvenience to have her around. I love spending time with her, playing with her and talking to her. It will be hard, of course it will be. I've never had any experience of childcare before, but it's not something I'm afraid of.'

'Well, we can have Wren for a sleepover tonight, give you guys some time alone,' Lizzie waggled her eyebrows, mischievously.

'That's not necessary. We can have time alone once Wren has gone to bed. I feel like the poor girl has been passed from pillar to post recently as we've been getting ready for the opening of the hotel. It would probably do her good to have some stability,' Pip said.

David and Lizzie exchanged smiles.

'Spoken like a true parent,' Lizzie said, fondly. 'But we insist. We haven't seen her for two months, she's growing up so fast. We would love to have her over and I'm sure she would love to come. We'll ask her, see what she wants to do.'

'OK. But I warn you now, if she tells you she normally sings all the *Frozen* songs before she goes to sleep, then she's lying.'

Lizzie laughed. 'Sounds like you're learning from experience already.'

❄ Chapter 18 ❄

Gabe looked over at Pip as the dessert plates were cleared away. It had been a funny night and he just hoped that his weird, wonderful and overprotective family hadn't scared Pip away. Although Pip had come back from seeing his parents much happier than when she had left, she was still a bit nervous about sitting down to dinner with his whole family as if she belonged there. For Gabe, he knew that she did and he failed to understand why she couldn't see that. Even before they got together, as kids she had been part of their family, and now she belonged there even more.

Luke had talked to Pip a bit. His mum and dad had been their usual warm, friendly chatty selves and to his surprise Neve had been chatting to her all night and making a real effort to be friendly. Pip had come out of her shell completely and they had listened to many a story of some of the wonderful and terrible hotels that Pip had stayed in over the years.

Wren clearly had not been as captivated by Pip's stories, as she was curled up on Pip's lap, her head on her shoulder, dozing off with her thumb in her mouth. Pip seemed really at ease as she stroked her hand down Wren's back.

His dad stood. 'Well, it's been a long day and I think we'll turn in.' He looked at Wren in Pip's arms and smiled. 'It looks like this little one could do with going to bed too.'

As his mum came to take Wren from Pip, Pip stood up and kissed Wren on the head.

'Goodnight beautiful,' Pip whispered as she passed Wren into Lizzie's arms.

Wren stirred slightly and opened her eyes. 'Nanny, can we go and get Winston too, he won't be able to sleep without me.'

'Of course darling, we can get anything you want.'

Gabe bent over and kissed Wren goodnight too. 'I'll see you tomorrow for breakfast, sweetheart.'

Wren nodded and closed her eyes again.

They said their goodbyes and left just as several other members of staff walked in. Gabe had called for a full staff meeting but promised to keep it quick ahead of the guests' arrival the next day.

He sat back down as he waited for everyone else to arrive. Pip seemed to hover between staying and leaving, but he caught her hand and tugged her back into her seat. 'You're part of the team too. Besides, I want to introduce you to everyone so they all know you're not just a guest.'

Pip looked shocked. 'You're going to introduce me? As what? Lover, friend?'

'I was going to go with girlfriend, if that's OK?' he said, quietly. 'They're going to see us together anyway, I'm not going to hide that.'

Pip stared at him for a second and then smiled. 'Girlfriend is fine.'

Neve leaned across the table to talk to Pip. 'I'm not sure if Gabe told you, but he showed me some of your photos.'

Gabe's heart sank a little; he had been going to tell Pip himself but his sister clearly had other ideas.

Pip looked back up at him in confusion. 'My photos? How did you show Neve my photos?'

'I emailed them to myself the other night when we were looking at them. I showed Neve this morning.'

Her face fell and he immediately felt guilty. She didn't see anything in her talent or skills as a photographer, but she had a rare and beautiful gift and he wanted her to realise that.

Neve obviously realised she had stepped on some toes with her announcement. 'Pip, those photos are incredible. Your talents are wasted taking photos of hotels, bedrooms and swimming pools. People would pay really good money to have something like your photos hanging in their homes. Gabe showed me because he thought it might be something I would be interested in for here. I have to say, I was very impressed with what I saw. I would gladly commission you to take photos of the island and maybe some of the other Shetland Islands too, and we would hang them in the lodges and around the hotel, to encourage our guests to explore the island. We'd put some on our website as well to showcase our resort in the best possible light. We'd also display them in some of Gabe's other hotels worldwide to encourage guests to come here.'

'We'd also be interested in buying some of the photos you've already taken,' Gabe said. 'They would be perfect for many of our hotels.'

Pip stared at him. 'You want to buy my photos?'

'Yes, we would pay good money too.'

'That's very kind but I don't need you to buy my photos just to be nice.'

'Trust me, that has absolutely nothing whatsoever to do with it,' Gabe said.

'I didn't even know they were yours when Gabe showed me; he just asked me to look at them, told me that someone had sent them to him with the view of him buying them and he wanted my opinion. I'm not blowing smoke up your ass here, Pip. I would never want to put photos in my hotel that were crap just to be nice. The photos I looked at were beautiful.'

Pip didn't say anything and Gabe didn't know whether she was angry or just taking it in. She had been on her own for so long, she clearly had no idea what it felt like when someone believed in her.

'I was going to talk to you about it. I wanted to ask Neve for an unbiased opinion before I did. I didn't want to get your hopes up, especially when you were so down on your talent to begin with.'

'I don't know what to say,' Pip finally said. 'I just took those photos for me, I didn't take them for other people to see. I wouldn't even know what to charge for a photo.'

'Well, just think about it. I can put you in touch with other photographers and they can discuss with you the kinds of prices they charge for something like this,' Gabe said. 'You don't have to decide now.'

'It would be a great help for us to have something like that on our website. It will really help us to stand apart from other resorts,' Neve pushed, and Gabe glared at her.

'If it'll help, of course I'll do it,' Pip said, suddenly galvanised into action. 'I can show you some of the personal photos of the island I've taken so far, see if any of those are good enough; if not I can take some more.'

Gabe smiled. 'Congratulations on your first commission for Stardust Lake Hotel.'

❄

Pip listened to Gabe as he talked to his staff, about the guests arriving the next day, his expectations and how every guest must be treated like royalty. He spoke about the mystery guest again and Pip could see how nervous everyone was about Mr Black. It was worrying to think that one man could make or break Stardust Lake Hotel on its opening weekend.

Gabe answered questions whenever he was asked and deferred to Neve too, as she was the manager and he clearly wanted people to know that. But throughout Gabe's speech, he was friendly, approachable and, although she could tell he was serious and passionate about the hotel doing well, he just came across as so damned likeable. As she watched the staff hang off his every word, she couldn't help smiling as she found herself falling further in love with him.

'I'll let you get off in a minute, I know some of you have jobs to do ahead of our guests' arrival tomorrow and some of you have an early start too, but before I do, let me introduce some new members of staff that most of you won't know. We had a couple of shortages, due to one reason or another, so Iris is now our reservations manager but she will also be helping out on reception too. This is Adam.' Gabe pointed out a tall, impossibly handsome man who was sitting next to Neve and clearly very happy about being here. 'He is going to be assistant manager for the next six months, he'll be helping out Neve and if you have any issues or queries, you can talk to him. He has been deputy manager for my hotel in London for several years, so he brings a wealth of experience to the role. This is our head receptionist, Cora, also from my London hotel and she'll be here for a few months too. And this is Pip, my girlfriend.'

There was a sudden murmur of interest as everyone looked over in her direction. She could feel her cheeks glow red. It must be weird for many of the staff who had just arrived back on the island. They had left only a few days before when Gabe was single and now he had a girlfriend and she was living with him. By anyone's standards, that was fast work.

Gabe carried on regardless of the mutterings. 'I'm sure you will see her around the place and she has kindly agreed to help out with the odd job and looking after the reindeer too.'

Pip glanced across at Luke and he smirked at her at the mention of the reindeer.

'I know some of you have already met our entertainers for tomorrow night's carnival as they arrived earlier, but for those that haven't they are staying in three of the larger family lodges, twelve, thirteen and fourteen. They should be treated as any guest, but just so you are aware that's where they are. Oh and lastly, the couple in Lodge Four are my mum and dad, just in case you see them walking around with Wren or hanging around the offices upstairs. That's it. I know the hotel is going to be a huge success because I absolutely have the best staff working here. Just continue to work as hard as you have been and I know our guests will be very happy.'

There was a small round of applause and Pip smiled. They all wanted this to work as much as Gabe.

The staff slowly filed out, some coming over to introduce themselves to the new members of staff, some coming to ask Gabe and Neve questions, and then they left too, until there was only a handful of them remaining.

Adam came over to introduce himself to her, the only member of staff that had. 'Pip, it's a pleasure to meet you, I've heard a lot about you. It's nice to know that someone has Gabe under control at last.'

Gabe laughed.

'It's nice to meet you too,' Pip said. 'Gabe speaks very highly of you.'

'Oh, it's all lies, I assure you.' He turned to Neve. 'I'll see you tomorrow, boss.'

Neve smiled. 'Eight o'clock, don't be late,' she said.

Adam laughed. 'I wouldn't dream of it.'

He left and Pip could see there was no animosity from him despite the fact that Neve used to be his equal and was now in charge of him. She hoped that Adam would be exactly what Neve needed to help her get over Oakley.

Neve and Luke stood up to go. 'Pip, come and see me tomorrow and show me some of the photos you've taken of Stardust Lake Hotel and the island so far.'

'I will, thank you.'

Neve smiled, Luke nodded at her and they both walked out, leaving her and Gabe alone.

'That was a good speech,' Pip said, as she stood up and looped her arms around his neck.

'Thank you. And you didn't mind being introduced as my girlfriend?'

'No, although it certainly piqued their interest.'

Gabe shrugged. 'Give them something to talk about. Besides, they needed to know who you were. If any of them see me cavorting with someone they think to be a guest that would be very hypocritical as I told them all a few days ago they weren't allowed to have relationships with anyone who was a guest.'

'And do you intend to do a lot of cavorting with me?'

Gabe smiled as he wrapped his hands round her waist and tugged her closer. 'Well, I think we have the house to ourselves for tonight, so how about a bit more cavorting?'

'Hmm, I could be persuaded.'

'Let me try to persuade you now.'

He bent his head down and kissed her. Immediately, that chemistry, that need for him ripped through her, as if it had been bubbling just below the surface all day and all it took was one kiss from him to ignite it again.

Gabe could sense it too as his hands tightened at her waist.

He suddenly snatched his mouth from hers and stared at her, his breathing heavy. 'I think we better take this back to my house.'

Pip nodded and Gabe grabbed her hand and walked out, past the reception and outside into the cold, which at least had the effect of cooling her cheeks, but not, it seemed, Gabe's passion as he walked as quickly as he could back towards his lodge. Pip had to jog to keep up with him and the faster she moved, the faster he walked, until they were both running back to his lodge. It would be clear to anyone watching what they were going to do, but Gabe didn't seem to care.

He pushed open the door, pulled her inside and closed the door behind her, pinning her up against it with his weight as he kissed her hard.

Without taking his lips from hers, his clever hands quickly removed her clothes as she helped him out of his jacket and shirt. Her nipples hardened against the feel of his smooth, velvety chest, the taste and smell of him invading all her senses.

When she was naked, his fingers slid between her legs and she moaned against his mouth as he very quickly brought her to a climax.

He pulled back slightly, staring at her as she came down from her high. He fumbled around with his trousers, releasing himself and dragging a condom out of his pocket.

God, she needed him inside her but she wanted to do something for him, as he had done for her. He was already rock hard and impressively erect as he tore at the condom wrapper.

She reached down and wrapped her hand around him. He froze, his breath catching in his throat. She had no idea what she was doing but she had watched films and read enough books to have some clue.

She ran her hand down his length and he let out a strangled groan. Keeping her eyes on his face to judge his reaction, she ran her hand back up to the top. His eyes were dark and apart from his heavy breathing he still hadn't moved.

Suddenly his hand gripped hers, holding it tighter around him. He moved her hand up and down showing her how he liked to be touched and after a few seconds he released her, bringing his mouth down on hers hard while she continued to stroke him.

But it wasn't long before he stopped her again, dragging her hand away. She clearly still wasn't doing it right even though his breathing was rapid.

'I'm sorry,' Pip muttered.

'Christ, don't be sorry, Pip,' Gabe said, quickly rolling the condom on. 'If you touched me any longer like that, I would have lost any control I'm desperately trying to cling on to.'

'Oh, I thought I was doing it wrong.'

'Believe me, you were doing everything right. Now put your arms around my neck.'

Pip quickly did as she was told and Gabe lifted her. She wrapped her legs around his hips and a second later he was buried deep inside her. He groaned with relief, his fingers tight under her bum as he started to move fast and hard against her. He shifted her higher so he was deeper, the angle suddenly hitting all those sweet spots, and she clung tighter to him as she quickly felt the climax building and then ripping through her with such ferocity that a second later she felt Gabe find his own release.

❄

Pip stared up at the man she loved as he lay on top of her. After they had made love against the door, Gabe had lit a fire and, under the glow of the flames and the twinkle of the fairy lights illuminating the otherwise dark room, he had started to slowly make love to her again. He was inside her now but seemed content to just lie there, happy to be connected to her in this way as he barely moved at all. Every time he moved against her, tiny ripples of pleasure moved through her body, which was wonderful and frustrating all at once.

He stared down at her as if in awe of her and she reached up to stroke his face. Almost as if he had forgotten they were in the middle of making love, her touch seemed to awaken that realisation in him and he started to slowly move, but he was in no rush; it was languid and slow as he lavished her with kisses, caressing her skin.

But as her orgasm had been bubbling beneath the surface for so long, it didn't take him long to send her over the edge, despite his slow administrations. He quickly followed, pulled out and rolled on his side, gathering her to his chest.

It was not possible to love this man more than she did. Everything felt more real, more powerful than it had twelve years before. She couldn't imagine ever not loving him or ever wanting to leave. This was her home now, with this incredible man and his beautiful daughter. As soon as she had that thought she couldn't help but smile. This was where she belonged, with this family, Winston and probably Blaze too. Excitement rushed through her like a great wave. This was where she wanted to be for the rest of her life. Although she would miss travelling around the world, there was nothing the world could offer her that could compete with the blissful happiness that she felt right now, lying in Gabe's arms.

It was too soon to tell him, though, she knew that. The next few days would be stressful for him and if he didn't yet feel the same she didn't want it to be awkward between them. She also had to figure out what she would do about her job. Travelling around the world was no longer an option, not unless Gabe and Wren came with her and she knew he wanted to make a home for Wren here. But she had to do something to contribute; she couldn't expect Gabe to support her for the rest of her life, and with no other job experience than her being a mystery guest for the last ten years and with no qualifications or training she didn't feel she had a lot to offer beyond her skill of helping to impregnate the reindeer.

Gabe caught her hand and entwined his fingers with hers, bringing her hand to his mouth and pressing light kisses across her knuckles and over her palm.

'What are you thinking?' he asked.

'About staying with you forever and what that would actually mean.'

He grinned hugely. 'It would mean you would make me the happiest man alive.'

She smiled. 'There are other things to consider though too.'

'Not for me.'

'What would I do here?'

'You could be my sex slave.'

Pip laughed.

'Why are you worried? I would take care of you.'

'I can't live like that, though.'

He frowned. 'With me taking care of you? Being reliant on someone else? Why is that so wrong?'

She stroked the tiny hairs at the back of his neck, soothingly. 'It's not that. I can't just live in this gorgeous house, eat all the lovely food and not give something back.'

'Why? Wren does. Mum and Dad do when they visit, you're part of my family. I'd give you whatever you need.'

'I'd need money, though.'

'What would you need money for?'

'Clothes, Christmas presents, birthday presents.'

'I'd give you money.'

'I don't want your money, that's the last thing I want. I'm not with you for that.'

'I know you're not, but I want to take care of you.' He smiled, sympathetically. 'You've always looked after yourself, I get that. And I know it will take a lot for you to understand that someone wants to take care of you, when you've never had that before, but let me be that person. I promise, I will never let you down.'

Pip frowned. It was going to take a lot of getting used to. 'I'll try.'

'And if you still need your own money, think about selling your photos to other hotels, or just sell them online. There'd be a real market for them. And I promise that's not just me being nice. I'll help you set up an online shop and just see how much you sell, I bet it'll be a lot.'

Pip nodded. 'OK, we'll give it a go.'

It seemed a push to think she could make real money from selling her photos, but she was willing to try anything if it meant she could stay here with Gabe for the rest of her life.

❄

Pip woke in the early hours of the morning, with the faint pink glow of the winter sunrise just touching the sky and a fully formed idea in her head. She was lying on Gabe's chest, with his arms tight around her. They had managed to move to his bed during the night, which she was glad for. The room was chilly but they were cosy wrapped up in each other's arms under the duvet.

She kissed his chest, wanting to share her idea with him but not wanting to wake him at the same time. He shifted beneath her, sensing she was awake.

He smiled when he saw her staring at him. 'Morning beautiful.'

'Hey, I have an idea.'

She saw the dark look of desire flicker in his eyes and she knew what kind of idea he was hoping for. She shifted to sit up out of his reach, straddling his hips. Although that did nothing to quell the arousal she could feel beneath her. He moved his hands to her hips, running his thumbs over her skin.

'Not that kind of idea.'

He laughed. 'Tell me your idea, let's see if it's better than mine.'

'I know how I can contribute to Stardust Lake Hotel. I can be your official photographer.'

He narrowed his eyes as he thought. 'In what sense? Taking those posed photos in front of the hotel name when the guests arrive?'

'No, absolutely not that. Natural photos. I would follow all our guests around the island as they go to the village, meet the reindeer, ride on the snowmobiles, go to the ice palace. It would be completely unobtrusive and not posed. I would just capture their enjoyment as they discover the delights of Juniper Island. At the end of their trip they could view all their photos and buy the ones they like. We could do some kind of deal – buy four get the fifth free or a CD with all their photos on for a set price. We can work out all the details later. But the guests could hire me too if they wanted to capture a particular moment or day, and there would be a set price for that too. The hotel would get fifty percent of any money that comes in and I'd get the other half, so I'd get a wage and have my own money and—'

'Hang on, it all sounded good until the percentage split. Fifty percent to the hotel? Do you have any business experience at all?'

She had thought that was a fair percentage, though she had just plucked the figure out of the air.

'We'd take five percent,' Gabe said in a manner that said there was to be no negotiation on that.

'Gabe, I might not know anything about business but I do know that five percent is ridiculously small. You would be providing me with customers and a place to sell my photos.'

'And you are doing all the hard work, providing the quality service and product. If you were to sell your photos on Etsy they would only charge three and half percent commission plus three percent transaction fee. As there would be printing costs for the photos and the cost of the CD if customers bought that, five percent is more than enough.'

'I want to pay more than that. I want to contribute towards my food and expenses.'

'I'm not taking your money off you, Pip. You will work hard to take those photos and if the customers like them enough to go and buy them then you should be the one that benefits from the money. Five percent. I'm not taking more than that.'

Pip opened her mouth to argue but Gabe sat up so they were nose to nose. 'I think it's a brilliant idea and it's something the hotel is just not offering, so that will be a huge help for us. I think the guests will love it too. I don't know how much business you will get, but if it proves successful we can look at the percentage split again in a year's time and re-evaluate if need be. That's if you're still here.'

'I think I want to stay.'

'You do? What about your amazing job travelling the world?'

'Turns out it's not that amazing when you haven't got anyone to share it with. This feels right with you. This feels more right than anything before in my life. I'm ready to stop running now.'

He smiled against her lips as he kissed her.

'I know Juniper Island hasn't got the skyscrapers and amazing restaurants of the big cities or the beaches and rainforests of other places around the world, but the food is pretty good and the views I think are…' Gabe trailed off as she put her fingers against his lips.

She traced her fingers down his neck and placed them over his heart. She looked back up into his eyes. 'Juniper Island has you and that's exactly where I want to be.'

He smiled.

'Now seeing as I have something very hard pressed into my bum, do you want to show me what your idea was? Let's see if I like it.'

He grinned and reached back to grab a condom. He lifted her and a few frustrating seconds later he was buried deep inside her.

He groaned, pressing his lips to her throat. As he moved against her, he leaned back and he stared into her eyes. For a brief moment, she could see real fear in his eyes, which made her feel slightly better about the fear she was feeling too. But it made her worried as well. What could she do to prove to him she was here for the long haul? Would he ever trust her enough to let her into his heart and let himself fall in love with her?

She wrapped her arms around his neck and kissed him softly. 'We belong together,' she whispered against his lips.

His hands tightened around her hips as he thrust into her harder and deeper. 'Christ Pip, I don't think I'll ever be able to let you go.'

She smiled. 'I don't want you to.'

❄

Pip sat on the sofa with her laptop on her lap. Gabe was in the shower and she had just finished the review for Stardust Lake Hotel. She read over it and smiled. It was the best review she had ever written – her affection for the island, the hotel and the tiny town shone from her words. Gabe would be delighted with this review when he saw it, even if he didn't know that it came from her. Anyone reading this would be booking their next holiday at Stardust Lake Hotel, keen to experience the beauty of the island themselves.

She scanned over it, tweaking a few words here and there, wanting to make sure it was perfect. Even though she knew that it was, she was struggling with actually sending it in. She bit her lip. Would this really be her last review? This had been her life for ten years, could she really walk away from it? She had made the resort on Juniper Island sound like paradise, a little haven in the snow, and she knew that for her it was. She had been moving on all her life because she had no home, but this was home for her now and she knew it always would be.

Pip opened up an email and attached the review. Upstairs, she heard Gabe get out of the shower and walk to the bedroom. She started writing an email to Wendy. It started in the usual way:

Please find attached my review for Stardust Lake Hotel and some photos you may wish to use...

Pip stared at the words and then a smile grew on her face as she continued to write.

It is with great regret that this will be my last review for The Tree of Life *magazine and I am hereby giving formal notice of termination of my employment with immediate effect.*

I'd like to thank you for the wonderful opportunities you have given me over the years. I have enjoyed my time with your magazine immensely, but due to personal reasons I will no longer be able to continue my employment.

Kind regards

Piper Chesterfield

Pip read it through and laughed. She suddenly felt free and liberated. She knew, unequivocally, that she was doing the right thing and telling Gabe that she was handing in her notice would be a sure sign that she wasn't going to run away again.

Her fingers hovered over the send button, but she knew that she owed Wendy more than a formal email.

She grabbed her phone and dialled her number.

'*Tree of Life*, Wendy Nagle speaking.'

'Hi Wendy, it's Pip, um, Piper.'

'Hey honey, how's it all going?'

Just then Gabe came running down the stairs. 'You ready to go over for breakfast… Oh sorry, I didn't realise you were on the phone.'

Pip covered the phone. 'I'll meet you over there, I won't be long.'

Gabe nodded and with a slight frown of confusion he left her alone.

'Hey, you still there?' Wendy said.

'Yes, I'm here, sorry. I've written the review.'

Wendy laughed. 'And?' Clearly she wanted more information than that.

'And… I'm going to stay here.'

'That's good, spend your sabbatical getting lots of hot sex from your lovely man. Can't think of a better way to spend your sabbatical than that.'

'I'm staying here for good, Wendy. I've just written out my notice. I'm sending it over with the review.'

There was silence from the other end of the phone and when Wendy spoke, the jovial, playful tone had gone.

'Are you sure you know what you're doing? This is happening so fast.'

'I love him. I think I always have. You have no idea how happy I feel right now. I know I'm doing the right thing.'

There was another long pause from Wendy. 'You know, I got engaged to Jamie a week after we first met. We married four weeks later. Everyone said that it would never last, that we were crazy. Next month we celebrate our fortieth anniversary. When you know, you just know. I can tell by your voice, how happy you are. Hold onto that happiness and never let it go.'

Pip smiled. 'Thank you. I'm sorry to let you down.'

'Don't worry about that. Arsehole Marcus won't be happy, but then he isn't happy about most things. I will miss our chats, though.'

'Well, they don't have to stop. I'm sorry I never took the time to get to know you properly before. If you fancied celebrating your anniversary at Stardust Lake Hotel next month, I bet I could get you a discount.'

'I'd love that. It would be great to finally meet you in person. Let me speak to my husband and I'll let you know. Piper, I'm really happy for you.'

'Thank you and I look forward to meeting you too.'

She ended the call, addressed the email to Wendy and Marcus and pressed send before she could change her mind. She waited for the fear and doubt to hit her, but it didn't. It was the best decision she had ever made.

❄

Gabe watched Pip playing with Wren as he finished off breakfast with his parents. It looked like it was some kind of *Frozen*-related game and he smiled as Pip seemed perfectly accepting of this new role in her life.

The island looked peaceful now, basking in the early-morning sunshine. Fresh snow had fallen overnight, dusting the hills with a new sparkling blanket. The breakfast room was almost empty, the other staff having already been and gone. The plane was leaving shortly to collect the first lot of guests. This was the quiet before the storm.

'How's it going?' his mum asked, gently.

Gabe dragged his eyes from Pip to look at his mum, but it was very obvious that his mum was asking about his relationship with Pip and not anything to do with the hotel.

Gabe sighed and his mum took his hand. 'You're falling in love with her, aren't you?'

He nodded. 'Yes. I thought I could hold back, try to protect myself from getting hurt, but I never stopped loving her and now she's here I'm falling even more in love with her than I was before.'

'She loves you too, any idiot can see that.'

'I'm not so sure.' He lowered his voice even though Pip was on the other side of the room. 'I don't know what this is for her. I've offered her a home, stability, even a ready-made family, which she has never had before. The sex is great, we're good friends. I wonder if it can ever be any more than that for her.'

'You don't trust her to love you back.'

'She says she wants to stay, but is she staying because of all that or because she loves me? I think at the moment I'm still trying not to get too excited about her being here because I know in my heart that if she doesn't love me, no amount of me being able to provide for her, no matter how much I love her and shower her with affection, none of that will be enough to make her stay.'

'You have to put aside this fear of losing her, because if you can't show her you trust her then you will push her away,' his mum said.

His dad nodded. 'I know she broke your heart the last time, but that was circumstances that were really out of her control. She's grown up now, she's not going to run away again. If you love her, tell her and be confident that what you both have will be enough to make her fall in love with you too.'

Gabe nodded, knowing that he had to put aside his fears once and for all.

Pip came over with Wren swinging from her hand.

'I better get to the airport so I can take some photos of the guests on their flight.'

Gabe nodded. 'Stephen is going to pick you up.'

Pip hesitated for a moment, clearly wondering whether to kiss him goodbye in front of his parents and members of staff.

He quickly stood up and kissed her softly on the forehead and briefly on the lips and she blushed with happiness.

He would do everything in his power to show her what it meant to be involved in a loving relationship and just hope it was enough.

❄ Chapter 19 ❄

Pip stood at the bottom of the steps of the plane with Stephen, waiting for the guests to board. Stephen looked smart as always in his long green coat and top hat. Pip had dressed as smartly as she could for the occasion, but she wondered if she should ask Gabe if she could have some kind of uniform to present a unified front.

She stamped her feet with the cold and blew into her hands. She realised she was worried about the guests, though Stephen seemed completely unaffected.

'Aren't you nervous?' Pip asked.

Stephen shook his head. He seemed unruffled about most things. 'Why would I be nervous?'

'Because these guests could be difficult, or they might not like it and they could tell their friends they don't like it. Some of them are journalists and they'll write about us in their papers or magazines. Then there's this Mr Black to consider; he could make or break us. I just want this to work for Gabe.'

Stephen nodded. 'Worrying about those things isn't going to change the situation. So we might as well try to enjoy it. There will be teething problems, there always is in these circumstances. But I also know that Gabe and Neve have worked their socks off to get everything ready, they both have a lot of experience in this area and I trust them to be able to pull it off. We can't change what Mr Black thinks of us. We can just give all our guests as enjoyable a time as we possibly can and hope for the best.'

Pip smiled at Stephen's laidback attitude. 'I'll try to take a leaf out of your book.'

Stephen nodded his head towards the steps and Pip glanced over as the first guests came down them. They were a young family, the parents maybe early thirties with a boy of five or six holding the dad's hand and a little girl of two or three fast asleep in her mum's arms. The little boy looked entranced by the red plane and Pip quickly fired off a few shots of him and the family as they took in the plane and Stephen.

'Good morning, Mr and Mrs Chambers, Master Nate, I'm Stephen and I'm going to be your flight attendant today. This is Piper Chesterfield, she is our official photographer for Stardust Lake Hotel. She'll be taking some photos of you during the course of your stay.'

Pip blinked. It had been a long time since she had been Pip, but just a few short days with Gabe and his family and she had so easily assumed that identity again that she had almost forgotten her identity of Piper. To be referred to as such almost seemed alien now.

Charmed by Stephen's easy manner, they all smiled.

Mikael suddenly appeared by Pip's side and offered to take the hand luggage from the family. She hadn't realised when she had first met Mikael that he was the pilot for Juniper Island Airlines. Mikael escorted them aboard where Pip knew that Elise and Carter, two teens from the village, were waiting to welcome the guests with mulled wine and hot chocolates. Everything was in place and Stephen was right, she had to learn to relax.

The next guest who came down the stairs was on her own. She was in her late forties and dressed in a suit that was too big for her. She scowled up at the sky as tiny little snowflakes danced and twirled through the air. She was obviously one of the journalists who had been told to come and cover the opening, but she looked like she wanted to be anywhere but here. Pip let her camera fall round her neck. The last thing she wanted was to take a photo of someone when they were miserable and probably tired. That would not be a good memory for her. Though she vowed she would get at least one natural smile out of her before she left the island.

'Good morning, Mrs Hughes. Welcome to Juniper Island Airlines. I'm Stephen and I will be your flight attendant today. This is—'

'Yeah whatever, can you let me get on the plane and out of this horrible weather rather than making me greet people I have no interest in getting to know,' Mrs Hughes said.

Pip was unable to stop her jaw from falling open in shock, though, yet again, Stephen seemed unbothered.

'Of course, Mrs Hughes, right this way.'

Stephen offered out his hand for her bag and took it from her and she stormed up the stairs as Mikael came rushing down them to escort her up.

Pip waited until the lovely Mrs Hughes was inside and out of earshot before she spoke.

'How rude.'

Stephen shrugged. 'The world is made up of rude people; fortunately the world is also made up of lovely people. You didn't take her picture?'

'There didn't seem much point. Besides, I thought her sour face might break the camera.'

The next guests were a young couple who were obviously still in that honeymoon stage of being head over heels in love with each other. It was lovely to see. The man was holding the girl's hand and staring at her as if he was completely and utterly in love with her, as if he wasn't aware of anyone else in the world but her. Pip fired off a few shots of them looking at each other, giggling at some private joke before they finally noticed Stephen and the plane.

'Good morning, Mr Richards and Miss Brown,' Stephen said. 'Welcome to Juniper Island Airlines.'

Stephen introduced himself and Pip and then Mr Richards escorted his girlfriend onto the plane. Pip couldn't help smiling at them.

The next couple were American, Pip could hear them talking as they came down the steps. The couple were probably close to retirement. The woman clearly thought the plane and Stephen were really quaint and cute while the man was taking lots of photos himself. Pip fired off a few shots of them both.

'Welcome to Juniper Island Airlines, Mr and Mrs Weatherby. I'm Stephen, I'm your flight attendant today, and this is Piper Chesterfield, our photographer.'

Mr Weatherby's eyes lit up at the prospect of a fellow photographer. 'What kind of camera is that?'

Pip felt embarrassed at being labelled as a professional photographer when this guy clearly knew his stuff. Just one look at his camera with his telephoto lens had Pip green with envy. She had always wanted to invest in some decent photographic equipment, but as she always had to travel light it wasn't really a luxury she could afford or practically take with her.

'It's just a Lumix,' Pip said, shyly.

'Lumix cameras are great, I love them,' Mr Weatherby said.

'I've got some great photos from this over the years,' Pip said, growing in confidence under his approval.

'What kind of stuff do you like to take pictures of? Landscapes, nature, architecture?'

'Oh, all of it. But I think my favourite thing to take is people. You can really capture the essence of a place from its people and how tourists engage and interact with the place too.'

Mr Weatherby smiled. 'I think so too.'

'Juniper Island is a beautiful place, I'm sure you will be able to take a lot of stunning photos here.'

'I hope so, we both want to see the ponies.'

'Oh, there are lots of them here wandering free around the island. Most of them are very tame and will be very obliging when it comes to having their photos taken.'

Mikael appeared then and helped them on board with their carry-on bags.

The next guests arrived through a side door with a member of the airport crew. Pip looked over as a girl of eleven years old wheeled herself to the foot of the steps in her wheelchair and a woman, presumably her mum, followed carrying a few bags.

'Hello Poppy and Mrs Matthews,' Stephen said before introducing himself and Pip.

'This plane looks fab,' Poppy said. 'And are we staying in a real glass igloo?'

Stephen consulted his clipboard quickly. 'Yes you are. The view is quite spectacular, I'm sure you'll love it.'

Mikael came back down the stairs and, between him and the airport crewman, they lifted Poppy and her wheelchair up the steps and into the plane as Poppy talked to them both throughout the whole thing.

A few more guests arrived, one with a daughter the same age as Wren, one elderly couple and one man on his own.

Pip and Stephen got on the plane and Stephen got to work making sure everyone had drinks and mince pies. She took some more photos of the guests as they started to warm to their surroundings. It was a strange mix of people who were there to genuinely enjoy it and journos who were there to report on the place. Pip just hoped that Stardust Lake Hotel would capture all their hearts as it had captured hers.

❄

By lunchtime all of the guests had arrived. Gabe had met most of the guests personally and although some of the journalists were obviously there only to review the place, everyone had seemed charmed by the little log cabins, open fires and the beauty of the island. There had been one guest, Mrs Hughes, who had complained about a few things, but that was always to be expected. He still had no idea who the dreaded Mr Black was, but as everyone seemed to be enjoying themselves there was no point worrying about it too much.

The one thing he was worried about was Neve. He watched her get up from the lunch table and run to the toilet holding her mouth. She was sick and had been for several days. She was trying to hide it, but she wasn't eating her food and this hadn't been the first time he'd seen her run to the toilet to throw up. Thankfully Adam was here to help support her and lighten her workload a little, but despite Gabe's insistence that she take a few days off, she refused to do so and it just made him so worried. The village doctor was away on holiday and wouldn't be back till after Christmas. He wanted Neve to visit the doctor on one of the other islands, but she kept saying she didn't have time. He'd offered to pay for a doctor to come out to the island, but Neve didn't want that either. Thankfully with their mum and dad here, they might persuade her to see a doctor or at the very least take a few days off to recover.

Gabe couldn't help wondering if the stress over the whole Oakley thing was at the heart of the sickness. He knew how painful and upsetting it was to try to get over a broken heart and he was so tempted to call Oakley and get him to come here and sort things out between them. If ever there was a couple that were meant to be together, it was Neve and Oakley. As far as he could see they should never have broken up in the first place.

He understood that Neve was scared, but he also understood what it meant to love someone completely and what it felt like when that love ended. If Neve and Oakley were meant to be together then they should try to find a way to make it work.

Adam came and sat opposite him with a cup of coffee in his hand.

'She's not well, is she?'

Gabe shook his head.

Adam took a sip of his coffee. 'I appreciate the fact that you might not want to tell people, but if she's pregnant then I need to know.'

Gabe nearly choked on his lunch. 'Pregnant? Christ, that thought never even occurred to me. If she is, she certainly hasn't mentioned anything to me.'

Adam nodded thoughtfully. 'I only ask because my sister was exactly the same way when she was pregnant with her first child, off her food, certain smells set her off. It's probably nothing more than stomach flu though.'

Gabe stared at his plate and then back at Adam. 'It would actually be something of a relief if she was pregnant. At least I wouldn't be worried about her being sick because she had contracted some awful disease. What a mess though, if she is.'

'I take it her and Oakley are no longer together?'

'She broke it off with him. By all accounts the poor boy is heartbroken.'

Adam shook his head. 'She's a fool. She's crazy in love with him. What possible reason would be good enough to end it?'

'I don't know. I think she thought he meant more to her than she did to him and wanted to get out before she fell completely in love with him. Although it's too late for that. I don't understand it. They were crazy for each other, any fool could see that.'

Adam sighed.

'I'm glad you're here,' Gabe said. 'She really needs you right now.'

'I'm glad I'm here too, maybe I can talk some sense into her.'

'Hopefully you can because lord knows I've tried.'

Adam finished his coffee. 'I'll do my best.' He nodded subtly in the direction of Neve as she came back from the toilet. 'Any problems or issues I need to be aware of in the hotel?'

Gabe shook his head. 'Everything seems to be going like clockwork.'

Adam nodded and stood up to leave, snagging Neve's arm on the way out.

Gabe attempted to finish his lunch but couldn't. If Neve was pregnant that wouldn't fit in with her grand plan for life. But then children never came to order. He'd never wanted children himself until Wren came along and now he wouldn't change a single thing. It would be hard for Neve as a single mum but he would support and help her, just like she'd supported him when Wren had arrived. Hell, if she was pregnant, Gabe would phone Oakley and tell him to get his arse on the next plane and come and sort things out with Neve. There was no way Oakley would leave her to raise his kid alone and he had a right to know. Of course all this worrying could be completely unnecessary, but if she was pregnant she would surely have to tell him at some point. Preferably sooner rather than later.

'Daddy!'

He smiled as his daughter made her presence known, her little feet running across the dining room. He turned and swung her up in his arms and she placed tiny little kisses across his face. 'Hello Princess, have you had a good morning with Nanny and Pops?'

Wren nodded. 'I've shown them the reindeer and the puppies and they really want to go to the ice palace. Can I go with them, Daddy?'

'No, I want to take you on Christmas Eve, that's the day after tomorrow, so you don't have long to wait.'

Wren pouted a little but seemed to accept it. His mum and dad came to sit with him.

'How's your morning been? I hope Wren hasn't forced you to watch *Frozen* too many times?'

His dad laughed. 'We haven't seen it yet today, but Wren was kind enough to sing us a few of her favourite songs…several times.'

Gabe sat Wren down in the chair next to him and kissed her head. 'Well, that sounds very nice. What are you going to have for lunch?'

'Do they have fish fingers today?'

'I'm not sure but I bet Chef would do them for you if you were to ask him nicely. I've got to go and send some emails, but I'll be back soon.'

Wren's face fell. 'Are you not having lunch with me?'

'No, but I'm spending the rest of the day with you. As soon as you've finished your lunch, me, you, Nanny and Pops will spend the rest of the day together.'

'The whole day?' Wren grinned.

'Yes.'

'And Pip too?'

'We'll see Pip tonight, but I think she'll be busy today.'

Wren frowned. 'I like spending time with Pip.'

'I do too. Hopefully she might stay with us a bit longer and we'll get to spend a lot more time with her.'

'I want Pip to stay forever.'

'I want that too, but it might not work out that way. Go and ask Chef if you can have fish fingers and I'll see you as soon as you've finished lunch.'

Wren wriggled down from her chair and ran off to the kitchen door.

'I'll see you guys shortly,' Gabe said to his parents and stood up to leave.

As he was leaving the restaurant, Pip was walking in. She was positively beaming and it filled his heart to see.

'Have you enjoyed taking photos today?'

'It's been brilliant. I think I've found my niche in life, this is what I'm supposed to do.'

He smiled, longing to reach out and touch her. But although he was quite happy to kiss her in front of the staff, he knew it would be unprofessional to do so in front of the guests who were starting to filter in for lunch.

'Do you have five minutes?'

Pip nodded. 'Yes, just five minutes, though. I need to grab a very quick lunch before a lot of the guests go down to the ice palace this afternoon.'

'Come up to my office.'

Pip frowned in confusion but followed him up to his office anyway. He stepped inside, leaned round her to close the door, then kissed her hard. She let out a gasp of shock for a second before she kissed him back.

There was something so wonderful about just kissing her, her taste, her smell, her warmth, the fact that she obviously enjoyed it as much he did. Her kisses were so sweet and innocent and her obvious affection for him completely disarmed him.

He groaned as he pulled away, leaning his forehead against hers and holding her close.

'Did you just bring me up to your office so you could kiss me?'

'I'm not even going to deny it. I couldn't kiss you downstairs in front of all the guests, certainly not in the way I wanted to kiss you and I couldn't not kiss you. You've been gone for just a few hours and I missed you already.'

He cringed inwardly at how pathetic he sounded. He was trying to play it cool with her, to not let on how he was feeling, trying to hold back from falling in love with her, but he was failing miserably. He didn't want to scare her off either with being too full on. But weirdly she didn't seem bothered by his need for her.

'I missed you too. So we have the fireworks and carnival after dinner, but maybe, after we've put Wren to bed, you can show me just how much you miss me then.'

He grinned. 'I look forward to it.'

'I better go. I'll see you at dinner?'

He nodded, kissed her again briefly this time and then watched her leave. He sat down at his desk and opened up his email account. He quickly fired off one email and had just opened up a new one when Neve walked in.

'Hey, how are you feeling?' Gabe asked.

'I'm fine. Please stop worrying about me. And I'd appreciate it if you didn't send Adam to sniff around me as well.'

'He's worried too.'

'There's no need. I'm fine.' She sat down in the chair opposite his desk and his eyes immediately found her stomach. Was it any bigger? It still looked flat to him.

'Can you remember which holiday company Pip said she worked for?' Neve said, snagging his attention away from what could possibly be his niece or nephew.

'I can't remember. Was it Ocean View?'

'That's what I thought she said.'

'Why do you ask?' Gabe asked.

'Because I've just been in touch with Ocean View about their new brochures and our prices and I told them their photographer was here. I asked them for which brochure they were considering using the photos she's taking and they didn't know anything about her. They said they didn't have any photographers out at the moment and they didn't know any photographers under her name.'

'Well that's weird. Maybe it was Ocean Wave not View.'

'Oh maybe,' Neve said.

'Or Seaview? There's a holiday company called Seaview, isn't there?' Gabe suggested. 'Maybe we got them confused. Or Pip got confused. She's freelance and she said she works for lots of different companies. If she was working for Ocean View last week and this week she's working for Ocean Wave she might have given us the wrong name by mistake.'

'Maybe. Though that doesn't explain how Ocean View hadn't even heard of her.'

'Well it does, if they hire her through an agency. They might not actually have any dealings direct with her.'

'That's true,' Neve said.

'I'll ask her tonight.'

'OK. I just want to make sure that whoever she is with has the most current information. Especially if she intends to quit her job. I want to make sure they have all the photos and information before she leaves.'

'Is she quitting her job?'

'Well, it sounded like she was. When we talked about her being our photographer this morning, it sounded like it was a permanent thing for her.'

'She says she wants to stay but…' Gabe trailed off.

'You don't believe she will?'

'I'm just not sure it will be enough for her. The island, life as a step-mum, me. I don't want her to regret giving up that glamorous life of travelling the world for me. Every time she speaks about her job, she is filled with so much excitement and happiness about her travels and I'm just not sure she will feel the same way about staying here.'

'If she loves you, she'd never regret it.'

'I suppose that's the trouble, I don't know whether she does.'

'Giving up that life to stay here is a big change for her. If she is already putting the wheels in motion to make that change happen after just a few days, I'd say the chances of her already falling in love with you are pretty high. Give her a chance.

I know I was against the two of you getting together at the start, but she wants this to work as much as you do.'

Gabe nodded. He knew she was right.

Neve stood up. 'Find out who she works for because with talent like hers, whoever she walks away from is going to be pretty pissed off at losing her. If they know they are losing her to us, they might be even more annoyed. I'd like to pre-empt that if I can.'

'She's freelance, I wouldn't think they'd be that bothered. Sure, she has a ton of talent, but there must be hundreds of freelance photographers out there that can step into her shoes.'

Neve opened her mouth to protest and, not wanting to cause her any more stress, he held up his hand to stop her. 'I'll find out.'

'Thank you.'

❄ Chapter 20 ❄

Gabe walked through the village with Wren sitting on his shoulders. There was a wonderful hum about the place as the guests moved from shop to shop, their arms filled with bags of goodies they had bought or their hands filled with sweets or cakes. With only three days until Christmas, people were obviously buying last-minute gifts or treats for the big day.

Everyone seemed happy and he knew the villagers must have already had a roaring trade on their first day.

The only fly in the ointment had been Mrs Hughes whose list of complaints had been steadily getting longer. The fact that there wasn't a swimming pool had been high up on her list of complaints. What did she expect them to do, magic one out of the air? She didn't like the pillows, she wasn't keen on the tree decorations in her lodge and she didn't appreciate that there was so much snow.

He had to give credit to Cora, Iris and Jake who had dealt with her complaints professionally and courteously, but he knew, from his experience in his other hotels, that mystery guests liked to complain about ridiculous things to see how the hotel staff dealt with the complaints. It made him wonder. Could Mrs Hughes be the mysterious Mr Black? It had never really occurred to him before that Mr Black could in fact be a woman. But it would explain why she was so intent on finding fault with everything.

She had even marched up to him not two minutes before, when she could clearly see he was playing with Wren, and complained about the temperature of the hot chocolate. He had apologised and said he would look into it even though he had no intention of doing any such thing.

'Daddy, why was that woman shouting at you?' Wren said, leaning into his head.

'Sometimes when someone is sad all their life, they forget how to be happy. Instead of enjoying the good things they look for the bad.'

Wren clearly thought about this for a second. 'Is Mrs Hughes sad, Daddy?'

'Yes, I think she might be.'

'Do you think we can make her happy again?'

'I hope so, Princess.'

'Can we get some churros with chocolate sauce?'

'Of course we can.'

'I love churros, they make me happy.'

'They make me happy too.'

Gabe smiled at her simplistic view on life. Who needed to be sad when there were churros to be had?

He walked into the churro and doughnut shop and Wren chatted happily to Maryline, the owner of the shop, while they were being served and then they walked back out onto the street just as his mum and dad walked out of the shop opposite, their arms filled with bags and boxes.

'Are you two buying all the stock from the whole village? There'll be nothing left,' Gabe laughed.

'Oh, shush, you, this is just a few things. Everything is so lovely, I can't resist,' his mum said.

'Gabe, this place looks so wonderful,' his dad said. 'Your grandad would be so proud of what you've achieved here, continuing his legacy like this. The village, the little lodges, the glass igloos. I think he would have really loved it.'

His mum nodded. 'It's so lovely. When you first said you were going to take over the hotel, I had no idea how you could possibly make it better, apart from a few repairs. I honestly didn't expect anything like this. All these people will tell all their friends and family about what a wonderful place this is. I imagine you'll be sold out for months and that's something your grandad never achieved.'

'Thank you, I'm so pleased you both like it. We spent so much time here when I was a child, I didn't want to damage those memories and I certainly didn't want to do anything that would ruin the island. I hope Grandad would have liked what we've done too,' Gabe said.

'I'm sure he would.'

Wren suddenly ran from Gabe's side and disappeared into the crowd of people. His heart leapt as she vanished from his sight and he quickly ran after her.

When he pushed his way through a few of the guests he saw her approaching Mrs Hughes. He ran over to stop her just as Mrs Hughes turned round at the sound of Wren calling her name.

'Mrs Hughes, would you like a churro?' Wren asked, offering up the cup of sticky treats.

Mrs Hughes stared at Wren in surprise.

'They make me happy,' Wren explained. 'And I thought they might make you happy too.'

Oh crap. He hurried over to apologise for his daughter just as Mrs Hughes helped herself to a churro.

'Make sure you get one covered in chocolate sauce, those are the best ones,' Wren said.

Mrs Hughes chose carefully and popped it in her mouth. She chewed for a second and then swallowed.

'Thank you,' she said and just before she turned and walked away, he was sure he saw her smile. Maybe Wren was right, maybe everything could be fixed with a chocolate-covered churro.

He knelt down in front of his daughter. 'That was very kind of you.'

Wren smiled as she pulled a churro out the pot to eat herself.

'But don't run off when there are lots of people around. I don't want to lose you.'

'Are you afraid of getting lost, Daddy?'

'I would be lost without you.'

Wren smiled. 'I'll hold your hand then, Daddy, then you can't get lost.'

Gabe didn't know whether to laugh or sigh that Wren had completely misunderstood, but with Wren holding his hand the problem was solved regardless.

Suddenly there were shouts and laughter from the end of the village. He stood up, taking Wren's hand and looked over towards the commotion.

Leo and his gang of reprobates were walking through the village, clearly not fazed by the sheer number of people out on the street. Leo was flicking evil glares at anyone he walked past. People were pointing and laughing and taking pictures as the ponies looked through the shop windows, clearly looking for something they could steal.

Gabe walked over, determined to shoo the ponies out of the village, despite the fact that the guests clearly thought they were hilarious. But before he could get close, Leo spotted a likely victim. Emma Brown and her boyfriend Anthony Richards stepped out of a shop, each holding a pancake. And before they could take a bite Leo ran up and snatched the pancake from Emma's hand and ran off with it in his mouth.

'Hey!' Emma shouted after Leo's retreating back while the other guests laughed, some people filming the whole debacle on their phones. Another of Leo's cohorts suddenly snatched a bag of sweets from someone else's hand and then, at a gleeful whinny from Leo, all the other ponies ran out the village after him, clearly to share the illegal contraband.

Gabe sighed as he walked up to the guests who had been mugged so he could reimburse them. Thankfully they all seemed to see the funny side, but clearly it had been too soon to assume everything was going smoothly.

❄

'The first day seems to have gone relatively without a hitch,' Pip said as she sat down to dinner with Gabe, Wren and his parents that evening. 'Well, I certainly didn't spot any problems. I know we have the grand opening after dinner but I can't foresee any difficulties.'

Pip exchanged a smile with Gabe as Wren climbed onto Pip's lap and carried on colouring in a *Frozen* picture. Wren had accepted her so easily into their life that Pip couldn't help feeling touched by it. She squeezed her tight and kissed the top of her head, love for her unfurling in her chest. Pip watched as Wren coloured in Elsa's blonde hair and then coloured the eyes in the same gold colour. It warmed her from the inside. 'What are you having for your dinner, honey?'

'Fish fingers,' Wren declared.

'No you're not,' Gabe said. 'You had that for your lunch.'

Wren pouted and Pip laughed.

'What are you having, Pip?' Wren asked.

Pip grabbed the menu and gave it a once-over. 'Mushroom soup to start, pasta carbonara and crème brûlée.'

Gabe went very still next to her.

'I'll have that too,' Wren declared.

'Good choice,' Pip said, then looked up to talk to Gabe's parents. 'Did you guys have a good day? Did Gabe take you down to the village?'

'He did,' Lizzie said. 'It's so wonderful down there. All the shopkeepers are so lovely and talented. The guests loved it. So many of them came back to the lodge with their arms filled with purchases. I think it's going to be very successful. It's so different to how it was before. We haven't been here for years and the whole island was almost in ruins, but it looks fantastic now.'

'Leo came to the village too, didn't he, Daddy? He stole a pancake from one of the guests. It was so funny.'

Pip looked over at Gabe. 'Did you have pony trouble?'

'A little. Luckily it was only a pancake and a bag of sweets from someone else. The guests thought it was hilarious. I bought them replacements and Luke came down and brought the ponies' favourite food to the trees outside the village to encourage them away from the shops, but I think we're going to have to come up with a more permanent solution to keep them out of the village from now on. We may have to fence the village in and have cattle grids over the roads. I think the villagers will be happy with that solution too, as they've all been terrorised by Leo and his gang at some point.'

'I still think it's hilarious that these tiny ponies are terrorising everyone.'

The waiter came and took their order and again Pip could feel the tension from Gabe when Pip told the waiter what she wanted. The waiter left and Pip looked at Gabe in confusion.

'That's an odd choice of dinner.'

Pip frowned. 'Is it?'

Gabe stared at her for a moment and then clearly changed the subject. 'Are you looking forward to the fireworks, Wren?'

Wren nodded and clapped her hands. 'I love fireworks.'

Pip turned her attention to Wren, knowing something was wrong, though she didn't know what.

❄

Pip stood opposite the line of guests as they all waited excitedly for the carnival procession to begin. The start time of the procession had been put back half an hour and Pip didn't know why and now it seemed it was more than ten minutes later than the new time too. She just hoped that everything was OK and nothing had gone wrong. She hadn't seen Gabe since dinner, and Adam and Neve were nowhere to be seen, so she couldn't ask them. The other staff who had been rushing around giving out drinks and cookies to the kids didn't know anything either. The guests looked happy enough though. They had all been plied with oversized hot chocolates in cardboard cups, which were helping to keep them warm. The hotel staff had made a temporary barricade for the guests to stand behind and they stood there now, stamping their feet and cupping their hot drinks. The excitement among the children especially was almost palpable and Pip took a few photos of them all as they waited.

Wren was playing opposite with Chester and they were chasing each other around and giggling uncontrollably as Boris and Mikael watched over them.

Suddenly music and singing could be heard and everyone looked around excitedly waiting to see the start of the procession. Pip took a few more photos of the guests, their excitement and happiness completely visible on their faces. It seemed even Mrs Hughes was looking forward to the event.

From around the back of the hotel two fire-breathers appeared, blowing arcs of fire into the dark night sky. The crowd predictably *oohed* with wonder and Pip momentarily transferred her camera lens to the fire-breathers. They were dressed all in gold with red and orange ribbons trailing from their arms and legs. Following close behind them were jugglers throwing clubs of fire into the air. It was magnificent. As they moved along in front of the guests, Pip took more photos of the performers and everyone's reactions to them.

The dancers were next, some ballet, some ballroom dancers, interspersed with more contemporary street-dancing, which involved lots of somersaults and throwing each other around. They were all dressed in emerald green outfits that sparkled in the light of the lanterns that lined the path, and somehow, though there was this mix of dance styles, it all blended together into a beautiful and seamless performance.

Next came a choir made up of several people from the village, the oldest members of the village right down to the youngest, all dressed as angelic choir members. They walked along in their white robes, carrying candle-lit lanterns, singing 'Silent Night', and Pip was stunned by their voices; the rendition was flawless. They stopped in front of the guests and stood until they had sung the last soulful note. But as Pip was smiling at the simplicity of their performance they suddenly all ripped off their choir robes, revealing glittering red clothes underneath, and launched into a rocking, jiving version of 'All I Want for Christmas Is You'. The guests lapped it up, clapping and dancing and laughing as the older members of the village danced as well as the younger ones. It was perfect, catering for all tastes in one performance.

More dancers followed on after the choir singers had moved off, this time dressed entirely in silver, and dancing with illuminated snowflakes. Some of the snowflakes were giant in size and some of them tiny, and the dancers were juggling or throwing them between them.

Four stilt-walkers came after them, two couples waltzing around each other despite the fact that they were balanced on six-foot poles of wood no more than a couple of inches wide. The men wore long black suit trousers that covered the whole stilts and the women were beautifully dressed in elegant ball gowns that almost touched the floor. It was utterly mesmerising.

Some of the villagers dressed as elves, complete with stripy red and white tights and pointy green shoes, followed after the stilt-walkers, each leading a tiny Shetland pony that had plumes of red, gold and green feathers on its head. The guests *oohed* and *aahed* again, the tiny ponies getting the loudest claps and cheers of the night so far.

The elves and ponies were followed by Santa on his sleigh being drawn by all nine reindeer in their shiny red harnesses. It was quite spectacular and the children all squealed and cheered as they watched him glide past, waving and giving the obligatory *ho, ho, ho*.

As the procession came to an end and the guests started following it down the path towards the ice palace, Pip noticed Gabe standing on top of the steps leading into the hotel reception area.

Gabe hoisted Wren on top of his shoulders as he walked past Mikael and Boris and came down to join her while they followed the guests down the hill.

'That was incredible,' Pip said.

'It was all co-ordinated by some big theatre producer. She flew up here a few weeks ago to go through a trial run with the villagers, although we hadn't seen how the procession would look complete with all the performers – this was the first time they did it all together.'

'It worked so well, the guests loved it. I even saw Mrs Hughes smile.'

'Well, that is a victory.'

'Did you enjoy it, Wren?' Pip asked, though the little girl's eyes were shining bright, her cheeks flushed pink with excitement. She was bouncing up and down on her dad's shoulders with a huge smile on her face. Pip didn't really need to ask.

'It was beautiful,' Wren said. 'And now we get to see Elsa's palace too.'

'Just the outside, Princess, we'll see the inside on Christmas Eve, that's just two days away.'

For once, Wren didn't seem that bothered by not being able to see it right away; obviously the excitement of the procession was still running through her veins.

The crowd just ahead of them parted slightly and for a brief moment Pip saw Luke walking with Audrey. From the way she was looking at him as he talked to her, it was quite clear she adored him. Pip took a few photos of them. If this was going to turn into something then it would be nice to record it from the beginning.

'I got some great photos,' Pip said as she let her camera fall round her neck. 'I took some of the guests and the performers. I think you could use most of them on your website too.'

'Would you use any of them for the travel company you work for?' Gabe asked.

Pip cringed a little. That lie was going to keep tripping her up. She knew she would have to come clean with it at some point, but she didn't like the idea of rocking the boat when everything was so new and fragile between them.

'Yes, I'll send it to them, though there's no guarantee that they'll use it.'

'Which company was it you said you worked for?' Gabe asked and the tone of his voice was not as casual as he clearly hoped it would be.

'Ocean View,' Pip said. 'Though I don't work for them any more, or anyone in fact, I handed my notice in this morning.'

'It's funny, Neve said she contacted Ocean View today and they didn't know anything about you.'

Pip frowned that he had completely missed the part where she had said she'd resigned, before registering that he had caught her in her lie.

'Oh, I always get confused which company has sent me where, I just go where I'm sent by the freelance agency I'm signed with. I send the photos to the agency too and they send them on, I don't really have any dealings with the travel companies directly.'

'That's what I said to Neve, that you'd probably got confused. I told her you wouldn't lie to us.'

He looked at her and she felt her stomach clench with guilt. It was such a tiny lie that didn't mean anything, but she knew she had to tell him the truth. However, with the excitement of the carnival and with Wren enjoying the evening's entertainment, now didn't seem like the right time.

'Look, Daddy, there's the palace, there's Elsa's palace,' Wren squealed with delight as she pointed and wriggled around on Gabe's shoulders. 'Oh Daddy, it's so beautiful.'

Gabe smiled and wrapped his arm round Pip's shoulders. She felt safe in his arms, one little lie was not going to break them, she knew that.

There was a small hut by the side of the ice palace and Pip saw Jake and Iris handing out more hot chocolates and hot mulled wines to the guests as they walked past, following the trail of fairy lights down the path towards the lake. The performers and Santa trailed off behind the ice palace, but the elves and the ponies stayed on the path leading the guests towards where the fireworks were going to take place.

'Why was the carnival delayed?' Pip asked as they approached the frozen lake.

Gabe smiled. 'You'll see.'

The elves led the guests to the wooden decking on the lake's shore and no sooner had the last guest stepped up onto the platform than red fireworks exploded into the sky on the opposite side of the lake, the colours reflecting off the frozen surface beautifully.

Wren clapped and cheered as another gold explosion took the place of the red one.

Pip took a few photos and then slipped from Gabe's side to take some pictures of the guests as they watched the colours light up the night sky.

After a few minutes, she returned to Gabe's side, leaning into him as he kissed her head. As the fireworks continued, a riot of colour suddenly appeared behind the explosions and the guests gasped with shock and delight as the Northern Lights seemed to preside over the proceedings. As silver, blue and gold rockets sparkled and glittered across the lake, the Northern Lights lit up the sky beyond with greens and blues, dancing and shimmering to their own private rhythm.

It couldn't be more perfect and as she looked up at Gabe and Wren, she knew that Gabe was right, the Northern Lights had called her home.

❄

After the fireworks display, Pip trudged back to the lodge with a very excited Wren on her back. The evening couldn't have gone better.

But something was wrong, Gabe had been so quiet all evening.

'Why don't I put Wren to bed and then we can have a glass of wine and talk,' Gabe said and something about the way he spoke suggested talk meant something serious and not a night of hot passionate sex as she had originally planned.

Pip nodded in confusion.

'I want Pip to put me to bed,' Wren said. 'I want her to read me a story.'

'I'd be happy to,' Pip said. 'Why don't you light the fire and get the wine ready? I'll be down soon.'

Gabe nodded and Pip carried Wren upstairs to bed. She helped her into her pyjamas and then lay down in bed with her, picking up the book Wren had been reading with Gabe. Winston leapt up onto the bed and curled up at their feet.

She was so tired from running around taking photos all day, but she knew she had captured some wonderful images for the guests. Conversely, Wren, it seemed, was still buzzing from the fireworks and Pip suspected that she would take a long while to wind down.

❄

Pip had been gone a long time and Gabe could still hear Wren chatting away upstairs. Obviously Pip was having some trouble getting her to go to sleep. He went up to Wren's room and found Pip fast asleep in Wren's bed and Wren playing with Winston next to her.

'Daddy!' Wren whispered. 'Pip fell asleep reading my story, so I thought I would read it to her instead, but the words are too hard so I decided I would make it up. Winston has been helping me with the end of the story.'

Gabe smiled. 'Why don't I take Pip to bed and then I'll come back and read the rest to you.'

Wren nodded as she moved her Elsa doll across the sheets towards Winston.

Gabe scooped Pip up and she didn't even stir. He carried her back to his bedroom, undressed her and tucked her under the covers. Her breathing was heavy and she clearly had no idea that he was there.

He watched her for a moment, her vulnerability in that moment achingly endearing.

It was stupid to think she was Mr Black just because of what she had eaten. They had laid a trap and she had been the one to accidentally fall into it. Combined with Ocean View denying all knowledge of her earlier that day, it had set wheels in motion in his mind, prompting thoughts that he shouldn't even be thinking about. He would simply talk to her about it all tomorrow.

He left her in his bed and went off to read to Wren.

❄

Pip woke to soft kisses being peppered down her spine. She opened her eyes in confusion and peered around the room, bathed in the morning sunshine. The last thing she remembered was reading Wren a story. But she had no recollection of coming to bed.

'What happened last night?' Pip said, rolling onto her back to look up at the man she loved as he transferred his kisses to her belly.

'You fell asleep reading Wren's story, I brought you in here and put you to bed.'

'Oh, sorry about that. Did you want to talk about something last night?'

His mouth paused just below her belly button. Then he leaned over her so he could kiss her on the mouth. She wrapped her arms round his neck and in a movement that was swift and confident, he slid one arm round her hips and the other round her shoulders as he lifted her up and sat her astride his lap so she was straddling him. She kissed him deeply as she ran her hands down his chest and he caressed her back. Obviously the time for talking was gone.

He grabbed a condom, slid it on and then lifted her slightly as he moved inside her. She groaned against his mouth and he pulled back slightly, leaning his head against hers.

'So, are you Mr Black?'

Pip burst out laughing. When he'd said he wanted to talk she hadn't been expecting that.

'Can you imagine if I was, that would be hilarious,' Pip said, though it was obvious Gabe couldn't see the humour in it.

'You would tell me if you were,' Gabe said, moving slowly against her and causing her to arch against him, desperate for more.

'Of course I would.'

It didn't sit well with her that she'd lied to Gabe the first night they'd met. They still thought she was a photographer and that lie was even worse than admitting the truth of who she really was, especially when they were willing to let her be their official photographer without any prior experience or qualifications. But they obviously saw a talent in her that she couldn't see herself. They surely wouldn't let her represent them in that way if they didn't think she was capable. But despite the fact they believed she had skills, the lie still lay undiscovered between them. She had wanted to tell Gabe that she was a mystery guest but the words seemed to stick in her mouth. When would have been the best time to admit she had lied? The day after she'd made love to him for the first time? The day she realised she had fallen in love with him again? The day all the guests were arriving? None of it seemed the best time and as it seemed like an insignificant lie and one that was not going to impact on him in any way, it didn't seem worth mentioning, though in truth she knew she was being cowardly. She was a mystery guest, just like Mr Black, and although she wasn't him, nor wielded the same kind of power he clearly did, Gabe still had a right to know who she really was, even if the review she had written and sent off yesterday morning had been the best she had ever written.

'What makes you think I'm Mr Black?' she said, burying her face in his neck as she tried to hold back the orgasm that was threatening to rip through her.

He ran his hands down to her hips, pulling her tighter against him. 'We set a trap. He loves to eat mushroom soup, pasta carbonara and crème brûlée. It's his test to compare hotels across the world. Of course not all hotels provide it, but in those that do he always eats those meals when he can. We thought if we provided all three he wouldn't be able to resist ordering them all and it would be clear who the dreaded Mr Black was. The only person who ordered all three was you. Well, you and Wren, but I think I can let her off.'

Pip hesitated, her mouth pressed to his throat. Those foods were her calling card. She would always try them wherever they were offered. She hadn't twigged last night that for the first time in ages all three had been on offer in the same place. But she hadn't been comparing the night before. She had just picked her three favourite things. It was too much of a coincidence that another mystery guest also tested out those three foods in different hotels across the world. Could she really be the dreaded Mr Black?

He pulled back slightly to look at her and she forced a smile on her face as she kissed him. Could she really be the mystery guest whose reviews held so much weight? Her reviews were in a tiny little article at the back of some magazine. She'd never even bought a copy of the magazine. She just wrote the reviews and handed them in. Surely if her reviews were so significant she would know about it.

'Who does he write for?' Pip asked, running her hands through the hair at the back of his neck and hoping she could distract him.

He moaned softly, thrusting inside her. '*The Tree of Life.*'

She froze, the bottom dropping out of her world. She was Mr Black and she'd had no idea. It was hard to believe that hotels had closed simply because of her reviews. Everyone had been so fearful of this Mr Black and it'd been her all this time.

She suddenly heard Wren's door slam open and her little footsteps as she ran down the stairs.

'Someone's awake,' Gabe said, pushing the hair off Pip's face. 'We better wrap this up. She'll be in here in a second demanding jelly and pancakes for breakfast and a game of Dragons or a *Frozen* sing-a-long before we go over to the dining room.' He pulled her tighter against him, urging her to come as he thrust into her harder and faster. But her mind was too messed up to connect with what they were doing. If Gabe found out she was Mr Black after all this time he would be furious. And having just promised him she wasn't would be the ultimate betrayal. She wasn't sure he would forgive her for that.

Sensing her mind was elsewhere, he slid his hand between them, running his finger over her most sensitive area and despite her confusion and fear she quickly tumbled over the edge. As he found his release, she clung to him and was surprised to feel tears on her cheeks. She couldn't lose him, not when she had just found him again after all these years.

Gabe shifted her off him, giving her a sweet kiss as he got out of bed.

He looked at her with concern. 'Are you OK?'

She nodded, numbly. She had to tell him. He would hopefully see the funny side and not get angry that he and the rest of the staff had been worrying about Mr Black all this time and she was actually him. She'd tell him she'd had no idea that she was Mr Black, which she hadn't. He would understand.

'I'm just going to grab a quick shower, can you check on Wren for me, see if you can persuade her to get dressed before we go over for breakfast? She might be more agreeable if you ask, she adores you,' Gabe said.

Wren. She didn't want Wren to walk in on them when they were talking about Mr Black. She wanted time to reassure Gabe properly, not just drop the bombshell on him and then have Wren come in and interrupt them.

'Do you have time to meet with me after breakfast?' Pip asked.

Gabe nodded, though she could see he obviously wanted to know why. 'We can talk now if you want.'

'I just need a few minutes to discuss the photography and stuff, it can wait until after breakfast.'

Gabe nodded and disappeared into the bathroom, closing the door. A few moments later she heard the shower running.

She felt sick at the prospect of having that conversation, but she had to tell him now and not let it drag on any longer.

She got out of bed and threw on her clothes, then peered out of the window to see what the weather was doing. The early-morning sunshine glinted off the frozen lake. Movement caught her eye and her heart dropped into her stomach as she realised what she was seeing. Wren was on the lake.

❄ Chapter 21 ❄

Pip screamed for Gabe as she ran out of the room and down the stairs. She quickly yanked on her boots, not bothering to do them up, and then ran out of the house.

Stumbling on the snow she ran as fast as she could behind the house and down towards its edge, screaming for help from anyone else close enough to give it.

As she drew closer she could see what Wren was doing. Blaze, Luke's mischievous puppy, had escaped again and had run onto the frozen lake. Wren had clearly seen him from her bedroom and decided to save him, heedless of the danger to herself. At the moment, neither of them was in trouble, but it would only take Wren stepping on a particularly thin bit of ice as she chased Blaze across the lake and she would go straight through it. Or what if Blaze broke through the ice and she tried to get him out? It didn't bear thinking about.

Pip ran down to the lake's edge, and yelled for Wren. Wren didn't even turn around, either because she couldn't hear Pip or she was too intent on getting to Blaze. Pip hesitated for a second and then stepped onto the ice. The ice didn't give at all, incredibly taking Pip's weight. She ran forward a few steps and then heard it crack beneath her feet. She froze, memories of that fateful day she had been trapped under the ice flooding back.

Just then Wren slipped on the surface of the ice and came crashing down on her side. She let out a wail of pain and the sound of ice splintering under Wren's weight echoed through the early-morning silence. Pip ran forward a few feet, but the ice cracked again beneath her feet. She quickly lowered herself to the ice, spreading her arms and legs out wide to distribute her weight. The cracking stopped.

'Wren, are you OK?'

Wren gave a little sob but she sat up to look at Pip.

'Honey, can you lie back down for me and spread your arms and legs out wide like a snow angel?'

Wren sniffled a bit but obviously thought this was a fun game as she let out a little giggle and lay down on her front, arms and legs out, facing towards Pip.

'That's right. Now can you copy me and try to move towards me with your arms and legs as far out as you can?'

Wren did as she was asked, finding it a lot easier than Pip.

Pip started moving like a soldier, crawling along the surface of the ice, but with her arms and legs out wide, hoping she could get to Wren before either of them disappeared through the ice. She could feel the ice shifting slightly under her weight but it wasn't cracking.

They started slowly closing the gap between them, though Pip was painfully aware of how far away from the edge she was getting. They were both too far to get any help now.

Blaze suddenly came back to Wren, jumping up and down, yapping and running round in circles, obviously thinking what Wren was doing was all part of some great game.

'Blaze, no,' Pip yelled but Blaze paid her no attention.

'BLAZE, COME,' yelled Luke's voice from somewhere behind Pip and she could detect the fear in his voice straight away.

Blaze tore across the ice at his master's command, which at least took some of the risk away from Wren. Pip continued her slow progress across the frozen surface towards Wren.

There were some shouts behind Pip and she knew that Gabe had arrived on the scene and by the sounds of it Luke was trying to stop him from coming onto the ice too. That was the last thing they needed, to add more weight to the already fragile surface of the lake.

She shuffled closer and Wren moved closer to her, giggling over how her tiny body slid over the surface with ease. When Wren let out a little 'Wheeee', Pip almost laughed herself. Almost.

She finally reached Wren, but she was so scared of breaching those last few inches in case the combined weight sent them both through the ice to their watery graves.

Suddenly a red and white rubber lifesaving ring skittered to a halt by their sides. It had a rope attached and she knew that Luke or Gabe would pull them both back to safety once they had hold of it, but Pip didn't want to risk their combined weight breaking the ice. The thought of losing Wren under the ice was terrifying.

'Wren, can you hold onto the ring, honey. Daddy will pull you back to safety.'

Wren slid over to the ring and wrapped her arms round it.

'Hold on tight, honey.'

But to her surprise, the ring didn't move.

She looked back at the bank where there was lots of shouting.

Boris was there, as were a few of the guests.

Both Luke and Gabe were yelling at her to grab the ring too. She shook her head but they were insistent.

Pip shuffled closer to the ring. She realised that Wren was dressed only in her pyjamas and she would likely get some kind of ice burn if she was dragged across the ice at speed.

'Wren, climb on my back and wrap your hands around my neck.'

Wren did as she was told and the ice shifted beneath them. Pip quickly wrapped her arms around the life ring and yelled at Gabe to start pulling.

The life ring shot forward as both Luke and Gabe yanked at the rope and Pip and Wren shot across the surface of the ice at high speed. The sound of ice cracking behind them made Pip hold the ring tighter as Wren, clearly unaware of the dangers, screamed with joy and delight at the fun ride. The cracking was getting closer, following them, and Pip could feel her legs dip into the water on several occasions before she was yanked onwards.

'Hold on tight, Wren, whatever happens don't let go,' Pip yelled, praying they would get back to the edge before the ice broke completely.

As they neared the edge, the boys carried on pulling so the ring slithered straight off the lake and onto the bank with her and Wren still holding tight. Wren leapt off Pip's back, jumping up and down with glee at how much fun that had been. Pip sat up, suddenly finding it hard to breathe.

Gabe grabbed Wren by the arms. 'What were you thinking? You know how dangerous the ice is, I've told you countless times.'

Wren's smile faded from her face. 'I know Daddy, that's why I had to help Blaze. I didn't want him to get hurt.'

Gabe pulled Wren into a big hug. 'Don't ever do that again. If you see Blaze or any other animal on the lake, you tell an adult and we'll save them. Don't go onto the lake alone, do you understand?'

'Yes Daddy,' Wren said, solemnly.

Pip was vaguely aware of Boris shepherding the guests away, but she still couldn't draw in any breath, panic and fear slamming into her chest, memories of her past clouding her thoughts. She'd had many panic attacks after the accident but she'd not had them for years. It was stupid to have one now when they were both safe, but she couldn't let go of how terrifyingly it could have gone wrong. The thought of Wren trapped under the ice like she had been all those years ago was paralysing. Pip still couldn't breathe and she gasped and clawed at her chest desperate for the much-needed oxygen.

Luke took his coat off and wrapped it round her shoulders and Gabe looked over at her and paled even more.

'Wren, can you go with Luke and make sure Blaze is alright,' Gabe said, shifting to Pip's side.

'OK,' Wren said and Luke scooped her up and threw her on his back, where she clung like a monkey. Luke flashed Pip a look of concern before he walked back to his house.

'Pip, you're OK and Wren's OK, thanks to you. Just breathe,' Gabe said.

But hearing him say that and knowing it was true was doing nothing to stop the tightness in her chest.

Gabe scooped her up and quickly carried her back to his lodge. He burst through the door and laid her down on the sofa. He knelt down by her side, holding her hand.

'You're safe baby, you're OK,' Gabe said, calmly. He scooted onto the sofa by her side and rolled her towards him. 'Look at me. You're safe with me. Breathe in through your nose and out through your mouth.'

Pip knew he was right. Wren was safe. She was safe. As Gabe started breathing deeply through his nose and out through his mouth, she attempted to copy him. Slowly the tightness in her chest lessened and eventually she could breathe normally again.

'I'm sorry,' Pip muttered, feeling beyond embarrassed.

Gabe stared at her incredulously. 'For what? Saving my daughter's life? You were so brave, I can never thank you enough.'

'For being pathetic. I've had panic attacks before, for months after the accident, every time I thought about getting trapped under the ice. But now all I could think of was Wren getting trapped like I did and it was crippling.'

Gabe's face softened. 'You have nothing to apologise for. That whole experience with your dad must have been terrifying and something like this must have brought it all back. I've had panic attacks too, remember. No amount of trying to be rational and logical can stop them.' He kissed her head and wrapped an arm round her shoulders, pulling her onto his chest.

'We need to get ready for work. It's Christmas Eve tomorrow, I'm sure there's lots to do.'

'Work can wait, I'm staying here with you.'

Pip closed her eyes as she lay on his chest, trying to block out the images of her memories and now her new fears of losing Wren. Gabe wrapped his arms around her and held her tight.

❄

Pip woke a while later when Gabe carefully removed himself from underneath her, shifted off the sofa and went to the front door. It was just starting to get dark outside and Pip had evidently been asleep for most of the day. Whenever she'd had a panic attack when she was younger, she always felt exhausted for the rest of the day. She smiled when she realised that Gabe had stayed with her for the whole time.

She heard him open the door and heard Neve's voice.

'Hey, is Pip with you?'

'Yeah, she's asleep.'

'Luke said she had a panic attack after what happened on the ice. Is she OK?'

'Yes, it was pretty scary, she couldn't breathe. She was scared of losing Wren under the ice. She's OK now, but I wanted to stay with her.'

There was silence from both of them for a moment.

'What's wrong?' Gabe said.

'Look, I don't suppose it makes a difference, you and Pip are together now and I don't want to ruin that, but I think you should know. I've just had an email from *The Tree of Life.*'

Pip's heart thundered in her chest.

'About Mr Black?' Gabe said.

'Yes. Marcus Wright just emailed to say that one of their employees was here to write a review and they had paid for her to stay until the day after New Year's Day. But their employee handed in the review yesterday along with their notice. Mr Black quit. *The Tree of Life* said that as their employee no longer works for them, they won't be paying for the remainder of their stay and that the guest would have to pay for themselves.'

There was silence from Gabe before he finally spoke. 'Did they give you a name? Did they tell you who Mr Black is?'

Pip cringed on the sofa, knowing that Gabe already knew the answer to his question.

'Yes. It's Pip.'

❄ Chapter 22 ❄

Pip leapt up from the sofa and both Gabe's and Neve's eyes found hers accusingly.

'I can explain.'

'You're Mr Black?' Gabe said, incredulously.

'Yes.'

His eyes turned to stone.

'You lied to me. I asked you outright if you were Mr Black and you said no.'

'I didn't know. I swear. It was only—'

'You didn't know? The fortnightly article is called "The Black List", how could you not know?' Gabe said, his voice rising.

'I never read it. I visit the hotels, I submit my reviews, I move on to the next hotel. I used to read it in the beginning, but they changed my sentences around so much and cut the reviews I had written and it used to annoy me, so I just stopped reading them in the end. They were paying for me to travel the world, so I just decided that they could do whatever they wanted with my words. I had no idea I was Mr Black.'

He looked away, angrily. God, what a mess, he was so furious and she couldn't see any way to calm him down.

'You came here to review Stardust Lake Hotel?' Neve said.

'Yes and as soon as I knew you guys were here I contacted *The Tree of Life* to say I couldn't do the review, but they insisted.'

'So you were never here to take photos,' Neve said.

She shook her head, feeling horribly guilty about that lie.

'You made me look a fool contacting Ocean View about your visit when they didn't know anything about you. I looked unprofessional to them.'

'You lied to both of us about that,' Gabe said. 'And the lies you told about being a photographer and travelling the world, are those photos you showed me even yours? What other lies have you told?'

Pip felt sick, everything was unravelling.

'Of course the photos are mine. The travelling the world part was all true, the stories I told you about the hotels I stayed in, and the places I've been, that was true too. Did you honestly expect me to tell you the truth within minutes of me arriving? My job is supposed to be a secret, I never tell anyone.'

'You've been here almost a week, you could have told me at any time,' Gabe said.

'Things were so weird between us and then I fell in love with you and I didn't want to ruin that. I didn't think it was really that important. I wrote the best goddamn review for this place that I've ever written. Me being a reviewer wasn't going to impact you at all, so why risk what we had by telling the truth upfront?'

'Because all the staff have been so worried about Mr Black and you could have put a stop to that at any time. Instead you let us carry on panicking about it.'

'Don't you think I would have told you if I knew I was Mr Black? I helped you to get everything ready for his arrival, I wanted this place to succeed as much as you did. I honestly didn't know. It was only when you mentioned the food he likes to eat this morning that I realised. I was going to tell you after breakfast and then saving your daughter's life kind of got in the way of that.'

'I can't be in a relationship with someone who lies to me. God, I trusted you. After you ran away twelve years ago, I never thought I could trust you again, but I did. I let you into my life and Wren's and you betrayed that trust. I don't even want to look at you right now.'

Pain sliced into her chest. He was breaking up with her.

He walked out of the door and slammed it behind him, taking Neve with him.

Pip stared at the door in horror. What the hell had just happened?

Tears filled her eyes. It was over.

The fear she'd had that it would end, that her heart would be broken and she would be alone again, slammed into her chest now.

Numbly, she went upstairs to pack. She put her suitcase on the bed and threw her few belongings into it. She'd never really unpacked, so there wasn't a lot to put back in the suitcase. And now she was moving on again from the one place she wanted to call home.

She stared at the suitcase. Before she came here, everything important in her life was in that suitcase, but now the things that were the most important to her were Gabe, Wren and Juniper Island and she couldn't take them with her.

She couldn't help the sobs that escaped her throat. She wouldn't get to say goodbye to Wren. She'd never see Gabe ever again. For the first time in her life she wanted to stay in one place and make a home. He was the only person who had ever made her feel like that and now he was willing to throw it all away. They were supposed to be together forever, how could he throw their relationship away like that?

Suddenly anger ripped through her. She wasn't going to let him go without a fight.

She flipped up the suitcase and emptied the contents on the bed. She turned it back upright and looked at the empty bottom. She had never completely unpacked once in the ten years she had travelled the world and to see her clothes and belongings out of her suitcase and in the house where they belonged was suddenly a liberating release.

She looked up as Gabe arrived in the doorway. 'Did you just say you loved me?' he asked, quietly.

She had said that and it was true. She did love him with everything she had. Though clearly he didn't feel the same way if he was willing to throw away what they had so easily.

His eyes glanced down to the suitcase on the bed and he paled. 'You're leaving? One argument and you're running again?' His voice was choked when he spoke.

'You just said you couldn't be in a relationship with someone who lies to you. You said you couldn't even look at me.'

'I didn't mean… I just needed some space from you for a while. Christ, Pip. I can't believe you're running away after everything we've been through. Well, if our relationship means that little to you then go. There's a plane leaving for Edinburgh in half an hour, make sure you're on it.'

Before Pip could say another word, he stormed away from her.

'Gabe, wait,' Pip said, chasing after him, but he was already charging down the stairs and a second later she heard the front door slamming behind him.

What the hell was wrong with this man?

She grabbed her coat and hat, pulled on her snow boots and stepped outside. It was already dark, snowflakes swirling through the sky, and although there were several guests milling about, going to dinner or heading towards the ice palace, there was no sign of Gabe or Neve.

She stormed into the reception and straight up the stairs that led to the offices. Though Adam was up there, there was no one else around.

'Pip, are you OK? I heard what happened on the lake this morning, you're a hero,' Adam said, as he spotted her.

Obviously word hadn't got round yet about her betrayal.

'I think my hero status has been revoked. I need to see Gabe, any idea where he might be?'

Adam looked at his watch.

'I'm not sure, maybe he's having dinner.' He stood up. 'Are you OK, you look like you've been crying?'

Pip shook her head. She didn't have time to get into the issues in her and Gabe's relationship right now, and if she stopped to explain she'd only end up crying again.

'Look, I'm not sure what's happened, but don't let Gabe push you away. He needs you. I've known him a very long time and quite frankly, you're the best thing that's ever happened to him.'

'I have no intention of letting him push me away. I just need to find him to tell him that.' She flashed Adam a smile as she registered what he'd said. 'Thank you.'

She turned and ran down the stairs and into the dining room, but though it was busy with guests and staff, Gabe wasn't anywhere to be seen.

She raced out of the reception into the cold and ran straight into Luke. He steadied her with his hands on her shoulders.

'If you're looking for Gabe, he's down in the ice palace getting ready to be Father Christmas,' Luke said. 'I've just seen him, he's in a terrible state.'

'Thanks to me.'

Luke shrugged. 'I've told him he's being an arse, if that helps.'

Despite everything, Pip let out a little giggle. 'He is an arse, but I love him.'

He smiled. 'Then go tell him that.'

Pip ran down the hill towards the ice palace. She saw all the families lined up outside, ready for their turn with Father Christmas. They were lavishing the reindeer with strokes and pats and the reindeer were clearly loving all the attention.

The door was roped off with a temporary barricade, barring the way into the ice palace until they were ready for the guests. Pip simply stepped over the rope and let herself inside. She walked through the ice forest, past the elves, snowmen, reindeer and candy canes until she got to the igloo in the corner.

She could hear voices from inside, Gabe's and Neve's, and she hesitated for a moment to listen.

'She's running away again,' Gabe said. 'I thought we had turned a corner, that she wanted to stay here with me. She said she was falling in love with me.'

'I know.'

'And she handed in her notice so she could stay here.'

'Yes.'

'And now, one bump in the road and she throws everything away.'

God, he sounded so heartbroken that Pip couldn't listen to any more.

Pip stepped inside the igloo and Gabe's eyes slammed into hers, anger and pain and emotion warring in his face.

She was momentarily distracted by the fact that he was dressed as Father Christmas – no beard yet, but he wore the red velvet fur-lined suit and the black shiny boots. His jacket was open, revealing a toned, bare chest. Neve was holding a cushion that they were no doubt going to use for padding. He was sitting on the throne as he had been that day they'd kissed in here.

She glanced over at Neve and noticed she was dressed as an elf, in a green velvet waistcoat, shorts and red and white stripy tights, with oversized pointy shoes. Pip almost giggled but the scowl on Neve's face stalled any laughter in her throat.

'You're still here?' Gabe said, coldly.

Tearing her gaze from Neve, she looked for the relief in his eyes, or any regret that he had tried to send her away, but there was none.

Neve stared between them and then, handing Gabe the cushion, she left them alone in the igloo.

Pip stepped towards Gabe. 'Twelve years ago, I made a rash decision which broke us apart. Fate or luck or love brought us back together and I'm not going to let another rash decision from you tear us apart again, so yes I'm still here. I thought you wanted me to leave so I went upstairs to pack but as soon as I put the suitcase on the bed I realised that this is my home, Juniper Island is my home, the town called Christmas, the horny reindeer, the evil ponies, your grumpy brother and overprotective sister are my home, and most importantly you and your beautiful daughter are my home and I'm not going anywhere. If you had stayed in my room for longer than five seconds, you would have realised that I wasn't packing, I was unpacking. I emptied everything I own onto the bed because I want to stay here and I was going to come and find you and tell you that you can't kick me out of my home. I gave up everything for you, my job, travelling the world. I wanted to prove to you that I'm here for good, that you can trust me not to run away any more, but you were always waiting for me to let you down. Despite what you said, you didn't trust me and the first chance you got to prove that you were right about your instincts, you grabbed hold of it with both hands.'

She walked up the stairs to the throne and sat on his lap. Thankfully he didn't push her off, though he didn't wrap his arms round her as she had hoped.

'I love you and I love your daughter and I want to be part of your life. But you have to learn to trust me because I'm here for the long haul. I get that you're angry, I shouldn't have lied about my job, but I honestly had no idea I was Mr Black. It's not going to always be sunshine and roses for us, we will fight and argue, but you can't push me away when that happens. You can't let our past cloud our future.'

Neve suddenly walked back into the igloo. 'Gabe, the children are waiting.'

He still didn't say anything, but his eyes were locked on Pip's.

'If you want to talk once you're finished here, then I'll be in our home waiting for you.'

She hesitated for a second, hoping he would say something, but he didn't, so she climbed down from his lap and the throne and walked out.

He didn't call her back.

❄ Chapter 23 ❄

It was almost midnight when Gabe came back, carrying a sleeping Wren in his arms. He was still dressed in his Father Christmas costume, though minus the beard, hat and cushion. He didn't say anything to Pip as she sat in the lounge waiting for him. He carried Wren upstairs to her bedroom and Pip was left wondering if he was coming back to talk to her or had gone straight to bed. Feeling her heart breaking all over again, she let her head fall into her hands just as he came running down the stairs. She looked up at him as he stood in front of her.

He immediately sank to his knees in front of her, taking her hands in his.

'I love you. I don't think I ever stopped loving you in the twelve years we were apart but I know I love you so much more now than I ever did before.'

Pip let out an involuntary sob, tears filling her eyes.

Gabe smiled slightly, brushing the tears from her cheeks.

'Seeing you with Wren, seeing how hard you've worked to help get everything ready, your passion for photography, I think I fell in love with you all over again. I never thought I could offer you enough to make you want to stay in one place for the rest of your life – asking you to swap travelling the world for a home on the tiny and remote Juniper Island seemed like an impossible dream. I was so scared that I would lose you all over again and I knew this time, if you walked away, the pain would be unbearable.'

He stroked his fingers over the back of her hand.

'To find out you lied to me about your job made me question everything, including whether our whole relationship was a lie too...'

'I'm sorry, I've always lied about my job, it was an instinctive thing and not something I gave much thought to after that...' she trailed off as he cupped her face in one hand, tracing his thumb over her lips.

'It's OK. I understand why you did it. And you were right, I was waiting for you to break my trust. I was so scared of losing you that I completely overreacted. I'm so sorry. I was too blind too stubborn and too hung up on the past to see that you wanting to be a photographer here, you giving up your job so you could stay here, was all the proof I needed to know that this, us, our second chance, meant as much to you as it did to me. I love you and I want to build a future with you by my side.'

Pip leaned forward and kissed him, crying with relief that they were going to be OK after all. He cupped the back of her head and kissed her back.

Eventually she pulled back, leaning her forehead against his. 'You're not angry that I lied any more?'

'Everyone lies. I've just been Father Christmas for the last four hours and listened to countless children telling me they had been perfect, well-behaved saints all year. Wren lied to you when she told you she always sings all the *Frozen* songs before she goes to bed every night. We lie when it's something we really want. You lied or didn't admit the truth because you really wanted me. I can't really be angry about that. I lied to you too. I said that we could never go back, that I couldn't feel for you what I had in the past because I was afraid of getting hurt all over again, but it was already too late. I already loved you.'

'I don't think you lied. I don't think we have gone back, I think we have moved forward. Maybe if we had stayed together twelve years ago we would have drifted apart because we weren't ready to have a serious long-lasting relationship back then. But we're ready now. We just have to make sure that we're one hundred percent honest with each other from now on.'

He smiled and leaned forward to kiss her just as the clock struck midnight. He pulled back slightly, kissing her nose sweetly.

'It's Christmas Eve,' Gabe whispered. 'I hope Father Christmas brings you everything you want.'

'I have my best friend, the man I love. You are everything I've ever wanted.'

Gabe climbed on the sofa with her. He undressed her kissing her softly, tenderly caressing her all over.

He pulled his mouth from hers to stare down at her. She smiled and he kissed her again, and without taking his mouth from hers, he made love to her like a best friend should.

❄

'IT'S CHRISTMAS EVE!' Wren shouted, jerking Gabe from his sleep. It was very early in the morning judging by the muted light filtering through the window. The woman he loved was lying naked in his arms on the sofa and his daughter was running downstairs towards them. He had just enough time to grab the blanket off the back of the sofa and cover him and Pip as Wren thundered into the lounge. Pip giggled into his arm as she peered over the top of the blanket at Wren, her face filled with so much excitement.

'Morning sweetheart,' Pip said.

'Hey Princess,' Gabe said, as Wren bounced up and down on the spot.

'I get to go to Elsa's palace today,' Wren said.

'You do, we're going straight after breakfast,' Gabe said.

'Let's go to breakfast right now,' Wren said.

'Breakfast won't start for a while yet. Why don't you go and get dressed and we can play in the snow for a bit before we eat.'

Wren pouted a little and then looked at him and Pip. 'Did you two sleep here last night?'

'We fell asleep on the sofa, yes,' Gabe said, knowing that after they had made love for hours the night before, neither of them had been able to make it back to their bed.

'Listen,' Pip said to Wren. 'I was supposed to be leaving after Christmas but how would you feel if I hung around for a bit longer?'

Gabe kissed Pip's shoulder, hoping Wren would be happy about it. Although if she wasn't, it wouldn't change anything between him and Pip. They would have to work through it somehow.

'Will you stay forever?' Wren asked, seemingly even more excited about that than seeing the ice palace.

'If that's what you want?' Pip said.

'Yes, I want you to stay forever. You make Daddy really happy and you make me laugh a lot. I'm going to get dressed,' Wren said, as she ran back upstairs.

'You get the official seal of approval,' Gabe said as Pip rolled over in his arms to face him. 'We should celebrate.'

'I think I better wait until I get Neve's approval before we celebrate. I know she feels I let her down.'

Gabe pulled her closer. 'I love my sister and my daughter, but there isn't a single person in the world that could keep me from being with you. Besides, Neve told me not to throw away what I had with you. She doesn't appreciate being lied to but the whole thing with Oakley is playing on her mind. She lied to him and breaking up with him has left her heartbroken. She says she regrets that more than anything and told me not to make the same mistake and let you go. If she's hard on you, I think it's her emotions over the situation with Oakley rather than you. Adam even thinks she might be pregnant.'

'Oh my god, poor Neve. Raising a baby will be hard on her own.'

'She might not be, but it would explain a lot if she is. Anyway, she won't be alone, we'll help her if she is. So be forgiving of her, even if she isn't with you. It might be a while before you two are the best of friends, but as far as we're concerned, I think she approves.'

Pip smiled, running her fingers down his bare chest. 'Well then, I think we should definitely celebrate.'

A thunder of feet and high-pitched yapping came tumbling down the stairs.

'Tonight, I promise. For now, we need to work out how to get upstairs and get dressed without Wren seeing us naked.'

❄

After breakfast, Pip, Gabe and Wren made their way towards the ice palace, with Wren practically buzzing with excitement.

With Gabe's arm round her shoulders and Wren holding her hand, Pip had never felt so content and blissfully happy in her life.

As the ice palace appeared in the valley below them, Wren let out a squeal of delight as the building sparkled in the morning sunlight.

Pip spotted Luke and Gabe's parents waiting for them. No sign of Neve yet, but Pip wondered if she was already inside. She felt nervous about seeing Neve, but she and Gabe were together again and nothing was going to change that.

Lizzie, Gabe's mum, gave her a big hug when they got near.

There were no other guests around as the ice palace wasn't officially open until after lunch and Pip loved that Wren would get to see it for the first time on her own.

They pushed open the door and Boris, Mikael and Chester were waiting for them just inside, all of them dressed in elf costumes. Pip laughed at Boris and Mikael. They were so big they looked ridiculous dressed as elves, but Wren didn't seem to mind and she ran forward to hug Chester.

Boris knelt down to talk to Wren.

'Chester wanted to give you your Christmas present now,' Boris said, as Chester handed over a badly wrapped parcel.

Wren tore at the paper to reveal a snow globe, one of Mikki's creations by the looks of things.

'Chester told Mikki what kind of snow globe he wanted for you and she made it specially.'

Wren peered at it and then let out a laugh of delight. 'That's me and Chester playing with Olaf the snowman.'

'Yes it is.'

'I love it, thank you Chester,' Wren said, hugging Chester tightly.

Neve appeared through the trees, also dressed in her elf costume. 'Father Christmas is ready for you now.'

Neve flashed Pip a small smile. As Gabe said, it might be a while before they were good friends, but she was relieved that things would be OK between them.

Wren giggled at seeing Neve in her costume but, unable to hold in her excitement any longer, let go of Pip's hand and ran on ahead.

'Daddy, look at this,' Wren squealed, pointing out the ice snowmen. 'Pip, come look at this.'

Wren came back to grab Pip's hand and pulled her through the ice sculptures, stopping to admire every carving, stroking the ice animals and squealing in delight over the fairies and trees and bushes.

Lizzie took loads of photos of her granddaughter as Neve, Luke, Gabe and his dad trailed after them, smiling indulgently at Wren's excitement.

Finally they reached the igloo and they stepped inside, Wren gasped when she saw Father Christmas sitting on the throne. Pip tried to look past the beard and the suit to see who it was but it was only when he started speaking that Pip realised it was Stephen.

'Good morning, Wren,' Stephen said in a deep voice and Wren went really quiet as she stared at him.

'Is he the real Father Christmas?' Wren asked Pip.

'Of course he is,' Pip said. 'How else would he know your name? Go and say hello.'

Wren let Pip go and tentatively stepped closer. When she was close enough Stephen lifted her onto his lap.

'And what do you think of my wonderful ice palace?' Stephen asked.

'I think it's marvellous,' Wren whispered.

'Good, I do too. Are you looking forward to Christmas?'

'Yes, I'm very excited,' Wren said, growing in confidence.

'And what is it you would like for Christmas this year?' Stephen asked, clearly getting into the role.

'A step-mum,' Wren said, loudly.

Pip froze. This could be awkward. But to her surprise, Gabe slung an arm round her shoulders and squeezed her tight. She glanced at him and he was smiling broadly.

Stephen chortled.

'Oh, that's quite a big present. Normally I bring bikes or dolls to children around the world.' He looked over at Gabe and Pip and smiled. 'I will try my best to arrange one, but you might have to wait a while for that to happen.'

'I can wait. But I don't want just anyone for my step-mum, I want Pip.'

Gabe laughed. 'I think that can be arranged.'

Pip's heart filled with love for him.

'Well, Wren, I have lots of presents for you on my sleigh that I'll deliver tonight. But I do have a little something for you that you can open now.'

Stephen reached down and gave her a small square box. Wren tore at the paper and lifted the lid to reveal a blue crystal tiara.

'It's an Elsa crown,' Wren gasped, immediately putting it on her head and then hugging Stephen tight.

She clambered down from his lap and rejoined Gabe and Pip.

'And Pip, is there anything you want for Christmas?' Stephen asked.

Pip laughed. 'No, I have everything I've ever wanted right here,' she replied, gesturing to Gabe and Wren.

'Are you sure there's nothing else you want?' Stephen prompted and Pip shook her head. 'Not even this?'

He gestured to Luke and from behind the throne Luke pulled out a silvery grey rocking horse with a red saddle.

Pip gasped and looked at Gabe.

He shrugged. 'It didn't seem right that you never got it.'

Pip stepped forward to stroke the horse's mane. It was beautiful and exactly like the one she had wanted as a child. Wren ran her hands over the horse too.

'It's lovely, can I have a go?'

Pip smiled. 'Of course you can, you can have a go whenever you want.'

Pip lifted her onto the horse's back and laughed as Wren rode it like a professional cowboy.

She moved back to Gabe's side and kissed him on the cheek. 'I love you.'

Gabe smiled. 'I love you too.'

After Wren had tired of riding on the horse and they'd said their goodbyes to Father Christmas, they started making their way outside. Pip found herself next to Neve.

'I am sorry I lied to you,' Pip said and Neve smiled.

'It's OK. Besides, you've made my brother happier than he has ever been in his life and I can't possibly hate you for that. You'll take good care of him, won't you?'

'I promise.' Pip hesitated for a moment. 'What about your happiness?'

'I'm going to go and see Oakley after Christmas. I should never have let him go and we really need to talk.'

Suddenly a noise filled the air, a deafening, ear-splintering sound like a machine gun and Pip looked up as a helicopter flew overhead.

It landed on a huge expanse of grass just past the main reception and well away from the lodges.

'Who the hell is that?' Gabe said. 'They shouldn't be landing there.'

The rotors stopped and the door opened. A huge blond man stepped down who looked to Pip like someone she recognised.

'Who is that?' Pip asked, as the man walked across the snow towards them.

Neve stood frozen still next to her, her face as white as the snow on the ground. She clearly recognised the man too, but she couldn't find the words to say who he was.

Gabe put his arm around Neve's shoulders. 'That's Oakley.'

Neve and Oakley's story continues in

A Town Called Christmas

A Moment of Inspiration with Holly

Many people ask me about the settings for my books, whether they are real and where I get my inspiration from for the locations that play such a big part in my stories. Mostly my settings are an amalgamation of many places I've visited with a large dollop of imagination to make it the perfect place for my characters.

❄

But the setting of Stardust Lake Hotel was based very much on a real location. Kakslauttanen Arctic Resort in Finland might not have the same romantic name as my hotel but it had everything that made my hotel so magical.

❄

I first saw Kakslauttanen in one of those 'must visit' posts that appeared on Facebook. I completely fell in love with the place, with the breathtaking videos and photos that seemed to be doing the rounds on social media. With its beautiful glass igloos to watch the northern lights from and cosy log cabins with their open fires . . . and in the snow it looked like a magical winter wonderland. I knew I had to visit and, once I had, I knew I had to include it in my story.

❄

I had already written a lot of the story when I visited and when I arrived it was like walking through the pages of my book and discovering the delights of the resort just like Pip. It had a stunning ornate log house where you'd go to meet Santa and an opportunity to meet and feed the beautiful reindeer, who were so gentle and inquisitive. Blue-eyed huskies were in abundance, ready to pull you on sleigh rides, and there was snowmobiling, too.

❄

In a weird twist of real life imitating art or vice versa, in *Christmas Under a Cranberry Sky*, Gabe invites artists to stay in the Christmas market to make and sell their art to the guests, and this is something I didn't know about the owner of Kakslauttanen, he invites artists from all over the world to come up there, stay at the resort and make sculptures or works of art; the place is covered in them, some of them were weird and abstract, some were more classic, recognisable sculptures but all of them were wonderful and beautiful.

❄

Sleeping in a glass igloo was not like any other experience I've ever had. I thought it would be cold but special glass ensured I was warm and cosy all night. And although I was not lucky enough to see the northern lights from the igloo, sleeping underneath a blanket of stars was an unforgettable experience.

❄

Inspiration for my stories comes from many different sources, TV programmes, music, pictures or places I've visited but sometimes I find a place that ticks every single box. So much of Kakslauttanen was in the Stardust Lake Hotel that I half expected to see the gorgeous Gabe come out and greet me when I arrived or to see the lovely Luke tending to the huskies. So a huge thank you to Kakslauttanen for providing the perfect, magical backdrop for my characters to fall in love.

❄

Thank you for reading and I hope you have a magical Christmas

Love Holly x

@hollymartin00

hollymartinauthor

www.hollymartinwriter.wordpress.com

Acknowledgements

To the wonderful Kakslauttanen resort in Finland, the real life Stardust Lake Hotel. The incredible beauty of this resort, the glass igloos and the log cabins were the inspiration for both of the books in the *A Town Called Christmas* series.

To my family, my mom – my biggest fan, who reads every word I have written a hundred times over and loves it every single time – my dad, my brother Lee and my sister-in-law Julie, for your support, love, encouragement and endless excitement for my stories.

For my twinnie, the gorgeous Aven Ellis for just being my wonderful friend, for your endless support, for cheering me on, for reading my stories and telling me what works and what doesn't and for keeping me entertained with wonderful stories and pictures of hot men. I love you dearly.

To my friends Gareth and Mandie, for your support, patience and enthusiasm. My lovely friends Jac, Verity and Jodie who listen to me talk about my books endlessly and get excited about it every single time.

For Sharon Sant for just being there always and your wonderful friendship.

To my wonderful agent Madeleine Milburn for just been amazing and fighting my corner and for your unending patience with my constant questions.

To my wonderful editor Claire for putting up with all my crazy throughout the whole process, for replying to every single email and for listening to me freak out with complete and utter patience. My editor Celine Kelly for helping to make this book so much better, my copyeditor Rhian for doing such a good job at spotting any issues or typos. Thank you to Kim Nash for the tireless promoting, tweeting and general cheerleading. Thank you to all the other wonderful people at Bookouture: Oliver Rhodes, the editing team and the wonderful designers who created this absolutely gorgeous cover.

To the CASG, the best writing group in the world, you wonderful talented supportive bunch of authors, I feel very blessed to know you all, you guys are the very best.

To the wonderful Bookouture authors for all your encouragement and support.

To all the wonderful bloggers for your tweets, retweets, Facebook posts, tireless promotions, support, encouragement and endless enthusiasm. You guys are amazing and I couldn't do this journey without you.

To Kielder Observatory who gave me some great information on the Northern Lights and how to predict when they appear.

To anyone who has read my book and taken the time to tell me you've enjoyed it or wrote a review, thank you so much.

Thank you, I love you all.

Turn over for a delicious Christmas recipe from Holly Martin

Christmas cupcakes

Makes 12

Ingredients:

For the cupcakes:
200g dark brown sugar
175g butter
600g mixed dried fruit
1 orange (zest and juice)
(optional) 100ml dark rum or brandy
80g pecan nuts, chopped
3 eggs
80g ground almonds
200g plain flour
½ tsp baking powder
½ tsp ground ginger
½ tsp ground nutmeg
1tsp cinnamon

For the topping:

400g rolled marzipan
400g white fondant icing sugar
Marmalade or apricot jam to spread

To decorate:

12 gold or silver muffin cases
Gold or silver sugared almonds

How to make them:

- Preheat the oven to 150C/gas mark 2
- Tip the butter, sugar, dried fruit, orange zest and juice into a pan. Pour over the rum or brandy and slowly bring to the boil, stirring gently to make sure the butter is melted. Keep stirring and let it bubble gently for a few minutes.
- Pour in the nuts, eggs and ground almonds, and then sift in the flour, baking powder and spices. Stir thoroughly, now your batter is ready to bake!
- Plop the mixture into cupcake cases and bake for 35-45 minutes until golden brown and springy to the touch.
- Whilst the cupcakes are cooling, roll out the marzipan and cut out 12 circles (of about 6cm, or the size of your cupcakes). Brush the cake tops with marmalade or jam, press down the marzipan circle on top.

- Add water to your icing sugar until it is thin enough to spread but won't drip down the sides. Swirl the icing on top of each cupcake and decorate with sugared almonds.

- **Enjoy**!

Ready for your next gorgeous read from Holly Martin? Then turn the page for a peek at

Christmas at Lilac Cottage

Chapter 1

The timer went off on the oven and Penny quickly dropped her sketch book and grabbed her oven gloves. Opening the oven door released a waft of gorgeous, rich fruity smells into the kitchen, making Penny smile with excitement. The mince pies looked golden, crisp and perfectly done. She quickly transferred them to a wire rack to cool and gave the warm mulled wine a quick stir as it simmered on the hob.

She looked around at the green-leafed garlands that covered the fireplace and the white fairy lights that twinkled from in between the leaves, the lights that lined the windows also lending a sparkling glow to the room in the dullness of the late winter afternoon. She knew that next door, in the annexe, looked equally inviting now that she had spent hours decorating it in suitable festive attire ready for the new arrivals.

Everything was perfect and Penny couldn't wait to meet them.

Henry and Daisy Travis had been referred to her by the agency in charge of finding tenants for her annexe. Although Penny would have preferred a single woman like her, the young couple came with great references and no children.

Not that she had an issue with children; she loved them. She had even thought at one point in her life that she might have some of her own but that had passed her by. She just wanted to make friends with people who were at the same point in their life as she was.

One by one all her friends had got married and had children, and each time a new child in the town was born it seemed to add weight to her solitary existence. Everyone had someone to love and look after. Penny had a fat, lazy dog called Bernard. The loneliness inside her had grown recently to an almost tangible thing. Whenever people asked if she ever felt isolated up on the hill on her own, she always batted it away with a cheery smile and talk of how she never had time to feel that way with her job. And while it was true that her job as the town's only ice carver did keep her very busy, she knew she took on a lot of work to try to distract herself from how utterly alone she really felt.

She had always lived in Lilac Cottage and she could never imagine living anywhere else. The view over the town of White Cliff Bay and the rugged white coastline that lent the town its name was stunning; she could look at it for hours and never grow tired of it. But the hustle and bustle of the town was a good ten minutes' drive from where she lived and, although she loved the remoteness of her home, she was starting to hate it too.

Renting the annexe out would be a good way to make some new friends and, even though they would still lead separate lives, Penny hoped they would be able to chat from time to time.

Penny checked her watch again, a nervous excitement pulsing through her. She had cooked lasagne for them and she hoped they could spend the night chatting over wine and a good meal and really get to know each other.

It was going to be perfect and she couldn't wait to start this next chapter of her life.

Henry slammed his hands on the steering wheel as another red light forced him to stop. In a town that was probably no more than a few miles long they seemed to have traffic lights on every corner and every single one of them had been red so far.

This had to be the worst moving day ever. The expression of you get what you pay for couldn't be more true today. As the annexe he was moving into was fully furnished, he only needed a small van to bring his other belongings. He'd stupidly hired the cheapest company to move his stuff and now the van was sitting in White Cliff Beach in the furthest reaches of Yorkshire instead of White Cliff Bay in rural Devon.

And what was with the people in the town? They asked so many questions. Stopping for petrol in the town's only petrol station, stopping at a supermarket, and then a café for lunch with Daisy, he had been accosted by about thirty different people who wanted his whole life story. Daisy was lovely and sweet and would chat to anyone and everyone, the complete opposite to him; he just wanted to tell everyone to sod off and leave them alone.

Daisy was staying with his sister tonight, which was a good job too as he was in a foul mood. All he wanted now was to get to this house, unpack the few things he had brought with him and fall asleep in front of the TV or over a good book.

He just hoped that Penny Meadows, his landlady, wasn't a talker. Living up on the hilltops all by herself and completely cut off from the town, he presumed she was some kind of hermit and liked to keep herself to herself. That suited him fine. He didn't want to make friends, he didn't want to chat to anyone. He just wanted to be left alone.

He turned onto the long driveway leading up to what he hoped was Lilac Cottage. He had got lost three times trying to find the blasted place and when he stopped to ask directions, people seemed to close ranks and send him the opposite way, as if they were trying to keep the place hidden. As he drove over the crest of the hill he saw it. The house was a pale purple colour. He had presumed the name Lilac Cottage would come from nearby lilac trees, not the actual colour of the house.

It looked like somewhere Barbie might live. With the lights twinkling happily in a multitude of colours from every tree, bush and fence surrounding the home, it just added to the sickeningly cutesy feel. Daisy would love it. He glared at the lights as if they were causing him great offence. Bloody Christmas. Humbug.

A silver Range Rover pulled up on Penny's drive and she nearly cheered with excitement. She ran to the front door to greet her new tenants, but then held back for a few seconds. Yanking the door open before they'd even turned off the engine might seem a bit over-enthusiastic. She didn't want to come across as too keen. She counted to ten, quickly, then opened the door. The man standing on her doorstep with light snowflakes swirling around him was. . . beautiful. He was so tall she had to crane her neck to look him in the eyes, slate-grey angry eyes hidden underneath long, dark eyelashes. He was muscular too. He had dark, stubbly hair and a deep frown that was marring his otherwise gorgeous features.

'I'm Henry Travis.'

Penny supposed she should say something but annoyingly any coherent words seemed to elude her. His frown deepened some more at her inadequate silence and she finally found her voice.

'Penny Meadows, pleased to meet you. Come in, I'll show you your new home.'

She ushered him in but, as she looked out, Daisy was nowhere in sight. Maybe she was coming later. She closed the door and stepped back into her front room, which seemed so much smaller all of a sudden now Henry was filling it with his enormous size. She tried to get past him to lead him into the kitchen but he was too big to squeeze past. He stared down at her with confusion as she tried to slide through the tiny gap and then finally he stepped to one side.

She walked into the kitchen, feeling awkward and clumsy in his presence.

'This is the connecting door,' Penny said lamely, showing him the obviously connecting door. Next she'd be saying things like, 'This is the door handle and this is the sofa.'

'But we have our own separate front door, don't we?' Henry said.

'Of course, but this will always be open so feel free to pop in any time.'

Henry's scowl deepened so much she could barely see his eyes. He stepped through the door, banging his head on the low door frame. He swore softly as he rubbed it.

'Oh god, I'm so sorry. I didn't realise it was that low.'

He glared at her as he stepped into his lounge. 'Jeez, it's tiny.'

Penny had always thought it was cute and cosy, but with his massive build the place looked like a doll house.

'Erm. . . through there is your kitchen and your front door, which leads out onto the back garden. So I suppose technically it's your back door.' She giggled, nervously, mentally slapping her forehead with how stupid she sounded. 'Upstairs are the two bedrooms and the bathroom.' Penny winced at how small the bathroom was going to be for Henry. He'd have to bend almost double to fit his head under the sloped roof of the shower.

He took two giant steps and ducked into the kitchen, shaking his head incredulously, probably at the size of it.

He looked back at Penny and must have seen the desperate hope in her eyes as his features softened slightly. 'It's lovely, and it's only for a few months so I'm sure I can remember to duck when I walk between the rooms until we find somewhere bet. . . bigger.'

Penny's face fell. 'You're not staying?'

Henry shook his head. 'We have our name down for a house in the town. Rob at the agency said he thinks he will have somewhere by March or April at the latest. Did he not tell you this was short term?'

Penny swallowed down the disappointment and shook her head. She had been trying for months to rent out the annexe without any success and in the end left it in the hands of the agency, and even they had struggled to fill it.

Now it seemed that, in a few months, Henry and Daisy would be gone, leaving Penny all alone again.

She forced a smile on her face, determined to make those months count. 'So I've put a bed in the second bedroom but if you wish to use it as a study or something else, then I can easily remove it.'

Henry looked at her as if she was stupid. 'No, we'll obviously be needing the second bed.'

Penny blinked. Maybe they had separate bedrooms. She knew lots of couples who slept apart for one reason or another. She could never imagine sleeping apart from her husband, but then she didn't have one of those, so who was she to judge?

'That's fine. I, erm. . . made some mince pies and some mulled wine if you wanted to have something to eat before you unpack.'

'No, I'd rather just get everything in before it gets dark. Most of my stuff won't arrive until tomorrow – the bloody removal people got lost and ended up in a different part of the country.'

'Oh, how frustrating for you,' Penny said. Maybe that explained the almost permanent frown. 'Well, I can help you bring things in from the car and I've made a lasagne for later, so if you didn't fancy cooking, you and Daisy are more than welcome to come round later to share it with me.'

'Daisy is staying with my sister tonight.'

'Well, you can still come over. . .' Penny trailed off. Was it inappropriate to share dinner with another woman's husband? It was just dinner but the cosy night in with her new neighbours was suddenly turning into something a bit more intimate now it was just the two of them. Henry obviously thought so too as his eyebrows had shot up at her suggestion. 'Or I can plate some up and bring it here for you to have on your own.' There was something even sadder about that, both of them sitting in their separate kitchens eating by themselves.

'I need to get unpacked tonight. Get it all out the way before all Daisy's rubbish gets here. She could fill this whole annexe with all her junk so I better get my stuff put away first. I'll probably just get a pizza and eat it whilst I work.'

Penny felt her shoulders slump in defeat, though she kept the bright smile plastered on her face. 'Well, let me help you with all your boxes.'

'I'd really rather. . .'

'It won't take too long with the two of us at it and as it's starting to snow now, maybe the quicker we get it in the better.'

Henry reluctantly nodded. She followed him out to the car and couldn't help her eyes wandering down to his bum before she tore them away. What was wrong with her? He was married.

She was disappointed that he hadn't even glanced at the incredible view yet, the sun covering the waves with garlands of scarlet and gold. He opened the boot and grabbed a box, passing it to her. With the easy way he handled the box, she wasn't expecting it to be so heavy, but the weight snatched the box out of her fingers and it tumbled to the floor, sending a pile of books over the gravel driveway.

'Oh god, I'm so sorry. I didn't realise it was so heavy.'

He stared at her incredulously. Penny sank to the floor and started scooping the books back up into the box, noticing wonderful delights from Ernest Hemingway, John Steinbeck, James Lee Burke, classics from Dickens and Thomas Hardy intermingled with Tolkien, Dan Brown and Iain Banks. She loved a man who liked to read.

Henry sighed, softly. 'Here, I'll get these, you take this. It's pillows so it should be a bit lighter for you.'

Penny took the box, unable to miss the sarcasm in Henry's words. This wasn't going well at all. She walked back into her house and into his lounge. She wondered where would be best to put the box that would be out of his way, but everywhere was going to be in his way – he filled the whole room. As it was pillows, she thought she could just put them upstairs for him. She turned and walked straight into him as he ducked into the room. She bounced off him, hit a plant on the shelf behind her and watched in horror as it fell to the floor, sending dirt cascading all over the cream carpet.

He rolled his eyes and sighed, heavily.

'Oh crap, I'll get my hoover, I'll clean it up.'

'Please don't take this the wrong way, but I think it's best if I just unpack myself. This place is small enough without the two of us banging into each other.'

'Of course, sorry, I'm not really helping, am I? Let me just clean this up for you and—'

'Just leave it.' Henry was clearly trying to stay calm when he was well and truly pissed off.

Penny nodded, stepping back out into her own kitchen. 'Well, feel free to cut through my house, it will probably be quicker—'

'I think I'll just use my own front door, start as we mean to go on.'

Disappointment slammed into her at that obvious statement of segregation.

'Shall I run through a few things with you, how the oven works and—'

'I'm sure I can work it out and I know where to find you if I get stuck.' He forced a smile onto his face. 'Thanks for your help, I'll see you around some time.'

He closed the door between them and Penny stood staring at his shadow in the frosted glass.

She rolled his words around her head. 'I'll see you around *some time*.'

She swallowed, sadly. Of course it was stupid of her to expect they might use the connecting door as their front door, that they would let themselves in through her kitchen and they'd chat over a cup of tea or dinner on a daily basis. They would have their own lives to lead. They had rented a property and that was it. Making friends with her was clearly not on the top of their to-do list, especially as they were planning on moving out soon.

She watched Henry look around the room and then he moved away. She heard the sound of furniture being dragged across the floor. The huge shadow of the bookcase was pulled in front of the door, blocking out all the light from the window, and then it stopped, resting against the door. He clearly had no intention of ever using the connecting door, now or in the future. He had made a blockade to keep her out permanently. Penny felt the tears that sprang to her eyes at this gesture and she dashed them away angrily. She had been rejected.

Chapter 2

Penny zipped up her jacket and walked into the cool room that was attached to the kitchen. The heating was on very low in here and she felt the cold envelop her straight away, but in her warm clothes she didn't feel it too much on her body. It was only her face and hands that felt it.

She looked around her newly converted room; it was so much nicer and roomier to work in here than it was before. The room was large, with the ice-block-making machines up one end that made the metre-long blocks of ice, and there was a large space in the middle for her to work. The floor and walls were tiled to maintain the coolness of the room and for easy cleaning.

She opened up one of the block machines: the water was oscillating slowly inside to keep the ice pure and clear. The water was partly frozen at the bottom, the perfect time to add some of the decorations her clients had asked for. This particular one wanted fairy lights, interwoven with snowflakes. She placed the glittery snowflakes in a rough pattern in the middle of the block and weaved the fairy lights in between them, weighing them down so they didn't float to the top of the water and taping the cable for the lights to the side. It looked magical and she knew it would look even more so once the piece was finished.

The walk-in freezer was up the other end and she opened the door. Several blocks stood along the back wall, waiting patiently to be turned from large ice cubes into masterpieces. Along the side were about ten sculptures that were finished and ready to go out.

She had been carving ice for about ten years and she never tired of seeing the finished pieces, never failed to feel proud of turning a block of ice into something beautiful. She even enjoyed creating her most commonly requested piece, the swan, which almost every wedding party asked for.

She grabbed one of the ice blocks, which was resting on a wheeled platform, and pulled it out into the cool room, closing the freezer door behind her. She snapped the brakes on the wheels and looked at her blank canvas.

This one was going to be a Christmas tree. She had already stuck the template on a few hours before, now she was going to carve it. She pulled on her gloves, slid her safety goggles over her eyes and picked up the die grinder to trace the outlines of the template. The thin drill bit on the end was the perfect tool to sketch out the design. She pressed very lightly because the main detail would come later.

She could lose herself for hours in here, spending time perfecting each curve, swirl, feather or leaf. When she was in here, the only thing that filled her mind was carving, chiselling, scraping, sawing and creating something intricate and beautiful. That was why she loved it so much, because there was no time to think about how the whole town of White Cliff Bay seemed to be moving forwards with their lives while Penny's life had stagnated, frozen in time. There was no time to focus on her loneliness, or the heartbreaking feeling that her loneliness was probably going to last a lifetime. She could get lost in a sculpture for hours and never have to think about these things. It was only when she stepped out of the cocoon of her cool room to warm up that the real world invaded her thoughts.

Having finished marking out the lines of the template, she picked up the chainsaw and started lopping off the big pieces she wouldn't need. She wouldn't think about Henry and his slate-grey eyes and she wouldn't think about how her loneliness had seemed to have inexplicably doubled since he had pushed the bookcase in front of the connecting door.

Henry hovered at Penny's back door, unsure whether to knock or not. As he raised his hand to tap on the door, Penny stepped out from some room off the kitchen. She was wearing black waterproof trousers and a black jacket, which clung to all her wonderful curves, making her look sexy as hell. She looked like she was about to get on a motorbike and drive off into the sunset. She pulled off a pair of workman's boots and unzipped the jacket. He quickly looked away in case she was naked underneath. After a few seconds he chanced a very brief look back and was relieved to see she was wearing a tiny vest and, as the waterproof bottoms came off, he could see she was wearing black leggings underneath too. She hung the clothes up in a closet and pulled on a huge, oversized hoodie, obscuring that sexy body from view. Her conker brown hair that had cascaded in curls down her back earlier was pulled up in a messy ponytail. She looked dishevelled and messy and utterly adorable. Her green eyes looked sad and he wondered whether he'd put that look there or whether she always carried it with her.

He looked down at the white roses he was carrying and wondered whether it was too much. He didn't want her to attach any romantic motives to the gesture.

Penny suddenly spotted him and he waved. She didn't wave back; the cheery persona she had presented earlier had vanished, the sparkle in her green eyes had gone out. She visibly sighed and then came to open the door

Tiny flakes of snow swirled around them, settling on her eyelashes and in her hair. There was something about her that he felt drawn to. She was beautiful, there was no denying that, but there was much more to it than that.

Henry held out the roses. 'I wanted to apologise for my behaviour earlier. As moving days go, this had to be the worst. Even before I got here, everything that could go wrong did go wrong. I was grumpy and tired and I'm sorry. I was wondering whether that offer of lasagne and mince pies was still open.'

Penny stared at him in confusion. 'I, erm. . .' She looked around as if an excuse would suddenly present itself. She didn't want him there and he felt like an utter arse. He had a lot of making up to do. As she clearly couldn't think of somewhere important that she had to be, she nodded reluctantly and stepped back to let him in.

He handed her the roses and she took them.

'I see you moved the bookshelf,' Penny said, trying and failing to keep her voice casual as if she didn't care. He had hurt her with that too.

'I can move it back, I just. . . I'll move it back.'

'No, it's fine, it's your home, do what you want.' She shrugged.

He hadn't even thought what Penny would think about him blocking the door – of course she would be upset by that.

'Listen, the last place we lived, we not only locked all the doors and windows at night, but we locked the bedroom doors too and I slept with a baseball bat under my bed. We moved here because it's a better area, it's better for Daisy. It's just going to take a bit of getting used to that everyone is so friendly and helpful. I'm sorry if I upset you. I'll move it back tonight.'

Penny stared down at the flowers and softened. 'I'll put these in some water and make us some dinner.'

Henry breathed a sigh of relief.

'Would you like a glass of mulled wine while you wait?' She filled a vase with water and plonked the roses in some haphazard arrangement.

'Yes please, it smells wonderful,' Henry said, sitting down at the large dining table. He watched her as she moved around the kitchen. There was something so captivating about her, he couldn't take his eyes off her.

'It's my own recipe, I just sort of threw some ingredients together.' Penny lit the hob under the saucepan and gave it a stir. 'It's sort of a Sangria and mulled wine mix. Red wine, rum, brandy, fruit juice, fruit, some spices.'

'Sounds very potent.'

Penny laughed and he liked that he could see the warmth and spark back in her eyes.

'Yeah, it might be. I haven't tried it. At least neither of us are driving.'

A giant, deep red, shaggy beast ambled into the kitchen, sniffing at the lasagne that was warming in the oven. Henry laughed; he had never seen anything so ridiculous-looking in his entire life.

'Wow, what breed is he?'

Penny laughed. 'I don't think even he knows. Half red setter, half English sheepdog, half Newfoundland maybe.'

'That's a lot of halves.'

'I know. He thinks he's a tiny lap-sized dog too, always climbs on my lap for a cuddle and then squashes me to death. He must weigh seven stone. Seriously, he could give pony rides to small children.'

'He looks like a Muppet.'

'Don't say that, you'll upset him, but yes, I know. The vet says he has never seen any dog so red before and with his shaggy fur he does look as if he's just walked off *Sesame Street*. Henry, meet Bernard. Bernard, this is Henry, our new neighbour.'

Bernard came and sniffed him with a vague interest. Clearly Henry met with Bernard's approval as he sat on Henry's feet, demanding to be stroked. Henry stroked his head and rubbed his chest. He looked up to see Penny smiling at him and then she quickly looked away.

He watched as she poured two large glasses of the mulled wine concoction and brought them to the table. She passed Henry his glass.

'Should we make a toast?' she asked.

'How about. . . to new beginnings.'

She stared at him and then smiled, chinking her glass against his.

His grey eyes were so intense, like he was studying her, searching for answers to some unanswered question. He took a sip without taking his eyes off hers and she noticed straight away that he didn't have a wedding ring.

'Thank you for decorating next door for Christmas, by the way. Daisy will love it.'

'My pleasure. I didn't get you a tree. I guessed that you and Daisy would want to get one together.'

'She'd like that, thank you.' Henry smiled and Penny felt her heart leap. She had never been the sort of girl to fall in love with a smile before, but there was something about his smile that filled his whole face. He was married, she had to remember that.

She focussed her attention on Bernard for a moment so she wouldn't have to look at the smile.

'So what brings you to White Cliff Bay?' Penny asked, taking a sip of the wine.

'Work mainly. I have a job at the White Cliff Bay Furniture Company, starting after Christmas.'

Her eyes widened. 'As a carpenter?'

He nodded. That at least explained the lack of a wedding ring; he worked with tools like she did, and wearing jewellery could cause injury.

'Wow, they are so selective about who they take on,' Penny said. 'I hear they have something like five hundred applicants every time they advertise. Isn't there some crazy interview process?'

'Yes, it kind of felt like *The Generation Game* with all these tasks that we had to do. We were shown once how to do a process and then had to replicate it within a certain time with the utmost quality and care. It was a whole day thing with the woodwork skills demonstration in the morning and a panel of seven interviewers grilling me for over two hours in the afternoon. I came out feeling like I had run a marathon.'

'They only take on the very best so you clearly did something to impress them. It will be a huge feather in your cap if you ever decide to move on. Everyone knows how prestigious the company is.'

Henry took a big swig of the wine. 'We don't intend to move on. I hope to stay in White Cliff Bay for some time.'

The way he said that, staring right at her, sent shivers down her spine. Was he flirting with her? She shook that silly thought out of her head, taking a big gulp of the wine. It was spicy and fruity and, as Henry said, very potent.

She tried to tear her eyes away from Henry's gaze but struggled to do so. She quickly turned away from the table to dish up the lasagne.

'Have you always been a carpenter?'

'Yes, I love it. There is something wonderful about creating something beautiful with your own hands. I've made and sold my own furniture but I've also made wooden jewellery and statues too. That's more of a hobby, though, but it's something I like to do in my spare time. I know I asked the agency about this, but they said you would be happy for me to use the shed as a sort of workshop?'

Penny nodded. 'Yes, it's huge and I only really use a small part of it. Feel free. I would love to see some of your jewellery and statues. My job is quite similar.'

'What is it you do, Penny?'

'I'm an ice carver.'

'Oh, that's cool. And do you get enough work in that line of business?'

She placed the plate of lasagne down in front of him and sat down to eat hers. 'Do I get enough to pay for this place, you mean?'

Henry's eyes widened slightly. 'Sorry, that came across as very nosy, didn't it? Ignore me. I hate it when people ask me about my work and my money. It's absolutely none of my business.'

'The house belonged to my parents, I grew up here, but they emigrated to Italy several years ago and left the house to me and my brother. He lives in the next town and I bought him out of his half of the house. I'm the only ice carver for miles and there are weddings every weekend, business functions, parties. I have to turn down many jobs because I just don't have enough time to do them. It pays very well.'

Henry looked surprised but she'd got used to those comments by now; no one took her job very seriously and certainly didn't believe that she could support herself on it.

'And, erm. . . is there a Mr Meadows?'

Penny stabbed a piece of pasta with her fork. Why did people assume that she needed a man to keep her happy? She was perfectly fine on her own.

'I'm presuming by the way you are murdering that piece of lasagne that I've stepped on a sore nerve there. My apologies.'

Penny smiled as she looked at the massacred piece of lasagne.

'I only asked because that hoodie looks way too big to belong to you,' Henry said.

'I just like big jumpers or hoodies. They're comfortable. There isn't a Mr Meadows, there never has been. Everyone in the town says I should be married with babies by now so it gets a bit wearing. I. . . I've had my heart broken in the past and I guess I'm wary of falling in love again.'

She stared at her dinner in horror. Why did she feel the need to divulge that to him? She barely knew the man. How much wine had she drunk to loosen her tongue that much? It wasn't even true. She wasn't not with someone because she was scared of falling in love again, she was just happier on her own. It was easier this way. She took the last sip of wine in her glass and went to the stove to pour herself some more.

'So you'll have to go to the Christmas Eve ball now you're a resident of White Cliff Bay,' Penny said, desperately trying to change the subject. 'Daisy will love it, there's music and fine food and dancing, and there's also a big ice carving competition there this year.'

'I'm not sure a ball is really my sort of thing. I'm too big to dance gracefully.'

'Everyone goes, you have to go. It'll be a great way for you to meet people and I'm sure Daisy will be upset if you don't take her.'

Henry still seemed undecided.

'It's for charity, you sort of have to go.'

He smiled at her again and she cursed herself for reacting like a silly schoolgirl with a crush.

'Well, if it's for charity then I can't say no, can I?'

Penny grinned and shook her head. Noticing he had finished his lasagne, she stood up and took his plate to the sink. 'Shall we go into the front room? It's a bit cosier.'

What was she doing? She didn't need to get cosier with this beautiful man, with this beautiful *married* man. But Henry was already standing up and moving in there, taking his new best friend Bernard with him.

She watched him go. She could do this, be in the same room with a man she was insanely attracted to without launching herself at him. A giggle burst from her throat at this thought. She had never launched herself at anyone in her entire life; it was unlikely she was going to start now. She was rubbish when it came to approaching men or even talking to them. Henry was easy to talk to. Although she was attracted to him, being married meant he was safe and she had spoken more to him tonight than she had to almost any man recently. She would just enjoy his company tonight and hopefully tomorrow she could pick up in the same place with his wife too.

She plated up two mince pies and followed him. She stopped when she saw him on all fours in front of the fireplace trying to light the fire. Good lord, his arse was a sight to behold. She couldn't help but stare at it as he wiggled it around setting twigs and papers in between the bigger logs.

Bernard seemed transfixed by his arse too and she quickly grabbed his collar before he decided that humping Henry was a good idea. She had almost forgotten that Bernard liked to hump most of the guests who came to the house. She didn't get too many visitors up here, but poor Jill, her cleaning lady, had been humped several times over the years, especially when she got on all fours to dust or clean. Bernard thought the whole thing was clearly a game and the more his victims tried to wiggle or escape, the more Bernard clung on for dear life, like he was riding a bucking bronco.

'Bed!' Penny said, pointing to Bernard's basket. Bernard seemed to sigh theatrically at having his fun thwarted.

'Bed, now.' Bernard slunk off with disappointment and climbed into his basket.

'Erm, that's a very nice offer, but we've only just met,' Henry said and then laughed as he watched her flush.

She sat down on the sofa and to her surprise he sat down next to her. There were three other chairs that he could have sat in but he chose to sit next to her. She wanted to get up and move away from him but that would appear rude. His smell was intoxicating, sweet but spicy, like cinnamon, zest and cloves. He smelt of Christmas, of the pomanders she used to make with her parents when she was younger and hang over the fire. She wanted to press her nose to his neck and breathe him in.

He didn't say anything, he just stared at her like a starved man would stare at steak.

He suddenly leant forwards and brushed his finger across her cheek. Electricity sparked through her at the softest of touches and she leapt back away from him.

Henry's eyes widened in horror. 'I'm so sorry, I'm not normally this creepy, I promise. I don't normally go round touching strange women. You had sauce on your cheek, I was just wiping it off. With hindsight I probably should have just told you.' He stared down at his wine. 'What did you put in this thing? It's gone straight to my head.'

Penny tried to find her voice, to try to say something to put him at ease, but she could still feel his touch on her cheek. Had it really been that long since she was touched by a man that her body reacted this insanely over a simple graze of her cheek?

She cleared her throat. 'I didn't think it was creepy.'

'You didn't?'

'A bit inappropriate, maybe, but not creepy.'

'Very inappropriate, I'm sorry.'

Silence descended and sparks seemed to crackle between them like the flames in the fireplace.

Penny passed him a mince pie, suddenly feeling nervous around him for the first time that night. He took it and bit into it, obviously still embarrassed by his overly tactile moment earlier.

'Mmm, this is delicious. I'm so rubbish at making mince pies, I just can't seem to get them right.' He took another bite and moaned softly with pleasure. 'So tell me more about this ball – will I have to wear a suit?'

She was relieved to move the topic back onto safer ground, although the sudden vision of Henry in a suit was doing nothing to stop these inappropriate thoughts from swirling around her head.

'Erm, yes, everyone gets dressed up in their best clothes.'

Henry pulled a face.

'I'm sure you'll look very sexy in a suit.' Good lord, what *had* she put in the mulled wine, some kind of truth serum? His eyebrows shot up, the mince pie frozen halfway to his mouth. 'I'm sorry, I'm rubbish around men, I really am. I'm trying to say things to you that I'd say to my girlfriends: "Oh, you'd look beautiful in that dress, those shoes look so good on you." Please don't take it the wrong way, I'm not chatting you up.'

He resumed eating his pie and Penny was surprised to see what looked like a brief flash of disappointment cross his face, but then it was gone.

She took a sip of the wine.

'What charity is it for?'

'It changes every year. This year we're raising money for research into miscarriages, stillbirths and premature babies.'

'That sounds like a very worthy cause. My sister, Anna, miscarried. I know how utterly heartbreaking it can be. She just had her second child, but I don't think the pain of it ever really goes away.'

She stared at him, a huge lump forming in her throat. He understood. He stared right back, narrowing his eyes slightly. When he spoke his voice was soft. 'I'm guessing you've lost a baby too.'

She swallowed. 'You're very astute. It was a long time ago, eight years, in fact. I was only twenty-one.' It had been a long time since she had spoken about it too but he seemed to command so much honesty from her. 'You're very easy to talk to. I never talk about this with anyone.

Chris and I had only been going out for three or four months but I just knew that he was my happy-ever-after, that we were going to be together forever. Then I fell pregnant. He didn't want to keep it, he wanted to travel the world, not be tied down by a baby. But there was no way I could get rid of it; from the moment that I found out, I loved that baby with everything I had. I was nearly four months when I lost it. Chris was so relieved, he practically cheered when I told him. I couldn't stop crying, for the baby, for his reaction to it. He left me a few days later. I was heartbroken.'

'I'm so sorry.'

'It's fine. Well, it's not, but it was a very long time ago. And looking back now, I'm so glad we never stayed together. He was wrong for me in every way. I cannot even begin to imagine raising a child with him. He was an arse. So maybe in some horrible way it was for the best.'

'I went through a similar thing myself when I was sixteen, got my girlfriend pregnant. She was horrified, kept saying that she wanted an abortion, that the baby would ruin her life. I couldn't bear the thought of that – this was my child and I couldn't believe that she hated this baby so much when it hadn't even been born. Thankfully her parents were Catholic and wouldn't let her have an abortion but they blamed me entirely and I wasn't allowed anywhere near her. They moved away and said the baby was going to be put up for adoption. I was absolutely gutted. I suppose I should have been relieved, a drunken fumble that turned into a pregnancy. I was sixteen years old with my whole life in front of me and her parents were giving me a way out, but I never saw it like that. I never saw my girlfriend again. Last I heard she ran away to Australia not long after the baby was born.'

Penny stared at him in horror. Was it worse that Penny had lost her baby or that Henry had a baby somewhere that he wasn't allowed to see? 'What happened to your baby?'

Just then Bernard leapt up from his position at the window and started barking furiously at something unseen outside.

Henry quickly moved to the front door as if he was ready to take on the world. She giggled at his over-protectiveness as he flung the door open and Bernard ran out into the night.

'It's just rabbits, Bernard hates them.'

She followed Henry to the door as he stood on the doorstep with his fists clenched, scanning the darkness for any threat. Bernard was sniffing around the rabbit holes, clawing at the grass with his big paws, with the obvious hope that one day one of the rabbits would run straight out the hole and into his mouth.

Seeing that there was no one waiting outside ready to kill them, Henry turned back and banged into her, nearly sending her flying. His hands shot out and grabbed her arms. She looked up at him, silhouetted against the night sky, tiny flakes of snow fluttering around him like icing sugar, his sweet, spicy scent washing over her as he was standing so close. She had bared her soul to this man tonight and, for the first time in a very long time, she wanted nothing more than to reach up and kiss him. Weirdly enough he looked like he wanted the same thing, as his eyes darkened with desire and then scanned down to her lips. What the hell? He was married. It was bad enough that she was having inappropriate thoughts about a married man; it was absolutely not OK for him to be having those same thoughts about her.

She took a definite step back. 'Well, it's getting late and I have to be up early tomorrow so maybe you should go.'

He stared down at her with confusion and she knew she had been sending some very mixed messages that night.

'Yes, of course. I'll let you get to bed,' he said, softly.

'And I look forward to meeting Daisy tomorrow,' Penny said, waiting for the guilt to cross his face at the mention of his wife. But there was no remorse there at all. He just nodded, walked through her kitchen and out the back door, not giving her a single backward glance.

She breathed in the cool night air, determined to clear her mind, then called Bernard in. He ran in, shook wet snowflakes all over her and then launched himself at the sofa where they had been sitting just moments before. She sighed and went into the kitchen.

How unfair was it that the first man in years that she'd had any kind of feelings for was beautiful, intriguing, intelligent, worked with his hands, kind and. . . married?

She was better off alone – that had been her mantra for the last eight years and she was sticking to it.

She jolted at a sudden noise from next door and she watched as the bookshelf was pushed away from the connecting door. He'd done that for her and she wanted to hug him and shake him in equal measure. He was married and it seemed he needed reminding of that even more than she did.

Daisy would be back tomorrow; hopefully that would stop any of that chemistry that was sparking between them.

Henry turned the downstairs light off and wandered upstairs to bed. There was something so attractive about Penny. Even wearing that oversized hoodie over black leggings and her hair pulled up in a messy ponytail, she looked adorable. She was fascinating too; he could have chatted to her all night. But she didn't seem to know what she wanted. Flirting with him one moment and completely back-pedalling the next. He didn't need another complicated woman in his life; Daisy was his entire world. But as he lay down in bed, it was Penny's smile and those intense green-gold eyes that he thought of before he drifted off to sleep.

Chapter 3

Henry strode along the steep, narrow, winding lanes with his niece Bea on his hip. She was too little to keep up with his long-legged stride so it was easier to carry her. She didn't seem to mind.

He passed cute little cottages that were jutting out onto the cobbled streets, their front doors opening right out onto the road. The homes were a higgledy-piggledy mess – there was no order, they just seemed to have one house piled almost on top of the next one. They were all brightly coloured, but none were the same style as the previous one he had passed; some were tiny bungalows whereas some were large three-storey houses. But it just sort of worked.

He stepped into a coffee shop and looked up at the board to see what was on offer. He had to smile when the limited choices ran to cappuccino, espresso and a few herbal teas. This was definitely not Starbucks.

'Jesus, who is that fine piece of arse?' said a voice behind him in a stage whisper.

'Jade, keep your voice down. I'm sure he can hear you.'

'But look at him, we never get men like that in White Cliff Bay.'

'That's Henry Travis, Anna Kent's brother, and that's his niece. He's moved into Penny's annexe.'

Henry winced that they were talking about him so openly, like he was a piece of meat.

There was a loud bark of a laugh from a third woman. 'I bet Penny thinks all her Christmases have come at once.'

'He's not going to go out with Penny,' Jade said. 'A man like that only goes out with beautiful women. Besides, she wouldn't have the first clue what to do with him. She wouldn't know how to please him.'

'And you would?'

'Oh yes. I could make him cry with joy.'

'You're so full of yourself.'

'Shut up, Beth, do you want to have a go?'

'I could do better than you.'

'Want to have a bet? A hundred pounds to whoever can get him into bed first.'

Henry stared at the counter incredulously as he waited for his turn in the queue. How old were these girls – twelve? He glanced briefly in their direction: three bleached blondes with long manicured nails and completely overdressed for a coffee shop on a Saturday morning. Their type did nothing for him.

'Deal,' said one, holding out her hand for the other to shake.

'Well, as I saw him first, I get the first go,' Jade said, standing up. Henry quickly looked away.

He heard the click-clack of heels over the tiled floor as she came towards him.

'Excuse me, you must be Henry Travis. I'm Jade Ambleside.' She held out a manicured hand for him to shake, which he ignored.

'Sorry, I've sort of got my hands full.' He gestured with his head towards Bea.

'Well, aren't you the cutest thing ever?' Jade said in a singsong voice. 'What's your name?'

Bea stared at her with unblinking eyes. She wouldn't speak to Jade. She didn't speak to anyone outside her home. It was a worry for Anna that Bea would chat non-stop inside the house to her family but as soon as she left the home she wouldn't say a word.

'Her name's Bea, she's very shy.'

'Oh, you don't have to be shy with me, sweetheart,' Jade sang, trying to pull a cutesy face. Bea just stared at her as if she was stupid. 'I love children so much, I love playing with them and talking to them. Kids love me.'

Henry doubted that statement to be true. He looked to the front of the queue where the same person who had been at the front when he came in was still happily chatting to the owner of the coffee shop.

'Henry, I think we should get together some time, for a date?' Jade said, thrusting her chest towards him.

'Like a play date? Do you have children too?' Henry said, deliberately misunderstanding her. 'Anna would love to take Bea to a play date with you. There's a kids' indoor play area on the far side of town – it's very noisy, very sweaty, but the kids love it. I'll tell Anna you'd be interested in going. Well, I must go, I'm in a bit of a rush. I'll get Anna to give you a call.'

He turned and walked out the shop. Maybe he should start wearing a wedding ring so people would know he was not in the market for a relationship. Though knowing women like Jade, that wouldn't stop her.

Feel the sunshine on your face and fall in love . . .

HOLLY MARTIN

Available in paperback now